It wasn't until he entered ~~~~~~~~~~~~~ ~~~~~~ ~~ ~~~~~~ bright mile that Kit realized how eagerly he'd been anticipating his next encounter with her. What he hadn't expected was to find her holding a baby.

If possible, she appeared even lovelier in the light of day, her face flushed and soft with pleasure, her luminous eyes the same shimmering green of the hills outside, her parted lips glistening like a mist-kissed Irish rose.

"Do me a favor," Meg whispered, offering her bundle to him. "Please hold Brian?"

Kit took a step backward, palms extended.

"It's for Tim," she said quietly. "If he were to see you, a grown man, he'll know there's nothing to fear from holding a baby." Giving Kit no chance to argue, she thrust the infant into his arms.

The baby began to cry. He was nobody's fool, Kit realized; Brian knew the ideal spot was in Meg's tender grasp.

"He's not an egg, he won't break," Meg said softly. "Go on, snuggle him close. All he wants is to feel safe and secure and loved." She smiled as the baby settled in Kit's arms, his cries fading to sniffles. "It's a rare joy, putting that smile on his face. Doesn't it make a part of you glow?"

Kit might feel a certain satisfaction in soothing the infant's woes, but he saw no reason to make a practice of it. He wanted to hand back the baby, but oblivious, Meg continued to coo over Brian, her soft-scented hair close to Kit's face.

Any glow he felt, he thought sardonically, came from his heated response to her nearness. . . .

—from "Where Dreams Come True" by Barbara Benedict

Taylor-made Romance from Zebra Books

WHISPERED KISSES (0-8217-5454-8, $5.99/$6.99)
Beautiful Texas heiress Laura Leigh Webster never imagined
that her biggest worry on her African safari would be the handsome Jace Elliot, her tour guide. Laura's guardian, Lord Chad-
wick Hamilton, warns her of Jace's dangerous past; she simply
cannot resist the lure of his strong arms and the passion of his
Whispered Kisses.

KISS OF THE NIGHT WIND (0-8217-5279-0, $5.99/$6.99)
Carrie Sue Strover thought she was leaving trouble behind her
when she deserted her brother's outlaw gang to live her life as
schoolmarm Carolyn Starns. On her journey, her stagecoach
was attacked and she was rescued by handsome T.J. Rogue. T.J.
plots to have Carrie lead him to her brother's cohorts who murdered his family. T.J., however, soon succumbs to the beautiful
runaway's charms and loving caresses.

FORTUNE'S FLAMES (0-8217-5450-5, $5.99/$6.99)
Impatient to begin her journey back home to New Orleans,
beautiful Maren James was furious when Captain Hawk delayed
the voyage by searching for stowaways. Impatience gave way
to uncontrollable desire once the handsome captain searched
her cabin. He was looking for illegal passengers; what he found
was wild passion with a woman he knew was unlike all those
he had known before!

PASSIONS WILD AND FREE (0-8217-5275-8, $5.99/$6.99)
After seeing her family and home destroyed by the cruel and
hateful Epson gang, Randee Hollis swore revenge. She knew
she found the perfect man to help her—gunslinger Marsh
Logan. Not only strong and brave, Marsh had the ebony hair
and light blue eyes to make Randee forget her hate and see
the love and passion that only he could give her.

*Available wherever paperbacks are sold, or order direct from the
Publisher. Send cover price plus 50¢ per copy for mailing and
handling to Penguin USA, P.O. Box 999, c/o Dept. 17109,
Bergenfield, NJ 07621. Residents of New York and Tennessee
must include sales tax. DO NOT SEND CASH.*

Jo Goodman
Hannah Howell
Carol Finch
Phoebe Conn
Barbara Benedict
Jane Kidder

ZEBRA BOOKS
KENSINGTON PUBLISHING CORP.

ZEBRA BOOKS are published by

Kensington Publishing Corp.
850 Third Avenue
New York, NY 10022

First Printing: June, 1996
10 9 8 7 6 5 4 3 2 1

Printed in the United States of America

CONTENTS

The Baby Dream

Jo Goodman

Annie never learned the truth until Ruby was dying. There had always been the dream, of course, but no one had ever intimated there might be a glimmer of truth in it. Now Ruby was telling her that a glimmer was how it all began. Twenty-two years ago, to be exact. This very month.

"I tried to do right by you," Ruby said. Her voice was hoarse but surprisingly strong. Years of training it to reach well beyond the footlights helped her speak clearly now. "We all did. You're so very special, Annie."

Annie Moses shook her head. "No," she said quickly, wiping perspiration from Ruby's fevered brow. "Not special. Don't say it again. Don't say anything." There was a certain desperation in her tone, as if the course of events could be altered if Ruby remained silent. Outside the door to their room she could hear movement in the hallway. The troupe was assembling there, waiting for Annie's announcement. It was a death watch.

Ruby heard the murmurs and shuffling feet too. She smiled. "The ghouls," she said not unkindly. "I'll wager they're hoping I'll pass before the eight o'clock performance." Her voice carried beyond the foot of the bed, under the door, and into the hallway. There was immediate silence. She was tickled by that and her smile deepened. Laughter, even weak laughter, was a joy denied her. Her small attempt at it dissolved in a coughing fit that exhausted her.

Annie watched helplessly. When the racking coughs had subsided, she held a handkerchief to Ruby's mouth and wiped away the blood that stained her lower lip. When she was done, Annie got to her feet and went to the window. She did not want Ruby to see her distress. She knew her face was pale, her features drawn. At least there were no tears. It wasn't Annie's way to cry

Annie leaned toward the window, pressing her forehead against the glass. She felt weary enough to close her eyes, yet there was comfort to be drawn from the view. In the distant harbor, over the rooftops of boardinghouses, brothels, and bars, Annie could see the tall, stately masts of the Mannering ships When their sails were unfurled as they headed downriver for the open sea, there were no other ships that could touch them for grace or beauty or speed.

Ruby watched Annie turn away, stronger now for the pause that had drawn her eyes to the harbor. Like the Mannering ships she admired, Annie was a tall, serene beauty with a proud carriage and effortless grace. Annie's sail was her extraordinary hair, bound now by a simple black ribbon, but unfurled on a windy day it defined the breeze that lifted it away from her face like rays of sunshine. "You shouldn't be here," Ruby said when she had gathered her reserves.

"You're repeating yourself," Annie said gently. "I shouldn't be anywhere else."

Ruby Doubletree knew she had to choose her battles carefully, and this was one she couldn't win. Annie was also a willow, bending but never breaking, courageous in the face of whatever life presented her, resilient in the wake of change.

She had been like that from the very beginning, Ruby thought. Annie's resolute spirit spoke more to her birth than it did to her upbringing. It was in the girl's nature, not in how she was nurtured. In truth, there hadn't been too much of the latter, and no matter how often Ruby Doubletree promised herself she would do better by Annie, she never did. There was always a performance to give, trunks to pack, lines to learn, playbills to distribute, costumes to mend, and creditors to elude.

Most moments Annie was an afterthought.

Except once, twenty-two years ago this month, there had been a moment when Annie Moses had taken center stage. Ruby closed her eyes and rested . . . and remembered. . . .

It was the glimmer of gold that caught her eye. No one who knew Ruby Doubletree was surprised when they heard it was the first thing she noticed. Among the Liberty Players it was accepted, mostly with affection, that Ruby was a bit of a mercenary at heart. She always attracted the richest theater patrons, even during lean times, and she was generous with their gifts, never failing to share her bounty with the troupe when her interest waned.

The sparkle of gold that caught Ruby's eye this time was floating on the Delaware. At first she thought it was a trick of sunlight on the water. She would always recall that the June day was horribly humid and the riverbank offered little in the way of relief. Even here, at the Delaware's edge, there seemed to be a haze rising from the water. The very air shimmered and distorted images in the distance. It was easy to convince herself that she wasn't seeing what she was seeing.

Ruby had never put a lot of stock in modesty. The theater did not lend itself to privacy. Shyness about one's body was more an affectation, something to be trotted out when trying to impress a suitor with one's near-virginal state. It had no place in a crowded dressing room or on the banks of the Delaware when one was about to make a heroic rescue.

Stripping down to her chemise and drawers, Ruby Doubletree flung herself into the river and struck out in the direction of that glimmer of gold. She was a good swimmer and cut her way through the water with crisp, clean strokes. Although she had her sights on a spot some twenty yards in the distance, she was aware that her friends had left their shaded picnic spot to gather on the bank. Their low, rumbling cheers carried over the water and caught her attention each time she raised her head for a breath.

Ruby paused just once. Gold glinted again as the river bobbed the basket that carried it. She cut a diagonal path through the water to head off the basket. There was little chance that she could catch it if it got past her. Ruby ducked her head and struck out again.

The basket floated into her arms and filled them. Treading water, Ruby embraced it, allowing it to support her as much as she supported it. Sure enough, the gold she had glimpsed was there. The problem was, it was not the only treasure.

Ruby Doubletree stared at the infant sleeping in the basket. A blue and white quilt swaddled the baby, covering everything but the tiny head. Sunshine caught the fine, silky threads of hair that were so pale, they were almost transparent. The infant breathed lightly, and a small, wet bubble appeared on the delicate bow mouth.

A true measure of the impact of this moment was not that Ruby Doubletree's heart turned over, but that she forgot all about the gold that had first captured her attention.

Pushing the basket in front of her like a float, Ruby paddled toward the bank where the Liberty Players waited for her. She ignored their offers of help and climbed out of the water unassisted, carrying the basket in the same embrace that she had caught it. Her fellow actors crowded around.

"I'm going to call him Moses," Ruby announced. "You know, like in the Bible. And I'm going to raise him myself."

Among the members of the acting troupe there was general, if silent, agreement that Ruby was out of her mind. It wasn't that anyone objected to the name. Given the circumstances, it seemed wholly suitable. It was the idea of Ruby Doubletree embracing motherhood that set the players back on their heels.

Without warning Ruby thrust the basket into Peggy Cook's hands. "All of you can help, of course." She missed the sigh of relief that was shared by the gathering as she took the gown Abel Wiggins was holding out to her. Ruby shimmied into the dress, drawing it over her head and wiggling until it settled over her damp, voluptuous figure. She smoothed it over her hips and breasts, ignoring the water stains that were seeping through. "Well," she said, satisfied. "That was refreshing."

The basket of baby was being passed around the small circle. The ingenue handed it to the seamstress, who gave it to the prop collector, who was the first to pay attention to the necklace dangling from the baby's small fist.

"Here," Abel Wiggins said deeply. Besides collecting props, he played most of the roles that called for a commanding, noble presence. His favorite was King Lear. "What's this?" He extracted the delicate gold chain and locket from the tiny dimpled fist and passed the basket and baby along to the wig dresser. "This might present a clue to the child's parentage."

Ruby plucked the locket out of Abel's hand and fastened it around her own neck. "As if I care a fig about his parents," she said. Patting the gold locket in place, she gave Abel a dead-on look. "As if they cared a fig about Moses. Do you think they simply misplaced that basket?"

Abel Wiggins did better when he had his lines memorized. Without a script he was capable only of blustering. He made some noises that he hoped sounded important, and let the matter drop.

Ruby wrung out her thick ebony hair and plaited it with deft fingers. "Moses belongs to us now, and if you ask me, that's what was intended in the first place. I'll wager no one wants him back, and if we were to go looking, we wouldn't be rewarded for our efforts."

Several heads nodded immediately. Others took a bit longer to see the sense in Ruby's words, but eventually they all came around. The baby encouraged that kind of response. He was a precious little bundle, already attaching himself to a dozen hearts with his sweet and incredibly quiet disposition.

Ruby tucked the locket beneath the neckline of her dress. Out of sight, out of mind. Plopping herself down on the grassy bank, she raised her hem to her knees and rolled on her stockings. Without being asked, Peggy ran to get Ruby's shoes. "It's all settled, then?" Ruby asked. Her chin was lifted regally, and the

graceful gesture she made with her upturned hand was subtly
reminiscent of a queen holding court. "For all intents and pur
poses, Moses belongs to me?"

The baby chose that moment to wake and let out an ear
piercing wail.

"And therefore to all of you," Ruby added quickly.

Mrs. Dodd, with her ample bosom and smoothly rounded
face, was most often called upon to take the matronly roles. She
reminded everyone that it was just acting when she passed the
basket back to the young male lead and aspiring playwright.
Tom Watt, the oldest of seven children, tickled the baby's chin
and cooed softly. He raised the blue and white quilt and slipped
his large hand under the baby's bottom. "Wet," he announced
to the troupe.

Tom set the basket down, knelt beside it, and removed the
quilt. Moses was quite naked. Amused, Tom scratched his head
and looked up at the sea of faces above him. Only Ruby wasn't
watching. She didn't know what to do about a baby's wet bottom
and wasn't of a mind to learn now. Tom's amusement deepened
as laughter rippled among the actors.

"What's wrong?" Ruby demanded. She leaned over the basket
and peered inside. "Oh, my God! What happened to his doo-
dle?"

Abel Wiggins was laughing so hard that the seamstress had
to support him. Mrs. Dodd's shoulders were shaking and Peggy
Cook had tears at the corners of her eyes.

Tom Watt reached over the basket of bawling baby and patted
Ruby on her shoulder consolingly. "You may want to rethink
your daughter's name," he said. His blue eyes were fairly dancing
with laughter. "Moses doesn't suit this little water baby."

Ruby shrugged Tom's hand off her shoulder. "The blanket
was *blue* and white," she said indignantly. "Apparently his
mother was confused as well."

"Her mother," Mrs. Dodd corrected, catching her breath.

"Whatever." Ruby sniffed and lent the mannerism a certain

regal presence. "I'm going to call her Annie," she said. "Annie
Moses. That's a good name, don't you think?"

They all agreed it was a splendid name. . . .

Annie stepped out into the hallway where the troupe was waiting. They looked at her anxiously, then looked away, guilt inter-
mingling with grief. For a long time no one spoke.

Abel Wiggins broke the silence. His voice was no longer a
rich baritone. It rumbled with bass notes now and rolled over
audiences like thunder. In the theater he delivered every line as
if it were a pronouncement from the gods. "She's gone, then,"
he said heavily. "Our Ruby's gone."

Annie slipped her slender arm under Abel's. It was the willow
supporting the oak. "You can see her now," she said quietly.
"I've dressed her hair just the way she liked it."

"In a moment. I can't . . . not just . . ." He drew in a steadying
breath. "Not just yet."

Annie nodded. Her gray eyes were clear and dry, but grief
marked her face in the very stillness of her features. She knew
they all found it difficult to meet her direct gaze. They were
more comfortable with passions on display than they were with
emotion held back.

Peggy Cook dabbed at her eyes with an embroidered handkerchief. Peggy hadn't played ingenue roles for ten years, but it
was second nature for her to project fragility and innocence
when pressured. The pressure had started the moment she saw
Annie was wearing the gold locket. "She told you?"

In answer, Annie merely touched the locket. She had slender,
graceful hands and a way of turning a gesture that reminded
them all poignantly of Ruby Doubletree.

"Don't hate her," Tom Watt said. He stood very close to Peggy.
They had been married for a score of years now, the only wedded
couple among the thespians. "Or us."

"I could never hate Ruby," Annie said. Her solemn features
lent weight to her sincerity. "Nor any of you. You're my family."

They filed past her one by one, sometimes reaching to touch her arm or squeeze her hand, but in point of fact it was Annie who comforted them. Ruby Doubletree had been the heart and soul of the Liberty Players, but Annie Moses was their rock.

It was later that evening, when Annie was alone in her room, that they came to tell her their decision. Annie let them in, tightening the belt on her worn cotton dressing gown and smoothing the lapels to close the neckline. She had never embraced the same thoughts on modesty as Ruby or any of the others.

They had prepared a script for Abel, just to make the proceedings smoother and add the weight of authority to what was, in fact, only their opinion. He cleared his throat, took center stage near the empty fireplace, and spoke from memory.

"It's time for you to find your family, Annie," he said. "We know how you think of us, how we think of you, but it's different now with Ruby gone, and we're agreed you should make the attempt. That's why she gave you the locket before she died. It's the link between you and your heritage. She kept it all these years out of fear."

"Fear?" Annie interrupted. She drew her legs under her on the wing chair and fingered the end of her long, thick braid. Her hair had never darkened much beyond the color that Ruby had first spied. Gold and platinum strands still mingled like cornsilk. "Ruby wasn't afraid of anything." Not even death, she almost added. Like all aspects of life, Ruby had found a way to embrace it.

"She was afraid of losing you," Mrs. Dodd said, stealing Abel's thunder and deviating from the script. "And that's the truth."

The seamstress nodded. "Not that she'd ever admit it, even to herself. But we knew what you meant to her. Never mind that story that you were her best friend's daughter."

"Ruby let her imagination spin out the story," Tom said.

Peggy nodded. "I half believed it myself."

"I never did," Annie said. Complete silence followed her announcement, and she realized she had shocked them. "Or at least I didn't after I discovered *A Fallen Woman's Tale* in the script trunk. I think I was eight, but I could read well enough to get the gist of it."

Mrs. Dodd pressed one hand to her bosom, her shock palpable. "So *that's* why Ruby's story seemed so familiar," she said. "Didn't we do that once in Boston?"

"Charleston," Peggy piped in. "It was too risqué for Boston. We all agreed."

Abel made blustering sounds and shook his head. "Didn't know," he said shortly. "Forgot all about it."

"I don't blame any of you," Annie said when she saw they were overcome by guilt. "I thought you were just protecting Ruby. I thought *she* was my mother."

That brought silence back.

"And so she was," Tom said after a time.

"No," said Annie. "You all were." She let her eyes go from one to the other, acknowledging the contribution each person had made to her upbringing. "I was very lucky. I *am* very lucky."

Abel Wiggins seemed to find his place in his prepared recitation. He blinked once, pulling on the corner of his shaggy salt-and-pepper eyebrows, and took to the stage again. "It doesn't change the fact that it's time for you to go your own way," he said. "Find your people as Ruby wants you to. It's not for us to keep you from it any longer."

"You're kicking me out?" she asked. Panic clawed at her insides, but nothing showed on her face. This was the last thing she expected. "Where would I go? What would I do?"

"We're not tossing you," Peggy said, her voice cracking slightly with emotion. "It's just that we're disbanding for a while. Ruby was . . . Ruby was the life of the Liberty Players. Without her . . ."

Tom Watt held his wife's hand. "We're not a family, Annie. We're merely people who have worked together, some of us more than a quarter of a century. We care about one another, love one another, but we're agreed we need some time apart."

She could feel the panic rising. Soon it would reach her eyes and they would see how frightened she was. "But I could go with one of—" She stopped before she made herself foolish. The truth was in front of her, and she was being slow to accept it. None of them was offering to take her. In their own way they were each self-sufficient. As a group they had depended on her, but alone she needed them. "Of course," she said quietly. "You must do as you see fit."

Before they lost their resolve, Abel said, "Ruby wanted it. It was her dying wish that we set you on a course back to your own people."

You're my people, Annie wanted to say. She remained mute, afraid she would start screaming and simply never stop.

Peggy crumpled the handkerchief in her hand. "There's a bit of money set aside. Ruby wanted you to have new clothes, set yourself up proper."

"Ruby never told me," Annie said, looking down at her lap. Her fingers were threaded together, the knuckles almost bloodless. "She only passed on the locket." She was wearing it now, but it was invisible to them, tucked beneath her voluminous nightshift and dressing gown. The gold had absorbed her body heat and it lay warmly against her skin. She had always thought of the locket as Ruby's, and it had value when she looked on it in that light. When she considered that it had been worn by Ruby only for safekeeping, that it was a gift from the person who had abandoned her, it was worthless.

"There's nothing in the locket but a scrap of hair pressed under glass," she told them. "There's no miniature portrait or name. The hair is probably my own. I don't see that the locket will help me."

Tom said, "There's the engraving on the front, Annie. You've seen it yourself over the years. All of us have one time or another."

"I've seen it," she said stiffly. "It's the letter M. All fancied up, but it's only an M."

The members of the troupe traded uneasy glances. It was Mrs. Dodd who finally put their discomfort into words. "It doesn't stand for Moses," she said. "If Ruby told you the story, then you must know she lied all these years about that."

Annie *had* realized it, only she didn't want to think about it. It was just that morning that Ruby had pressed the locket into her hand and made the revelations.

"You've always had the dream," said Peggy. "Since you were a wee thing, there's always been the dream. From the moment you could talk about it, Ruby knew she was only borrowing you."

Abel sighed deeply. "We *all* knew. The truth is, we hoped to borrow you a bit longer." Sturdy, robust, barrel-chested Abel Wiggins blinked back tears and cleared his throat.

It was too late for Annie to take back anything she had ever said about her dream, yet it was her fervent wish to do just that. Still, she heard words coming from her mouth that she wasn't certain she wanted to say, a question she wasn't sure she wanted answered. She withdrew the locket from against her skin and brought it out where they all could see. "If the *M* doesn't stand for Moses or Mother," she said, "then what does it stand for?"

The uncomfortable silence returned. There was some shuffling as they looked anywhere but at Annie.

"Aren't you going to tell me?" she asked at last.

Abel had to clear his throat again. The lump that was lodged there made speaking difficult. "We're thinking you already know the answer."

Annie frowned, genuinely at sea. "Know the answer?" she asked slowly. "How would I—" She stopped, raised her hands to the back of her neck, and unfastened the locket. She held it in the heart of her palm and studied the fluid engraving on the surface. The *M* leaned slightly to the right and lay amid a flourish of curls, like a stamen surrounded by so many petals. She stared at it for a long time, feeling the silence in the room as a pressure on her chest. An ache began at the back of her eyes and she was aware of her own labored breathing. Peggy was kneeling beside her now, and Annie realized that she was in danger of fainting.

As if from a great distance she watched her fingers slowly

fold over the locket. Her own voice came to her from even farther off. "Mannering," she said.

Ian Reynolds leaned against the taffrail of the *Somerset* and surveyed the busy dock. Normally he would have found some satisfaction in the frenetic pace and purpose of so much activity. Not this morning. Nor any other morning these past three weeks. That's how long it had been since the *Glendower* had been missing. All hands lost. His cousin and his cousin's wife, passengers returning from London, gone with every other good soul aboard.

Ian and Adam Mannering had not been particularly close. Indeed, Ian had met Leticia Mannering only once. Adam preferred to manage the London office of the Mannering line and leave the more volatile nature of Philadelphia business to the family's black sheep. Leticia also preferred London, so it was easy for Adam to justify abandoning the American branch in favor making a home abroad.

That made Ian's present circumstances more stunning. For some reason that Ian had yet to fathom, Adam and Leticia Mannering had named him guardian of their infant son. Jefferson Mannering had not been with his parents on the *Glendower*. Leticia had written that the baby did not travel well, but Ian suspected that it was Leticia who did not travel with the baby. A mother's selfishness, a father's indulgence, had saved young Jefferson's life. Ian found he couldn't be sorry about that and stopped assigning blame for things that were beyond the control of mortals.

Captain Henry Dallas spied Ian at the taffrail and crossed the deck to join him. "You look in a fine black mood," he said. Captain Dallas had been with the Mannering line too long to be a respecter of moods. Unless a man was preparing the noose for his own neck, Dallas wasn't of a mind to talk him out of it. He simply noted that Ian was scowling and moved on with the business at hand. "There's a delay with the iron and steel we're supposed to carry to Charleston. It doesn't appear we'll have it until tomorrow morning at the earliest."

Ian nodded. The fact that his scowl didn't deepen meant he was taking it in stride. "Tell Samuel Reade that his delay in delivering his own goods will cost him extra. If he doesn't agree, then he can find another line to take the shipment. One delay here will cause another delay in Charleston. There's no guarantee that Villeurs will want to ship his cotton if we're late arriving."

Dallas rubbed his chin with the back of his knuckles. The answer was what he expected—more or less. "You're not going to talk to Reade yourself?"

"I just told you to do it." Ian heard the terseness in his voice but made no apology. Dallas wasn't the sort of man likely to be offended by it. Straightening, Ian turned his back on the dock and thrust his hands into his pockets. His feet were planted apart and his lean body swayed easily with the gentle rocking of the ship. A strong ocean breeze flattened his dark hair for a moment. Like most things in life, Ian faced it head-on. On a day this warm, it was welcomed.

Captain Dallas watched the head of the Mannering line lean into the wind. The black mood was dissipating. Ian Reynolds took to salt spray and sea air the way some men took to ale. Dallas let him enjoy it. There was no sense interrupting a man well into his cups.

The breeze subsided. "Jake arrived last night," Ian said without looking at the captain. "On the *Seneca*. With his nurse. They're at the house now."

"Jake? I thought Adam's boy was Jefferson."

Ian shrugged. He had wide shoulders but a loose way of moving that suggested a certain careless ease. He stepped back, rested one hip on the taffrail, and crossed his arms in front of him. "I call him Jake. He's too tiny for more name than that."

"You must be relieved to have him here." In retrospect, it was a stupid thing to say. Ian's black mood had not brought relief to mind, and Dallas could admit to himself that he deserved the sour, disbelieving look Ian cast in his direction.

"The nurse is leaving later today. She doesn't want to stay even a week to get the boy settled with someone new. Leticia must have filled her head with stories. She thinks we're barbarians."

Dallas liked that. "We are."

Ian ignored him. "The best I could get her to agree to was to interview women I send over."

The captain of the *Somerset* rolled forward on the balls of his feet as the deck slanted beneath him. "So? Send them to her while there's time. You know lots of—" He stopped because he began to see the problem. "Oh." He raised his hand to his chin again, this time to steady a smile that was in a moment of revealing itself. "I see."

"Oh," Ian said, drawing out the single syllable. "I *see*." He shook his head, raking back his thick, inky hair. "I'm glad I don't have to put it into words for you."

Dallas put it out there anyway. "You don't know the right sort of women."

Ian's blue-gray eyes took on a decidedly flinty look, but he said nothing.

Careless of the repercussions, or perhaps oblivious of them, Captain Dallas added, "Whores and wenches."

"I know a number of gently reared women," Ian said. "Daughters from families of consequence."

"I didn't forget them," Dallas said. "They're the wenches. Heartless little bluebloods who'd like to get their hands deep in your pockets." So there was no mistaking his meaning this time, he added, "And they're not looking for the same thing as the whores."

Ian found himself hard pressed not to laugh. He held up his hands, surrendering. "All right," he said. "I'll not debate your cynical vision of womankind, but I'm not admitting agreement either."

"Coward." Captain Dallas rested his weight back on his heels. His arms went behind his back, and the expression on his craggy, square-jawed face was thoughtful. "What are you going to do?"

"Ask around, I suppose. My housekeeper may know some-one. Mrs. Ward's familiar with just about everyone working in the homes around us."

"The old busybody," Dallas said under his breath. Mrs. Ward guarded Ian's home like a Notre Dame gargoyle, scaring off visitors with stony silence and a stare that could shatter glass. What Dallas didn't mention was that all his advances in the widow's direction had been firmly rebuffed. More clearly, he added, "She's the one to ask."

"Mr. Reynolds sent you?" Jane Howard asked. She laid the baby in his crib and straightened, brushing the front of her crisp apron while she pointedly took measure of the nursery's guest.

Under Miss Howard's narrow-eyed scrutiny, Annie felt un-gainly and gauche. She did not let it show. In her mind she held the vision of the Mannering masts and let her posture speak to a pride she didn't really feel. This was the second time she had been asked if she was sent by Mr. Reynolds. Mrs. Ward was distracted and didn't seem to notice her hesitation. In conse-quence, Annie was sent to the nursery straightaway.

It was easier to lie the second time. "Yes," she said. "Mr. Reynolds sent me."

"Very good." The clipped accent spoke well of her. "Sit down, please." She pointed to the rocker while she took the stiff, high-backed chair at the writing desk. "At home there would be tea, of course. But here . . ." She shrugged her narrow shoulders. "You have references?"

Annie was startled by the question. It registered on her face only as a slow blink. She was careful not to look away. Although she had never aspired to join Ruby or the rest of the Liberty Players onstage, she had learned something about acting over the years. "It was short notice," she said. "I didn't bring them with me."

Jane Howard accepted this explanation. "Tell me about the family who employs you now," she said. "How many children?"

There was the slow blink again, but Annie's eyes remained clear gray and guileless. At least she had a better understanding of the nature of this interview. She hadn't given the sleeping babe a second thought since the nurse put him down. "Two," she said. "A boy and a girl. Margaret and Thomas. Thomas is three now. I've been with the Watts since his birth."

"And the Watts?" she asked. "What is their position?"

Of course that would be important, Annie thought. Jane Howard was the sort of woman who measured her own worth through the status of the family that employed her. It was a shame that titles were inappropriate in this case. They surely would have impressed.

Annie spun out her tale, letting it convince by the quiet reserve with which she told it. She took a page from Ruby Doubletree and stayed close to the script in her head. She recalled the Liberty Players had performed *The Union Club* in most of the eastern cities from Savannah to Boston. It was about a family who could trace their heritage to the *Mayflower* and did so with irritating regularity. Annie was certain that Jane Howard had never seen it.

Halfway through her recitation, Annie knew she had her audience. The position as young Jefferson Mannering's nanny was going to be hers. It occurred to her much later that she had managed it all without having to show the locket once.

Ian Reynolds left his horse with the groom and used the back entrance to gain access to his home. He half expected Mrs. Ward to meet him at the door and take him to task for leaving her to tend to Jake. He had an apology prepared, not that it would be appreciated or even accepted. The events of the day formed a downward spiral. After news that the steel and iron shipment would be delayed, there was news of another delay affecting the Boston run. That kept him busy until noon. He would have gone to his offices, but a fight broke out on the dock among hands working for competing lines and required settlement at higher evels. The battle came down to Ian and William Tyler of Concord Shipping. Ian had a lump on the back of his head, and Tyler was sporting a black eye. Hours later they worked out their real differences in Yancy's Tavern on Market Street.

Trading shot for shot at Yancy's was the reason Ian had missed seeing Miss Howard off. Now he had to face down Mrs. Ward. His sore head practically guaranteed he wouldn't be able to manage the thing with dignity. He took solace in the fact that William Tyler's wife was a harridan and his worthy opponent was getting his due right now. He even permitted himself to feel a little superior, coming out ahead because at least he didn't have to sleep with Mrs. Ward. Tyler wouldn't escape his nemesis so easily.

Ian took off his coat, slung it over a kitchen chair, and plucked an apple from the bowl of fruit on the table. There was the lingering sent of fresh baked bread and Yankee pot roast in the air. He breathed deeply, but when his stomach roiled he accepted that the apple was his best choice.

He nodded briefly to one of the kitchen girls when he passed her in the hallway. "Where's Mrs. Ward, Cathy?"

"Retired to her room, sir." She made a quick curtsy and went on her way, stopping to give him a backward glance when he was well past her and wouldn't be able to hear her sigh. She knew Ian Reynolds didn't dally with the help. It didn't stop her from wishing he would make an exception in her case.

Ian's boots tapped lightly on the carpet runner as he took the main stairs two at a time. His hand ran smoothly along the polished banister. At the top of the stairs he turned left toward Mrs. Ward's room in the east wing. He was halfway there when he saw the door to the room they had designated as the nursery was open. On impulse he stepped inside.

Annie looked up when the shadow crossed her doorway. She was sitting in the rocker holding Jefferson in the crook of her arm. He was wide awake but content to be held. Even though it was late, the room had become noticeably darker only in the past half hour. Summer sunlight had lingered in the nursery as

long as it was able, then Annie replaced it with oil lamps on the
mantel and bedside table.

"I see Mrs. Ward found someone," Ian said. He watched her
lashes lower slowly, then rise again in kind of a serene acknowledgment. He didn't know her well enough to understand that
she was shielding her surprise. "I'm Ian Reynolds . . . Jake's
guardian."

Annie said the first thing that occurred to her. "Jake? Miss
Howard told me his name was Jefferson."

Ian stepped closer to the rocker. The scent of baby mingled
with lavender. He looked at the baby, but he was drawn to the
lavender. "I think Jake suits him better." The infant smiled.
"See? He approves."

It was probably gas, but Annie didn't explain that to her new
employer. Nothing could be served by being disagreeable the
first day out.

Ian whisked the apple behind his back as he made a slight
bow. "Ian Reynolds," he said. "Mrs. Ward explained that Jake's
my cousin?"

"Actually it was Miss Howard," Annie said. She found herself
unable to look away from the blue-gray eyes that were studying
her face. The directness of his gaze should have been uncomfortable, especially when she had misrepresented so much to
make a place for herself under his roof. Unconsciously Annie's
hand went to her throat. Beneath the severe, high-cut bodice of
her day dress, she could feel the outline of the locket. She reminded herself that she had a right to be there, at least until she
found something that told her she didn't. "She said Jeff . . . I
mean Jake was a second cousin, I believe. She told me about
his parents. I'm sorry." She hesitated a heartbeat, then added
softly, "For both of you."

He had the oddest sense she really meant it. Careless of her
comfort, he studied her a moment longer, taking in the details
of the oval face, the milky complexion, the pale hair. He would
have understood if she had shyly turned away under his scrutiny;
the fact that she stared right back made her more interesting.

Satisfied that the care of young Jake hadn't been turned over to some fey creature, Ian nodded, responding to her condolences. The hand behind his back, the one that held the apple, was brought forward, and Ian began polishing it on his sleeve. He thought he saw a glimmer of a smile raise the corners of her mouth. It was quickly masked. He wondered what she found amusing. "You've had dinner?" he asked.

"Hours ago."

"I suppose Mrs. Ward had a few things to say about me missing the meal."

Annie doubted it was proper to repeat the housekeeper's exact words, but she could feel a smile nudging her lips again. She looked down at the baby instead and adjusted his blankets.

Ian stopped the apple polishing. "You don't have to say anything. I can see that she did." He took a bite of the apple. "Mrs. Ward has certain liberties where I'm concerned," he said. "I couldn't change her if I wanted to. She was my nurse once upon a time."

This information startled Annie. Her head came up and she tried to see him in a new, smaller light.

Ian had no difficulty interpreting the look she gave him. He swallowed his bite of apple and grinned a little crookedly. "My point exactly," he said. "As hard as it is for you to imagine me as an armful the size of Jake there, Mrs. Ward finds it even harder to believe I'm out of short pants."

The image that came to Annie's mind was quite ridiculous. Instead of seeing the man in front of her as a young boy, she saw the grown man wearing short pants. She managed to tamp down her smile, but she could do nothing about the laughter in her eyes. Quickly ducking her head, Annie gave her full attention to the infant in her arms.

Ian watched her raise Jake to her shoulder and pat him on the back. The baby rested his soft, warm cheek against her collarbone and closed his eyes. A tiny bubble formed on the infant's pink mouth. She touched it with a slender finger.

"Baby dew," Annie whispered. She nudged Jake's silky crown of hair with her own cheek.

Ian was struck by the natural simplicity of her movement, the beauty inherent in her nurturing gesture. It would have been an intrusion to say or do anything. Ian remained still and said nothing. After more than a minute he heard Jake's gentle breathing change cadence. Something stirred in Ian.

"I'm Annie Moses," she said quietly, raising her cheek. She continued to pat the sleeping baby's back.

Still coming to grips with an unfamiliar restlessness, Ian nodded faintly. "Miss Moses." He looked around the room. The bedchamber was rather spartan in its furnishings and not very appealing as a nursery. "Mrs. Ward told you you would have free rein in here?" he asked.

"She suggested I might want to do some things. She didn't seem to think the room was suitable."

"And you do?"

"It's bathed in sunlight most of the day," she said. "I always think that's suitable." Except for the footlights, the theaters where she had gown up were invariably dark, and the boarding-houses rarely captured more than a slender beam of sunshine. "Jake and I will be going outside a great deal. Fresh air is good for an infant."

"But you will still be spending time in here." He glanced at the narrow bed. "You must make it comfortable for yourself. I'll see that Mrs. Ward has funds for your use."

"Thank you," she said. "It will be a pleasure."

Ian's blue-gray eyes narrowed thoughtfully. Although she had replied with gracious simplicity, he had the sense she was masterfully masking her excitement.

Annie wasn't conscious of her sigh or the faint, almost dreamy smile that touched her lips. It would be like having a place of her own, she was thinking, a place where she could hang brightly colored curtains and paint the wainscoting white. She was going to change the wallpaper and add paintings to the walls. There would be a chest of toys for Jake and a basket of books for

herself. She could build a home for herself and Jake in this room.
It would be . . .

Annie came out of her reverie to discover she was alone with
Jake. The door was being closed. A moment later there was the
faint sound of footsteps in the hallway. They receded gradually.
Annie cocked her head to one side to take in young Jake's che-
rubic face. "I shouldn't wonder that he thinks I'm daft, going
off into another world like I just did," she said. "I shouldn't
wonder at all."

"Nesting," Captain Henry Dallas said. He leaned back against
the taffrail of the *Somerset*, arms folded across his chest as he
regarded Ian Reynolds consideringly. "She isn't daft," he went
on, squinting slightly against the early morning sun as it peeked
around the ship's mast. "Or at least no more daft than any other
woman when she gets to thinking about building herself a nest.
Mark my words, Ian, that's what she was doing."

"Nesting," Ian said pensively. He wasn't as alarmed by the
prospect as Captain Dallas apparently thought he should be.
"Well, it's good to know she isn't daft."

Henry Dallas studied his employer for several moments.
"That's it?" he asked. "That's why you came down here this
morning, roused me out of my bunk? Just to ask me about young
Jake's nanny?" He rubbed his chin with the back of his hands,
his curiosity raised when he saw Ian's complexion ruddy a bit.
"Here now," he said suspiciously. "What's this woman like? I
take it she's not a prim lemon face like Miss Howard. Now,
there's a woman I was glad to see take her leave of this shore."

"Not half so glad as she was to leave," Ian said, recovering
himself. He pushed away from the taffrail, thanked Captain Dallas for his time, and left the *Somerset* for his offices at the Mannering warehouse. He acknowledged to himself that it was a
narrow escape. He had piqued the captain's interest in Miss Annie Moses, and for reasons he did not fully understand himself,
he wasn't prepared to talk at length about Jake's nanny.

As it turned out, Captain Henry Dallas was able to answer his own question about Annie Moses later that morning. He spied her just as he was leaving the gangwalk of the *Somerset* headed to Crowe's Tavern for a plate of stew and a spot of ale. He didn't know who she was, but she turned his head the same as the heads of a dozen other sailors, dockworkers, and fishermen on the harbor pier.

The day was already uncomfortably warm, but on the wharf the river breeze gave some relief. It was sunshine glancing off the crown of her cornsilk hair that first caught the captain's eye. She had just removed her bonnet. As he watched, she leaned over the baby carriage she had been pushing and laid the bonnet inside. Over the din of work on the dock he couldn't hear the words she was saying to the infant, but there was an expression of reassurance on her face and a smile of infinite gentleness that made even an old salt like Henry Dallas think of his mother.

She could have been anyone. Yet Captain Dallas didn't believe she was. He hurried down the gangwalk to introduce himself and hustle her off the wharf. Perhaps she *was* a bit daft, he thought. Nannies didn't push the infants in their care on busy wharfs. This sort of activity was generally confined to the park where there were shade trees and benches and other women similarly engaged.

He walked up to her and tipped his hat. "Ma'am," he said. "May I be of some assistance?"

Annie straightened slowly. She had an urge to look over her shoulder to see if anyone was there. She was not convinced it was she who was being addressed. "Well, yes," she said slowly. "I wonder if you might direct me to someone who will take us aboard a Mannering ship?"

The captain's heavy brows were lifted a notch before they were drawn together. He rubbed his chin, frowning. "A Mannering ship?" he asked. "Now, why do you want to board one of them? None of them are taking passengers now."

"Oh, we don't intend to go anywhere," she said. "We'd just like to tour one of the ships."

Captain Dallas stole a glance at the infant in the carriage. The brim of Annie's bonnet and the wicker hood of the carriage threw most of the baby's face in shadow. Even so, Dallas could make out a pair of alert blue eyes staring back at him. "We'd like that, would we?"

Annie wasn't certain if he was talking to her or the baby, but she answered for both of them. "Yes, we would," she said firmly. "I don't believe you're taking our request at all seriously."

He blinked at that. She had raised her chin a bit, straightened her shoulders, and looked for all the world as if she were prepared to take him to task. He did not relish the idea of going toe to toe with Miss Annie Moses. More than ever he was convinced he was speaking to Mrs. Ward's choice of a nanny for Jefferson Mannering. This was just the sort of no-nonsense spirit the widow would admire. "Captain Henry Dallas," he said, making a slightly bow. "Of the Mannering flagship, the *Somerset*. At your service."

Annie flushed a little at that. "Annie Moses," she said. She pointed to the carriage. "And Jefferson . . . *Jake* Mannering."

Discovering he had been right all along, Captain Dallas permitted himself a small, satisfied smile. He decided that Crowe's Tavern could wait. So could his lecture about the proper place to take an infant for a stroll. "This way, Miss Moses."

Annie clutched the rungs of the ladder as the doors to the library were abruptly parted. "Oh," she said breathlessly, twisting her head to see who had entered. The book she had started to remove from the shelf slipped back into place. "It's you."

Ian Reynolds stepped inside, closed the doors behind him, and leaned against them. His casual posture belied his irritation.

Annie was not proof against the splintered steel of his eyes. Forgetting about the book that had drawn her to the upper shelf in the first place, Annie descended the ladder slowly. "Mrs. Ward gave me permission to come here," she said. "It seems I have overstepped my—"

It spoke to his level of agitation that he didn't care that she had invaded his sanctuary. "I spoke to Captain Dallas just above an hour ago," he said. His tone was deep, tense with barely suppressed anger. "He says that he took you and Jake on a tour of the *Somerset*, so don't think you can deny you were at the harbor this morning."

Annie's face remained unchanged, although a surge of heat flushed her cheeks. "I have no intention of denying it," she said.

"Mrs. Ward says she didn't approve of you going," he said.

"That's true, but perhaps not the way you think. I didn't ask her permission. I wasn't of the opinion that it was necessary."

Ian pushed away from the door. There was a small sideboard in the library that was stocked with liquor and wine. He poured himself two fingers of whiskey. He raised the glass but didn't drink, watching her instead. "And I wasn't of the opinion that you had cotton between your ears. It's an opinion under revision."

That deepened Annie's flush. She said steadily, "I take it you object to my visit to the ship."

"Miss Moses," Ian said carefully, setting his tumbler aside. "I don't care if you parade your wares up and down the harbor for every woman-starved sot and sailor to ogle, but I damn well do care if you expose my cousin's child to that sort of pandering." It wasn't what he meant to say at all. He was hearing the words for the first time as he spoke them; they had never been a clear thought in his head. He had intended to tell her that it wasn't safe for her to go unaccompanied, that she had put herself and the infant at some risk by going there alone. He had been prepared to offer himself as escort and guide in the future.

But that was before he had opened the library doors and seen her perched with delicate precision on the upper rungs of the ladder. It was before he had glimpsed the trim ankles and slender calves peeking out from beneath her raised petticoats. It was before he had witnessed her near fall as she was startled and before the breathy little voice, tentative smile, and wide gray eyes were turned on him like a series of lighthouse beacons.

Annie simply stared at him now, mute. Only that morning she had gone to the boardinghouse and collected her trunk of clothes and personal effects. The Liberty Players were not even there to wish her well, and she had no time to stop at the theater, where they were rehearsing their last play together. She left a hastily scrawled note to relate her good fortune in acquiring a position with Ian Reynolds. They would be congratulating themselves that evening after the performance for having made the right decision to force her out of the nest. Annie couldn't imagine herself going back or explaining her failure. She was truly on her own now.

Annie smoothed the navy blue material of her gown over her midriff before she let her hands fall to her sides. Calmly, with a serene dignity that would have pleased Ruby Doubletree, Annie said, "I wanted Jake to experience his heritage. He *is* a Mannering and he should know his birthright." Having said her piece, Annie crossed the room with a regal bearing and opened the library doors.

"Where are you going?" Ian asked. "I didn't dismiss you." His father had talked to the servants like that, Ian remembered. It didn't seem to matter that he had vowed to do it differently, approach every situation with evenhandedness and composure. When his back was to the wall, he heard his father's voice coming from his own throat.

Annie paused on the threshold and looked sideways at Ian Reynolds. He was raking back his hair with his fingers. His hand stayed at the nape of his neck and rubbed it momentarily, tilting his head to one side and closing his eyes briefly. There was a sigh, but it wasn't of relief, merely of impatience. Annie's fingers whitened on the door handles as she waited to be excused.

"Come back here," he said. "And shut the doors. You're neither excused from this room nor dismissed from employment." He studied her, the edge of flint still in his eyes. "Unless you desire to quit. That would be your choice."

Annie stepped backward into the library and let the doors fall closed. In the silent room they clicked into place as if she had slammed them. "I want to stay," she said quietly.

One month passed, then another. Jake smiled in earnest now and crawled freely. His infectious gurgling laughter delighted the household staff. Annie often found herself being the lone voice advocating firmness and discipline in the care of young Jake. Without it, she reasoned, he was in danger of becoming horribly spoiled.

Annie redecorated the nursery. The room was bright now, with light blue walls and white woodwork. The window seat was given a plump brocade cushion and a new, colorfully braided rug was added to the sitting area in front of the hearth. Annie refused to part with the rocker, or search for another, so the groundskeeper refinished it. The narrow bed was replaced with a larger four-poster from another room, and the adjoining dressing room was furnished with amenities like a Chippendale armoire and highboy.

A scarred and battered sea chest with the stylized Mannering *M* on the lid held all of Jake's toys. The worn chest was a gift from Ian. He had carried it into the nursery, unannounced and without fanfare, and placed it at the foot of Jake's crib. Annie was sitting on the window seat, reading, while Jake napped, and by the time she gathered her wits, Ian was at the door on the point of leaving. His brief parting comment was "So he'll know his heritage, Miss Moses."

The exchange was typical of their interaction. They rarely saw each other except in passing, and the comments were stiff and formal, coolly polite, and just a little tense. Annie could not help but notice that her employer's reserve was strictly maintained only where she was concerned. With the rest of the staff Ian Reynolds was relaxed, even friendly. Mrs. Ward acted on his behalf more than once in settling personal problems that cropped up from time to time. No one doubted it was Ian's money that helped the head groom pay his gambling debts or that it was

Ian's influence that secured a position for the new cook's husband on the Mannering line.

For his part, Ian observed that Annie Moses always had a kind word to say in passing, unless she was passing him. He escorted her to the harbor on two occasions, but he could see there was no joy for her in the excursions. Captain Dallas remarked that she had had no end of questions when he guided her through the *Somerset*. When Ian accompanied her, she hardly spoke.

Ian noticed that she read a great deal. He never investigated the basket of books in the nursery. He knew her tastes ran to Shakespeare and Jonson and that she especially liked the comedies. He knew she enjoyed philosophy and history. He knew it because of the empty spaces in his library where she had removed one or another of his leather-bound volumes.

He never ran into her again there. She slipped in and out of his sanctuary unnoticed, choosing her times carefully to take or return a book. He never glimpsed her hanging on his ladder, stretching for a volume just out of her reach, her ankles turned just so, the smooth line of her slender calves displayed amid ruffled petticoats.

Ian Reynolds didn't have time to think about what Annie did with her day. He made time solely for that purpose. He imagined her sitting with Jake in the nursery, sunshine forming a penumbra about her cornsilk hair. The braid would fall forward over her shoulder and the baby would grab it, draw it toward his mouth and suck once or twice before she pulled it away. He could see her pushing the carriage through the park, taking a picnic luncheon beneath the trees by the river, then strolling along the bank with Jake in her arms.

Ian visited the nursery to see his infant cousin several times a week. Annie took time to answer his questions about the child's development, then she invariably found some reason to leave him alone with Jake. She would return promptly in twenty minutes, her quick return suggesting to Ian that she did not believe he really enjoyed his visits with Jake and made them only out of duty. He did nothing to disabuse her of the notion. More than once he was almost caught out on the floor rolling a cloth ball in Jake's direction. Somehow he always managed to be upright when Annie returned, and if Jake was chortling with childish abandon, Ian left Annie to wonder what it could mean.

Two months was long enough for Annie to learn something of the Mannering history. Her most important discovery, at least to her way of thinking, was that if she were a Mannering, she was of no blood relation to Ian Reynolds. It was a comfort to know she shared no sire with the arrogant head of the Mannering line. It was Ian's stepmother who was the Mannering, and Ian's father, James Sutton Reynolds, who had infused the shipping line with enough money some twenty years earlier to keep the Mannering vessels quite literally afloat. Sarah Mannering Reynolds had borne her husband no children, and when she and her husband had been killed in a carriage accident three years before, Ian Reynolds found himself fighting for control of the line his father had saved but took little interest in.

Annie supposed the arrogance she observed was an inherited trait, like his aquiline nose and flinty, remote stare. By all accounts, he took after his father. His mother, Mrs. Ward noted, was a restrained, fragile woman who took to her bed for weeks at a time following Ian's birth and for eight years after. If the housekeeper was to be believed, it was inactivity and boredom that killed Ian's mother. There was no chance they would be Ian's undoing. They were two circumstances he did not suffer gladly. He was up at dawn and often did not return to his Chestnut Hill manor until the dinner hour had passed. Annie was as aware as the rest of the staff that with Adam Mannering's death there was upheaval in the company again and there were those Mannering heirs with their eyes on the prize once more.

In the two months that Annie Moses had lived under Ian Reynolds's roof, she had never known him to come home for luncheon. That's why it was a surprise to run into him in the gallery.

Annie stopped short on the threshold when she saw she would not be alone. The gallery was a favorite place of hers, a quiet room where she could find solitude while Jake napped. Unlike some of the other staff, she did not mind the gilt-framed portraits that crowded the walls. She had heard the maids complain about the eyes that seemed to follow them as they dusted, but Annie never had the sense she was being watched. It was rather a warm feeling she enjoyed from spending time in the room. She could make herself believe it was family surrounding her, not strangers.

"I'm sorry," she said, backing up immediately. "I didn't know . . ."

Ian was sitting in a large wing chair, his lean frame unfolded casually, one leg resting over the brocade arm, the other stretched out negligently in front of him. His head rested against the back of the chair. Weary lines creased the corners of his mouth like commas framing a clause. He had one hand raised to his temple. He was massaging it absently.

His eyes were closed. Even before she had spoken he had recognized her presence. It was the lavender. "Don't go on my account," he said quietly. "I don't mind."

It was the fatigue that edged his expression and deepened his voice that Annie responded to. Here was proof at last that Ian Reynolds was human, that his tolerance and endurance did indeed have an end. Annie sat down on one of the small sofas, perching on the edge like a wary bird, hands folded in her lap to keep from fidgeting

Ian opened his eyes slowly. His hand moved from his neck to the bridge of his nose. He rubbed it with his thumb and index finger. "Do you come here often?" he asked.

"When I can," she said. "Jake doesn't always nap when I'd like. Sometimes there are other things to do." Three sentences, she thought. It was the most she had spoken to him that week. She watched him complete his weary gesture and his hand drop to his lap. It rattled the papers lying there. It was the first time she noticed them.

"What other things?" he asked. "How do you spend your day?"

Annie wondered what prompted the question. Genuine interest? Perhaps he was only looking for a diversion. If that was the case, he would be sorry. There was nothing diverting about her day.

She had hesitated so long, Ian didn't think she was inclined to answer. "I know what you do with Jake," he prompted. "Tell me what you do without him. What pleasures are in your day?"

"I read," she said. "Plays mostly. I like—"

"Comedies," he said, closing his eyes again. "Yes, I know. Go on."

Annie saw the weary creases flatten out as he rested again. She looked at his angled jaw and strong line of his exposed throat. She had never considered that he might be vulnerable, but with his eyes closed and the steely nature of their color sheathed, she saw him differently. "I like to sew," she told him quietly. She created scores of costumes over the years for the Liberty Players. It was an activity she missed in the early days of her arrival at the manor house. "I've made some shirts for Jake. I'm making short pants for him now, for when he's a little older." She hesitated. "I made this dress."

He didn't open his eyes. He knew it was dove gray, almost the exact shade of her eyes. It had a high neckline, offset at the throat by a black bow. The sleeves were tight and the bodice defined her willowy shape, closely following the slender contours of her breasts and waist. Just above her hips the skirt flared. The effect was one of guarded reticence. It made Ian wonder what she would be like without the gown to restrain her. His mind was wandering into dangerous territory. He indicated with a small wave of his hand that she should go on.

"I write letters," she told him.

One of Ian's dark brows rose a fraction. He had always thought of her as most singularly alone. It was a revelation to find she had friends . . . family . . . perhaps a lover.

"My friends left the city six weeks ago," she said. The Liberty

Players had not disbanded after all. They struck out for points south and were entertaining in theaters in Richmond, Charleston, and Atlanta. "They won't be back for several months."

"All your friends?" It was an intriguing notion that she was as alone as he had first thought.

"Well, yes," she offered reluctantly.

"Family?"

Family and friends. They were one and the same. "They're gone too," she said.

"Dead?" he asked. He was looking at her now. "Or gone?"

She thought of Ruby Doubletree. She stared at her folded hands. "Dead," she said. There was a dry, aching lump at the back of her throat. Annie swallowed it with difficulty. When she raised her face her features were composed and she was dry-eyed. "I used to go to the harbor," she told him, continuing to describe her day. "Even before I came here. I liked to watch the ships putting out to sea. The Mannering ships were always the most beautiful." She didn't say it to ingratiate herself. She said it because in her eyes it was true.

It was on the tip of his tongue to thank her. Many of the ships were of his design, though he doubted she knew that. Instead, he said, "I never noticed you there." Ian felt sure he would have.

"I never went there to be noticed."

Though she said it simply, without sarcastic intention, it was impossible for Ian not to recall the things he had said to her, the accusations he had leveled at her head. It was an opening for an apology, but the words stuck and the moment passed. Her eyes strayed to the portraits on the opposite wall. Ian followed the line of her vision. "That's Dora Mannering," he said. "My step-mother's grandmother. She was fifteen when that portrait was done. I met her once when I was very young. She still had laughing eyes."

Annie nodded. The eyes did laugh. They were gray eyes, rather like her own but not so solemn. They also presented the only similarity Annie could find between herself and any of her supposed family. "There are more Mannerings here than Reynoldses," she said. "I've wondered about that."

The papers in Ian's lap rustled a bit as he straightened. The leg that was hooked over the arm of the chair was removed and joined the other stretched out in front of him. His posture was more relaxed now, less weary. "That's because my father gave Sarah a free hand in this room. He had no real interest in either of the families, but he loved Sarah to distraction. He didn't care what she put on the walls."

"You called your stepmother Sarah?" She wondered if he would consider the question impertinent and refuse to answer or, worse, take her to task for it.

"I had a mother," he said. "That was the point Sarah made when she married my father. Sarah wanted to be my friend and that's what she was. Father disapproved, but it was another round lost to Sarah. She was nineteen when she married him. I was eight. There were fewer years separating us than there were between Sarah and Father. I think he finally agreed that she had done the right thing."

Annie looked to the wall again. She already knew there was no portrait of Sarah in the room but she did not know why. Ian anticipated her question.

"She sat for a portrait only once, before her marriage. She never wanted it displayed. I don't even think she brought it with her. She said she wanted no reminders of what it was like to be young."

"But she *was* young," Annie said.

"Sarah?" he said, shaking his head. "No. She was very old." He looked at Annie, studying the grave face, the clear gray eyes. "A bit like you in that regard. Far older than her years."

Annie wasn't certain if she was being insulted or complimented. Perhaps he meant neither. "Mrs. Ward told me that Sarah Mannering was very gay, that she brought life into this house."

A faint smile changed the shape of Ian's mouth. "That's true,"

he said. "She was. She did. But that was her public face." The
smile faded. "She worked hard at it."

Curious, Annie was on the point of asking another question,
when she saw Ian straighten, pulling his feet closer to the chair
and raising the papers from his lap. She caught the hovering
question and remained silent, recognizing the discussion was
closed or at least that Ian intended to control it.

His index finger traced the corner of the papers he held.
"These arrived at the warehouse a few hours ago," he told her.
"My lawyer delivered them." He didn't look at Annie or the
papers. His gunmetal glance studied the portraits. "The Mannerings have banded together to dispute Adam's will. They want
the guardianship of Jake, in spite of my cousin's wishes."

Annie felt her throat closing. For a moment she couldn't
speak, and when she did, she didn't consider her words. "Someone wants to take Jake from us?" Annie flushed and waited for
Ian to take issue with her phrasing. She had no defense. In her
mind she had spoken the truth. Young Jake was not a child on
loan. He belonged to both of them.

But Ian didn't take issue. He merely studied her face again,
something like approval settling over his blue-gray eyes. "It's
not Jake they want precisely. That would make it easier to stomach. The Mannerings want what he represents to them. Control
of the line."

"But how can Jake . . . he's just an infant."

"When my father flooded the Mannering shipping line with
money he did it for only one reason. It was Sarah's bride price.
They sold her to my father in return for his financial assistance,
but they did not desire his interference in the day-to-day operation of the line." Ian dropped the papers on the table beside him
and leaned forward in his chair. He rested his forearms on his
knees and regarded Annie frankly.

"Father and Sarah were satisfied with this arrangement. He
got Sarah and she got away from her family. My father never
begrudged them the money that saved their empire, but they
were never comfortable with their own indebtedness. It didn't

sit well with them that they had required bailing out. The less my father cared, the more the Mannerings hated him for it. What he could give them so easily, they resented passionately."

"Who are *they?*" Annie asked, looking from Ian to the portraits. She wanted to know faces. She wanted individuals to blame.

"Adam's father, for one," said Ian. "Fletcher Mannering. Sarah was his sister."

"Then he's Jake's grandfather."

"Yes," he said tersely. "Jake's grandfather." He didn't like being reminded that he could claim no blood tie with his infant cousin. A judge might not look upon that favorably. "Louisa Mannering, Fletcher's wife and Jake's grandmother. Tyler and Marcus Mannering. Adam's brothers. Georgia Mannering, Fletcher's sister and Jake's great-aunt. At the death of her parents she became the self-appointed head of the family."

Annie's eyes darted from one portrait to another and finally came to Georgia Mannering. "She was Sarah's sister too," Annie said softly. She tried to find something of the woman she imagined Sarah to be in her sister's portrait. She could see no gaiety or lively interest in the features as painted by the artist. The portrait showed a woman in her thirties with a handsome face, if not a beautiful one, the corners of her mouth already tightening from the effects of a disapproving mind. Annie spoke her thoughts aloud. "A force to be reckoned with."

"Indeed," Ian said dryly. "There was no love lost between her and Sarah."

Somehow Annie knew. She just knew. She turned to Ian. "Georgia was in love with your father."

He nodded slowly, eyeing Annie thoughtfully. She had an intuitive sense he appreciated. "He might even have married her if my own mother had died sooner. She was my mother's friend and a frequent visitor to the house, caring for Mother, comforting Father. I think she expected a proposal. She may have even had my mother's blessing."

It sounded rather ghoulish, Annie thought. This time she kept her thoughts to herself.

Ian went on. "My mother, however, was not so cooperative that she was willing to die in order for her friend to marry her husband. She lingered for years in that sickbed of hers. She didn't have visitors, she granted audiences."

Annie had no doubt that he included himself and his father among those who had to make appointments to visit the sickroom.

"By the time she died," he said, "Sarah was a woman grown and my father's eyes never lighted on Georgia. He never regretted his decision and Georgia never forgave him. It was her idea to elicit such a heavy price for Sarah's hand. She was determined to see him pay for his betrayal."

"There was no betrayal," Annie said.

"In Georgia Mannering's eyes there was. For Fletcher Mannering it was strictly a business transaction. For Georgia it was deeply personal." He bent his head and stared at the floor. His broad shoulders heaved once with the force of his sigh. When he raised his eyes he speared Annie with his flinty gaze. "Some things don't change. They have their own reasons for wanting Jake. I suspect it's the very reason that Adam put his son into my care. For all that Adam was a Mannering, he had occasional moments of rebellion. We stole away on a ship once and got as far as Narragansett Bay before we were discovered. I was ten. He was a year younger. Everyone thought it was my doing." He grinned a little at the memory. "I wish it had been. It would have made taking the punishment a little easier."

Annie noticed that he did not seem particularly regretful.

Ian's grin disappeared. "Adam wanted me to have his son for a reason. I didn't understand it at first, but now that the Mannerings are making their move, it's clearer to me."

"How will taking Jake help the Mannerings?" asked Annie.

"Adam's shares are now Jake's and as Jake's guardian I control them. When my father agreed on the Mannerings' price for Sarah, he also negotiated forty-nine percent of the company. The

Mannerings agreed because Sarah's shares were part of the forty-nine percent and there was no method for him to gain control. They also knew that my father was not interested in managing the operation but that his forty-nine-percent share would mean he would not allow it to go under either."

Annie's hands unfolded in her lap and she smoothed the material over her knees. "So for the first time in the history of the Mannering empire, the control has fallen out of their hands."

Ian nodded again, satisfied with her conclusion. "When my father and Sarah were killed a few years ago, there was no mourning period before the Mannerings swooped. They tried to buy me out, only nothing I owned was for sale. My role in the company until that time was that of an employee. As a young man I sailed under Captain Dallas. Later I commanded the *Glendower*. I liked the open sea and I think I would have been content to stay there."

Annie glanced at the portraits again. Where there were smiles, they were stiffly set. The eyes, with the notable exception of Dora Mannering's, seemed predatory to her now. She turned back to Ian. "If they hadn't pushed you," she said. She had no difficulty imagining him in command of one of the Mannering vessels. Even if he had never taken her on a tour of the shipyard, she would have been able to see him there among the masts and yardarms. He walked the deck with the ease of long practice, and maneuvering in the close quarters of the passageways and cabins was second nature to him. His walk was fluid, rolling, like the sea that cradled his ship. And it was his ship. They all were. She didn't doubt that either. There were Mannerings working in the offices at the warehouse, but Captain Dallas told her they rarely boarded the vessels any longer. In most things related to the design and construction, he said, they deferred to Ian Reynolds.

Annie imagined they must resent deferring to Ian just as they had resented the gift of his father's money. Ian Reynolds had made the Mannerings realize he was necessary to the survival of their company. Now, with Adam's shares shifted to him through Jake, Ian *was* the company.

"What are you going to do?" Annie asked. She glanced at the papers on the end table.

Restless now, Ian stood. He rubbed the back of his neck with his palm. "My lawyer says that Adam's will is very clear about his intentions. The Mannerings will have a difficult time breaking it, blood relation or no. In part because the line is doing so well, they have money to fight it." He shrugged. "I have money too."

"So you'll fight it in court?" she asked.

His hand dropped to his side. "If it comes to that. I'm hoping it won't, or that if it does, I'll have something else in my favor."

"Something?"

"Some*one*," he corrected her. "Mr. Edwards thinks a judge may be more inclined to support Adam's wishes if I demonstrated I had a proper home."

Annie's brows raised slightly. "A proper home?"

"A wife," Ian said, watching her closely.

"Oh." Annie's eyes lowered. She bit her lip. Any moment someone would come to the door and announce that Jake was stirring above stairs. She could leave then, gracefully, and pretend this conversation had never taken place.

"I wondered if you might be willing?"

There was a roar in her ears, so Annie couldn't be certain she'd heard him correctly. She finally took flight, springing to her feet. "I think I hear Jake," she said. "I should go."

He closed the distance between them, taking her by the arm. She did not try to wrest away from him but held herself very still in his light grasp. "Miss Moses . . . Annie . . . may I call you Annie?"

She nodded, staring at his hand on her arm. She knew she could pull away, yet she didn't. He had never touched her before, never led her to believe that he might want to. His hand was warm, dry. Just as she thought it might be. Her own palms were damp.

"Captain Dallas will tell you I don't know many women," he said, his tone carefully neutral. He saw Annie risk a skeptical look in his direction. "Whores and wenches. That's what he'd say."

Annie began to recover some of her poise. "No, he wouldn't," she said. "Not to me he wouldn't. Captain Dallas is not so ill mannered." Ian removed his hand and Annie lowered her arm.

"Dallas says you're a proper lady," Ian told her. "I'm inclined to agree with him. I know you're good with Jake. Mrs. Ward says you don't miss a trick, and that's high praise in her book. There's been a change in the air since you arrived. I thought at first it was just Jake's presence that was making the difference, but it's you too."

Annie's face was pale. Her lower lip trembled slightly. "Please excuse me, Mr. Reynolds. I must go to Jake." She fled the gallery, and this time he did not call her back.

It did not surprise her that the dream came to her that night. She had had it many times over the last two months. In the course of her young life she had had the recurring dream every few months. Upon her arrival at Ian Reynolds's home she began having the dream every few days. She had thought it had little to do with Ian Reynolds and everything to do with Jake Mannering. Now she was not so sure.

In her dream it was always the hand she saw first. It was a slender and delicate hand, a woman's hand. There was an emerald ring on the smallest finger and the gold filigree setting fascinated her as much as the emerald did. Fingers brushed her cheek, drifted across her skin. It was a light caress, slow. A parting gesture. She was being bid farewell. Something wet touched her cheek. A tear. Someone was crying. It could have been she. It could have been the woman leaning over her.

The features above her were hazy. It was impossible to make out any single line. The arched brow slid into the curve of the nose that blended into the cheek. The mouth was puckered. The features blurred further as the woman bent closer. Something was pressed in Annie's small fist. There was a voice. Words that meant very little. "It has to be."

She was floating then. Bumping along on clouds. Bobbing. Bobbing. She clutched the thing in her hand. Her fingers ached because she held it so tightly. . . .

Annie woke. She bolted upright. Her cotton nightshift was damp. Tendrils of her pale cornsilk hair clung to her neck. She lifted them away and plucked at the bodice of her shift. Her right hand was cramped where she had curled it in a tight fist. She shook it out and felt for the locket at her throat. It was still there. At least this time she hadn't yanked it off.

When she had first told Ruby Doubletree about the dream it had been dismissed. After all, Ruby assured her, what was there to suggest that any part of the dream had a counterpart in reality? Now Annie realized that Ruby had been afraid she would remember something more substantial and begin asking questions that Ruby didn't want to, or couldn't, answer.

There was little danger of the dream becoming more clear. It was as it always had been. Increased frequency was no harbinger of clarity. She could not make out her mother's face, if indeed it was her mother. There were no clues in the dream save the emerald ring and the locket. She had the latter and no confidence that she would ever be led to the other.

Sliding her legs over the edge of the four-poster, Annie steadied herself, then stood. She padded over to Jake's crib. The baby was sleeping soundly. She scooped him out anyway and held him against her breast. The child was not the one in need of comfort now, she was.

Annie walked to the window seat and parted the drapes. The window was open halfway. A gentle breeze fluttered the fringe on the drapes and billowed the sheer curtains. It stirred the fine, silky strands of hair on Jake's head. She pressed her mouth against his temple.

"What do you think, Jake?" she asked quietly. "It would be almost as if I were your mother."

The sleeping child was silent. His cheek rested on her shoulder.

"I couldn't have foreseen any of this when I came to this house," Annie told him. "I came because I thought it was a good place to start. I didn't imagine it might end here. Every time I asked a question about the Mannering line I was directed to talk to Ian Reynolds. He doesn't even realize that others think of him as more Mannering than the Mannerings themselves." She rubbed the baby's back soothingly as she paced the floor in front of the fireplace. "Perhaps that's what your own father knew about Ian. He has the founding spirit of the Mannering line. He loves the sea, the ships. He works so hard for something that bears his stamp but not his name. It has your name, Jake. You're a Mannering. He's working for you!"

The baby raised his head briefly, turning so he could lay his other cheek against her. She cradled his head in the palm of her hand. "I didn't know about you either," she whispered. "Mrs. Ward thinks I was Ian's choice. He thinks I arrived at her request. Heaven knows what will happen if they sort it out between them. I don't suppose that even marriage to Mr. Reynolds will help me then."

Annie rested her cheek against the baby's silky hair. "You're not going to help me sort it out, are you?" She sighed. "Or perhaps you already have."

How could she abandon him? It was not a possibility. If she refused Ian's proposal and he lost Jake, then she would also lose him. But then, marrying Ian did not guarantee the desired outcome either. The Mannerings might still be able to take Jefferson. "That's what they'll call you," Annie told him. "Jefferson. That name will make you proper. Jake will give you character."

She laid the baby in his crib. She brushed his sweet, downy cheek with her fingertips, much as she dreamed someone had done to her. In Annie's case it wasn't a farewell gesture. "I won't abandon you," she said. "It doesn't have to be."

Annie sought out Ian Reynolds the following morning. He was alone in the dining room drinking a cup of coffee. A newspaper was laid out on the table but he wasn't reading it. He was staring out the window.

"I've thought about your proposal," she announced without preamble. "I want you to know I'm agreeable."

He didn't have time to put down his coffee cup before she was gone.

Ian came home early. At work he had been distracted and unable to concentrate. Noise from the warehouse below his offices irritated him and interruptions were annoying. He was impatient with the clerks and almost rude to one of the shippers. It was at that point he thought he'd better leave. He realized he was quite capable of sinking the Mannering shipping line with no help from the Mannerings.

Calm covered him like a favorite blanket when he walked into the nursery. All the petty aggravations of the morning were forgotten. The missed schedules, the unexpected repairs, the insurance claims—the business upsets of the afternoon—were pushed to the back of his mind. Ian didn't question the sense of peace that came over him. He simply allowed himself to enjoy it.

Annie and Jake were lying on the four-poster. Annie didn't stir as Ian approached the bed. Jake was wide awake, however, and he grinned happily when he saw Ian. As if the child could understand, Ian placed a finger to his own lips to insist on quiet. Jake gurgled, stretched, and put two fingers in his mouth.

"Good boy," Ian whispered, lifting the child away from Annie. Her heat and fragrance lingered against Jake's skin. "Lucky boy," Ian said in Jake's ear.

Ian set Jake down on the braided rug amid the child's uncollected playthings. Jake immediately grabbed a cloth ball, clutched it against his cheek for a moment, then pitched it at Ian. Hunkering down, Ian rolled it back. It was just outside of Jake's reach, but the baby made a clumsy lunge for it anyway. Ian laughed as Jake toppled on his side.

Strains of that deep, nearly silent laughter sifted through Annie's sleep and ended her dream. She woke abruptly, sensing the
shift in the room and the absence of the baby beside her. Her
eyes flew open and then she was still.

Ian was lying on his side, stretched out beside Jake. He was
building a tower of blocks. Jake watched, apparently fascinated
by the construction's progress, then without warning struck the
tower down, spilling blocks in all directions. Ian didn't scold or
even appear frustrated by the demolition. He simply gathered
the blocks and began rebuilding. Annie realized what she was
witnessing was not a first-time occurrence. Ian was constructing
the tower knowing full well that Jake was going to topple it. It
was part of the ritual, part of the play.

When it happened again, Ian and the baby grinned simulta-
neously. Annie felt her own breath catch. With their bright, unaffected smiles, they could have been father and son.

"I think we've disturbed Annie's slumber," Ian said to Jake.
He raised his head, saw the flicker of Annie's lashes as she tried
to close them, and nodded. Pointing conspiratorially in the direction of the bed, Ian said, "I'm sure of it. She's playing possum
now." He gave Jake a push on his padded bottom and the child
began scooting across the rug toward the bed. Ian sat up, crossing
his legs in front of him tailor-fashion and began pitching the
blocks back into the sea chest. He made enough noise to be
certain that Annie was roused.

Jake pulled himself up using the bed frame, raised himself
on tiptoe, and peered cautiously over the edge of the mattress.

"Peekaboo," Annie said.

Laughing, Jake fell backward and landed on his rear. A small
grunt punctuated the fall, but Jake was scrambling up again in
the next moment.

Annie sat up and swung her legs over the side of the bed. She
pushed at her skirt when she saw Ian's gaze drop to the length
of her uncovered calves. It was not the residue of sleep that
flushed her cheeks now. It occurred to her that Ian's presence in

the nursery was vaguely improper. "You should have wakened me," she said, coming to her feet.

Her tart criticism had no impact on Ian. He shrugged. "Jake said you were tired. It seemed best to let you sleep."

Annie was picking up Jake. It took a moment for Ian's words to register and another moment for her to understand he had blithely placed the blame on an infant who had yet to utter a single intelligible word. She kissed Jake on his temple as much in the way of an affectionate greeting as to hide her smile from Ian. Carrying Jake to the changing table, Annie made short work of cleaning and powdering the infant. She patted the baby's belly, scooped him up, and set him on the floor beside Ian. "Next time," she told Jake, "tell your cousin that you want him to change your nappy."

"Father," Ian said.

Straightening, Annie stared down at him. A frown puckered her eyebrows. "What?" she asked.

"Father," Ian repeated. "I want to adopt Jake. I've been thinking about it most of the day. Since you're going to marry me, I think it's what we should do."

Annie backed away a little, startled by this piece of news. "Oh, but—"

Ian's blue-gray eyes darkened and narrowed fractionally. Jake had crawled into his lap and he held the baby still. "You haven't changed your mind, have you?"

Annie didn't respond immediately. There was winter in Ian's voice and frost in his eyes. Annie shivered, chilled by both. She shook her head slowly. It was all she could do not to cross her arms protectively in front of her. "No," she said finally. "I haven't changed my mind."

Ian sent Jake off in the direction of his treasure chest of toys and stood. He noticed Annie held her ground but looked as if she wanted to take another step backward. "Are you afraid of me?" he asked.

"No!" But she said it too quickly and she saw that he knew it too. "Perhaps a little," she conceded. Annie turned away and began arranging items on the changing table. None of it needed her attention, but she required the diversion.

Ian said nothing. He simply watched her, waiting, and quelled the urge to tug on the single thick braid that fell down her back. It was easy to imagine wrapping the end of it around his fist and pulling her against him. She would have to come to him then, he thought. She would have no choice.

"You really don't know anything about me," Annie said as she lined up jars of creams and powder on the table. "You might want to take back your proposal and find someone more suitable."

"Suppose you tell me," he said.

Annie skirted the table and went to the writing desk. She had spent most of her morning composing a letter to the Liberty Players. Proof of her frustrated efforts lay crumpled in the basket beside the desk. She ran a finger along the edge of the half-finished missive that was her last attempt and looked at Ian. "I've been trying to write to my friends," she told him. "My family. And when I put these recent events into words I find myself wondering at the wisdom of your proposal and my decision to accept it."

Ian was watching Annie's finger trace the edge of the vellum. It was the delicacy of the movement that captured his attention, the gracefulness in the gesture. His eyes lifted to her anxious ones. "What is it you think I should know?" he asked.

Annie drew in a deep breath. "My friends are actors," she blurted out before she lost her nerve. "They raised me. They're the only family I've ever known." She raised her chin a notch and braced herself as if for a blow. "I'm not ashamed of them," she said. "I love them. I love who they are and what they do, but I'll understand if you think it makes me ill suited to be Jake's mother. You may not consider me proper enough, no matter what Captain Dallas thinks of my character."

Ian listened gravely, his head tilted slightly to one side as Annie confessed the skeletons in her closet. It was an effort not to smile, not so much at what she said, but at her earnestness.

'Mrs. Ward never mentioned that to me," he said. "I wonder why?"

Annie begged the question. "You would have to ask her."

He shrugged. "I'm certain she found it all unremarkable, or she would have said something. It's not as if you were on the stage yourself." He saw her stricken look. "Were you?"

Annie swallowed. "Walk-on parts," she said. "A servant. A messenger. Things like that. I had no talent for delivering dialogue. Mostly I painted scenery and designed and mended costumes. No one had much head for finances or schedules. I organized the troupe."

Ian had no difficulty believing that. "I see."

Yes, Annie thought, but what was it he saw? She waited.

He waited.

"Well?" she asked.

"Well?" he repeated. "I haven't heard anything to make me change my mind. You're quite suited to be Jake's mother." He noticed she did not look relieved by any measure. "Is there something else?"

Annie's gray eyes dropped away. A delicate wash of color touched her cheeks. She wished Jake would not be so easily amused by his blocks and balls and would demand her attention. She glanced at Ian again, and there was a touch of defiance in her tone when she spoke. "I'm a bastard," she said.

Ian's dark brows rose a fraction. He raked his fingers through his hair. He had suspected as much when Annie told him she was raised by an acting troupe. "It doesn't matter," he said.

"Of course it matters. The Mannerings—"

He interrupted her. "The Mannerings will find out and they'll make it an issue, but it doesn't have anything to do with you. It's about your parents, and I'm not asking either one of them to be Jake's mother."

Annie simply stared at him. He was forging ahead in spite of everything. She couldn't think clearly enough to ask why. Annie found herself sinking slowly into the chair behind the desk, her legs no longer capable of support.

"Tell me about your mother," Ian said.

The one she knew? Annie wondered. Or the one who had abandoned her? "She's dead."

Jake was tugging on Ian's leg, pulling at his leather boot top to raise himself up. Ian sat in the rocker, raised his leg with Jake still clinging to it, and bounced the baby up to his knee. Jake laughed gleefully as he was momentarily airborne. Ian dandled him on his knee, perfectly oblivious of the fact that Annie's heart was in her throat. "That isn't what I asked," he told Annie.

"What?" Jake's perch on Ian's knee seemed precarious to her at best. It was all she could do not to snatch him up.

"I asked you about your mother," he said, pulling Jake more securely onto his lap. The infant made a face as the bouncing and jostling was ended. He tried to climb up Ian's chest, then settled for pulling at the buttons on Ian's coat. Once Jake was quiet, Ian's full attention returned to Annie. "Tell me something more."

"Her name is . . . was Ruby Doubletree." She saw the name meant nothing to Ian. "She was an exceptional actress and a finer person. She dedicated her entire life to the stage and to keeping the Liberty Players going. She loved the theater and the travel. The troupe played in Boston and Concord and New York. In the winter we'd go south to Charleston and Atlanta and Richmond."

"But home was here?" asked Ian.

"I've always thought so," Annie said softly. "I don't know that Ruby and the other players considered it that way, but for me Philadelphia has always been home."

Ian stopped ruffling the crown of Jake's head. His blue-gray eyes shifted to Annie. He studied her for a moment. "Good" was all he said.

They were married three weeks later. The mid-September morning was bright with sunshine, the sky cloudless and seamlessly blue. Annie wore a modest white gown she made herself.

seed pearls embellished the fitted bodice, but otherwise the organdy was exquisitely plain. Her willowy figure was enhanced by the tight sleeves and full skirt. She wore a white bonnet with a pale blue sash and carried a Bible that was lent to her by Captain Dallas and an antique white lace handkerchief that was a gift from Mrs. Ward.

The ceremony was held in the garden of the manor. Pink and white hedge roses bordered the back of the great house and lined the flagstone walk. Along the fence, regal spires of blue and purple delphinium attracted butterflies to the gathering. Ian took Annie's cool, slender hand under a white arbor woven with silver-pink blossoms of clematis. As a breeze shifted tendrils of Annie's pale hair, Ian was unaware of any fragrance in his garden except the light scent of lavender.

Captain Henry Dallas stood as Ian's best man. The exchange of vows was witnessed by Ian's lawyer, two longtime friends from his Princeton days, his paternal great-aunt, and Mrs. Ward, who held Jake and occupied him successfully. Most of the household staff watched from windows at the back of the house. The Mannerings had been invited. None of them chose to attend.

The kiss was chaste. Annie's lips were cool and dry. She felt the heat of Ian's mouth on hers, was almost startled by it, but then the kiss was over and she was left with Ian's lingering heat and the tantalizing taste of him.

There was a champagne wedding breakfast where the requisite toasts were made. Annie was bereft when Mrs. Ward whisked Jake away to the nursery, but she continued to smile gamely and accept the wishes that were offered.

Ian's aunt and friends left after a few hours. Captain Dallas coerced Mrs. Ward to take a carriage ride with him along the river drive. Ian excused himself and shut himself up in the library with his lawyer. Annie looked around the empty parlor. She felt a sudden rush of loss. It was a familiar feeling, something like what she experienced at the end of a theater run when the scenery was struck and the trunks were packed and she was standing alone on a bare and hollow stage. She stepped outside the room, shut the doors quietly, as if letting the curtain fall, and began slowly mounting the stairs to the nursery.

Ian found her later having her lunch on a tray at the window seat. "You changed your gown," he said. It was the first thing he noticed, and the words simply fell out of his mouth.

He sounded almost disappointed. "Well, yes," she said uncertainly. "I couldn't wear it all day." He hadn't changed, she noticed. He was still wearing his black tailed jacket and gray waistcoat. His shirt was snowy white against his darker skin. Ian's only concession to comfort had been to loosen his cravat. Annie thought he looked a bit disreputable, like a rake returning at noon from a night of debauchery at the gaming hells and bordellos. She also thought he looked impossibly handsome.

"You look warm," Ian said, seeing her complexion flush. "Are you feeling well?"

Annie raised a glass of ice water and sipped. It would have served her better if she had been able to press the glass against her heated skin. "Fine," she said. She cleared the catch in her throat. "I'm fine."

"I see someone's had the sense to bring you lunch. You didn't eat much at breakfast." Ian took off his coat and draped it over the back of the rocker. Jake was mewling pitifully in his crib. Ian picked him up and cradled him easily in the curve of one arm.

"I wasn't hungry then," she said, watching Ian placate Jake with a few softly spoken words. It was so easy for him, she thought. Even this came easily to him.

"Dallas gave me an idea," Ian said. "I thought you might like to go for a drive this afternoon." He saw her hesitate. "We can take Jake."

"All right."

"But tonight," he told her, "we're going to the theater and we're leaving Jake behind."

Annie realized there was nothing to say because he hadn't asked her permission at all.

* * *

Returning from the theater, Annie reflected that no matter the circumstances of her marriage, she had had a lovely wedding day. The carriage ride along the river was as slow and meandering as the water it followed. Annie sat opposite Ian. She wore a lavender poplin dress shot with cherry and a silk shawl about her shoulders. An Italian straw bonnet trimmed with puffs of tulle and flowers framed her face. The gown and the bonnet were gifts from Ian, part of the wardrobe he insisted she purchase in the weeks before the wedding. She was able to forget that he had a purpose in dressing her a certain way or showing her off in the parade of open carriages at the river. Annie allowed herself to enjoy the moment and take pleasure in his company.

It was the same at the theater. She had thought it would be difficult without Jake to fill the awkward moments. That might have been true, but there were no awkward moments. They saw *Lady of the Lake,* a play Annie had seen a dozen times before but never from the vantage point of a box seat. Everything about it seemed new and fresh, and her only regret was that she wasn't seeing the Liberty Players present it.

She had written them about her impending marriage but not about the reasons for it. Annie let them think what they would, but she did not extend them an invitation to visit her at the manor. She knew the extent of her talent for acting and it would not see her through to face them. They would discover for themselves that she was a good mother for Jake but no wife to Ian Reynolds.

Ian noticed the change in Annie's expression as he helped her down from the carriage. For most of the drive home her gray eyes had taken on a dreamy, distant look that he found mysterious and intriguing. The look was gone now, as if it had never been, and yet nothing had been said or done. "Is something wrong?" he asked.

She shook her head. "No," she said. Her smile was tentative, a trifle wistful. "I suppose I'm sorry it's ending. The day, I mean. It's been rather more than I expected."

Then she had expected very little, Ian thought. He raised her hand, slipped his arm through hers, and escorted her inside. They were met at the door by the butler. Ian gave over his hat and coat. "I think I'll take a drink in the library," he said. "Would you like to join me?"

"No," Annie said. It was a tempting offer, to let the day linger, but she declined. "Thank you, but no. I'd like to retire now."

"Very well." Ian stood in the entrance hall, watching her until she was halfway up the stairs, then he stepped into the library in search of a stiff drink. He took his time choosing and preparing it, then sipped it slowly. He purposely sat with his back to the mantel clock and measured time in his own mind. What was a decent interval? he wondered. How much time did she need? If Annie had been his mistress, he would have known to follow immediately. She would have undressed in front of him or asked him to help. If she had been a whore, he could have expected to be taken to the room when she was already in the bed, the sheets still warm from her previous paid encounter. And if she had been one of high society's protected daughters, Ian's experience told him they wouldn't have made it as far as the bedroom. Those young women of his acquaintance invariably wanted their pleasure on the carriage ride home.

Ian set down his drink and raked his fingers through his hair. He rubbed the back of his neck, wondering if other husbands approached their wedding night with this same mixture of anticipation and uncertainty. No answer occurred to him. He knew only that it was true of him and that he had felt this way since she had accepted his proposal.

Risking a glance over his shoulder at the mantel clock, Ian assured himself he had waited a proper amount of time. He went to find Annie.

She wasn't waiting for him in his bedroom. He could find no evidence that she had been there at all. There were no earring studs on the bedside table. No shawl draped over the wing chair. The bed covers were turned down and a small fire burned in the fireplace, but these things had been done by servants at his request.

Annie's clothes filled the armoire in the dressing room, and her chemises and stockings and ruffled nightdresses shared drawer space with his things in the Chippendale highboy. A vanity had been moved into the room, and Annie's brushes and combs were arranged neatly on top. A small basket held her hair ribbons. A frosted bottle of delicate lavender scent sat beside the basket.

This also had been his doing. He had asked for all of Annie's things to be moved into his own suite of rooms while they were at the theater. Ian had thought she would be more at her ease surrounded by the familiarity of her own belongings. Now she wasn't there to appreciate his consideration.

He knew where he would find her and he cursed himself for not realizing it immediately and giving her more time. It was natural for her to check on Jake upon their return. If the child was fussing, then she would have wanted to stay with him. Ian's smile was rueful. "Only one of us can have her tonight," he said under his breath to an empty room. "My turn, Jake."

He found her in the nursery. Jake was sleeping soundly in his crib. It was Annie who looked as if she had been set adrift. She was standing in the middle of the room when he entered. Two candles on the bedside table threw her body into slender relief. Her bonnet was lying on the bed. Her shoes were on the floor beside it. She was still dressed, unable to manage the hooks and eyes at the back of her gown without a maid. She looked up when he entered, unaware of the stark, wretched aloneness that was her expression.

Ian stepped into the room. He left the door open behind him a crack. "Annie," he said gently.

"All my things are gone," she said slowly. She was off center, confused, but there was more than that. There was sadness. A sense of loss. "I don't know—"

He approached her and took Annie's hands in his. They were cold. He could feel a faint tremor vibrate her body, like a taut string that had just been plucked. "Your things are with mine," he said quietly. If anything, her pale gray eyes became wider, her expression more bewildered. "I thought it would please you."

She stared at his face, searching for the explanation his words did not provide. She shook her head slightly, partly in negation, partly to clear her head. "But why would you do that? Why would you think it would please me?"

Now it was Ian who frowned, his dark brows furrowing over his narrowed eyes. "You're my wife, Annie. Your place is with me."

She tugged a little, trying to remove her hands from his warm grasp. He held her fast. "My place is here."

Ian heard the edge of panic in her voice. "Sometimes it will be," he said. "But not now. Not tonight." He let go of one of her hands and raised his own to touch her face. He brushed the arch of her cheek with his knuckles. Her skin was faintly damp, and for the first time he realized she had been crying. "Oh, Annie," he said softly. "I thought you knew."

"Know?" she asked. "How would I know? *What* should I know?"

"That I intend this to be a real marriage."

Annie freed herself from his hold and never doubted it was because he permitted it. She hugged herself. "You never said . . ."

"No," he admitted slowly. "I suppose I didn't."

"And now you're—" She couldn't finish. She didn't know quite where she expected her thought to go. If he had told her from the outset that he had intended something other than a marriage of convenience, would she have begged off? Hadn't she wondered these last weeks what it might be like to be his wife in fact? Annie looked away, afraid he would see the truth in her eyes before she was prepared to admit the answers herself.

Ian held out his hand and beckoned Annie with the smallest movement of two fingers. He watched her hesitate, leaning forward, then pulling back, uncertain and wary. He let his hand

emain extended and practiced a patience he didn't feel, hoping
n the end she would reward him.

She did.

Annie placed her hand in Ian's and allowed him to lead her
rom the room. In the hallway he slipped one arm around her
waist and with the slightest pressure at her back guided her to
his own room in the opposite wing of the manor house.

Ian's bedchamber was twice as large as the nursery. An entire
sitting area with a small sofa, two chairs, an end table, and fireplace was to the right. The room was balanced on the other side
by another fireplace, a writing desk, a polished mahogany highboy, a vanity and padded stool, the enormous four-poster, and
bedside tables. Annie's eyes alighted on the vanity because it
was the one place where she recognized her own belongings. It
was suddenly easier to draw a breath. Ian was right. It helped
to see familiar things.

He showed her the adjoining dressing room with another chest
of drawers and the massive armoire. He opened the doors and
let her see her gowns were there, that he had made space for her
stockings and petticoats and shoes among his own things. She
was at once disconcerted and reassured, and something of the
conflict showed in the face she raised to his.

"Thank you," she said gravely. "It was kind of you to think
of it."

Ian studied Annie's upturned face. A measure of color had
returned to her cheeks and offset the pale gold and platinum
stands of her radiant hair. Her mouth was wide, the lips parted
just enough to suggest an invitation. In contrast to the invitation
were her large gray eyes. They watched him. Alert now. Guarded.

"It was selfish," he said. "I thought of bringing your things
here because I wanted *you* here."

"But you said . . ."

He shook his head, stopping her. "I know what I told you,"
he said. "The truth is I thought it would be easier for me if it
was easier for you." Ian didn't know what his honesty would
cost him. He half expected that she would step back, reconsider

her decision to follow him. He hadn't really prepared her for
this, he thought. While he'd known from the outset that he intended to have her in his bed, he also knew he'd managed to
conceal that intention from her.

He looked at her mouth again. Until that morning he had
never even kissed her.

Ian bent his head. He could have sworn she raised herself up
a little to meet him. His mouth covered hers. Her lips were warm
now and pliant, and where she had touched them with her tongue
they were damp. Her hands came up to his shoulders and lighted
there, the fingers fluttering like a butterfly's wings before they
were still.

She pulled back a fraction. Her eyes were closed. She tasted
him on her lips. Annie raised her lashes and looked at him. His
eyes were very dark, the blue-gray irises just a slim ring of color
around the widening centers. His own mouth was parted and
she could hear the faint rush of breath past his lips. He lowered
his head again, bridging the small space of air between them.
She did not think she was ready for the touch of his mouth again,
but then his lips were on hers and she found she was wrong.

Somehow they came to stand at the foot of the bed and he
was withdrawing his kiss to turn her around. His hands held her
shoulders and he laid his mouth across the curve of her neck.
His lips were warm and the contact was like a brand on her skin.
He let his hands fall lightly down her arms, palm her waist, then
rise again, skimming the velvet bodice that covered her midriff,
ribs, and breasts. He cupped her breasts and felt the tremor of
her body and the sharp intake of air. He let his hands fall down
again and his mouth move up her neck to just below her ear.
She leaned backward, into the protective embrace of his body.
His thighs cradled her.

He gave her a moment and then he began to unfasten the
hooks and eyes at the back of her gown.

Except for the small fires laid in the hearths, the room was
dark. Annie was glad for it. Close quarters in the theater and
boardinghouses often made privacy a luxury. Annie knew what

to expect, but she wasn't prepared to surrender her modesty. At least she didn't think she was. Ian's mouth near her ear, his hands at her back, his fingers brushing her skin through the eyelet lace of her cambric chemise, were working against her resolve.

The velvet theater gown fell in soft folds at her feet. He unfastened her petticoats, all four of them, and let them fall away. Ian lifted Annie out of the puddle of material and set her down facing him. She was wearing her chemise and drawers and stockings. He knelt in front of her and removed her stockings. His hands slid under her chemise and took the drawers. When he stood again she was facing him wearing only the cambric chemise. Her arms hung loosely at her sides. She didn't know what to do with them.

Ian took her hand and led her to the vanity. She sat on the padded stool, her image reflected in the mirror. She could watch Ian, watch him pluck the pins from her hair, watch him sift the strands between his fingers as they fell around her shoulders. Firelight colored the side of her face with gold and orange tones. It infused her hair with the same glow. Ian's touch was tentative, as if he expected to feel heat at his fingertips. Once he ran his finger along the golden chain of her locket. She laid her hand over it, holding it in place beneath her chemise, then she forgot about it when he bent, raised her face, and kissed her long and deeply.

Straightening, he finished removing the pins. Annie picked up the brush and pulled it through her hair. Ian went to the bed and sat on the edge, watching her while he removed his shoes and stockings, and later, while he unfastened his vest and shirt. Annie turned on the stool and came to her feet in a fluid, graceful motion. She laid the brush on the vanity and approached the bed.

Ian drew her between his open legs. He placed his hands on her hips and her fingers went to his shoulders. Her breasts were level with his mouth. He increased the pressure on her hips and she was drawn closer. His mouth closed over her breast. Annie's breath caught. The cambric material became deliciously abrasive as it was dampened by his tongue. Her fingers tightened on his shoulders. She closed her eyes. Her nipple hardened and her breast swelled. The hot sucking of his mouth held her captive.

She made an inarticulate cry as Ian tumbled her onto the bed. She would never quite be able to say how it was that he took her chemise or when exactly he became as naked as she, but she would always remember the feeling of shameless abandon, of wanting and desire that guided her hands and mouth and body.

Her body was lithe and supple and fit sleekly against Ian's hard frame. She was stretched flush to him, held in the cradle of his arms and thighs, her breasts taut against his chest. She kissed him deeply, the way he had shown her, using her lips and tongue to press a like response from him. His body rubbed hers, rocked her hard so that she was forced to grab the headboard for purchase. He held back then, gentling her and denying himself.

He kissed her carefully, almost chastely, and waited for the roar of blood to dull in his ears. He raised his head and nudged her nose with his. Her eyes were like polished onyx and he imagined he could see his reflection. "I may hurt you," he said.

She nodded. "It's all right," she whispered. "I was expecting it." Indeed, it was the *only* thing she had expected from their consummation. She squeezed her eyes shut. Her entire body tensed.

Nothing happened.

Annie opened her eyes cautiously and tried to see Ian through her lashes. A rueful smile hovered at the edges of his mouth. "It's not going to be *that* bad," he said.

And it wasn't. There was a sharp sensation when he first entered her, but he eased himself in carefully and then there was only a feeling of aching fullness. He taught her his rhythm and their bodies moved in unison. She did not close her eyes again, but watched him instead, and saw the face of hunger and desire and, finally, fulfillment.

He lay on top of her a moment, searching her features. What he saw there were the shy stirrings of pleasure, not the same satisfaction he had known. Ian eased himself out of her and lay on his side.

A deliciously warm feeling spread throughout Annie when he positioned her body to the curve of his. His breath ruffled her hair. "It will be better the next time," he said.

"Oh, but—"

"Trust me," he said softly. "You have to raise your expectations."

Annie woke suddenly. The haunting dream drove her upright and made her gasp for breath. She was alone in the bed. Her hand automatically rose to her throat to grasp the security of the locket.

"Looking for this?"

It was Ian's voice. She raised the coverlet to shield her breasts and turned in the direction of it. He was leaning forward in one of the wing chairs in the sitting area. A candle was lit beside him. The gold chain and locket flashed as he let it fall from one hand to the other.

"The clasp was loose," he said. "It must have broken while we were . . . occupied."

Annie sensed that he had used the last word deliberately, as if he might have described it earlier as making love, but now, in light of discovering the locket, he was thinking about it differently.

"I didn't take it off your neck," he told her. "I might have had I ever seen it clearly, but I didn't."

Annie's stomach was churning. She wanted to dive under the covers, but it had never been her way to avoid a painful scene. She was the one who took every turn in life head-on. The acting troupe that raised her, even Ruby Doubletree, only played at it at six evening performances and one matinee.

Annie slid her legs over the side of the bed and dragged the coverlet around her naked body. She went to stand in front of Ian. He was wearing his trousers. His feet were bare. His shirt

was buttoned only halfway. His hair was tousled and his eyes
were still heavy-lidded, evidence of his recent interruption from
sleep.

She held out her hand, palm out.

Ian's fist closed over the locket and he leaned back in the
chair, refusing to give it to her. "Did you have a nightmare?"
he asked. "Something to do with this necklace?"

Annie let her hand drop to her side. "Not a nightmare exactly.
Just a dream. A very old one. One I've had as far back as I can
remember." She gathered her hair to the left side of her shoulder
and began to braid it loosely. "And yes, it has something to do
with that necklace."

"Where did you get it?" he asked. His voice was sharper than
even he had intended. He saw Annie flinch, her fingers hesitating
just a moment. He made no apology for his anger. She had to
know what a shock it was to him to find the locket.

"My mother gave it to me."

"Liar." He came up out of the chair. Annie almost fell as she
recoiled, startled by the aggressive move. Ian caught her by the
elbow, capturing her as much as steadying her. "This never belonged to Ruby Doubletree."

"I said my mother gave it to me. Ruby wasn't my flesh-and-
blood mother, only the woman who took me in."

Ian's gunmetal-gray eyes narrowed. His grip on Annie's elbow
eased but he didn't let her go. "You're one of them," he said
lowly. "One of the Mannerings."

"I don't know," she said honestly.

"Did they pay you to set me up?" His mind was working
furiously, wondering how they may have thought it would help
their cause. "Is it some trick to get Jake and the line out of my
control?"

"No!" She wrested her elbow out of his grip and stumbled
backward. "No! Nothing like that! The Mannerings don't even
know I exist!"

His glance was more suspicious now. "That necklace is en-

graved with the Mannering *M*. I didn't mistake that. And there's
a lock of hair inside. Is it yours?"

"I suppose it is. I don't know. How *could* I know? I was only
a few days old when I was found with the locket."

Some of the tension drained out of Ian. His hand was still
tightly closed over the necklace, but he was thinking more
clearly than he had been a moment earlier. Either Annie Moses
was a better actress than she or the Liberty Players had ever
suspected, or she was telling the truth.

Ian pointed to the chair behind Annie. "Sit," he said. "And
tell me about your dream."

Annie's chin came up in a display of bravado, then she sat as
if it were her choice. She tucked the coverlet more securely
around her breasts and curled her legs under her. Ian did not
immediately return to his own chair. He stood over her, waiting
for her to begin before he backed away. She found it difficult to
speak with him towering so near, but she never doubted that she
would. He was owed an explanation.

So she told him everything. He heard about the discovery of
the basket on the Delaware River twenty-two years before and
he learned how she came by her name. She told him about her
unusual upbringing, about how Ruby and the troupe did their
best to raise an abandoned child, about how at last they had all
come to depend on her. In low, almost hoarse tones she told him
how she had always been drawn to the Mannering ships, how
they represented something fine and steady and honest. There
was so much in her experience that was painted and propped,
constructed and knocked down. The Mannering ships were real
in a way little else was.

When she could speak clearly again she explained about the
recurring dream and the significance that was made known to
her only before Ruby died. She told him how the locket had
been pressed into her hand and of the emerald ring on the hand
that had put it there and pushed her away.

Annie spared herself nothing in the telling. She admitted that
she had accepted the job as Jake's nanny knowing that Mrs. Ward

and Ian each thought the other responsible for finding her. She confessed she had used her position to discover what she could about the Mannerings in the hope of finding her place among them, if not her birthright.

Ian listened to it all without speaking, his face impassive. There was no expression in the cool, implacable blue-gray eyes. When she was finished, her voice trailing off because there was no real ending, simply nowhere else to go, he stood and went to the bedside table and withdrew a silver-plated flask from the drawer. He poured a measure of whiskey into a shot glass and carried it to her. He drank his own straight from the flask.

The whiskey burned and soothed Annie's throat. It was a marvelous drink that could do both those things. She watched Ian cap the flask and lay it down. She wished he would say something. When he did she wished he had said anything else.

"Why did you marry me?" he asked. "Was it for Jake or to be part of the Mannering line?"

Annie came to her feet. She was cold suddenly. A shiver prickled her bare shoulders. Her cornsilk braid slipped over her shoulder and fell down her back in a straight line. In front of the fire she hugged herself, her back to Ian. "Both those reasons," she said quietly, honestly.

Behind her, Ian took it as a physical blow, his shoulders heaving once.

"And neither of them."

Pain shuttered his eyes and his senses. He almost didn't hear her. "What?" he asked. "What did you say?"

Annie turned. "Neither of them," she repeated. *This could break me. If I give him this and he doesn't want it, it will break me.* "They were not enough," she said. "Alone or together, they weren't enough for me. I had to love you."

The silence was enormous. Watching him, she hardly dared breathe. He was so still, his eyes steady on her face, and she could not know if her confession meant anything at all.

"My God." His words had the intonation of thanksgiving. Ian crossed the space that separated them and pulled Annie into his arms. He kissed her mouth, her cheeks, the crown of her head. His lips brushed her closed lids, her temple, and her mouth again, and this time he found the wavering shape of her smile. "My God," he breathed against her lips. "Annie."

She returned his kiss measure for measure. Her heart was lifting, in danger of bursting. There was a roar in her ears. Raised against Ian, caught in his secure embrace, she was weightless. There was no up or down, no center of gravity. Her fingers threaded in his hair and her palms framed his face. She kissed him again. And again. There was a pressure in her chest and she had no air. With his mouth over hers he was drinking her air. He took her braid in his fist and gently pulled, angling her face and breaking the kiss. She breathed deeply, long drafts of air filled her lungs. It was as if she had been drowning.

Ian carried her to the bed and laid her on it. When he had stripped out of his clothes, Annie was waiting for him, the coverlet opened and spread from her arms like wings, ready to take him in.

She accepted him with joy and without reservation. He covered her with his body and she held him in the circle of her arms, her thighs parted and drawn around his hips. She rubbed his back, clutching him. Her fingertips pressed whitely into his skin as he came into her. His name hovered on her lips and he saw it there, and urged his body forward.

"Ian." It spilled out of her. There was a sigh the second time. "Ian."

He watched her face as he gave her pleasure she wasn't expecting. She had only anticipated the warmth of their intimacy. She didn't know yet about the splendid rush of pleasure or the intensity of sensations that would pull her taut as a bow. Her eyes closed, her throat arched. He kissed the hollow, sipping at her skin. Where they were joined there was heat mingling with urgency and he pressed on even when she cried out that it was too much and shook her head in negation. He pressed her until her body was shuddering beneath his.

Later, after their heartbeats had slowed and pleasure was like a heavy, comfortable blanket across their naked bodies, Annie rested in Ian's loose embrace, her head on his shoulder. Beneath the sheet she traced the defined ridges of his chest. When her fingers moved to his abdomen, he sucked in his breath and placed a hand over hers.

He shook his head. "No," he whispered. "It's too much."

She stopped and let her hand remain where it lay. She smiled. It wasn't a bad thing that her touch was more than he could take just then.

Ian glimpsed her smile. "That's right," he said. "Be pleased with yourself."

Annie snuggled, pressing her cheek against his warm skin. "Mmmm," she hummed sleepily.

The vibration of her lips on his chest was almost too much. He felt he might seize her, take her again, and he knew it was too soon. He waited. She was almost asleep when he finally spoke.

"I love you," he said. "I have since the first. I think I suspected as much when I behaved like an idiot the day you took Jake to the harbor."

Annie's eyes were open now. She raised her face slightly and looked up at him. "But that was only my second day here."

"I told you, I felt that way from the first." He stroked silky tendrils of hair at her temple. "I was only slow in realizing it." Ian wound a pale curl around his index finger. "When the Mannerings came at me with their lawyers and their money and wanted to take Jake away, I thought I might lose everything . . . then you were there and I saw an opportunity to have it all."

"You might have told me you loved me," she said.

"I thought it would frighten you. You seemed so contained. There was room for Jake, I thought, but I didn't know if you had room for me." He felt the splash of something wet on his skin. "Annie? Are you crying?"

She knuckled her eyes. "No."

He smiled at her denial. "All right," he said gently. "You Mannerings are so proud."

Annie sat up, unable to appreciate his attempt at humor. "Don't say that."

"What? That you're proud?"

"That I'm a Mannering. You don't know that I am."

"And you don't know that you're not." Ian sat up as well and leaned against the headboard. He searched under the covers and found the locket where he had dropped it on the bed along with Annie. "This was made for a Mannering," he said. "There's no mistaking the *M*. Here, let me put it on you again. It's yours." He waited patiently while she considered it.

"You don't mind that I might be one of their bastards?"

"I don't hate them, Annie. Jake's a Mannering. So was Sarah. We'll probably never know about you. I don't suspect any one of them will be eager to make a claim after so many years."

"I know." Annie offered Ian her throat and he slipped the locket around her neck. He fiddled with the damaged clasp and secured it as best he could. "I used to think I might find my connection to the Mannerings among the portraits in the gallery."

"I thought that might explain your interest." He took her in his arms again. She looked very fetching wearing only the gold locket and a sheet that was slipping by slow degrees. "The truth is, you don't look like any of them."

"Even Sarah?" she asked. "I've never seen her portrait."

He heard the edge of hope in her voice that she could not quite hide. "I'm sorry, Annie. Not even Sarah. If you're a Mannering, then you favor the parent who wasn't."

Annie was quiet for a long time. Ian thought she had fallen asleep, when she said, "I thought I would be more disappointed."

"You're not?"

She laid her hand on his chest. This time it was not too much. "No," she said. "I'm not. I'm Annie Moses . . . Annie Reynolds." She raised her face and smiled at him. "Every woman should be so lucky."

* * *

The insistent knock on their bedroom door woke them both. Ian glanced at the mantel clock. It was past ten. He couldn't remember ever having slept so late. A sideways look at Annie languorously stretching her beautifully curved body reminded him of all the reasons he had. He pulled up the covers. "What is it?" he called.

Annie was more alert now. "Is it Jake?" she asked. "Is something wrong?"

Mrs. Ward opened the door enough to poke her head inside. "It's them," she said. "They've all come. The parlor's hardly fit to accommodate them." Her pursed, disapproving mouth softened as she caught sight of Annie's flushed face. "And Jake's just fine. Cathy's looking after him right now."

"I'll be right there," said Annie.

The housekeeper's brows rose a little, and she looked at Ian questioningly.

"It's all right, Mrs. Ward. Annie wants to see Jake. I'll talk to the Mannerings alone." When the housekeeper was gone, Ian responded to Annie's stricken expression. "There's nothing to worry about. They can't take Jake from us right now, even if they've come to do just that, which I most heartily doubt."

"Then why—"

He stopped her with a brief kiss. "Go to your son, Annie. I'll deal with the Mongol horde."

They were indeed all there. As Mrs. Ward had informed him, the parlor hardly contained their numbers. Fletcher Mannering was there with his wife, Louisa. Adam's brothers, Tyler and Marcus, flanked the sofa like bookends. Their wives filled the space in between. Tyler had also brought along his eldest son, who worked in the warehouse offices. Fletcher's cousins, Edward and Allen Mannering, stood at the sideboard, eyeing the stock of liquor in spite of the early hour.

Sitting regally in the large burgundy armchair at the center of the gathering was Georgia Mannering herself. Her back was is stiff and straight as the ebony cane she held in front of her. Her delicate hands rested on the ivory knob, an intricately carved lion's head that looked as if it might actually be able to roar.

There was no pretense of greetings when Ian entered the room. Georgia Mannering tapped her cane once and the parlor fell silent. Her narrowed eyes surveyed Ian coolly, and even though she was sitting and he was standing, she had a way of looking down the length of her nose at him. "Is it true?" she demanded.

"I'm afraid you'll have to be clearer, Miss Mannering," Ian said. "Is what true?"

She tapped the cane. "Don't be dense. Did you really get married yesterday?"

"As none of you saw fit to attend the ceremony . . ." He purposely allowed his voice to trail off and regarded them all with the slimmest of smiles.

"I told you it wasn't a hoax, Georgia," Fletcher said. He was built more solidly than his angular sister and his voice was deep with a rough, hoarse edge. "As soon as I heard, I warned you he meant to do it."

Georgia Mannering ignored her brother and spoke directly to Ian. Her mouth flattened when she looked at him. There was too much of his father in him to make him comfortable to look upon. "Did you know anything about her before you took this precipitous, unwise action?" she asked sharply.

"Enough to know the action was neither precipitous nor unwise," said Ian.

"We had her background investigated," Fletcher said. "She's a bastard, you know. And raised by an acting troupe." He could not have been more disdainful or horror-struck if he had said Annie was raised by wolves. "She's after your money. There can be no doubt about her intentions. That puts all of us at risk, Ian. You. Mannering Shipping. My grandson." He said this last with deliberate emphasis. "I won't stand for Jefferson to be cared for by a harlot."

"You forget yourself, Fletcher," Ian said. "You're speaking of my wife."

The doors to the parlor were parted just then, and Annie entered the room, Jake lifted in her arms. Ian held out his hand to her. She took it and allowed him to draw her to his side. Her smile was warm. She was not oblivious of the effect her entrance had on the gathering, but she ignored it all the same.

Jake was fascinated by the locket Annie wore on the outside of her lavender gown. He had already tried to grab it several times that morning. It was only now that Annie, in spite of the serene presentation she made, was finally distracted enough to let him get away with it. He swatted it once with his right hand and made a grab with his left. The locket was secured in his tight fist only a moment before the gold chain snapped. Surprised, Jake let go and the locket and chain were sent spinning across the room. They landed at Georgia Mannering's feet.

Annie handed Jake to Ian and acted quickly to retrieve the necklace. She wasn't fast enough. Stooping in front of Georgia Mannering, Annie was forced to jerk back her hand as the grande dame of the Mannering clan brought the tip of her cane squarely down on the locket. Annie raised her face and stared at the older woman without giving any quarter until her eyes were drawn to the emerald ring on Georgia's right hand. That was when she backed away.

Georgia's rigid spine posed no problems for her as she bent to get the necklace. She studied it for a moment, opened it with a manicured nail, and studied the contents. She closed it slowly, then placed it in Annie's hand. "A nice piece," she said gravely. "Simple though. Something a young girl might wear. I don't know that it suits you."

Annie murmured her thanks for the locket's return and backed away. Georgia Mannering's scrutiny was unnerving. Even when Annie turned to Ian she could feel Georgia's eyes on her.

Fletcher Mannering cleared his throat and spoke to Ian. "Do you think her presence here changes anything?" he asked. "I *will* get my grandson from you. You can't expect that we'd allow a woman of her sort to raise him. Adam didn't know you intended to marry a bas—"

Georgia's cane slapped the floor hard this time and drown out Fletcher's last word. She rose to her feet without any assistance. "Enough," she announced. "You will not do anything. *We* will not do anything. It's over. Ian has what he has. You should thank God he has been able to make the best of it."

Fletcher looked thunderous. He was used to falling in with his older sister's wishes, but he was not used to being countermanded or reprimanded in front of others. He saw other members of the family looking to one another in bewilderment. At least he was not alone in that.

The Mannerings filed out, Georgia leading the way. Ian saw them to the door and watched them drive off. When he returned to the parlor Annie was sitting in the same chair where Georgia had sat, Jake playing with the locket at her feet. She looked more numb than shaken.

"Are you all right?" he asked.

Not trusting herself to speak, Annie merely nodded.

Ian eyed her suspiciously, then rubbed the back of his neck and let the tension seep out of him. "That was the damnedest thing I ever saw," he said. "I wonder what Georgia Mannering was thinking?"

The answer came three days later. Annie was in the gallery with Jake when the package arrived. The dimensions were a grand two and one-half feet by almost four feet. The depth of the package was several inches. It was wrapped in brown paper, tied with a white cord, and heavy enough for Mrs. Ward to require two maids to assist carrying it in.

"There's a note that's come with it," Mrs. Ward said. She handed it to Annie. The vellum was antique white and it was folded and sealed with bloodred wax stamped with the distinctive Mannering *M*.

After Mrs. Ward and the maids left, Annie dropped the note

on an end table and moved to the floor to keep Jake from tearing at the package. He had already found one loose end of the cord and was tugging. "Not so fast," she said, pulling him back. "Perhaps we should wait for Ian." But the note was addressed solely to her, and by implication so was the package. She glanced at the clock. Ian would not be home for several hours. Annie realized she hadn't much more patience than Jake. "All right," she said finally, as if giving in to the child's curiosity and not her own. "Let's see what the Mannerings thought was important enough to send me."

On his return home, Ian found Annie in the gallery. "Mrs. Ward says you've been in here all afternoon." He dropped a kiss on her mouth when she raised her face to him, and plucked Jake off her lap. Ian sat on the sofa beside Annie, tickling and jostling Jake until the child was laughing and flailing his arms gleefully. "And I missed you," he said, pressing his forehead against Jake's. Jake looked at him so solemnly that it was Ian who laughed. He set the child on the floor and let him crawl away. Ian turned slightly to Annie. "There was a package from the Mannerings?" he asked.

"And a letter," she said. "From Georgia." Annie pointed to the long gallery wall where the portraits had been rearranged to make room for Georgia Mannering's surprising gift.

The painting was mounted in a heavy gold-leaf frame embellished with intricately carved blossoms and leaves. The main subject of the work was a young woman. She had thick auburn hair, cut short and arranged artfully in soft curls that framed a delicate, heart-shaped face. Her head was tilted just slightly to one side, as if she were listening or faintly amused. Her blue eyes and dark lashes were so exquisitely rendered they actually seemed to flicker. There was the beginning of a smile as the right corner of her mouth was lifted infinitesimally higher than the left.

She was sitting in a high-backed chair much larger than she was. Her feet were curled under her and the stocking toe of one foot peeped out beneath the hem of her empire-waist dress. One of her bare hands rested on the arm of the chair. The other was stroking the fur of the sleeping kitten in her lap.

Around her neck she wore a locket. The artist had captured the suggestion of sunshine from a window that was not part of the painting. The Mannering *M* was outlined in a pencil-thin beam of light.

"Sarah," Ian said softly, more to himself than to Annie. "She must have been sixteen, maybe seventeen when that was painted."

"Fifteen," Annie corrected him. "Georgia says she was only fifteen."

Ian nodded. His eyes moved deliberately from the artist's rendering of Sarah Mannering to the only other subject in the painting—the artist's representation of himself painting Sarah.

The easel was set up a few feet from Sarah's chair. The artist sat on a stool in front of it, his back almost entirely to the viewer of the painting. He held a palette in one hand and was giving the canvas a brushstroke with the other. Only a quarter of his face was shown in profile, but more than that wasn't necessary to identify him. The same beam of sunshine that highlighted the Mannering *M* brought radiance to the gold and platinum strands of his cornsilk hair.

There could be no doubt that the artist of Sarah's portrait was also the father of her child. Annie's father.

At a loss for words, Ian could only shake his head. He reached for Annie's hand and held it. He understood now why she had spent all afternoon in the gallery. "What are you thinking?" he asked Annie.

"It's a little overwhelming," she said softly. "And Georgia Mannering . . . she must have experienced something very similar when she saw me."

Ian imagined that was true. "You are very much your father's daughter," he said. "At least in appearance. I think your resolve is Sarah's."

Annie leaned against him, shoulder to shoulder. "Thank you for that," she said.

His arm went around her. It was a good feeling to be able to support Annie. "What did Georgia have to say in her note? You must have had questions when you saw this. Does she answer them?"

"Mostly." Jake was creeping around the end table, trying to pull himself upright. He fell on his bottom, gave a small grunt of surprise, then went at it again. Annie smiled at his courage and resiliency and let him be. "Sarah was only fifteen when she became pregnant with me. His name was Andrew Wilson. He was twenty-two and hired by Joseph Mannering to do a portrait of his youngest daughter. Georgia says Andrew seduced her, but she also says that Sarah would disagree with that. She wanted me to know that Sarah imagined herself in love."

"I'm surprised Georgia told you that. She must have something to atone for if she's making painfully honest admissions about the family."

Annie glanced at Ian. He knew the bent of the Mannering mind quite well. "You're right, of course. She's trying to clear her conscience." Annie burrowed a bit deeper into the sofa and laid her cheek against Ian's shoulder. "Sarah came to Georgia after she discovered she was pregnant. My father had already gone on to another commission—with no promise to return—and Sarah had nowhere else to apply for help. Georgia aided her in concealing the pregnancy with the understanding that Sarah would get rid of the child . . . get rid of me."

Ian stroked Annie's arm. "Sarah must have been terrified, but I still can't imagine her setting you adrift on the Delaware."

"It's hard to say what went through her mind," Annie said. "But yes, I imagine she was frightened. She was just a child really—growing up fast to be sure—but really still a child. Protected. Spoiled. Probably a little selfish. It's amazing that she decided to keep me."

Confused, Ian's dark brows drew together. "Decided to keep you?" he said. "I don't understand. She *put* you in the river."

Annie raised her head from Ian's shoulder. "No, she didn't.

Sarah had no part in that. It was Georgia who set me adrift on the Delaware."

"Georgia? She *told* you that?"

Annie shook her head. "She didn't have to. She was wearing the emerald ring from my baby dream. I couldn't tell you that I'd seen it." Her eyes lowered to her lap. "God forgive me, I didn't want to believe that she could be my mother." Annie leaned over the edge of the sofa and picked up Jake. He was making whimpering noises, a sure sign that he was weary of being ignored. Annie fingered his silky hair and patted his back. "She couldn't bring herself to admit it in the letter. I suppose she wants me to think it was Sarah who did it, but I know the truth."

"Poor Sarah," Ian said, shaking his head. "I always sensed she was shielding some deep, abiding pain, but I never suspected she had known the loss of her child."

"Do you think your father knew?"

Ian nodded, never doubting for a moment that he didn't. "I suspect they had a very honest marriage." He sighed. "Georgia doesn't understand that sort of honesty. She wouldn't have wanted a scandal visiting the Mannerings. She was probably thinking of marrying my father even then and what it would mean." One corner of his mouth lifted in a smile that was without humor. "I can imagine her telling Sarah that she had found a couple to raise you or some such nonsense. No wonder Sarah was so eager to leave her family behind. What a bitter irony it must have been for Georgia when Sarah caught my father's eye."

Annie laid her cheek against the crown of Jake's downy hair. "I feel a little sorry for her," she said. "Sarah had your father. I have you. And we have Jake here. What has Georgia Mannering ever had but a life passed without living?"

Ian leaned forward and kissed her. "You're very generous," he said, raising his head a fraction. "That's not a trait generally associated with the Mannerings." Jake thumped on Ian's chest to get him to move back from Annie. Ian laughed. "See what I mean? Not what you would call selfless. Perhaps your father—"

Annie stopped him when she shook her head. Her voice was

soft with reminiscence. "No," she said. "I don't think so. If I'm generous, it's because of Ruby Doubletree. She and the Liberty Players taught me by example."

Ian straightened suddenly. "My God, I nearly forgot," he said. He patted himself down and pulled out a flyer. He unfolded it and held it up for Annie to see.

It was creased and crinkled and in the top center was a small puncture where it had been posted with a nail, but the words were there in bold letters quite easy to read.

**The Liberty Players
announce the production of an original play
by Tom Watt and Company**
Baby Dreams
In which a Foundling makes a Success of Life

Annie didn't read any further. She was shaking her head, smiling. "We have to go, of course," she said. "Just to see if their ending is better than the one I have planned."

Ian lifted Jake off her lap and put him on his own. When the baby was distracted by the buttons of his coat, Ian managed to steal another kiss. And another. "You have a plan?" he asked huskily.

"Hmmm." She hummed her pleasure against his mouth. "I had a baby dream last night."

"Oh?" There was concern in his voice.

"No," she said, smiling. "Not that dream. In this one I was holding Jake's sister."

"Jake's sister?" This time his head came up. "But you can't possibly know if you're—"

Annie cupped Ian's face in her palms and lifted her mouth to his. "I know," she said. "Some things I just know."

That night in the enormous bed where they shared laughter and loving, Ian got his wife with child. Nine months to the day she delivered their daughter. It was a baby dream come true.

About the Author

Jo Goodman lives with her family in Colliers, West Virginia. She is the author of fifteen historical romances (all published by Zebra Books) including her beloved Dennehy sisters series: *Wild Sweet Ecstasy* (Mary Michael's story), *Rogue's Mistress* (Rennie's story), *Forever in My Heart* (Maggie's story), *Always in My Dreams* (Skye's story), and *Only in My Arms* (Mary's story—to be published in September 1996). She has also had a short story in Zebra's bestselling Christmas anthology *A Gift of Joy* (which included Fern Michaels, Virginia Henley, and Brenda Joyce). Jo is currently beginning work on an exciting new trilogy, focusing on three brothers. She loves hearing from her readers, and you may write to her c/o Zebra Books. Please include a self-addressed stamped envelope if you wish a response.

Edina and the Baby

Hannah Howell

One

Scottish Highlands—Summer, 1420

"Gar? Where are ye, laddie?"

Edina MacAdam cursed as the sharp leaves of a tall thistle found the small, unprotected strip of soft white skin between the top of her knee-high deerhide boots and the hem of her tucked-up skirts. She looked around the wooded hillside as she idly scratched the irritating small bumps raised by the plant's unwelcoming touch. Her wolfhound had left her side and bounded up the hill, evidently tracking something that had excited him. He had disappeared into the thick growth of trees at the top of the hill and, now, even his barking had stopped.

After checking that her string of rabbits was firmly secured to her sword belt, she took a deep breath and plunged into the shadowed forest. It took several moments to quell the urge to run right back out, her terror of the forest almost blinding, but she had to find her dog. Gar was the only companion she had. Forcing back the dark memories of how her lovely but heartless mother had left her in the dark forest to run off with her lover, Edina concentrated on finding her dog. The day that had bred her fears had occurred fifteen years earlier, when she was barely five. It was time to shake free of such childish terrors. Her heart pounding in her ears and the cold sweat of fear trickling down her back, Edina stepped deeper into the forest.

"Gar! Curse ye for a witless beast! Where are ye?"

A sharp yelp answered her. Edina turned toward the sound.

Calling repeatedly to her pet, she followed his sharp answering
barks, softly cursing the forest for trying to mislead her with its
echoes and the way it concealed the true direction of a sound.
When she finally saw Gar sitting beneath a tree, she was torn
between the urge to hug the dog in relief and soundly scold him.
Then she saw the bundle of rags he sat next to. Even as she
cautiously approached, one tiny, pale, dimpled arm appeared and
a little hand grabbed a clump of Gar's thick fur in a way Edina
knew had to be painful. Gar just glanced at the small hand, then
looked at Edina and yelped.

"A bairn," she whispered as she crouched on the other side
of the child.

She reached out to touch the cooing child, saw the dirt on her
hands, and grimaced. Edina trickled water onto her hands from
the goatskin she carried, then rubbed them clean with the skirts
of her soft gray gown. After gently detaching the baby's hand
from Gar's mottled gray fur, she picked the child up in her arms
and found it impossible to silence her dark memories.

As clearly as if it were happening before her eyes, Edina could
see her mother riding away with her lover, laughing at her cries.
She had stood where she had been left for hours, unable to believe that her mother was not going to return. The sounds of the
forest had changed from enchanting to threatening with each
passing moment. In her terrified child's eyes the trees had become grotesque, dangerous shapes trapping her, alone, within
their shadowed home. Her dour uncle had not found her until
the next day and, by then, her fear had deepened until it had
scarred her very soul. It did not help her to conquer her fears
when every time she looked into a mirror she saw her mother.
Edina was not sure how exactly she matched the woman's looks,
but she knew she had the same thick, unruly raven hair and the
same faintly slanted, clear green eyes. That was more than
enough to revive the painful memories. The lack of love and
attention she got at her uncle's home insured that she had nothing
with which to soften those harsh memories.

"Did your mother toss ye aside?" she whispered as she undid

the child's swaddling and carefully looked him over before covering him back up again, relieved to find no injuries. "At least ye are too young to ken what has happened to you and where ye are. Ye willnae be scarred by the painful memories or the fear. Why do they do this to their bairns, laddie? Mothers arenae supposed to cast aside their bairns likes the bones of a finished meal."

She held him close, carefully stood up, and began to examine the area closely, looking for any sign that might tell her why a child of six months or so had been left to fend for itself in the forest. "Mayhap I blacken your mother's name unfairly," she said as she crouched and frowned down at the clear sign of hoofprints on the moist forest floor. "There may be an even darker reason for ye to be left here to die."

Just as she was trying to figure out how many horses had been there, she heard a sound that chilled her blood. Someone was riding toward them. She could hear the sound of horses crushing the leaves and undergrowth beneath their hooves. Even as she set the baby down, stood protectively in front of him, and drew her small sword, she heard men's voices. She patted Gar's big head as he stood beside her. She straightened her shoulders and waited, determined that no one would touch the child until she was sure he would be safe—and loved.

Lucais MacRae raised his gaze from the ground where he had been searching for tracks and reined his horse in so sharply, it startled the horses of his two companions into rearing slightly. As his cousins Ian and Andrew struggled to calm their mounts, Lucais studied the vision before him. He had spent three grueling days searching for his nephew, and the last thing he had expected to find was a belligerent little woman and a massive dog standing between him and what he had been seeking.

She was a tiny woman in both stature and height, made to look even tinier by the trees towering all around her. Thick, raven black hair tumbled around her slim shoulders in a wild, silken tangle. Her soft gray gown fitted snugly over full breasts, and her thick hair brushed against a tiny waist. The way her skirts were kilted up revealed slender, well-shaped legs. Her small, heart-shaped face was dominated by wide, heavily lashed eyes of a green so true and rich, he could see the color even from where he stood. He knew that they would be breathtaking up close. It would be easy to dismiss her for some pretty little lass, no more and certainly no threat, except for the small sword in her delicate white hands. She not only held the weapon as if she knew how to use it, but the expression on her pretty face told him that she was fully prepared to do so.

He dropped his gaze to the rag-wrapped child on the ground just behind her small, booted feet. Lucais could not see the baby's face, but the thick chestnut curls spilling out of the top of the wrappings told him that it was his nephew Malcolm. When he looked back at the girl, he felt suspicion and anger push aside his attraction and surprise.

"I have come to take my nephew home, wench," he said, and pointed at the baby.

"And what proof do ye have to tell me that he truly is your blood kin?" she demanded.

Edina fought the urge to take a step back when he glared at her, the strength of his anger frightening her. He was a big man, tall and lean yet strongly built. Thick chestnut hair that gleamed red whenever the sun touched it hung past his broad shoulders. The dark plaid draping his hard body was pinned with a brooch that identified him as a MacRae of Dunmor. The lean lines of his handsome face were taut with emotion. The clenching of his strong jaw, the light flush upon his high, wide cheekbones, and the tight line of his well-shaped mouth clearly identified that emotion as a dangerous fury. She glanced briefly at the way his long-fingered hand gripped the hilt of his sword, found herself a little too interested in the shape of his long legs, and quickly returned her gaze to his face. It was a poor time to find a man disturbingly attractive, she decided, especially since that man looked as if he would like to take her head from her shoulders.

"Look at the bairn's hair," he snapped.

"I have. He has a fine crop of curls, but brown isnae such a rare color that it alone marks him as your kin." Edina was surprised that she could look him in the eye and so sweetly dismiss his rich hair color as common. "Ye cannae expect me to just hand ye a helpless bairn because ye tell me to or because ye both have brown hair."

"And just what concern is it of yours?" he demanded as he dismounted in one graceful move. When he stepped toward her, however, the dog bristled and bared his large teeth in a low, threatening snarl, and Lucais stopped moving. "I might ask ye what ye are doing here, deep in the forest, with only an ugly dog and a bairn."

"That handsome beast is Gar, and I found this wee bairn whilst hunting." She lightly touched the rabbits hanging from her sword belt to strengthen her claim.

"A few rabbits dangling from your belt doesnae mean ye are innocent of any crime. It could just mean that ye paused now and again in the committing of the crime to do a wee bit of hunting."

Edina briefly feared that he knew she was hunting on another clan's lands, then shook that fear aside. He did not know who she was, for she wore no identifying brooch, badge, or plaid, so he could not know that she was poaching. "What crime? I have committed no crime."

"I have searched for my nephew Malcolm for three long days, and, when I finally find him, ye are here standing over him. I would not be amiss in suspecting that ye might have had something to do with his kidnapping."

"Nay? Ye would be an idiot. Ye are MacRaes from Dunmor. That is o'er a day's ride from here. Look about, fool. Do ye see a horse?"

It annoyed Lucais that he could find her low, husky voice attractive when she was so sharply insulting him. "Ye could be the one who was given the bairn after the kidnapping and ye brought him here to this desolate place intending to leave him

here to die. Now ye try to keep us from saving him." He took
an instinctive step back from the fury that whitened her pale
skin and hardened her delicate features.

"I should kill ye for that insult," she hissed, fighting to tame
her anger, for she knew she needed a clear head if she was to
be an adequate protector for the child. "I would ne'er leave a
bairn alone."

"Then why do ye hesitate to return him to the arms of his
own kinsmen?"

"I am nae so sure that ye are his kin, and I certainly have no
proof that those arms are safe ones."

Edina was beginning to doubt that this man was a threat to
the child, but she feared that his handsome face might be influ-
encing her opinion. She could not believe she could be so
quickly and fiercely attracted to a man who could hurt a child.
That child's life was at stake, however, and she had to be sure.
The fact that he and his two companions had made no move to
simply take the baby away from her, something she was sure
they could do without too much danger of injury to themselves,
was in their favor, but even that was not enough.

"Lucais," said the redheaded Andrew, drawing his angry
cousin's attention his way. "We go nowhere with this trading of
accusations and the day speeds by. Mayhap ye and the lass can
come to some agreement so that we can take poor, wee Malcolm
to a warmer, safer place. We must spend at least one night sleeping upon the ground. If we linger here much longer, that could
become two, and that willnae help poor Malcolm."

The wisdom of Andrew's words could not be ignored, and
Lucais took a deep breath to calm himself before again looking
at the belligerent young woman keeping him from Malcolm.
"Can we agree that the child must be kept safe?"

There was still a hint of anger in his deep, rich voice, and
that made his attempt to be reasonable all the more admirable
in Edina's eyes, so she nodded. "Aye. That is what we both claim
to want."

"And the trouble lies in the fact that I dinnae believe you and ye dinnae believe me. Ye dinnae wish to give the child to me and I dinnae wish to give the child to you, a woman I have ne'er met and dinnae even ken the name of."

"I am Edina MacAdam, niece to Ronald MacAdam of Glenfair. And, aye, ye have the right of it."

Lucais gave her a mocking bow. "And I am Lucais MacRae, Laird of Dunmor. So, we are at an impasse."

"Do I have your word that ye willnae kill me if I sheath my sword?"

"Aye. I swear it. Are ye willing to believe in my word?"

She shrugged as she sheathed her sword. "I cannae be certain that I do, but, if ye break your word, I will have the pleasure of kenning that ye will go to hell for giving an empty oath. And your name will be weel blackened, if it hasnae been already."

"Ye watch your tongue, lass," snapped young Ian, his thin face tight with anger. "The name of Lucais MacRae is an honored one. There isnae a mon in all of Scotland who wouldnae be proud to have Lucais stand at his side."

"Thank you, cousin," Lucais murmured to the youth, who, at barely nineteen years of age, was not as skilled as he was eager to be a knight. He caught Edina rolling her eyes at the boy's effusive praise and was surprised to have to swallow a laugh. "We need an answer to our problem, mistress," he told her. "As my cousin Andrew so wisely indicated, the day wanes and we must be on our way or chance two nights on the road. 'Tis summer, but the weather isnae always this fair and warm. A night caught out in a storm could harm the child."

Keeping a close watch on the three men, Edina picked up little Malcolm. "I can keep the bairn with me until ye have ended the danger he is in."

"Nay. I dinnae ken ye or your people. He is my sister's child. I will protect him."

"Aye, and ye have done such a fine job of it thus far." She ignored his anger and thought for a moment, finally reaching a decision that both satisfied and terrified her. "I willnae leave this bairn until I am sure he is safe and ye willnae let me keep him with me. That leaves but one other answer. I must come with you."

Two

Edina grimaced and tried to stretch without disturbing the child sleeping at her side. She did not think she had ever slept on harder or colder ground. Just as she was cursing herself for riding off to a strange place with men she did not know, little Malcolm opened his big gray eyes and smiled at her. Edina sighed and knew she would make the same choice no matter how often she was presented with the problem.

As she sat up, trying not to reveal how stiff and sore she was, she looked at the three men crouched around the fire. They were roasting the last of her rabbits, she noticed with a scowl. She also noticed that she felt no fear of them. After riding behind Lucais for several hours, little Malcolm in a sling on her back, she had begun to believe that he spoke the truth. He had been neither friendly nor trusting, but he had not even tried to hurt her or shake free of her. Although he had been lacking in courtesy, he had been gentle each time he had helped her mount or dismount or put Malcolm in his sling and secure it. He had also been kind to the child and to Gar. He had even brought supplies of clothing, clean changing rags, and goat's milk for the boy. Everything indicated that he was a concerned uncle, but Edina was not ready to give Malcolm into his full care yet. Someone had left the child out in the forest to die, there was a real threat to the life of the child, and she could not turn her back on him yet.

After rolling up the bedding Lucais had grudgingly given her, she left Gar to watch over Malcolm as she slipped into the cover of the forest to relieve herself. When she returned she found that Lucais had cleaned and dressed the baby and was preparing to feed him. She stood in front of him, her hands on her hips, and scowled at the tender scene. Her attraction to the man was increasing, rapidly growing too strong to push aside. She wished he did not act so sweet around the child, for it only enhanced his attractiveness, and she did not want to want him. Even if he proved to be a very good man, she could never have him. Not only was she poor and landless, but she had certainly not endeared herself to him by thrusting herself into the midst of his troubles.

"Your dog neither snarls nor bristles," Lucais said as he looked at her. "He trusts me."

"Ye think so?" she drawled. "Try to walk away with the bairn."

She smiled as Lucais picked Malcolm up, stood up, and started to walk away. He had barely taken two steps before he was confronted by a snarling, threatening Gar. After a moment of trying to stare down the dog, he whispered a curse and handed Malcolm to her.

"How did ye get him to do that?" he asked, frowning when Gar immediately relaxed.

"He is a clever dog," she replied, patting Gar on the head. "He will help me keep this bairn safe."

"I can protect my own kin." He cursed when she just looked at him, one delicately arced brow lifted. "My sister Elspeth was unwise," he said even as he wondered why he was bothering to explain anything to her. "She took a lover when she was young and heedless, a mon she could never wed, for he had a wife already. Finally, she turned to a mon who had courted her for a long time and they were married. I ne'er learned what turned her, whether her lover had done something wrong or if she had just grown older and wiser and realized that she did not wish to spend the rest of her days as that mon's leman. She and her young mon Walter were happy and Malcolm was soon born, her lover troubling them only now and again." He shook his head, puzzled and still fighting his raw grief. "Elspeth and Walter were not afraid of her old lover, seeing him as no more than a nuisance, and I soon did the same."

Edina fed Malcolm as she listened to the sad tale, hearing Lucais's pain and struggling against the strong urge to try to comfort him. "But her lover was a danger to her, wasnae he?"

"Aye. I dinna ken what finally changed him from a nuisance to a threat, but 'tis clear that jealousy and rage finally overwhelmed him. He killed Walter and Elspeth and took Malcolm. There must have been a hint of sanity remaining, and he could not put a child to the sword."

"Nay. He just tossed the poor wee bairn into the forest so that he could feed the animals or die on his own slowly." She believed him and, as she settled Malcolm against her shoulder and rubbed his back, she scolded herself for trusting too quickly. "Do ye ken who the mon is?"

"Aye. Simon Kenney, a mon who would be poor and landless save that he made a rich marriage."

"And why havenae ye killed him yet?" Edina was a little surprised at her bloodthirst, but then Malcolm patted her cheek with one damp little hand, and she understood.

"I cannae find the mon," Lucais reluctantly admitted.

"Ye arenae having verra good luck at finding things, are ye?" she drawled. "Mayhap ye should make use of Gar."

Lucais decided to ignore that insult and glanced at her dog. "Where did ye get a name like Gar?"

"From Maida, my uncle's cook. When I brought my wee puppy to the kitchens to show him to her, she said he was so ugly, *he gars me grew*—makes me tremble. So I called him Garsmegrew, but 'tis a mouthful, so it soon became just Gar. He grew into a fine, handsome beast," she said as she patted the dog's head.

There was a distinct gleam of laughter in her beautiful eyes. Lucais was not sure he was pleased to discover that he was right, that her eyes were breathtaking when seen up close. There was a faint slant to their shape, her lashes were long, thick, and as glossy a black as her hair, and the green was the color of ivy.

Afraid he was in danger of revealing his ill-timed attraction to her, he turned his attention to her dog, and nearly smiled. Gar was big, his shaggy coat was a mottled gray, and he was indeed a very ugly dog. When the animal was snarling and baring his impressive teeth, he was threatening enough to make any grown man hesitate. Although the animal was nothing much to look at, he was well trained and a good protector for his mistress. That alone made him a worthy animal. Lucais idly wondered how easy it would be to win the dog's trust. He suspected he could never pull the animal from Edina's side, but he might be able to woo the animal just enough to get him to stop threatening him. He allowed Gar to sniff his hand, then cautiously patted the animal, inwardly pleased with that small sign of progress.

"Ye had best break your fast," he told Edina, ignoring her look of suspicion and the way she pulled her dog a little closer to her side. "There is some rabbit left. We must ride for Dunmor soon."

Edina frowned as he walked away, his two young cousins following him as he strode into the surrounding forest. For a moment she was surprised to be left alone with their horses and goods, then shook her head and went to eat some food. She might not be able to see Lucais and his cousins, but she was certain at least one of them was watching her closely. Instinct told her that Lucais was beginning to trust her, to believe that she sought only to protect the baby, but he did not trust her enough to leave her completely unguarded.

As she struggled to eat and keep Malcolm's little fingers away from the fire, her food, and the wineskin, she tried to plan what she would do when she reached Dunmor. If she could not yet trust Lucais, she certainly could not trust any of his people. That meant that she would have to keep Malcolm with her at all times. She tried not to think about the possibility that Lucais was Malcolm's true enemy, that she was blinded by her own attraction to the man. If Lucais was the enemy, she was riding into the very heart of his camp, and there was little chance that she would be able to save Malcolm.

Edina blinked and shook her head, only faintly aware of Lucais's soft laughter tickling her ear. He had insisted that she and Malcolm sit in front of him when she had started to grow sleepy. Such closeness had distracted her only briefly, for she had been too tired to dwell on it for long. Now, however, as she woke up, she was acutely aware of how she was tucked up between his long, strong legs, her back warmed by his broad chest, and how his muscular arms encircled her as if in an embrace. She rubbed her hand over Malcolm's back, trying to cleanse her mind of disturbing thoughts about Lucais's embraces with thoughts of tending to Malcolm.

"There lies Dunmor," Lucais announced, giving in to the urge to touch his lips to her soft hair, finding it as silky as he had imagined it would be.

A small chill of alarm slipped down Edina's spine as she looked at his keep. It was set upon a stony rise, giving it a clear view of the surrounding lands. To the north was a tiny village, and hearty Highland cattle grazed contentedly in the fields surrounding the castle's thick walls. It was a strong keep and, she thought with an inner sigh as they rode through the big, iron-studded gates, a rich one. It was one thing to think that a man was out of her reach, it was quite another to see the proof of that in one huge pile of stone.

The way the people of Dunmor boisterously welcomed Lucais and his cousins, and their elation over Malcolm's good health, made Edina further question her suspicions about Lucais. The people would do what their laird told them to, but she knew he could never make them all pretend to be happy. As they dismounted in the heart of the crowd, Edina clung to Malcolm and struggled to regain some sense of belonging with the child, some sense of her right to be there. Her eyes told her that Malcolm would have all she had lacked as a child—love, ready ears for his questions, stories, and even his complaints, and ready arms to hold him close and soothe his hurts and fears. He might not be completely safe, however, she told herself, and soon felt a little more confident.

A small, thin young woman named Mary, who was all brown hair and brown eyes, was selected to show her to a room and see to her needs. Lucais made only one attempt to extract Malcolm from her arms, accepted failure with an apparent calm, and sent her on her way. As she followed Mary into the keep and up the narrow stone steps that led to the bedchambers, Edina looked around at the rich tapestries and fine weaponry hanging on the thick stone walls. She followed Mary into a bedchamber, looked at the big, curtained bed, the fireplace, and the sheepskin rugs, and shivered. She had never seen such wealth, and she felt intimidated.

After meekly asking for a bath, Edina sat down on the high soft bed and waited for Mary to fulfill that request. She took several deep breaths and fought to subdue her feelings of being small and unimportant. Edina knew she had just been overwhelmed by Dunmor, its wealth, and its air of contentment. This was the sort of place she had often dreamed of, and Edina decided that it was very unsettling to see one's dreams come to life. The cynical part of her began to revive, and she also decided that such perfection was worthy of suspicion. Just because everyone and everything at Dunmor seemed perfect did not mean there could never be a snake in the garden. Edina was sure that Malcolm could have a very good life at Dunmor, but there could easily be someone behind one of the smiling faces she saw who wanted Malcolm's life to be very short or who was willing to help the man who sought that. Until she was sure that Malcolm was completely safe at Dunmor she would stay with him.

"Are ye sure ye should have let her take the bairn with her?" Andrew asked as he, Ian, and Lucais washed in Lucais's bedchamber.

"She willnae hurt the bairn," Lucais said as he dried himself, surprised and a little alarmed at how confident he felt about that, for that confidence was not based upon any facts.

"So, do ye trust her now? Ye dinnae think she has anything to do with Simon?" Andrew donned his braies and poured himself and the half-dressed Ian some wine from a decanter on a table next to the huge bed.

"All I trust in is the fact that she willnae kill Malcolm, not whilst she is so completely surrounded by MacRaes."

"Are ye sure? I think ye are beguiled by a verra bonny pair of green eyes."

Lucais wondered about ignoring that as he donned his braies and helped himself to some of the wine his cousins were drinking so heartily. As he sipped his drink and studied his cousins, who were sprawled so comfortably on his bed, he decided that the full truth would serve better. His strong attraction to Edina was a weakness. It might be a good idea to have someone watching him and Edina to ensure that he did not give in to that weakness and that Edina did not try to use it against him.

"She does indeed have the most beautiful pair of green eyes I have ever looked into. I find most everything about the lass verra intriguing and alluring. My instincts tell me that she has nought to do with Simon, but I am not sure I should completely trust my instincts concerning her. Those instincts are also telling me that I want to lay her down in the heather and not rise from her slender arms for days."

"Oh," Ian said in a small, hoarse voice, causing both of his older cousins to laugh.

"Do ye think your loins could overwhelm your wits?" asked Andrew. "Do ye think that is why ye believe that she willnae hurt Malcolm whilst she has him alone with her?"

"Nay. She could have struck the child down back in the forest ere we could have stopped her. She did not. That could mean that she is honestly trying to protect the child, or she knew we would immediately kill her and has no wish to die. That holds true here as weel. To survive she must get away from here or continue this game."

"And so we watch her closely to see if she does try to leave with the child or if someone tries to come to her."

"Exactly. We watch her every minute. She is never to be without a guard. Ye need not be too secretive about it, as I am sure she expects it, but a little subtlety would be good. Then she might think she can elude us and we will finally see with our own eyes if she can be trusted."

"A good plan, but there is one little flaw. There is one place where we cannae watch her, certainly not with any subtlety—her bedchamber."

"We will have eyes there, too. I will ask Mary to bed in there with her. It was my mother's bedchamber, and there is a place for a maid to sleep close at hand. It is not something that will raise any great suspicion on Edina's part."

"And what will you do if she is in league with Simon?"

"If she is in league with Simon, I fear we will be given little choice about her fate. It will eventually come to the point where we must choose between her life and Malcolm's. I may lust after her far more than I have ever lusted after a woman before, but ye need not fear that I will hesitate in making that choice, and making the right one. The moment she sides with Simon, she will be the enemy."

Three

It was not easy, but Edina smiled at Mary, set a sleepy Malcolm in the woman's arms, and walked out of the bedchamber she had shared with the woman and child for a week. Her mind told her that she was foolish to worry, that she could at least trust Mary not to hurt the baby, but her heart was not ready to agree. The one who sought to harm Malcolm did not appear to be within the walls of Dunmor, but he was out there somewhere, she was sure of it. The watchful attitude of everyone at Dunmor confirmed that feeling. She was not the only one who scented the danger to the child. It was past time for her to step away from the child a little, however. If nothing else, she needed to take the risk to see if anyone tried to take advantage of it. Keeping a constant watch on Malcolm while the people of Dunmor kept a constant watch on her was not getting anyone anywhere, not even in deciding who could be trusted.

As she stepped out into the sunlit bailey and took a deep breath of the clear summer air, Gar trotted up to her and she patted his head. The dog still allowed no one to go very far with Malcolm, but he showed no other signs of wariness. The animal had, in truth, settled in quite well at Dunmor. He saw no threat, and that made Edina relax a little. She really needed a little rest from her self-appointed post as Malcolm's guardian. To ease the final pangs of guilt she felt about leaving the child alone, however, she ordered Gar to go to her room and watch the baby.

Enjoying the warmth of the sun, she walked around the bailey. Lucais had graciously sent word to her uncle to let him know why she was at Dunmor and assuring the man that she was safe. Her uncle was not a loving man, but he did have a strong sense of duty and she knew he would be concerned about her. She no longer had to worry about him, and could put all of her attention on the matter of Malcolm's continued safety.

After a thorough examination of the bailey, all the assorted buildings, and even venturing onto the walls to survey the surrounding lands, Edina found a shaded, secluded place near the walls of the keep and sat down. It was pleasant to be outside alone—if she ignored the way Ian shadowed her every step—and she wanted to enjoy it for just a little while longer. A cool breeze snaked its way around the walls, and she closed her eyes, savoring the way it took the summer heat from her skin. She was feeling drowsy and content, when she suddenly sensed someone was staring at her.

Cautiously, Edina opened her eyes and looked up. Lucais towered over her. There was a look of curiosity mixed with amusement on his face as she staggered to her feet. She frowned when he suddenly stepped closer, pressing her against the wall.

"What do ye want?" she asked, inwardly cursing the huskiness in her voice as his long body lightly brushed against hers.

"Ye have taken a rest from being Malcolm's constant guard?" he murmured as he closely studied her flushed face.

"I feel I can trust Mary and I have set Gar at his door."

"Ah, aye, the ever-faithful Gar."

"Howbeit, I believe I have been idle long enough."

He just smiled when she shifted slightly, silently asking him to move so that she could leave. Lucais was pleased to catch her alone, unguarded, and out of sight of the others. He had watched her for a week, whenever he and his cousins were not hunting Simon. Her voice, her eyes, even the way she moved, stirred him. She had begun to invade his dreams, dreams that had him waking up in a sweat, hungry for her. No matter how often he had told himself it would be a big mistake to give in to the attraction he felt for her, he had not been able to put her out of his mind. He had caught her watching him enough to make him think she felt the same interest. Now, Lucais decided, was the perfect time to test that theory.

"Malcolm is probably still asleep."

Edina gasped when he leaned forward and touched his mouth to hers. "What are ye doing?"

"Something I have thought about since the day ye first marched into my life."

That was a flattering thought, and it made her relax a little. A moment later she realized that had been his intention. She tensed when he put his lips against hers again. She knew she ought to hit him or kick him, and sternly remind him of the respect owed a lady. The problem was, with a disturbing and increasing frequency since arriving at Dunmor, she had thought about kissing him. Here was her chance to know if her idle dreams matched or exceeded the real thing. In a moment of what even she saw as pure recklessness, she decided to let him play his little game with her for a while. As he pressed his lips harder against hers, she curled her arms around his neck.

Her heart raced as he pulled her into his arms, lifting and pressing her body more fully against his. When he nudged at her lips with his, she opened her mouth, groaning with delight when he began to stroke the inside of her mouth with his tongue. The way he moved his big hands over her body, nearing but not overstepping the line to real intimacy, fired her blood. Her senses swimming, she clung to him and returned his kiss.

When his heated kisses slipped to her throat and he shifted so that her body was caught in a suggestive position between his body and the wall, Edina finally grasped at a thread of common sense. She pushed him away, and her sigh of relief when he immediately obeyed held a hint of regret. The kiss had been far more stirring than she had ever imagined, blinding her with the depths of the passion it roused within her. There was a flushed, taut expression on his face that told her he had felt much the same. That was dangerous, and, realizing that, she found the strength to step out of his reach.

"I believe that was enough of that," she muttered, taking a few deep breaths to completely steady herself.

"Oh, aye?" Lucais leaned against the wall of his keep and smiled at her. "To me it tasted like just the beginning."

"I came here to protect Malcolm, not to become—" She hesitated, not sure how to word what she wanted to say.

"Not to become my lover?"

"Of course not."

"That kiss we just shared told me elsewise."

It probably had, but Edina had no intention of admitting to what she had felt, and his arrogance in thinking he knew annoyed her. "That kiss was but idle and reckless curiosity. It was also the only one ye will get."

She turned and walked back to the front of the keep, trying not to look as if she were retreating, but eager to get back inside its thick walls as quickly as she could. Lucais's soft laughter followed her, and she resisted the urge to return and kick him. His kiss was still warm upon her lips, still alive and heating her blood. Edina knew it would be very unwise to get within his reach until she had overcome that.

Lucais smiled, straightened up from the wall, and frowned when he was suddenly confronted by a grinning Andrew. "How long have ye been here?"

"Only long enough to catch a few words and see the lass hurry off," Andrew replied, his blue eyes alight with laughter but his expression serious.

"No harm in stealing a wee kiss."

"Nay, although I think it was more than that. Ye were both flushed and unsteady. Aye, it may have been only a kiss ye stole, but I think it has left ye verra hungry for more."

"And what if it has?"

Andrew grimaced and threaded his fingers through his curly red hair. "If the lass is as innocent and earnest as she appears to be, then ye are attempting to seduce a weelborn maid. That could bring ye a great deal of trouble. If she is helping Simon, then ye are showing her a weakness she could use. Just be wary, cousin. Either way ye step, there looms a problem."

Lucais had no answer for that, as it was the truth. He did not think it would deter him, however. That one sweet kiss had fired his blood, and he knew he could not simply push that aside. He wanted to taste the fullness of her passion, hungered to know if the promise in her kiss could be met. Edina was certainly trouble whether she was innocent or guilty, but Lucais knew that if the chance arose to make love to her, he would not hesitate to grab it.

Edina shut the door behind her after she entered her bedchamber and sagged against it. The last few steps to her room had been hard ones to take. A large part of her had wanted her to turn around, run back to Lucais, and savor more of his kisses. Only the certainty that it would go far beyond kisses had kept her going. She needed time to think, and that kiss had shown her that she could do little of that held in Lucais MacRae's arms.

"How is Malcolm?" she asked Mary when she saw the girl frowning at her in curiosity.

"Still asleep," Mary replied, watching Edina closely as she walked to the bed and sprawled on top of it. "Are ye all right? Ye look as if ye got too much of the sun. Ye are verra flushed."

"I met with your laird. He has a true skill at making me get flushed."

"At times ye talk as if ye dinnae like him. He is a good mon. This trouble with Simon has sorely grieved him. He loved his sister and was most fond of her husband. When he realized the wee bairn was gone, he ne'er rested, searching everywhere."

"Aye, so I have been told." Edina had to admit that everyone at Dunmor seemed honestly fond of their laird, which would imply that he was indeed a good man.

"Some men wouldnae have tried so hard. After all, the laddie now claims a large holding that borders us on the west. Some men would want to keep that for themselves."

"Aye," Edina said as she slowly sat up and frowned at Mary. "They would indeed."

"Wee Malcolm is fortunate to have a kinsmon who will tend it, and him, most carefully until the lad is of an age to claim it."

"It wouldnae fall into Simon's hands?"

"Nay. Why should it? Simon is no kin to Malcolm. Why should ye think he would gain?"

"It would explain why he killed Elspeth and Walter and left the wee bairn to die."

Mary nodded as she walked to the door. "It would, but that is not why he now has their blood on his hands, nor why he will probably try to kill the bairn once he kens that Malcolm has survived. Simon is mad, insane with jealousy and hate. There is no explaining such things."

There was not, Edina thought after Mary left. Greed for land explained such murders far more clearly. Before, there had been no reason for either Simon or Lucais to kill Elspeth or Walter or the baby. Now she saw a reason for Lucais to commit such murders.

She cursed and fell back onto the bed. It helped to have a reason, but she heartily wished it was one that pointed the finger of blame squarely at Simon. She was torn, part of her horrified that she would even think Lucais was capable of such crimes and another telling her not to be a fool, that it was something she could not ignore. Edina rubbed her forehead as she struggled to decide what, if anything, she should do. It was hard to decide when she did not even want to believe it.

Slowly, she sat up, then stood up. What she needed was more knowledge, knowledge about Lucais and about Dunmor and its people. Edina knew the people of Dunmor would never say anything bad about the laird, but what they said could still help her. She could learn about Lucais's past, about his likes and dislikes, and even about his character by weeding through the things his own people said about him. It was time to stop just standing guard over Malcolm and take an active part in finding out exactly who wanted the child dead. The moment Mary returned, Edina was determined to go and search out a few truths.

It was late before Edina returned to her bedchamber. For the first time since she had arrived at Dunmor she had taken her evening meal in the great hall. Her intention had been to study further the laird and his people. Instead, she had spent most of the meal torn between desire and annoyance over Lucais's blatant attempts to seduce her. She had wavered between saying yes and wanting to scream at him to stop tormenting her.

Mary helped her undress, don one of Lucais's late mother's nightgowns, and wash. After kissing little Malcolm good night, Edina crawled into bed feeling utterly exhausted even though she had done little more than talk to people. As she listened to Mary settle down to sleep in the little alcove near the fireplace, Edina tried to sort out her confused thoughts.

She had learned nothing bad about Lucais, which did not really surprise her, but it promised to make it more difficult to come to any decision. Simon was loathed by everyone, but that was not really enough to condemn him either. Everyone at Dunmor thought the man guilty of murder, although no one had mentioned any real proof that the man had actually done the killings. If there was some clue that had set Lucais on the man's trail, most of the people of Dunmor did not know what it was.

It all left her very confused. She was not sure what part of her she should listen to—her heart, her mind, or her instincts. The fact that she desired Lucais made her unwilling to fully trust anything except her mind, and it did not hold enough facts to make a decision.

There were a few things in Lucais's favor, although they were not hard, cold facts. Gar trusted the man. She simply could not bring herself to fear him. If Lucais was the murderer, then why had he done nothing to hurt her? Why had he even allowed her to come to Dunmor and keep Malcolm by her side? If there was something suspicious about all of that, she could not think what it was.

What she needed, she mused as she snuggled down beneath the covers, pausing only to pat Gar on the head before he lay down on the floor by the bed, was one strong piece of proof. She needed some act, some word, or some fact that would clear her mind of all doubt about Lucais. It had to come soon too, for instinct told her that this peace could not last much longer. No one questioned that Malcolm's life was in danger and whoever wanted to kill the child would try again. Edina desperately hoped that she would know exactly who that person was before the next attack came.

Four

Malcolm giggled as she stood over him and shook the water from her hair. Edina could not believe she had been allowed outside the walls of Dunmor with the child, but she was not about to question her good fortune too loudly or it could disappear. It was always possible that after staying at Dunmor for two weeks, people had begun to trust her.

"Gar, get back here," she called, and sighed as the dog disappeared into the trees on the far side of the brook she had been splashing in.

As she dressed she decided she needed to have a stern talk with her pet. Gar had become so comfortable at Dunmor, so pampered by the MacRaes, that he was not doing a very good job of guarding her or Malcolm anymore. Gar saw no threat and, although she found some comfort in that, for it implied that she was not sitting in the midst of the enemy, she had to strengthen her commands. There could yet come a time when she would need his aid.

She was rubbing her hair with a drying cloth when a faint sound made her tense. Immediately kneeling by the child and pulling her sword from its sheath, she carefully looked around. It could be just someone from Dunmor keeping a guard on her, but she needed to be sure. Still watching, she finished dressing and picked up Malcolm. The joy of her moment of freedom was gone now.

Knowing that Gar would find his own way back to Dunmor, she decided that it was past time she and Malcolm returned to the safety of its high walls. She had barely taken three steps toward the keep when she knew she had waited too long. Six mounted and well-armed men rode out of the trees bordering the brook. Edina carefully set Malcolm down by her feet and faced the men squarely, her sword in her hands. She knew she did not have any chance of defeating six men, but she was determined to make them pay dearly for Malcolm's life.

"And where did Lucais find you?" demanded a tall, bone-thin man who rode to the fore of the others. "I dinnae ken who ye are."

"And I dinnae ken who ye are either, but I hadnae realized this was a courtesy visit."

"Ye are no MacRae."

"Nay. If it troubles ye so, I am Edina MacAdam of Glenfair. Does it help to ken who is about to kill you?"

The man laughed. "Ye have more spirit than wit, wench." He gave her a mocking bow. " 'Tis a great pity we couldnae have met at a better time and place. We could be lovers instead of enemies. I am Sir Simon Kenney."

"Lovers? I think not, Sir Simon. I ken what happens to the lovers ye grow weary of or who displease you."

The way his expression turned cold made Edina nervous. The man was obviously quick to anger. If she faced only him, that could have worked to her advantage. Now making him angry would make her death arrive all the sooner. She inwardly cursed and wondered where her dog and her guards were when she really needed them.

Lucais looked at the men slowly encircling Edina and softly cursed. "Ian, how could ye have let her come this far from Dunmor alone?"

Ian flushed with guilt. "Ye said we didnae need to guard her too closely."

"That didnae mean ye could let her wander about as if all is weel and there isnae a madmon lurking about."

"That madmon isnae lurking anymore," Andrew drawled, putting a stop to the argument. "We have three men behind Simon and his men, and we are in front of him. Ye are the one who must decide when we attack, Lucais."

"At least everyone will not think me some fool for the way I ordered so many men to arms just because one tiny woman and a bairn were out walking," Lucais muttered, dragging his fingers through his hair. "An attack could get Edina and Malcolm killed."

"There is no question that they will also die if we dinnae do something soon."

"If only we had something to briefly distract Simon and his men." Lucais looked around one last time before he gave the order to attack, an order he feared would be a death sentence for Edina, and his gaze settled on a familiar mottled-gray shape creeping toward Simon and his men. "Look, 'tis that cursed dog."

"Is he going to attack?"

"Aye, Andrew," Lucais replied, finding it hard to keep his voice low as excitement and anticipation rushed through his veins. "That ugly dog has ne'er looked more bonny. He is about to give us the diversion we need."

"He could get hurt," Ian murmured even as he readied himself for the attack he knew would come at any moment.

"I pray that doesnae happen, for 'twill sorely grieve Edina," said Lucais, never taking his eyes from the dog, tensed for the moment when the animal would spring, for that would be when he would order the attack. "Howbeit, better a dog than a woman and a child. Now, ready, lads, for the moment that beast lunges I will give the battle cry. All eyes will turn to the dog and whatever hapless soul he chooses to sink those teeth into, and that is when we will attack."

Edina felt the sweat soak her back as Simon just studied her. There was a chance that he was trying to put her off her guard and then he would attack. She decided she had a better chance if she tried to grasp some control, if she could somehow choose the time he charged her. The easiest way to do that, she decided, was to anger him. He had already shown her how easy that could be. It was a weakness she could have used well at some other time, but now it could at least serve to ensure that she was not cut down too easily. If she could make him attack, she could at least take a few of Simon's men with her, perhaps even Simon himself.

"Why do ye hesitate? Do ye fear a wee bairn and a woman?" she asked.

"I but wonder what ye are doing here and why ye are ready to die for that child," Simon said in a tight voice, revealing that her words had already stirred his anger.

"Not everyone can kill a bairn or leave them to rot in the wood."

"Ah, so that is how he has returned to Dunmor. Ye had the misfortune to find the bastard."

" 'Tis your misfortune. Come, let us dance. I grow weary of waiting for you. I cannae understand why any mon would be so cowardly as to slay a child, but, mayhap, 'tis that verra cowardice that causes ye to hesitate now."

Simon edged closer, his thin face white with fury. "Ye sorely beg to die, wench. Mayhap I but do the lad a kindness. A bairn should be with its parents, should it not? I mean to take him there."

Just as Edina was sure he was about to lunge at her, a gray shape hurled itself at the man on Simon's right. She gaped along with Simon and his men as Gar's attack sent the man tumbling off his horse, screaming with pain as Gar savaged his sword arm. A heartbeat later a deep, fierce battle cry rent the air. Edina had no idea whose battle cry it was, but she did not hesitate to take advantage of this further distraction. She grabbed Malcolm by the back of his gown and ran toward Dunmor.

Out of the corner of her eye she saw three familiar figures race from the trees straight toward Simon and his men. The moment they were between her and Simon she paused, sheathed her sword, and pulled a crying Malcolm into her arms. She rubbed his back, calming him as she waited for Gar to trot up to her. Lucais, Ian, Andrew, and three other men from Dunmor were pressing Simon and his men hard. It was tempting to stay and see how the battle went, but she had to think of Malcolm's safety. At least now she was certain who the enemy was. After giving Gar a rewarding pat for his bravery, she trotted back toward Dunmor, praying every step of the way that Lucais would win, that he would kill Simon and put an end to the threat to Malcolm's life.

"Curse it a thousand times," yelled Lucais as he stopped, bent over slightly, and tried to catch his breath. "We will never catch the bastard."

After a moment, Lucais straightened and looked at his men collapsed around him. Somehow Simon and one of his men had escaped. Desperate to get the man, he and his men had tried to chase him down, but they were no match for men on horseback. This time he would have to be satisfied that only Simon and his men suffered in the attack. Malcolm and Edina were undoubtedly safely behind the walls of Dunmor now, and none of his men had suffered any more than a few cuts and bruises.

"Weel, we had best get back to Dunmor," he finally said, smiling slightly when he saw that three of the men had already begun to walk back, leaving him and his cousins behind.

Andrew stood up from where he had collapsed on the ground and brushed himself off. " 'Tis a great pity that the coward still lives, but at least we ken one thing now that we werenae sure of before."

"Aye? And what is that?" Lucais asked as he and his cousins started back to Dunmor.

"Edina is exactly what she claims to be. She has no part in Simon's murderous plots. She found Malcolm, saved him from dying in the wood, and believes it her duty to stay at his side until that danger is gone."

"Aye, from what little I heard, Simon didnae ken who she was or understand what she was doing there." Although this proof of Edina's innocence elated him, Lucais found that it left him a little confused as well. "I have to admit that I share Simon's confusion. Aye, she has it in her head that it is her duty to stay at Malcolm's side until she is sure he is safe, but why would she have that idea? Why not just be satisfied that he is with his kinsmen? She must ken by now that we willnae hurt the child, yet she stays."

"There is something behind her determination, but I cannae say what it is. I just sense that she does this for more reasons than the child's safety." Andrew smiled crookedly and shrugged. "I make no sense, I ken it. I just ken that there is some reason we cannae guess at. Mayhap something that happened in her past that makes her so determined. She doesnae just speak of Malcolm's safety. She mixes it all up with his comfort and care."

Ian nodded as they approached the high gates of Dunmor. "I think I ken what Andrew is trying to say. The only way to ken what is in her head is to ask her though, dinnae ye think?"

"Aye," agreed Lucais, espying Edina waiting just inside the bailey and walking straight toward her. "How is Malcolm?" he asked even as he looked her over carefully for any wounds, relieved to find none.

"Weel, he was a wee bit upset o'er the rough way I picked him up and ran with him, but he has recovered." Edina inwardly breathed a sigh of relief when she saw that he was no more than bruised and scratched. "Is Simon dead?"

"Nay. We lost him."

"Then it is not over yet."

"Not yet. He was mounted and, when he managed to break free of the battle, there was no hope of catching him, although we did run after him for a ways."

"I still dinnae understand how anyone could kill two people

and try to kill a bairn, but I saw what pushes him to such cruelties. He is filled with anger. He nearly stinks of it."

"And, sadly, he has decided to unleash it upon my family."

"After a fortnight where nothing happened, I had hoped that he would not seek out Malcolm, that whatever had made him kill your sister and her husband had been sated and he would leave the bairn alone. He will never cease trying to kill the child. The brief moment of humanity that stopped him from taking a sword to Malcolm before has gone."

"We will watch. Now I must clean this dirt off and I want to give Gar a verra large bone."

Edina smiled as she followed him inside of the keep. "I didnae ken who was attacking at first, only that it allowed me to flee. But ye used Gar's attack to signal your own, didnae ye?"

"Aye. He drew all eyes his way. Before that we risked your life and Malcolm's." At the bottom of the stairs he paused to look her over again. "Are ye sure ye are unhurt?"

"Aye, I am fine."

"There will be no more walks outside of these walls unless ye take armed men with ye."

"None, not until that mon is dead."

"Good. Now go and let Mary see to your scratches."

She nodded, a little surprised that she had any, then recalled that she had paid little heed to rocks, brambles, or anything else in her way as she had run back to the safety of Dunmor. As she climbed up the stairs to her bedchamber, she watched Lucais disappear into the great hall. When he had walked up to her she had felt shy, at a loss for words. The proof of his innocence still filled her mind and heart, and she had feared she would say something about it. It was not something she should speak of, for it would reveal to him that she had suspected him of being the sort of coward who would murder a child. Even though her suspicions had been weak and wavering, and he had known that she did not fully trust him speaking of such things aloud would only cause hurt and insult.

As she stepped into her bedchamber, she saw Mary tucking Malcolm into his crib and asked, "Is he unhurt?"

"Aye, mistress. Ye and the laird saved him from Simon, did ye not?"

"Aye, I suppose. I was just a little worried that I might have bruised the poor lad, as I was rough with him when I tried to rush him out of harm's way." She stepped over to the crib and looked down at the sleeping child, relieved to see no obvious signs of her rough handling.

"Better a few wee bruises than a cut throat."

Edina shivered at the thought and moved to the wash bowl to clean the dirt from her hands and face. She was glad that Lucais was the good man everyone said he was, that her instincts and her heart were right in their judgments. However, that left her with a man who wanted to kill a child simply because he was twisted with jealousy and anger. Such a thing was beyond her understanding, and, if she did not understand it, how could she fight it?

Five

A soft curse escaped Edina as she slipped out of the keep and started to walk around the bailey. It had been a week since the confrontation with Simon, and in that short time her life had been turned upside down. Lucais had changed. He had been a little flirtatious before, stolen a kiss or two, but now he seemed to be doggedly pursuing her. At every corner he was there, smiling, flattering, touching. What really frightened her was how much she was enjoying it. She needed to get away from him so that she could think clearly.

Clutching her cloak more tightly around her to ward off the chill in the late August night air, she scowled at the ground as she walked and struggled to sort out her confused mind and heart. One thing she was sure of was that no one was suspicious of her any longer. Just as the battle had shown her that Lucais was innocent, so it had shown the people of Dunmor that she was equally innocent. Since she had nursed a few suspicions about them, she did not feel insulted that they had nursed a few about them. A child's life was at stake. One had to be very careful about whom one trusted.

The trouble with knowing that Lucais was innocent was that the knowledge had taken away the one restraint she had used to hold back the feelings she had for him. The possibility that he was a threat to Malcolm had been enough to make her hesitate. Now each time he smiled at her, all her feelings flooded through her, making her weak, causing her to melt in his arms. She could no longer ignore it. She loved him. It should make her happy, but there was no indication that he returned her feelings. He was also too high a reach for her. Men like him did not take a poor, landless, orphaned girl for a wife.

She had to fight the urge to flee Dunmor. Malcolm was still in danger, and although she now knew that Lucais and the people of Dunmor could protect him, she had made a vow to stay with the child until the danger had passed. She also knew that she would not be able to sleep at night if she did not stay until she was absolutely sure that the child was safe. Fleeing was no answer.

"Slow down, woman," said a familiar voice from directly behind her a moment before Lucais caught her by the arm and halted her blind march around the keep.

Edina looked up at him and her heart sank. She wanted him. The desire he stirred in her haunted her dreams. It was so much a part of her that she was sure he was aware of it. Her only comfort was that he could not know it was born of love. He had not asked for that, and no matter what else happened she wanted to be able to cling to at least some tiny shred of pride. It would devastate her to offer him her love, only to have him reject it, and she had the feeling she was going to be suffering enough pain very soon.

"I have a question I have been meaning to ask," he began a little hesitantly, threading his fingers through his thick hair as he frowned down at her.

"Weel? Ask it, then," she said. "I will either answer it or tell ye to go away."

Lucais smiled faintly, then grew serious again. "Why have ye taken on this duty of being Malcolm's protector? Aye, at first I could understand. Ye didnae ken what was going on, or who ye could trust. But now? Why? He is no kin of yours."

Edina only briefly considered telling him it was none of his business or making up some grand tale of vows and honor. She did not want to bring up all the old, painful memories of her childhood, but decided he was owed the truth. He had tolerated a great deal from her, allowing her into his home, and even respecting her claim of being his own nephew's protector, a role that was his by birth.

"I fear some of what makes me act as I do is that I too was left in the forest." She smiled faintly when his eyes widened, and he slipped his arms around her in a silent gesture of comfort. "My mother told my uncle that she was going riding and took me with her to make the tale seem the truth. When we got into the forest to the south of my uncle's lands, my mother met with her lover. She set me down on the ground, turned, and rode away with the mon, never looking back."

"How old were you?"

"Five. I waited, ne'er moving from the spot, but she ne'er returned. I waited the whole night and much of the next day, and then my uncle found me."

Lucais could not believe what he was hearing. Such cruelty was beyond his understanding. He felt a need to soothe that hurt, but knew he could not. It did explain her strange, fierce determination to stay with Malcolm until she was sure he was safe and loved, however. The urge he had to find the woman and punish her for her cruelty also told him that his feelings for Edina went a lot deeper than lust.

He inwardly smiled, amused at his own vagaries. He wanted her even then, and that did not surprise him. The desire he felt for her had been there from the beginning, growing stronger every day. At the moment, however, he was also feeling things like outrage over what had been done to her, fury at the ones who had done it, and an overwhelming tenderness. Very soon he was going to have to sort out his own heart and mind, decide just what he was going to do about Edina MacAdam, because the moment the threat Simon presented was eradicated, Edina would leave. Now, he decided, was not the time, and he turned his full attention back to her tragic story.

"Did ye e'er see her again?" he asked.

"Nay." Edina sighed and leaned against him. This was the first time anyone had ever offered her sympathy concerning her mother's desertion, and she decided it did not hurt to enjoy it for a little while. "When I was twelve my uncle called me to him and told me that my mother had died, stabbed by a jealous wife. He said she had lived like a whore and that it was justice that she had died like one. We ne'er spoke of her again."

"What of your father?" he asked in a slightly hoarse voice, not sure whom he detested the most, her mother or her uncle, who was obviously a cold man.

"He died but months after I was born. I ne'er kenned the mon. From the way Maida the cook spoke of him from time to time, I dinnae think he would have been much better than my mother." She leaned back and smiled at him. "Dinnae look so sad. I was kept weel enough. I was clothed, fed, and housed. Many a bairn left orphaned doesnae get e'en that. Howbeit, when I saw wee Malcolm lying alone in the wood—" She shook her head.

"I understand. I am almost sorry I asked," he murmured, and shook his head. "Ye have had an unhappy life, havenae ye?"

"It wasnae so bad that ye need to pity me," she said, starting to tug away from him only to have him hold her a little tighter.

"Dinnae confuse sympathy with pity, bonny Edina." He touched a kiss to her forehead. "I might pity ye if all that had happened had turned ye into some terrified wee lass who cowers when she sees her own shadow, but ye arenae that."

"I am afraid of the forest," she whispered.

"Most people are, even if only at night. I am eight and twenty and I wouldnae be eager to spend a whole night alone in the forest. Ye were no more than a bairn and, if your lack of size now is any indication, little more than a bite or two for any beastie that might have found ye." He met her scowl with a brief smile. "Nay, I am but passing sorry that ye had to grow to womanhood among such an uncaring lot. The way your uncle told ye of your mother's death tells me that he is a cold mon. Ye couldnae have found much comfort there."

"He is a good mon, truly," she said as she eased out of his hold, finding such tender proximity dangerously arousing. "He ne'er beat me and he gave me all that was needed to stay alive.

I think he just doesnae ken how to be, weel, happy or kindly. Dinnae forget, he was the one who came searching for me, took me home, and raised me."

"True. Mayhap he just didnae ken that there is a wee bit more needed to raise a bairn than food, clothes, and a roof," he said as he took her by the hand and started to lead her back to the keep. "Mayhap that was all he e'er got, and he was ne'er shown another way."

"Ye have decided that I have walked enough, have ye?" she asked, but she made no attempt to break free of his light grip.

"Aye. The summer fades quickly and there is a bite to the air."

"I am stronger than I look. A wee chill in the air willnae cause me to fall ill."

"Ye have also not had any food this night."

When he passed the door to the great hall and led her up the stairs, she frowned. "Have they cleared the tables, then?"

"Nay, I have had the cook prepare us something that is just for us."

Her suspicion grew in one large bound when he opened the door to his bedchamber. She tensed as he tugged her inside. This was far too intimate and far too close to a bed. It was undoubtedly just how he wanted it, and a large part of her did as well, but Edina knew she had to fight that reckless part of her.

"I dinnae think this is a good idea," she said, and turned back to the door.

Lucais grabbed her by the hands and tugged her over to a small table set in front of the huge stone fireplace that warmed his room. "I swear to ye, loving, that I will do nought that ye cannae agree to," he vowed as he gently pushed her down into a chair.

And that was the real problem, Edina mused as she watched him sit down across from her and pour each of them some wine. She could easily be persuaded to agree to most anything Lucais asked of her. Smiling faintly, she touched her silver goblet to his when he raised it in a silent toast. It had been difficult enough for her to turn from his gentle seduction when they had been surrounded by people as in the great hall or the bailey. Now they were enclosed in privacy, warmed by the glow of a low-burning fire, and facing each other over a fine meal. Edina was not confident that she had the strength to resist his wiles. She could try to flee to her room, but, as he smiled at her over the savory roast lamb they dined on, the door through which she could escape suddenly looked miles away.

Lucais saw the soft look in Edina's eyes and inwardly smiled. He easily pushed aside the small twinge of guilt he felt over his attempts to seduce a wellborn maid. Edina wanted him; he was certain of it. The desire was there to see in the way she looked at him, and it was clear to feel every time they kissed. He had no intention of forcing her to his bed, but he was going to do his best to make her give in to that desire and come into his arms willingly.

Six

"I have spent most of the evening speaking of old battles," Lucais murmured as he moved the table out of the way and sat down on the sheepskin rug by the fireplace. "Come, our bellies are full and 'tis time to take our ease." He patted the rug by his side. "Now 'tis your turn to tell me of your adventures."

Edina eyed the spot where he wanted her to sit. The unease she had felt when he had first tugged her into his room had been lulled by conversation and good food, but now it returned in force. There was a warmth in his gray eyes that told her talk was not all he wanted from her. The moment she sat down beside him she was silently offering him the opportunity to gain what he really sought.

She glanced at the door and thought about leaving, claiming a need to seek her own bed and a good night's sleep. It almost made her smile when she realized that she could not do it, she could not retreat again. He offered no more than passion, but she ached for it. Soon Simon would be defeated and there would be no reason for her to linger at Dunmor. She would return to Glenfair and all its coldness. Here was a beautiful man offering her warmth, no matter how fleeting, and Edina decided she wanted some. Even if it were for only one night, she wanted to be held in his arms, to taste the fullness of the passion promised in his kisses. She also wanted love, marriage, and babies, but had little hope of being offered that. Edina knew that if she tried to gain it all, she would end up with nothing, not even a sweet memory. Inwardly taking a deep breath to steady herself, she sat down beside him.

"I fear I have no great adventures to tell ye about," she said, silently cursing the tremor in her voice that revealed her nervousness and desire.

"Have ye led such a calm, peaceful life, then?" Lucais reached out to undo the strip of deerhide she had tied her hair back with, smiling gently at her when her eyes widened.

"Aye." She swallowed hard when he began to comb his fingers through her hair, plainly enjoying the feel of it. "The most exciting thing I have e'er done is a wee bit of poaching, but I have ne'er been caught at it."

"That is what ye were doing when we found you." He refilled her goblet and draped his arm around her shoulders, lightly tugging her closer.

"Aye. My uncle's lands are verra small, and sometimes there isnae any game to be found on them."

"Ye will get yourself hanged."

"Aye, I have feared that at times, but then the fear passes and I do it again."

"Weel, try to cling to the fear a little harder in the future. Hanging is the gentlest of punishments visited upon poachers, and I dinnae think your beauty and sex will save ye. Not every time anyway."

She nodded and shivered when he touched a kiss to the hollow by her ear. Her heart was pounding so hard and fast, she wondered that he did not hear it. Fear and anticipation raced through her veins alongside her increasing desire. Edina almost smiled when she realized that now that she had made her decision to be his lover, she was a little annoyed that he was moving so slowly. She lifted her gaze to his, saw the warm, steady way he was watching her, and briefly feared that he could read her thoughts.

"Lass, I fear I dinnae have the wits left to keep on talking, and ye arenae helping to keep the conversation alive."

"I think my wits are a wee bit scattered just now as weel,"

she whispered, her breathing growing heavy as he inched his mouth closer to hers.

Lucais threaded his fingers through her hair on either side of her head and looked deep into her eyes. He could read a desire in their clear depths that he was sure matched his. As he brushed his lips across hers and felt her tremble, he decided the game of seduction had grown very tiresome.

"Ye ken what I seek, dinnae ye, dearling?" he asked in a soft voice as he covered her upturned face with soft, warm kisses. "I dinnae think I have kept it a verra close secret. Nay, especially not during this last week we have been together."

"Not since ye were certain that I was innocent, that I wasnae working with Simon."

"Aye, though it shames me to admit that I held such suspicions about you."

"Dinnae be shamed. I held them about ye from time to time too."

Lucais laughed even as he moved his kisses to the pulse point in her long, graceful throat. "I want ye, Edina MacAdam. God's tears, I want ye so badly that I wake in the night all asweat with the need. I think ye want me too."

"I should say nay and leave just to dim that arrogance."

He lifted his head to look at her, smiling faintly when he saw the amusement in her expression, but then he grew serious. "But ye willnae say nay, will ye?" He stroked her cheek, a little surprised to see that his hand was shaking.

"Nay, I willnae say nay. It may be unwise, reckless, e'en stupid, but I willnae say nay to you, Lucais. I fear I havenae got the strength to do as I should."

"Thank God for that," he said as he stood up, and scooped her up into his arms. "Although," he added as he walked to the bed and gently set her down on it, "I should prefer to think that ye arenae weak, that this isnae happening because of weakness. I should prefer to think that ye just have the strength to reach out and take what ye want."

"That is a much better way to think on it," she murmured as she welcomed him into her arms.

A soft groan rose from the very depths of her body as he kissed her. There was such passion in his kiss, such sweet tenderness, she was lost in it, so lost that she paid no heed to the removal of her clothes. With each touch of his hands on her body, with each heated kiss, he kept her blinded until they were both naked. It was not until he took off his braies and slowly lowered his body onto hers, the feel of his flesh meeting hers for the first time searing away the haze his kisses had encased her mind in. She shuddered and blushed beneath his gaze as he looked over every exposed inch of her.

"Ye are lovely, sweet Edina, all black silk and white linen."

"Ye arenae such a poor sight yourself, Lucais MacRae," she said, smoothing her hand down his side, the feel of his warm, hard skin sending her reeling.

He touched a kiss to her breast and she gasped, the warmth of his lips flaring through her body. She could feel a faint tremor rippling through him and knew he was caught as tightly in the grip of desire as she was. The way he touched her, caressed her skin with his lips, told her that he was struggling to go slowly. When he enclosed the hard tip of her breast in his mouth and drew on it, she decided she did not have the will or the strength to go slowly. She slid her hands down his back to cup his taut backside and laughed huskily when he came alive in her arms, all hesitation gone.

A heedless passion took control of her. She met his every kiss and touch with one of her own, equaling the ferocity of his lovemaking in every way. There was a wildness to their need for each other, and she reveled in it. It was not until she felt him press to enter her that a hint of sanity broke through. She wrapped her body around his, gasping with a strange mix of pleasure and pain as he joined their bodies. When he broke though the barrier of her innocence, the sharp pain of that loss made her cry out, but it became of little importance very quickly.

Edina held him close, smoothing her hands over his broad

back as she savored every sensation caused by the unification of their bodies. It was as if her body had been sleeping for twenty years and had suddenly been brought to life. When she shifted, drawing him deeper within herself, she heard him groan and felt him shudder. It was only then that she realized he was so taut that she could feel the veins standing out on his arms.

"Arenae ye supposed to do a wee bit more?" she asked with a mixture of curiosity and amusement.

Lucais looked into her eyes, saw the faint glitter of laughter, and grinned. "Aye, just a wee bit more." He quickly grew serious and brushed a kiss over her mouth. "Is the pain gone?"

"What pain?" she whispered against his mouth.

When he moved, the last of Edina's amusement was swept away. She clung to him as he moved, greedily meeting his every thrust. A brief spasm of confusion and fear broke through the desire that so completely possessed her when her need grew almost painful, her body tightening with an anticipation she did not understand. Then something inside her broke free and she was lost. Edina was only faintly aware of crying out Lucais's name, and of the way he suddenly held her still, pushing deep within her as he shuddered and called out her name. Her inability to think clearly, to even know what was happening around her, did not really fade until Lucais had cleaned them both off and returned to the bed.

Edina cautiously opened her eyes as Lucais gently brushed the tangled hair from her face. He did not look disgusted or surprised, only gently amused, so she began to think that what had just happened to her was normal. She slowly reached up to touch his cheek and realized she was making sure that this was no dream, that he was real. That made her smile at her own foolishness.

"Does something amuse you?" he asked, brushing a kiss over her cheek.

"Only myself. I just realized that I touched you to be sure that ye arenae a dream."

He chuckled and briefly kissed her when she blushed. "And I have been touching ye so much for the verra same reason."

"Ah, I am disappointed."

"Why?"

"I thought ye were touching me for another reason."

"Ye must let a mon rest, dearling," he said, laughter shaking his voice as he turned onto his back and pulled her into his arms.

Edina looked at him and idly wondered how she could love him so deeply when he gave her no love in return. She smoothed her hand down his chest to his taut stomach, toying with the tight dark curls encircling his navel as she marveled at her own greed. Her body ached from her first taste of lovemaking, and yet she was hungry for more. She suspected some of that greed was born of the knowledge that this could not last for long, that her time with him was fleeting.

As she slid her hand around to his waist, she leaned down and touched a kiss to his rippled stomach. He shivered and she smiled against his warm skin. There might be weeks left in which they could be lovers, but there could also be only hours. Edina decided that she would give in to her greed and worry about the right or wrong of it later, when she was all alone at Glenfair.

"How long do ye need to rest?" she asked as she slipped her hand beneath the coverlet and curled her fingers around his staff, feeling her desire return as it hardened beneath her touch.

"I think I have rested enough," he replied in a hoarse voice as he pulled her back into his arms.

Edina laughed when he turned so that she was sprawled beneath him and greedily welcomed his kiss. "Aye," she said hoarsely when he tore his mouth from hers and began to kiss his way toward her breasts. "Your strength does appear to have returned."

"Lass, do ye mean to love me to exhaustion?"

"What a lovely idea."

"Weel, I challenge ye to try. We have time enough."

She threaded her fingers through his thick hair, arching toward his mouth as he lathed and sucked the aching tips of her breasts, and heartily prayed that he was right. Instinct told her, however, that their time together was rapidly slipping from their hands. Edina hoped that if all she would be given was this one night, that she had the strength to be satisfied with that.

Seven

A cold draft brushed against Edina's back, and she muttered a curse as she tugged the blanket around herself. When she heard the sound of someone approaching the bed, she tensed and warily opened her eyes even as she pressed closer to Lucais. A blush heated her skin as she looked up into Andrew's face. She and Lucais had spend the whole night making love, and she was sure that was obvious to the young man. Even as she cursed herself for going to sleep and not slipping back into her own room, she noticed the somber expression he wore, and nudged Lucais.

"Andrew is here," she said as Lucais groaned softly and tried to pull her back into his arms.

Lucais came awake and sat up so quickly that she had to scramble to keep herself modestly covered by the blanket. Her heart was in her throat and she was not sure why. There were any number of reasons for Andrew to look so serious and to seek out his laird so early in the morning.

"Malcolm is gone," Andrew announced.

When Edina cried out in alarm and started to get up, Lucais grabbed her and held her still. "No need to go and look, dearling. If Andrew says he is gone, he is gone." He looked back at his cousin. "Tell me everything."

" 'Tis clear that Simon had someone here that he could use. Mary was knocked on the head and the bairn was taken from his wee bed. No one saw anyone go into the room or come out with the bairn. Mary thinks it happened but an hour or two ago. She cannae say for certain. She was rising to tend to him, for she was sure she had heard him cry out just before sunrise, and that is when she was struck down."

"No one saw anyone leave with the child?" Lucais demanded as he climbed out of the bed and began to dress.

"Nay, but if it was someone from here, he or she would have kenned how to slip away without being seen."

"Gar didnae stop them?" Edina asked.

"Nay, he was asleep." Andrew frowned. "In truth, he was just waking and was a wee bit unsteady. He should have done something, shouldnae he?"

"Aye," agreed Lucais. "He still stops even me from taking the child out of the room."

"Something else a person from Dunmor would ken, and they clearly did something to remove that threat. Something in the dog's food mayhap."

"Go, ready the horses. We may find a trail we can follow. And begin a search for who is missing. We must learn who the traitor is."

"I ken where he took the bairn," Edina said, her voice softened by surprise that she could think so clearly when she was so afraid for Malcolm.

"How could ye ken where Simon will take him?" asked Lucais, waving to the departing Andrew to wait a moment.

"I think he told me that day by the brook. Truly," she insisted when he frowned. "He said, 'A bairn should be with his parents. I mean to take him there.' Where are your sister and her husband buried?"

"Are we there?" Edina whispered as Lucais reined in, slowing his mount from the furious gallop he had maintained for two hours to a walk.

"The burial site is just through those trees, in the yard of a wee chapel where Walter's kinsmen are always buried," Lucais answered in an equally quiet voice as he signaled to the ten men riding with him to move and encircle the area.

"Is he there?" She waited impatiently for an answer as Lucais exchanged a few signals with Andrew, who appeared a few yards ahead of them, then disappeared into the trees again.

"Andrew says he is."

"Is Malcolm still alive?"

"Aye." She sensed the anger gripping Lucais so tightly and eased her hold on his waist. "I am sorry."

"Ye have nought to feel sorry for," he said as he dismounted and helped her down.

"I should have stayed close to Malcolm as I had vowed to do. Mayhap with two women in the room he wouldnae have been stolen away."

"Or ye would have been knocked on the head as weel." He gave her a brief hard kiss, then began to move toward the churchyard that was on the other side of a thick growth of trees. "Now, dinnae forget that ye are here only to care for the bairn. Not to try and save him or to fight, just to care for him when we get him away from that madmon."

Following close behind him, Edina nodded and idly patted Gar's head as the dog finally caught up to her. As they crept toward the churchyard, she prayed that little Malcolm was unhurt. Despite Lucais's assertions that she had nothing to feel guilty about, she could not stop blaming herself for the danger the child was in. If anything happened to Malcolm, she was not sure she could forgive herself.

When Lucais stopped and crouched down, she silently edged up next to him. It took all her willpower not to race out into the churchyard they looked out on. Simon stood before two graves, Malcolm crying at his feet. He held a sword in his hand and six mounted men watched the wood that surrounded them. At any moment Simon could cease talking to the grave and kill the child, and there would be nothing they could do but watch.

"Ye cannae reach him," she whispered.

Lucais cursed softly, for it did look bad. He suddenly turned and looked at Gar. The dog had worked to divert the men before, but he was not sure it would work a second time. Simon was a

lot closer to Malcolm than he had been to Edina and the child
that day at the brook.

Edina saw the direction of his stare and also looked at her
dog. "If he is seen, Simon can kill Malcolm ere any of us can
reach him."

"I ken it. Do ye think he can get near one of the men without
being seen?"

"Simon has himself weel encircled with watchful eyes this
time. I cannae be sure."

She looked at the men in the churchyard, then back at her
dog. The idea forming in her mind could easily mean Gar's death.
Edina patted his big shaggy head and felt like weeping. It was
a horrible choice to make, but the child's life was more important. She briefly hugged the dog, then looked at Lucais.

"There is something he can do that might at least give ye the
chance to save Malcolm. Gar can put himself between Simon
and the bairn."

Lucais clasped her hand, squeezing it in sympathy, for he
knew how much she loved her dog and she could be sending
the animal to its death. "How?"

"I will tell him to go and fetch Malcolm. I will get him to
race into the churchyard and try to grab the child and run with
him."

"Would it be better to tell him to attack Simon?"

"Nay, for all Simon needs to do is cut him down as he runs
at him. One of those men will see him. If Gar runs for the child
instead, it might confuse them, giving ye that brief opening
needed to pull Simon away from the bairn so that poor wee
Malcolm can be pulled out of harm's reach. Simon may still kill
Gar, but my dog's body will then be between Simon's sword and
Malcolm for one brief moment."

"Tell Gar what he needs to do and I will pass along the word
to my men."

Lucais disappeared into the underbrush for a moment and
Edina hugged her dog again. Softly she told him what he had
to do, finding his eagerness painful. He trusted her completely

and could not know that she was asking him to risk death. Even as Lucais reappeared, he nodded, and she sent Gar on his way.

Her heart pounding, Edina clasped her hands tightly together as she watched. It surprised her a little when Gar approached slowly, as if stalking an animal. When one of Simon's men cried out a warning and everyone looked toward Gar, the dog lunged. He ran straight for Simon, who readied himself to cut the dog down as soon as he was in sword's reach. For one brief moment Edina thought Gar had misunderstood her command, then he veered. She gaped in wonder even as Lucais cursed when Gar darted around a screaming Simon, grabbed Malcolm by his little nightshirt, and kept on running. Simon and his men moved frantically to catch the dog, and that was when Lucais and his men attacked.

When Simon and his men turned to protect their own lives, Gar trotted back to her, little Malcolm swinging from his mouth. Edina quickly took the baby in her arms and hugged her dog. Following Lucais's orders to go to the horses and wait if she got Malcolm back safely, Edina rose to her feet. She paused only long enough to look at the men fighting in the churchyard. Already three of Simon's men had been cut down, and Lucais was facing Simon sword to sword. Edina realized that she did not fear Lucais losing this battle and turned to go to the horse, soothing a frightened Malcolm as she walked.

She had just finished changing Malcolm, and was feeding him some goat's milk when the men from Dunmor returned. A quick look at the men revealed no serious injuries, and she turned all her attention to Lucais. He came to stand in front of her, bending slightly to pat Gar.

"This dog may be the ugliest animal I have e'er set eyes upon, but he is surely the smartest. Ye shall have to breed him. 'Twould be a true shame if he was the only one." He reached out to ruffle his nephew's curls. "Is he unhurt?"

"Aye. He was just hungry, wet, and frightened. Is Simon dead?"

"Aye. It is over."

It was over, she thought, fighting to hide the sudden sadness that nearly overwhelmed her as she secured Malcolm in his sling and mounted Lucais's horse behind him. She was glad that Simon would no longer threaten Malcolm, that the child was now safe. But the end of Simon also meant the end of her time with Lucais.

Once back at Dunmor, she used the excuse of caring for Malcolm to slip away from Lucais. She took the child up to her bedchamber, murmuring her good-byes to him every step of the way. The moment she entered the room she handed Malcolm to Mary and used the woman's distraction with the child to collect up her meager belongings and slip away.

Everyone at Dunmor was caught up in the joy of Malcolm's safe return and the death of Simon. No one paid her much heed as she crept down the stairs, hurried through the wide doors of the keep, and dashed across the bailey. As soon as she got outside of the gates, she ran, determined to put as much distance between her and Dunmor as she could. There was no outcry from the walls, for they had been emptied upon Lucais's return. Edina knew that there had never been a better time to make her escape, and she pushed aside all pain and regret and took full advantage of it. Later, when she could stop running, she would think about what she was doing.

"Where is Edina?" demanded Lucais as he marched to the head table in the great hall and faced his two young cousins. "Have any of you seen her?"

"Nay, not since we rode in through the gates," replied Andrew.

"We thought she was with you or with Malcolm," said Ian.

"She is nowhere to be found." Lucais poured himself a tankard of ale and took a deep drink to steady himself. "I have spent this last hour trying to find her."

"Do ye think she has left?" asked Andrew.

"Aye, I do. She isnae at Dunmor, that is certain." He ran his hands through his already badly tousled hair. "I dinnae understand."

"Weel, she did say that she would stay until the child was safe and she was sure that he would be weel cared for. She kens all that now. Still, ye would have thought she would say fareweel." Andrew frowned and looked at Lucais. "Unless she feared someone might make her stay for all the wrong reasons."

"Ye mean me. Do ye think I am a *wrong reason.*"

"Aye, if all ye wanted was a lass to warm your bed."

"That is not all I wanted, and she kens it."

"Ah, ye talked to her about that last night, did ye?"

"We didnae do much talking last night." Lucais began to feel uneasy. "I had thought that there would be time to think about this and to talk. I ne'er thought she would just run away."

"She probably saw that it was the perfect time to get away without any awkward good-byes or ye trying to make her stay just to warm your bed."

"Will ye stop saying that?" Lucais snapped, but Andrew just shrugged, unmoved by his cousin's temper.

"If ye want more than that, then ye have to tell her so."

"Mayhap she doesnae want any more." The mere thought that Edina had wanted no more from him than a brief moment of passion was uncomfortably painful, and Lucais tried to shrug the thought away.

Andrew made a derisive sound that was echoed by Ian. "She will take whate'er ye want to give her, or would, save that she has a lot of pride for a wee lass. Ye are probably the only one that hasnae seen how she looked at you. There was more than passion shining in those bonny eyes. And she was a weelborn maid, an innocent no doubt. That kind of lass doesnae leap into a mon's bed just because he has a pretty smile. Of course, since she isnae here, ye cannae ken what she thought or felt."

"Ye think I ought to chase the lass," Lucais said even as he decided that he would do just that, right to the gates of Glenfair if he had to.

"I think ye ought to. I would. I would run her down and tell her all that is in my heart, for that is what she needs. 'Tis your decision. Of course, she is poor and landless and ye willnae gain anything but her if ye wed her."

"I think that will be more than enough," Lucais said as he started toward the door.

"Talk to the lass," called Andrew.

"Aye," agreed Ian. "She hasnae had a verra happy life and she needs to ken that ye are offering her more than a warm bed and, mayhap, honor and duty."

As he strode to the stables to get his horse, Lucais idly wondered how his cousins had come to know Edina so well. The moment his horse was ready, he swung up into the saddle and galloped out of Dunmor. If Edina needed sweet words, he would do his best to give her some, but he would get her back to Dunmor even if he had to drag her back. The moment he had realized that she was gone, he had known that he needed her and that the sweet passion they shared was only a small part of that. Lucais just prayed that she felt the same.

Eight

With her hand shading her eyes, Edina looked toward the hills in the distance and sighed. There was still a long way to go. She was not afraid of the journey. The weather could be harsh in early September, but she knew how to find or build a shelter. Late in the summer the land teemed with food if one knew where to look, and she did. She had Gar, her weapons, and was a skilled hunter, so she did not fear hunger. What twisted her insides into painful knots and made her head ache with the urge to weep was the fact that she was walking away from everything she wanted and needed. At the end of her journey was Glenfair, her cold, dour uncle, and his equally cold, dour people. She had always been alone, but now she knew she would suffer deeply from it. Now she knew that the love, friendship, happiness, and caring she had often dreamed of could really exist. It was going to be torture to live without it.

"Do ye think I have made a mistake, Gar?" she asked the dog sitting at her feet.

"Aye, but I begin to wonder if ye have the wit to ken it."

Edina was both frightened and elated by the sound of Lucais's deep voice right behind her. It also surprised her that she had not heard his approach and that Gar had given her no sign that they were no longer alone. She had not thought that she was that deeply sunk into her own musings. When she slowly turned to face Lucais and saw that he was on foot, his horse nowhere in sight, she felt a little less upset about how he had managed to sneak up on her.

"Ye didnae follow me all this way on foot, did ye?" she asked, curiosity briefly overwhelming her unease.

"Nay, I left my horse back among the trees. He will be safe enough. These are still my lands." He crossed his arms over his chest and looked down at her, one dark brow raised in an expression of slight derision. "Ye havenae gone verra far."

"Weel, I have been walking only for two, mayhap three, hours."

"And ye intended to walk all the way back to Glenfair?"

The bite to his words began to annoy her, and she put her hands on her hips, staring at him belligerently. "Aye. Mayhap ye failed to notice that I dinnae own a horse. The only way I can get back to Glenfair is to walk there."

"Ye didnae think ye should tell me that ye were leaving? One usually pauses to thank one's host before fleeing his home."

"I said faretheeweel to Malcolm," she replied, some of her belligerence fading as she fought a sense of guilt over the way she had crept away from Dunmor.

"Oh, aye, ye spoke to the only one who couldnae understand and certainly couldnae tell anyone that ye were leaving."

"I came to Dunmor to be certain that Malcolm was safe and that he would be weel cared for. That has all come to pass, so there is nae any reason for me to stay another day."

"Not even to say a proper faretheeweel to your lover?"

Edina cursed the blush that immediately warmed her cheeks. "One night of madness doesnae make ye my lover."

"Weel, then let us make it two so that ye can reconsider your decision to creep away like some thief."

Before Edina fully understood what he was saying, Lucais grabbed her and tossed her over his shoulder. That abrupt move and her own surprise kept her breathless for a moment as he started to walk back in the direction of his keep. She was not sure why he was acting so offended or even why he had come after her, but as she regained her senses, she decided that she did not like the way he was toting her about like an old blanket.

"Put me down, ye great oaf," she snapped, and punched his

broad back, cursing when he did not even flinch. "Gar," she called, and frowned when she looked around and did not see her dog. "Where is that foolish beastie?"

"He trotted off into the wood, nose to the ground." Lucais lightly slapped her on the backside when she wriggled violently in his hold. "Enough, or ye shall tumble to the ground and break your bonny, empty head."

"Empty head?" She hit him again, then watched in growing suspicion as he took a blanket roll from the back of his saddle and tossed it on the ground, spreading it out with a few nudges from his feet. "Just what are ye planning?"

A soft screech that was a mixture of alarm and annoyance escaped her as he picked her off his shoulder and gently tossed her onto the blanket. Before she could get away from him, he pinned her there by sprawling on top of her. Her attempts to hit him were stopped with an embarrassing ease when he lightly grasped her by the wrists and held her arms down on the blanket. Edina glared at him, struggling to cling to her sense of outrage and ill use and not be distracted by how good it felt to have his big, strong body pressed so close to hers.

Lucais saw her beautiful eyes darken slightly, the hint of passion in their clear depths contradicting the anger on her delicate face, and he inwardly smiled. That small sign that she wanted him still was enough to restore his battered confidence and soothe some of the pain she had inflicted by leaving so abruptly. His cousins might be right. He just needed to tell her how he felt and offer her more than passion.

At the moment, however, the feel of her soft, lithe body had him eager to do something other than talk. Mayhap, he told himself, it would not hurt to remind her of the sweet fire she was walking away from. And, when lying in his arms, sated from the fierce passion they shared, she might also be more inclined to listen to what he had to say. If nothing else, he decided as he lowered his mouth to hers, he craved one last time in her arms before she walked out of his life forever.

Edina gasped when his mouth covered hers, unwittingly giving him the chance to deepen his kiss immediately. A part of her was outraged. That little voice spoke of sin, warned her about allowing herself to give in to passion without love, and urged her to say no. As Lucais released her wrists and smoothed his big hands down her body, a louder, stronger voice told her cautious self to be quiet. Edina groaned softly as desire rushed through her veins, silencing the argument in her head. She wrapped her arms around Lucais's neck and returned his impassioned kiss.

It was not until they were lying flesh to flesh, their clothing scattered over the ground, that she grasped a fragment of clear thought. She briefly wondered how they had gotten undressed so fast, then struggled to think about what she was doing and not about how much she wanted to do it. The night she and Lucais had spent together had been beautiful. In a strange way, the need to go and save Malcolm had enhanced the sweetness of it. There had been no morning regrets, no wrong things said or done to spoil everything, even the memory. This time they were alone with no chance of interruption, and this time she could not use Malcolm as a reason to stay close, hoping for more than passion.

Lucais slowly kissed his way to her breasts, and Edina shuddered. There had been no promises, no words of love. Lucais could have sought her out because he hungered for another taste of the passion they shared, and for no other reason. As he drew the hard tip of her breast deep into his mouth, she decided that she did not care why he was there. Another taste of the passion they shared would just add to the memories she could cherish when she was alone again. She wrapped her body around his and let passion rule her.

Lucais held Edina close as he regained his senses. Never had lovemaking been so sweet or so fulfilling. He could not understand how she could walk away from that. When he felt her start to tense and shift slightly in his hold, he knew he had to start talking, demanding a few answers from her, and being painfully honest himself.

"Edina," he said, touching a kiss to her forehead as he gently but firmly held her still when she tried to move out of his arms. "We must talk. Since we first set eyes on each other we have suspected each other and desired each other. We have protected my sister's child, beaten my enemy together, and talked about little parts of our lives. Now we must swallow our pride and our doubts and talk about what is to happen between us."

She peered at him through the tangled curtain of her hair, not sure what he meant. A little knot of fear formed in her stomach. If he was planning to ask her to be his lover, to stay with him as his leman, she was not sure she had the strength to refuse.

"What about us?" she asked, her voice little more than a whisper.

"This might be a wee bit easier for me if ye didnae look so frightened," he said, and smiled crookedly.

"Uncertainty makes me frightened."

"Edina, do ye think I ran after ye just for this, sweet as it is?"

"I am not sure why ye are here." She took a deep breath and decided to be completely honest. "I cannae stay if all I am to be is your leman. 'Tis best if I leave now."

"I wouldnae chase my leman down if she left me. I would just go and find another." He brushed a kiss over her mouth when her eyes widened slightly. "Aye, I want ye in my bed, but I also just want ye." He grimaced. "I have ne'er spoken of such things with a lass before, so I ken that I may not say it weel, or prettily."

"Say it badly or any way ye choose," she whispered. "Just say it."

He laughed and pulled her into his arms. "I was nae really sure until I found ye gone, but I love ye, Edina MacAdam. I want ye to stay with me as my wife."

"Are ye sure? I have no dowry." She was not surprised that she found it hard to speak, her voice choked with tears, for she was elated, stunned, and afraid that she had not heard him right.

"Ye are all I need. I have lands and I am wealthy enough to satisfy all my needs." He looked at her, frowning a little when he saw a tear roll down her cheek. "I was hoping that ye would answer in kind."

She hugged him with her whole body. "Idiot. I love you. Aye, I will marry you. I have just dreamed of hearing ye say such things so often that I feared I had imagined them." As she got her emotions under control, she looked at him and smiled slightly. "Actually, I do have a small dowry." She glanced at Gar as he trotted up to sit beside them. "A big, furry one."

Lucais laughed and reached out to pat the dog. "A prize any mon would welcome. We shall have to find him a fine bitch to breed with."

"And then we shall have puppies tumbling underfoot. Puppies, and Malcolm, and mayhap a bairn or two of our own?"

"As many as ye want." He gently kissed her. "And they will ne'er be left alone, nor will their mother."

Edina did not think she could ever love him more than she did at that moment. "I do so love you, Lucais."

"And I you, my wee forest maid."

She smiled and looked around at the trees encircling them. The forest was where her mother had cast her aside. The forest was where she had found Malcolm and where she had met Lucais. And now it was in the forest that they pledged their love. Perhaps, she thought with an inner laugh of pure joy as she gave herself over to his kisses, there is something good to be found in the forest.

About the Author

Hannah Howell lives with her family in Georgetown, Massachusetts. Her previous Zebra historical romances include *Only for You* and *My Valiant Knight*. Hannah's newest Zebra historical romance, *Unconquered*, will be published in October 1996. Hannah loves hearing from her readers, and you may write to her c/o Zebra Books. Please include a self-addressed stamped envelope if you wish a response.

Lullaby of Love

Carol Finch

One

Post-Revolutionary War
Charles Town, South Carolina

Donnovan Maxwell heaved a long-suffering sigh and drummed his blunt-tipped fingers against his desktop. Irritation and displeasure crinkled his sun-bronzed features. For two endless days he had been ensconced behind his desk, interviewing the string of sour-faced spinsters who applied for the position of governess and nanny for his eleven-month-old niece. What Donnovan had imagined to be a simple task had proven exceptionally difficult and time-consuming.

The previous month Donnovan's younger brother and sister-in-law had sailed off to reestablish and expand their mercantile trade in the West Indies—and had been lost in a storm at sea. Enduring the bitter blow of losing what was left of his family, Donnovan had been overwhelmed by the responsibility of caring and providing for young Alicia.

For the past eight years Donnovan had commanded a militia, waging guerrilla warfare on the British—Banastre Tarleton in particular. Donnovan had learned to cope with the sound of muskets exploding around him, the unnerving whistle of flying cannonballs, and the scent of death. He had cut himself off from his emotions in order to fulfill his obligations as a soldier and commander.

Caring for a young female child simply was not within Donnovan's realm of experience. He had been raised in an all-male household after losing his mother when he was seven. He had dealt only with a regiment of trail-hardened soldiers who swarmed in and out of the swamps and forests to strike their blows against the British and rescue prisoners of war. He'd been nicknamed Stone Dragon, and he'd made certain the name and reputation struck fear in his enemies' hearts.

Understanding himself for what he was—a tough, sometimes vicious warrior trained for battle—Donnovan realized he was not acclimated to raise Alicia to be a proper, dignified lady. The task required a woman's gentle hand and tender sensibilities.

Unfortunately, hiring just the right woman for young Alicia Maxwell was fast becoming as tedious as sloshing through the swamps.

"Perhaps a glass of mint sling is in order, Captain." Horatio DeWitt set the mug on the edge of the mahogany desk and smiled sympathetically at his one-time commander.

Intense golden eyes rimmed with coal-black lashes lifted to the ex-soldier who had been Donnovan's second in command. Strong fingers closed around the glass in a gesture of self-discipline.

"I'm beginning to think 'tis not one suitable female in Charles Town who can fill this position as governess," Donnovan grumbled.

Horatio's lips pursed in a commiserative smile. "Aye, Captain." His gaze shot toward the door, where a long line of women awaited an audience with the master of the town house. "They're an unpleasant lot, aren't they? After listening to all these females spout out the duties they *won't* perform, and the fringe benefits they insist upon enjoying, it does leave a man to wonder if perhaps we should assume the task of raising young Alicia ourselves."

Donnovan took a welcomed swig of the mint sling and nodded somberly. " 'Twould seem we have been too involved in the business of waging war to understand the way women think and function. Until now I had been under the impression that would-be employees strived to please rather than flouncing in with a list of demands clenched in their upraised fists. Their tactics are in direct conflict with the precise chain of command and protocol observed in the militia."

Horatio chuckled. "Though I've often heard love and war are a great deal alike, I never realized the simple acquisition of a nanny could be a battle too."

"If I thought my staff of veteran soldiers could properly raise my niece, I would have packed Alicia off to the plantation already. But I doubt my brother would have approved.

"More's the pity that my sister-in-law refused to hire a governess to act in her stead before they set sail to the West Indies. Jessica intended to entrust Alicia to my care for a month, not the next seventeen years."

Horatio sighed heavily. "Aye, 'twould have simplified matters for us, but I can't fault Jessica for wanting to raise her own child rather than turning the responsibility over to a nanny. 'Tis a shame that none of us are authorities on grooming a little girl to become a respectable lady."

Donnovan glanced down at the gold watch clasped in his callused hand. If he didn't locate an acceptable governess in the next two hours, he wasn't sure what he was going to do. Another day of tiresome interviews with domineering, combative females would be worse than a life sentence in hell.

But then, Donnovan reminded himself, he knew what hell was like—had survived it. He had been to war, viewed its cruelty and the death of his comrades and friends firsthand, and then suffered the loss of his family. Any emotion once stored in his heart and soul had evaporated so long ago that he wondered if he would ever be able to feel again.

There were times when Donnovan swore he *had* become the Stone Dragon. He, like the Swamp Fox and the Gamecock, had become the subject of myths and legends. Relying on guerrilla warfare against the British, Donnovan had been on a personal vendetta as well as under orders to defend his homeland against the English hordes.

Banastre Tarleton, who had massacred more than a hundred

American soldiers at the Battle of Waxhaws, had cost Donnovan one brother. A violent storm at sea had cost him the other.

Donnovan had concentrated most of his hit-and-run operations against "Bloody" Tarleton for bayonetting the rebel soldiers to death while under the flag of truce. Tarleton gave no quarter, and Donnovan had vowed to make that ruthless bastard's life hell every chance he got.

Anger—the sole emotion Donnovan allowed himself to experience the past eight years—roiled inside him like a thundercloud. Willfully, he tamped it down and focused on the business at hand.

"Are you ready for the next prospective governess, Captain?" Horatio questioned.

Donnovan nodded his raven head. "Aye, and let's pray that somewhere—in the long line that streams out our door and down the street—'tis one paragon of femininity who can provide Alicia with the proper upbringing her mother and father would have wished for her."

"A pity the good Lord called Jessica and Stephen to His service so soon."

Donnovan silently agreed as Horatio strode toward the foyer. But life—Donnovan had discovered—was not always fair. He'd been forced to grow up beneath his father's stern hand, paving the way for his two younger brothers. He had watched his father wrestle with the tormenting loss of his wife and lash out at his own sons. Adam Maxwell had loved his wife so completely that an existence without her had become nearly unbearable. Donnovan had vowed never to care so much for a woman that losing her could ruin his life and dramatically affect those around him.

And then came the war, testing Donnovan to his very limits, teaching him that uncontrolled emotion led to vulnerability and disaster. And if 'twas true that he had turned to stone—as the legend stated—then he dared not complain. That absence of emotion allowed him to maintain a cool head under fire. His ability to think and react quickly in the face of danger had spared the lives of many of the men under his command.

The Stone Dragon had achieved and served his purpose. And now he faced yet another task and obligation—his niece Alicia. Donnovan braced himself to interview the middle-aged woman swathed in black. She reminded him of a hook-nosed witch—without her broom. Even before Donnovan began questioning Miss Prickle he knew she would never do. Alicia Maxwell would *not* be raised under this witch's disapproving gaze and heavy hand!

Hannah Rothchild hiked up her hampering skirts and shot off with a renewed burst of speed, leading the search posse on a merry chase through town. Whatever fate awaited her couldn't possibly be worse than what she'd left behind. And somewhere behind that gloomy cloud her life had become, there had to be a rainbow—or so Hannah optimistically told herself.

"There!" The booming shout scattered Hannah's thoughts. Neck bowed, skirts billowing, Hannah dashed around another corner in the city's wealthy residential district. 'Twas then that she saw the line of women camped out on the doorstep of a palatial three-story brick home complete with freshly painted shutters, stately colonnades, and well-manicured gardens.

Hannah made a beeline toward the house. When she cut in line, the string of females sniffed and snorted in objection. But no matter what, Hannah intended to avoid the search party sent to apprehend her. Whatever position these women clambered to fill, Hannah desperately needed the job—and its refuge. Scrubbing floors and scouring chamber pots held greater appeal than tolerating the situation that had gone from bad to worse.

"Now, hold on there, young lady," came the gruff voice of the prune-faced woman beside Hannah. "Your place is at the end of the line. You'll wait your turn like everybody else!"

When hands—like eagle talons—clamped onto her forearm, Hannah wormed loose. She paid no heed to the flock of women who clucked in condemnation. She simply elbowed her way through the crowd and then burst through the office door as if she owned the place.

Tenacity was something she had learned and relied upon during the past ten years. Iron-willed determination and unswerving optimism had sustained her when life's game of cards dealt her one disappointing hand after another.

"I expect to have the Sabbath off, and I insist—"

The hatchet-faced Miss Prickle, who was planted before the desk, swiveled her head around when she heard the door open and shut abruptly. As if Hannah's unannounced arrival were no more significant than a gnat's, Miss Prickle continued in her haughty tone. "I insist on having my evenings to myself to meditate and reflect."

"I'll work Sundays and evenings," Hannah declared—to whoever was sitting behind the desk, eclipsed by the broad-shouldered and even broader-hipped spinster.

'Twas just then that Hannah noticed the gray-haired man who stood beside the door. There was a smile on his ruddy features, a twinkle in his hazel eyes.

"In fact," Hannah continued, a mite out of breath, "I'll work for nothing more than room and board, seven days a week."

Glaring daggers, Miss Prickle rounded on Hannah. "This happens to be *my* interview, and you can wait outside with the rest of the lot. I mean to have this job!"

Hannah squared her shoulders when the hook-nosed spinster stamped toward her, but she became distracted by the fashionably dressed man who rose from his chair behind the desk like a genie from his bottle. Eyes like shiny gold nuggets focused on Hannah. A ruggedly handsome face etched with chiseled features and framed by jet-black hair demanded her fascinated attention. Despite the oncoming threat of the older woman, Hannah stood there, staring like a thunderstruck idiot at pure male perfection.

In all her twenty-three years, no man ever had such a stunning and dramatic effect on her. She felt as if she were staring at a six-foot-four-inch stone statue. And yet those tawny eyes were so intense and hypnotic that she knew he surely must live and breathe. Something instinctive and innate struck hard and deep. 'Twas like a page from a whimsical fairy tale—the missing page from her less than fairy-tale life.

Before Hannah could regather her composure, Miss Prickle shoved her toward the door. Hannah stumbled back, catching the heel of her well-worn shoe on the tattered hem of her gown. She fell on the floor like a misplaced rug. Petticoats spiraled around her like a white cloud as air gushed from her lungs in a whoosh. Her gaze lifted over the glaring witch to see the intriguing figure of a man staring down at her unladylike sprawl on his Belgian carpet.

"Horatio, kindly escort Miss Prickle away," came the deep, resonant voice that aptly fit the massive figure of a man. "I don't believe she can fulfill my requirements."

Miss Prickle snorted scornfully as she towered over Hannah. "And I can guess at the extra duties you'll expect from *this* wench. Should've known you wanted to fill two positions with one employee." Harrumphing, Miss Prickle squared her broad shoulders, tilted her pointed chin, and stamped off.

"Cranky old bat, isn't she?" Hannah remarked as she climbed to her feet to modestly rearrange her gown.

For just an instant Hannah swore those chiseled lips were about to curve into a smile. But they didn't. The man of stone didn't change his impassive expression. However, the gray-haired assistant standing beside the door camouflaged a snicker behind a cough. He, at least, seemed to have a sense of humor.

"So . . ." Hannah said as exuberantly as she knew how. "Am I hired. . . ."

Her voice trailed off when a squawk erupted from behind the glass door leading to the terrace. Hannah's gaze leapt to the hulky shadow of the man who was trying to retain his hold on the worming bundle of a child. Hannah broke into a grin when the vivacious child stuck out her feet, indicating she wanted to be set down—that very moment. The bulky figure doubled at the waist, carefully placing the little girl on the bricked patio. The instant the man opened the terrace door, the toddler surged inside, jabbering nonstop in a language that was impossible to translate.

Hannah dropped to her knees to greet the bewitching child at eye level rather than towering over her the way Miss Prickle had loomed over Hannah. The little girl—with a pink bow dangling off the side of her windblown hair that perfectly matched the color of the imposing man behind the desk—charged directly at Hannah. As if they were long-lost friends, the child outstretched her arms and fastened them around Hannah's neck, snuggling contentedly against her chest.

Hannah experienced an instant kinship with the child. For the space of a few seconds, she returned the unexpected hug this delightful child had bestowed on her. Hannah, who had been searching for a port in a storm, appeared to be a port for someone else.

'Twas destiny, Hannah told herself optimistically. This must surely be the elusive rainbow for which she had searched, the silver lining in the dark clouds hanging over her head. For once, perchance, she could make her bed in a home where she was wanted and needed. 'Twould be a welcome change, to be sure.

Now, if only the man of stone would stop staring at her with that inscrutable expression and crack a tiny smile, maybe she could find sanctuary from a life that kept taking one bad turn after another.

Donnovan appraised the attractive female who reminded him of a lively leprechaun. For the past two days his home had been besieged by a gaggle of women he would not have hired—neither in good conscience nor desperation—to care for his young niece. And here, like a bolt from the blue, came this green-eyed elf who, like the sun, lit up the room when she burst into it.

A mass of red-gold curls, all askew, was piled atop her head.

The glorious strands seemed to catch fire and burn with each
fascinating tilt of her head. Compared to the women he had been
interviewing, this lovely intruder was a breath of spring air. And
amazingly, Alicia had taken to her instantly. Alicia was still
clinging to the young woman, her head buried against the curve
of the woman's swanlike throat, perfectly content in the arms of
this stranger.

Yet Miss Prickle's comment about a governess serving a dual
purpose stuck in Donnovan's mind. He refused to base his se-
lection on fairness of face, fullness of breasts, and roundness of
hips. For sure and certain he was hiring a governess, not a mistress, and he did not want his integrity dragged through a caul-
dron of gossip stirred by Miss Prickle's tongue.

Estes Fitzgerald grinned broadly from his position beside the
terrace door. "We should've thought of this sooner, Captain.
Letting the little tyke choose her own governess would've saved
us some time." Fitz pushed away from the wall and straightened
the cravat Alicia had rendered cockeyed. "I guess that's that.
Shall I finish packing the child's belongings?"

Donnovan hesitated. "As much as Alicia appears to have accepted our unexpected applicant, she's not exactly what I had in
mind."

Horatio DeWitt jerked upright. "Neither was that slew of
militant females who've darkened our door the past two days.
This lass is definitely the best of the bunch."

True, Donnovan admitted, but 'twas something about this intriguing female with the pixielike features that disturbed him,
left him wary. Her theatrical entrance indicated she did not practice—or preach—Donnovan's regimented, disciplined approach
to life.

Donnovan proceeded, in logical order, from one duty to the
next. He did not appreciate being on the wrong end of unexpected surprises. As a military commander, he'd been trained to
surprise and conquer, never to be startled and disarmed. This
woman had done exactly that. She made him feel . . .

Donnovan chose not to analyze what this vibrant imp made

him feel. Instead, he garnered his defenses and asserted his authority. "What is your name, young lady?"

"Hannah Roth—" She grinned up at him, her emerald eyes sparkling like polished gems. "My name is Hannah Roth. And I would be honored to become Alicia's governess."

"Even on the Sabbath and in the evenings," Horatio inserted, smiling wryly at Donnovan. "Who could ask more from an employee?"

"*I* could," Donnovan said stiffly. Hands clasped behind him in military fashion, he strode around the desk to stare down on Hannah like an imposing mountain of granite. "You *do* have references, don't you, Miss Roth?"

"What more does she need?" Estes Fitzgerald put in quickly. "Alicia likes her."

"Thank you, Fitz." Donnovan frowned darkly. "Why don't you make yourself useful by bringing us a tray of tea."

The middle-aged man took his cue and disappeared around the corner of the terrace, carrying out the orders Donnovan was accustomed to giving.

"Tell me something," Hannah requested. "Do you always spout off like a whale when you wish your bidding done?"

Donnovan inwardly bristled at the mocking question and the teasing glitter in those spell-casting eyes. 'Twas just as he had predicted. This sassy, free-spirited female was trouble wrapped in an enchanting package. Sure as the world turned, Hannah Roth would disrupt his precisely arranged life and challenge his authority with insolent questions, tempered with the kind of mischievous smile that would do a leprechaun proud.

"Tell me something, Miss Roth, do you have the slightest appreciation for orderliness and proper chains of command?"

"Ordinarily?"

"Aye," he bit off, annoyed by the beguiling twinkle in her eye and the devastating smile that cut dimples in her flawless face. He felt the impulsive inclination to smile back, but he refused to grant Hannah the slightest indication that she could charm or manipulate him.

"Nay, I'm afraid not," Hannah said, rising gracefully to her feet, still cuddling Alicia in her arms. "I have a natural tendency to be outspoken—"

"Truly? I hadn't noticed."

"And my respect for authority must be earned, not blindly given—"

"Obviously."

"And my pet peeve," she confided with just the right hint of challenging directness, "is being interrupted before I can punctuate a sentence during conversation. I should think that even those in positions of authority should have the common courtesy to let a person finish what she is trying to say."

Donnovan slammed his mouth shut. From the corner of the room he could see Horatio battling to smother his grin—and failing miserably.

"I desperately need this job," Hannah went on to say. "And I've already been charmed by your daughter—"

"She is my niece," he corrected her.

"Her misfortune."

"Pardon me?" Donnovan strained to decipher the quiet words that had been murmured into Alicia's dark, curly hair.

And then it came again, that impish smile that made the room light up like high noon in the desert. "You are lucky to have been blessed with such a lovely young niece." Green eyes locked with intense amber. "Am I hired or not, *Captain?*"

"Not . . . without serious reservations," Donnovan stipulated as he sidestepped around the all-too-beguiling female, "but aye, you have the job. Now, if you will excuse me, I need to pack for our immediate journey to my plantation."

"We are leaving town?"

Donnovan broke stride and pivoted, only to find his betraying gaze focused on Hannah's bewitching face. "Aye, we are, as quickly as possible. Is that a problem?"

"As it happens, Captain, I'm looking forward to a change of scenery. *As quickly as possible* suits me perfectly, except that all I have in the way of a uniform is what I'm wearing."

"Your proper uniform will be provided."

Donnovan's thick brows furrowed over his squinted eyes. He critically appraised Hannah—overlooking not even one insignificant detail—as if she were a map that would lead him to the enemy's stronghold. All he received in his attempt to figure this woman out was another of those dazzling smiles. It seemed she hid her true thoughts and feelings behind a cheerful grin, while he employed the stony façade of indifference.

"Since you offered to work without salary, I will supply your wardrobe," Donnovan insisted.

Sparing Hannah one last glance, Donnovan strode into the hall to announce that a governess had been hired. When the passel of females had filed out, Donnovan marched upstairs to finish packing.

Hannah Roth was going to cause him trouble, Donnovan predicted as he neatly folded his clothes and tucked them in his trunk. He had developed a dependable sixth sense during his forays in battle. He would have to remain on constant vigil, ensuring Hannah didn't disrupt his structured, organized life.

Donnovan found himself wondering if perhaps he should have selected one of the dour spinsters who congregated around his town house. Even while they voiced their demands, he had still felt as if *he* were in control, that *he* would have the final word. The older women had claimed to be sticklers for precision and order. Hannah Roth, he speculated, would be nothing of the kind.

Forcing himself not to dwell on the image of sparkling green eyes, flaming gold hair, and dimpled smiles, Donnovan gathered the last of his belongings. Once the entourage reached his plantation on the Santee River, he intended to have little association with the governess. Alicia would monopolize Hannah's time. Restoring the plantation to its prewar state of efficiency would occupy Donnovan. He would leave Hannah to his second in command—Horatio DeWitt.

He would ensure the arrangement worked, Donnovan told himself confidently. But under no circumstances would Miss Prickle's scandalous prophecy come true. Donnovan had not hired Hannah as a prospective mistress, only as a governess. Attractive though she was, he was not about to complicate the issue.

Donnovan Maxwell was a man of honesty, integrity, and unshakable self-discipline, even when confronted by the most impossible odds and forbidden temptations. And that, he assured himself firmly, was *not* the shining example of famous last words either!

"Is the man of stone always so cool and remote?" Hannah blurted out the instant Donnovan was out of earshot.

Horatio nodded. "He wasn't nicknamed Stone Dragon for naught."

Hannah's eyes widened in recognition. That explained quite a lot. She'd heard the legends about the fierce guerrilla soldier who fought like a hellhound, nipping at British heels until the enemy evacuated their camps in the colony. According to the tales that had circulated around Charles Town, the Stone Dragon emerged from the swamps and appeared from the dense timbers like a mythical creature, breathing fire on his foe before vanishing into nothingness.

Small wonder Hannah had likened her new employer to solid rock. He had been a soldier to boot—a man who expected his commands to be carried out without question or objection. Still, 'twas better than dealing with a man whose intentions toward her had grown frighteningly alarming the past few months, Hannah consoled herself. She had been forced to take drastic actions before making her hurried escape.

"Would you care for tea, Miss Roth?" Fitz asked as he lumbered through the terrace door.

She smiled down at the child who had fallen asleep in her arms. "I think perhaps I should put Alicia down for a nap."

"First door on the left at the head of the stairs," Horatio directed as he plucked up a cup of tea. "We'll be up momentarily to gather the last of the child's belongings."

Hannah had not been gone more than a minute, when an abrupt rap resounded on the front door. Fitz hurried through the foyer to find a four-man posse staring anxiously back at him.

"We were told that a young woman with red-gold hair, dressed in a shabby green gown, was seen entering this house," the spokesman of the brigade said without preamble. "Is she here? We are under orders to take her into custody."

Fitz frowned. "Custody for what?"

Footsteps echoed on the tiled hall as Horatio calmly approached. "That explains it, then," he said as he halted beside Fitz. "The girl barreled in here, and then exited through the back door without so much as a by-your-leave. We wondered what the commotion was all about, but 'twas over as quickly as it began."

"How long ago?" the second guard inquired urgently.

Horatio shrugged a thick shoulder. "Fifteen to twenty minutes is my best guess. We were interviewing a string of prospective governesses, when the girl came and went like a dust devil. I suggest you check the alley. There are several nooks and crannies for a fugitive to hide there."

The troop of men darted off the porch and disappeared around the corner of the house.

"Came and left like a dust devil?" Fitz snickered. "I had not realized your talent for lying, Horatio. You're exceptionally good at it. 'Tis a pity our friend Jeffrey Wilcott didn't take advantage of your skills while he was spying for us and reconnoitering the British. Any particular reason why you deceived that patrol and spared the lass?"

"Aye." Horatio closed the door and pivoted toward the stairs. "If Alicia likes Hannah, 'tis good enough for me. And Hannah will be good therapy for the captain. Perhaps her infectious brand of spirit will pry him loose from the rut he's been stuck in."

"I found myself thinking the same thing," Fitz confided as he followed in Horatio's wake. "The captain could use a little spark and amusement in his life. The burden of responsibility he's shouldered the past few years has caused him to take himself entirely too seriously, even after the threat of war has passed."

"Then we are agreed," Horatio murmured conspiratorially as he glanced toward Donnovan Maxwell's closed door. "The captain need not know about this incident unless absolutely necessary."

"What incident?" Fitz asked with a mock-innocent smile.

Horatio grinned slyly as he ambled toward Alicia's nursery. Whoever or whatever Hannah Roth was running from, she had found a haven here. Horatio had been puzzled by Hannah's unannounced arrival and her eagerness to work for only room and board. But he refused to believe the vivacious lass could be guilty of a crime. She simply didn't seem the type.

Hannah's immediate affection for Alicia indicated she possessed a kind and loving heart. Having just such a female underfoot was going to do Donnovan a world of good.

Horatio was certain he had seen a carefully guarded—but unmistakable—flare of awareness the instant Donnovan clapped eyes on Hannah. That, Horatio assured himself, was why Donnovan had balked at hiring Hannah. Though Donnovan found fault with every other applicant, his only objection to Hannah was that someone might question his ulterior motive for employing such a fetching female.

That in itself indicated Donnovan did feel tempted, unwillingly attracted. The sad truth of the matter was that Donnovan never permitted himself the pleasure of a woman's companionship except in a man's most necessary sense. If anyone could crack the Stone Dragon's rock-bound heart and teach him to laugh and live again, Horatio was betting Hannah Roth could.

Indeed, Horatio was experiencing a lighthearted sense of satisfaction himself, just knowing Hannah would be gracing the halls of Maxwell Plantation. After witnessing so much death and destruction during the war, Horatio was looking forward to sharing his space with the personification of sunshine and refreshing spirit.

Two

With Alicia nestled comfortably on her hip, Hannah strolled through the gardens, following the dirt path that led to the Santee River. The two weeks she'd spent at Maxwell Plantation had eased the tension that had hounded her since her previous employer had returned from battle to hover uncomfortably close. Gone was the stress of dealing with a man who had begun to make blatant overtures with such alarming regularity that Hannah had cringed each time she was summoned from her daily duties.

'Twas definitely a change of lifestyle when she arrived at Maxwell Plantation, Hannah reminded herself. She had repeatedly dodged her previous employer's groping hands, especially when he was drinking, which he did often—and to the extreme. But Donnovan Maxwell avoided physical contact altogether.

Ironic, wasn't it, that Hannah found herself wanting to share more of her new employer's company, when she had wanted less of the scoundrel who had succeeded in making life so miserable that escaping was the only solution. Donnovan Maxwell, on the other hand, had taken such a wide berth around her that 'twas a wonder he hadn't toppled off the edge of the earth. Although Donnovan gave her no cause for complaint, she was oddly disappointed in the lack of attention she received from him.

Even young Alicia wasn't offered Donnovan's encouraging smiles or casual touch. Watching Donnovan avoid Alicia reminded Hannah of her own childhood, her own feelings of hurt and disappointment. Perhaps Alicia was too young to realize she was being deprived of her uncle's affection, but if the situation didn't improve, Alicia would think she was being kept at arm's length because of something she had done wrong.

The similarities between Alicia's tragic loss of family and her own tugged at Hannah's heart. She wouldn't have wished the succession of misfortune that had become her life on anyone, especially this adorable child. 'Twas that hope that happiness waited somewhere in her future that had always sustained Hannah. She looked at Alicia and saw herself—a confused child who didn't understand why her safe, secure world had come tumbling down around her.

Alicia, like Hannah, was teeming with love and spirit, searching for affection, acceptance, and contentment. Well, Hannah told herself resolutely, she would ensure Alicia wouldn't suffer as she had. If she could save even one child from a bleak existence of manufacturing one's own hopes and dreams for a better life, then she would have served a noble purpose on earth.

Somehow or other, Hannah was going to break Donnovan's barriers down and *teach* him to love Alicia, *convince* him to make her an integral part of his life. She had done her best to draw Donnovan's attention to Alicia. She had shown Alicia how to make mud pies, and the child had proudly presented her soupy creation to Donnovan. Unfortunately, the slippery pie had slid from Alicia's grubby hands and splattered on Donnovan's boots and breeches. He hadn't scolded the child, but he had certainly remarked on the fact that he suspected Hannah had put Alicia up to the prank.

And then there was the "turtle incident," as Hannah had come to call it. Alicia had discovered a turtle making its way across the meadow. She had snatched it up, amazed when the creature shrank into its shell. When Alicia toddled off to show her treasure to Donnovan, Hannah had pointed out that he and the turtle had a great deal in common. The comment had earned her a disgruntled glare. Of course Hannah had gone on to say that if he and the turtle would both emerge from their shells the whole lot of them might get to know each other better. Donnovan had done an immediate about-face and stalked off to attend the many duties that occupied him. Hannah had made her point, but Donnovan still hadn't softened toward Alicia. . . .

Hannah's thoughts evaporated when Alicia tipped her head back and pointed toward the birds fluttering in the trees.

"Whippoorwills," Hannah informed the curious toddler.

Squealing in delight, Alicia stretched up on tiptoe as if to touch the feathered creatures beyond her grasp. "Wh-ip," she tried to repeat.

Hannah glanced pensively from the child to the tree bough. "Shall we see what the world looks like from a bird's point of view, Ali?"

Scooping Ali up in her arms, Hannah approached the tree. The wide bough—between broad, outreaching limbs—provided a perfect seat for Alicia. Tucking the modest, high-necked gray gown that Donnovan had provided for her between her legs, Hannah fashioned makeshift breeches by securing the back hem into her belt. Shedding her shoes, Hannah pulled herself up beside Alicia.

Giggles and indecipherable phrases tumbled from Alicia's lips, indicating she was thrilled with the adventure. Hannah was rediscovering the simple pleasures of life through the eyes of this curious and energetic child.

While her former employer had been away, Hannah had been too caught up in time-consuming tasks to notice her surroundings. Her duties of caring for Alicia provided the opportunity to stop and smell the roses—as the adage went.

Alicia was good for her, Hannah decided. 'Twas a pity the self-imposed Donnovan Maxwell took himself too seriously to appreciate his niece and this panoramic plantation. The man definitely needed someone to rattle his rock cage. Never let it be said that Hannah hadn't made a valiant effort. Unfortunately, Donnovan had made a spectacular display of avoiding her and his niece since the "turtle incident."

Hannah pointed to a spot on the branch. "Look, Ali, a nest."

Rising, Hannah took Ali by the hand and led the way along

the thick limb. A chorus of chirps flooded from the straw and mud nest situated in the fork between two branches. Before Ali could grasp one of the fragile creatures by the neck—she was notorious for clutching the kittens in the barn in such a manner—Hannah guided small, eager fingers over the birds' feathered heads in a gentle caress.

Dark eyes lifted to Hannah, glittering with wondrous pleasure. Affection tugged at Hannah's heartstrings—and not for the first time. This child, who had been surrounded by only men—men who didn't seem to know what to do with her—was a wellspring of spirit and constant delight. If Hannah never found a husband to give her children of her own, at least she had Ali—for a time.

Hannah snapped back to attention when a tiny hand shot toward the nest again, intent on scooping up every last chirping creature for a zealous hug that might prove fatal.

"Their mama and papa would be displeased if we harmed these fragile babies." Hannah gave her head a firm shake when Ali glanced up at her. "Let them be, Ali."

Providing distraction, Hannah propelled Ali toward a higher branch that hung above the river. Hannah broke off a twig and tossed it into the water. Ripples streamed across the glassy surface in waves of silver. When she handed Ali a twig, the child mimicked the action, yammering in pleasure when she made her own shimmering ripples.

For a few minutes they sat upon the limb, feet dangling, viewing the world from a bird's perspective. Aye, Hannah decided, she needed to commune with nature as much as Alicia did. Each daily outing had been good for the soul as well as an education for this bright, intelligent child.

The sound of hooves brought Hannah's head around. While Ali jabbered and plucked at leaves, Hannah monitored Donnovan's approach. He sat a horse the same way he sat at the head of the table each night at supper—self-contained, invincible, unapproachable.

Hannah couldn't resist tweaking the Stone Dragon, just for

the sport and challenge of provoking a reaction, some evidence
that this fascinating but reserved man wasn't made of rock.

Hannah had the feeling Donnovan wanted to reach out, but
he simply didn't remember how because he was out of practice.
There were times when she thought she detected the smallest of
smiles, when she playfully taunted him, when Alicia's childlike
antics amused him. But the man seemed uncomfortable, unsure
of how he should behave now that he had returned to civilian
life.

When Donnovan halted directly beneath her, Hannah glanced
down to meet that expressionless stare, feeling the uncontrollable rise of mischief Donnovan provoked. She knew without
question that she was about to be reprimanded for hauling Ali
into the tree. Indeed, the only thing Donnovan ever said—when
he deigned to speak directly to her—was to criticize the uncon-
ventional outings she provided for Alicia.

"Miss Roth," Donnovan began in that carefully controlled
voice that made Hannah want to shake him, "I have indulged
you and your shenanigans for precisely fifteen days, but you
have pushed me to the crumbling edge of my patience with this
stunt."

"Have I?" she replied saucily. " 'Tis difficult to tell when
you wear that mask of bland indifference so well. How am I to
know if I please or displease you when you never change expression or tone of voice, hmm?"

She noted with immense satisfaction that a muscle quivered
along the strong line of his jaw and his tawny eyes flashed momentarily. 'Twas a small victory, one that tempted her to draw
even more of a response from a man who would not allow himself to display emotion. Why that seemed so necessary Hannah
wasn't prepared to say. It just was.

"Believe me, Miss Roth, I am extremely irritated to find my
niece and her governess—with bare legs dangling—hanging
over the river into which they could easily fall. Alicia has already
suffered the loss of her parents. I will not have her endangered
by your idiotic excursions. You allow Alicia to wallow around

like one of my pigs and slop mud on me. I resisted the urge to retaliate when you likened me to Alicia's pet turtle, but I have tolerated your permissiveness and insolence long enough. This, Miss Roth, is the last straw. Bring my niece down from there this instant. I am shipping you back to Charles Town within the hour."

"And do you intend to see to Ali's upbringing yourself?" she challenged. "You don't even spare the time to give the poor child a hug before I put her to bed. She needs to know you care, but you avoid her like the plague."

Another muscle leapt in his jaw. It seemed Donnovan was having more than the usual difficulty concealing his emotions.

Hannah gave herself high marks for effort. Donnovan may not like her, but never let it be said that she didn't dare to bring his lack of association with Alicia to his attention—constantly.

"How I choose to deal with my niece is none of your concern." There was, Hannah noted, a thread of underlying irritation, though Donnovan tried his level best to restrain it. "Now, haul yourself down here before I am tempted to climb up and break your defiant neck before you accomplish the deed by yourself!"

Hannah blinked when his command ended on such an emphatic note. Now she was getting somewhere! The devil perched on her shoulder nudged her, daring her to do more.

"I doubt you have the gumption, Captain." Eyes sparkling, Hannah met his piercing golden stare. "In order to snap my defiant neck—as you choose to call it—you would have to touch me. That, I believe, would be an impossibility for you. You aren't, after all, the least bit demonstrative, not in affection or in bad temper. In fact, I cannot tell when you are murderously mad or drop-dead bored. So how am I to know when I have unduly angered you until 'tis too late?"

"You, young lady, are dangerously close to witnessing—and experiencing—me at my very worst!"

Hannah beamed down at him. Donnovan Maxwell had actu-

ally raised his voice. The booming sound echoed along the riverbank and rose to the treetops. Startled birds took to wing.

To Hannah's surprise, Donnovan reined his steed to the
water's edge and stood up on the saddle. Two long, powerful
arms shot upward to snatch Alicia from her perch. While the
child squealed in protest, Donnovan held her at arm's length,
crouched, and then slid onto the saddle. With lithe grace, he
swung to the ground to deposit Alicia's rounded bottom on a
soft clump of grass.

All that, Hannah noted, had been accomplished with the most
impersonal contact possible. A pity her former employer
couldn't take instruction from Donnovan Maxwell. He refused
to touch unless absolutely necessary, Hannah realized with a
disbelieving shake of her head. Her life had certainly gone from
one extreme to the other, hadn't it? One thing remained the same
though. She was still dealing with difficult people and situations.

"Don't move, Alicia," Donnovan ordered in the same demanding tone he employed while commanding the militia.
Alicia's wide-eyed gaze drifted up his towering height. Her lips
quivered, indicating she was about to break down and whimper.
"And no tears either. Maxwells don't cry."

Wheeling about, Donnovan glared bayonets at Hannah. "You
have exactly thirty seconds to get down here, woman."

His brisk tone caused Alicia to burst out in a howl—whether
Maxwells were permitted to cry or not.

"Pipe down," Donnovan insisted, casting his niece a silencing
frown.

Alicia piped down immediately, but her bottom lip trembled
and tears streamed down her rosy cheeks.

"I'm waiting, Miss Roth. *Get . . . down . . . here!*"

His clipped demand was a direct challenge. Hannah tipped
her chin to a belligerent angle. "Come up here and *make me*,
Captain."

Muttering under his breath, Donnovan jerked off his jacket
and draped it over the saddle. When he bounded into the tree
bough with the muscular grace of a panther, Hannah experienced

a sense of awe rather than fear. Perhaps 'twas folly to be so confident of herself, but she didn't truly believe Donnovan intended to strangle her while his niece looked on. 'Twould simply be too traumatic for a young, impressionable child.

More amused than intimidated by the domineering male arrogance that etched his handsome features, Hannah came to her feet and scampered to the far-reaching end of the limb. When the branch crackled beneath Donnovan's weight, he halted. His expression changed to something akin to alarm, and Hannah found herself inordinately pleased by that. It occurred to her just then that she very much wanted to have a noticeable effect on this self-contained man—not for the mere challenge, but because something about him called out to something deep and instinctive inside her. She wanted to matter to the Stone Dragon.

Hannah stared deeply into those amber eyes that were fanned by impossibly long black lashes. Somewhere behind that granite mask—beneath the layers of callousness that war had forced on this legendary commander—was a lost soul that desperately needed the breath of life breathed back into it.

Perhaps Donnovan wasn't aware that he needed Hannah to rile him, to razz him, to evoke his concern, but he did. Donnovan Maxwell needed to feel *something*—anything to reassure himself that he wasn't simply a legend but a man capable of emotion, a man capable of displaying affection for the niece who hovered at his booted feet each time opportunity presented itself.

The insightful realization gave Hannah newfound confidence. She grinned elfishly. "Step closer, if you dare, Captain Dragon. I'm eager to see if your threats are all bluff. If 'tis my neck you really want, then come and get it."

"Woman," Donnovan growled ominously. "You are truly asking for it."

"Aye, I am. Now, let's see if you are going to step out on a limb to meet my challenge, or slither away like a coward."

"Coward?"

He actually *howled* in offended dignity. Good for him, Hannah thought delightedly. Donnovan's pressure-release valve had popped, causing him to demonstrate emotion for a change.

"You annoying little . . ." His voice evaporated as he surged toward her with a give-no-quarter glare.

The limb swayed and crackled beneath his weight, causing Hannah to teeter precariously. Yelping, Hannah staggered to gain her footing—and failed.

Donnovan rushed forward, attempting to grasp her hand. Their outstretched fingers failed to connect. Hannah swan-dived through the vast expanse of air, watching the river leap up to slap her in the face. Just before she splashed down, she heard Donnovan bellow her name—not "Miss Roth" but "Hannah."

'Twas the first time he had ever uttered it.

Hannah plunged into the river's depths, feeling the most incredible sense of satisfaction, visualizing the stricken look on Donnovan's face. The man was all gruff bluff, she decided. If the trembling in his voice was any indication, he did care about her—just a little—even if she was prone to tease him unmercifully. But, after all, 'twas for his own good. . . .

While Alicia clapped her hands in delight and toddled toward the river's edge to see the glittering ripples, Donnovan scrambled down the tree. His heart was pounding nonstop. He should never have allowed that ornery female to provoke him. She had the most amazing knack of getting under his skin, even while he watched her from a safe distance, gazed at her from across the supper table, or stared up at those shapely bare legs that had been draped over a tree limb. She teased him with witty taunts, challenged him, tested his self-control . . . and aroused a gnawing hunger he had valiantly contained.

Donnovan hastily bounded from the tree bough and hit the ground running. He noted that Alicia stood on the riverbank, still applauding Hannah's aerial acrobatics. His anxious gaze was fixed on the spot where Hannah had gone down—and hadn't come up.

Concern clouded Donnovan's mind like a suffocating fog. He didn't know if Hannah could swim, didn't know if the channel where she landed was deep enough to prevent her from knocking herself unconscious. All he knew was that there was no sign of her.

Donnovan was accustomed to feeling responsible for other people's lives. He'd spent years protecting the men under his command, his family—even at risk to himself. But the thought of this spirited elf vanishing forever struck deeper than it should for his own peace of mind. He couldn't afford emotion in the face of this disaster, only unerring rationality. But dammit, his legs felt like jelly as he dashed into the shallows.

For more than two weeks Donnovan had found his gaze instinctively drawn to those sparkling emerald eyes. He fed on that dimpled smile—the pure essence of mischievous spirit—but he had never given himself away. To lose the secret pleasures Hannah provided would send him plummeting back into the dark, empty cavern his life had become. Somehow or other Hannah had become his lifeline, a bright flame in the darkness. If she perished—along with his brother and sister-in-law—nothing was ever going to be the same again. . . .

Tormented by that thought, Donnovan plunged into the river. He groped the depths, and then experienced wild, ecstatic relief when his hand collided with cool flesh. His fingers clamped around Hannah's arm to tow her back to the surface. The instant his feet touched solid ground, he scooped her into his arms. Her head rolled against his heaving chest, resting against the thunderous beat of his heart.

Alicia was still clapping and giggling when Donnovan bent his wet head to Hannah's chest to ensure she was still breathing. The feel of his cheek brushing against the full swell of her breasts caused a muffled groan of longing to betray him. She felt unbelievably good in his arms, as if he were cradling some vibrant and much-needed spirit that had eluded him so long ago. More than that, he felt the alluring attraction he had nobly ignored. It hammered at his body and soul like a carpenter driving spikes. 'Twas not the time or place, to be sure. But then, lust wasn't known for its rhyme, reason, or good judgment, Donnovan reminded himself as his lips skimmed Hannah's unresponsive mouth.

His gaze dropped to Alicia, who reached up with miniature hands, as if eager to hold Hannah in her arms. Touched by the open affection and pure innocence of his niece, Donnovan knelt on bended knee so the child could see her dearest, most trusted companion.

"Ma-ma . . ."

Donnovan swore his knees had caved in when Alicia uttered the word. When Alicia reached out to comfortingly pat Hannah's cheek, Donnovan swallowed the unfamiliar lump that clogged his throat. To Alicia, Hannah had become the mother and father she had lost. The child's affection was clearly evident. She had accepted Hannah without reservation or restraint.

'Twas a pity, Donnovan thought, that he had lost the ability to be as open and demonstrative as Alicia—and Hannah. If he hadn't known it before, he was now vividly aware that the faith, trust, and affection of a child was the closest thing to perfection this side of heaven.

Lord! Donnovan thought with a jolt. His association with these two females had transformed him into sentimental sap. Although he didn't know how to relate to either of them—felt awkward and uncomfortable around them—he was, nevertheless, affected by both of them.

"So, Captain, you aren't afraid to touch after all. I must say I'm relieved to know it. I wondered if you would let me drown in your effort to avoid any sort of physical contact."

Donnovan silently fumed when wet, sooty lashes fluttered up and an impish smile cut becoming dimples in Hannah's cheeks. He dropped Hannah like a hot potato.

Luckily, she didn't have far to fall.

"Witch," he scowled at her.

"Dragon," she playfully flung back. "Am I, perchance, creeping beneath those scales of yours again?"

"Curse it, you were playing possum!" he snapped.

Hannah grinned unrepentantly. "Am I still fired?"

Donnovan gave his head a firm nod. "And 'tis for the best. Under your idiotic care Alicia will likely be climbing trees and diving headlong into puddles just because she has seen you do it."

Donnovan was gathering more steam, fueled by that elfish smile that constantly provoked responses from him. "I had high hopes of raising my niece to be a dignified young lady, not some reckless hoyden. Thus far, you've had her crawling around in the hayloft to torment kittens, plucking the blooms off the flowers in my garden, and sliding down the banister like a cursed monkey!"

"You heard about that too, did you?"

"I have heard and seen everything you've done in the name of educating my niece," he muttered, revealing more in that comment than he intended. "And neither of you is ever on time for meals. You allow this child to eat with her fingers. She throws food that she refuses to eat, and she drops globs of it to the floor, just to watch it fall. She has the table manners of a heathen, for God's sake!"

"She's not even a year old," Hannah reminded him. "I hesitate in handing her a fork for fear she'll poke herself in the eye or hurl it like a dagger."

"With you as her example, she'll probably be a hell-raising misfit by age two!" he snorted sardonically.

Hannah tilted her wet head to the side, regarding him from a different angle. "Don't you think you're overreacting just a bit? Good heavens, you rarely allow yourself the normal range of emotions, and here you are raving like a madman."

"I am not overreacting!" he blared in denial.

"I am only trying to teach Ali to enjoy and appreciate her natural surroundings. She's just a child—"

"And so, by God, is her governess!" Donnovan bounded to his feet, looming like a stone mountain. "I had expected my regimented style of living to be observed and practiced on this plantation."

"I will never march to the beat of your drum, Captain. Alicia and I are not soldiers under your command. You expect too much from us. Furthermore, I will not raise Ali—"

"Her name is Alicia," he corrected her. "That ridiculous nickname brings to mind rat-filled corridors in dirty streets!"

"I will not permit Ali to become a dimwitted twit whom men of this world can dominate and intimidate," Hannah continued forcefully. "As you recall, we just waged a war in the name of independence."

"May God save us all if you decide to lead some sort of harebrained feminine rebellion," Donnovan scoffed sarcastically.

To his surprise, Hannah bolted up to her bare feet, her damp head tossed back in militant challenge, her clothes clinging to her lush body like paint. Donnovan was hard pressed to ignore the tempting vision, but, thankfully, years of iron-willed discipline prevailed.

"I have decided to launch my crusade right here, Captain, beginning with you and your stone-clad ideals about how the world—and the women in it—should conform to your expectations."

"You can't," he took supreme satisfaction in flinging at her. "If you'll recall, you're fired. 'Tis obvious that I must see to Alicia myself to spare her from becoming a rebellious, uncontrollable little monster."

Hannah went very still, her snapping gaze locked with glittering gold. "You would raise Ali in your own image? You would squelch her natural heartwarming zest for life? You would purposely turn Ali into the stone you have become? Do you wish her to be such a pathetic creature that she cannot love or be loved?

" 'Tis one thing to wish such a bleak existence on yourself, Captain, but quite another to suck the refreshing breath of innocence from a child. Maybe you don't think you need to show

Ali that you love her, but you do. She desperately needs a substitute for the father she's lost."

"You forget your place, woman," Donnovan growled, wincing at her stinging words.

"I don't have a place in this world. But even if I did, 'twould not be up to you or any other man to tell me where it is," she plunged on. "Those of you who marched off to battle have failed to give credit to the women who stayed behind to oversee and manage homes and businesses, adequately filling your shoes. In some cases—I might add—we filled them better than you filled them yourselves. My previous employer, for instance. I took his failing business and made it prosper. My thanks was his—"

Hannah halted in midsentence, leaving Donnovan to wonder how she had been repaid for her efforts.

"If you think we will shrink back into your shadows after we've met the challenges you left in our hands, then you and the rest of the male gender are mistaken. And if you don't stop behaving like a hidebound fool, refusing to accept the affection Alicia wholeheartedly offers you," she added emphatically, "I'm going to give you up as a lost cause."

"Thank the Lord for granting small favors," he said on a smirk.

Her head came back up, silently scrutinizing him. Donnovan could see the indignation dissipating with each passing second. He regretted that, he really did. He dealt far better with Hannah when they were at odds. 'Twas safer, easier. He felt more in control—of himself at least. He wondered if any man could ever exert control over *her*. Hannah Roth was like a runaway horse galloping down an endless highway—and God help the man who was along for the ride!

"So that's your game, is it, Captain?" she said, considering him.

"I have no idea what in the hell you're babbling about."

"Don't curse in front of Ali—"

"Why not? I expect that will be one of the lessons you insist on teaching her in your crusade to ensure she believes she's a man's equal."

That infuriatingly bewitching grin returned in full force. Donnovan swore he'd lost the only skirmish he had hoped to win against Hannah. Silently, he watched Hannah scoop Alicia up and deposit her on his horse. Bold as you please, she straddled the saddle like a man, and then reined toward the manor.

"I expect you to be gone by the time I walk home," Donnovan called peevishly after her.

"Then you can expect to be disappointed, Captain. You'll have to physically throw me out if you want me gone."

" 'Twill be my greatest pleasure!"

"You need me here as much as Alicia does."

"I need no one!" Donnovan shouted to the treetops.

Hannah halted the bay gelding and twisted around in the saddle. Her smile went all through Donnovan—excavating so many emotions at once that he didn't know which one to fight first.

"Ah, but you do," she said with great conviction. "I have decided to like you as openly as I have come to love Alicia. You show promise, Captain. You simply need to be shown the way."

Donnovan swore his eyes had popped from their sockets when she made her grand declaration. Stunned, he watched Hannah trot off on his horse, with Alicia playing patty-cake and giggling happily in her arms.

Hannah had decided to like him? Why on earth would she? He had been nothing but aloof and remote, erecting barriers to keep her at a safe distance. Damnation, he didn't want her affection, because he was afraid he couldn't return it, wouldn't know how or where to start. And he knew all too well that when a man cared deeply he could be hurt just as deeply. When a man buckled to emotion, he lost the ability to think rationally, to react quickly. He became vulnerable to the crippling effects of wasted emotion.

Hadn't he just experienced several of those debilitating emotions while he rescued that ornery elf who'd been faking unconsciousness?

To make matters worse, he had nuzzled against her breast,

thoroughly enjoying the feel of her curvaceous body, under the pretense of checking for a pulse. He had humiliated himself, exposed his weakness. In a state of war that would have gotten him killed. A man who made crucial mistakes rarely lived to repeat them.

'Twas in that weakened moment that Hannah must have concluded the man of stone had a few cracks in his veneer. Now Little Miss Noble Crusader had decided to save him from himself—or some such nonsense. Well, he was going to prove to be very difficult, Donnovan promised himself. He was not going to succumb to the wit and charms of that woman. He had accepted his responsibilities—no more, no less. Letting go of years of military training and practiced techniques of mental and physical self-preservation was too difficult, too dangerous. He was what the cruelty and rigorous demands of war had made him. Anything else was foreign and unfamiliar. Donnovan could function in his regimented world, remaining emotionally detached while he tended to the business of providing for those who depended on him.

If Hannah thought for even a split second that she could burrow her way into his heart and then become the mistress of Maxwell Plantation just to enjoy the position and luxury he could provide, *she* was mistaken.

Wasn't that just like a woman—even the newly liberated variety—to prey on a man of wealth? Some things, Donnovan cynically reminded himself, never changed.

That must be her game, he concluded. True, the man in him responded to Hannah's arresting physique—even when he'd purposely dressed her in those drab, shapeless gray gowns. Also true, he was disarmed by her undaunted spirit and mischievous smile, but Donnovan vowed to stand firm. The British army hadn't been able to get the best of him.

And, by God, neither would Hannah Roth!

Amusement danced in Fitz's and Horatio's eyes when Donnovan trounced up the front steps, his saturated boots squeaking with each precise step.

"According to Hannah, you saved the day, Captain," Fitz commented. "Even if you did wind up looking like a drowned cat."

"Hannah claims she owes you her life for rescuing her when she fell into the river," Horatio put in.

"Hannah exaggerates," Donnovan muttered as he surged past his longtime friends. "And if you start believing the Gospel according to Hannah, you'll be as much of a nuisance to me as she is."

"Captain?"

"What?" Donnovan growled, halting in midstep.

"Hannah also said you intended to release her from her duties because you think she's a troublemaker." Horatio stared Donnovan squarely in the eye. "I don't think that's a good idea."

"Alicia would be lost without her." Fitz added his two shillings' worth. "Hannah is a joy and pleasure to have around. She's unbelievably handy in the kitchen too. I'm not sure you're even aware that she has been providing the pastry and breads we've been raving about. And I swear I've died and gone to heaven each night when I hear Hannah singing Alicia to sleep. That woman has the voice of an angel. You might realize what an asset Hannah is if you paid a bit more attention to—"

" 'Tis my decision to make," Donnovan said in a tone that brooked no argument.

Horatio stared into the distance, avoiding that golden-eyed glare. "Irritated though you are with Hannah, I don't think you'd want to send her—"

" 'Tis quite enough," Donnovan interrupted gruffly. "I intend to dismiss Hannah, the sooner the better."

"Before you do, 'tis something you should know," Horatio insisted.

Frowning, Donnovan found himself shuffled into his office. While Horatio closed the door behind them, Donnovan stood dripping on the carpet.

"Well? What is it I should know that you think is going to

drastically alter my decision?" Donnovan asked impatiently. "Give me one good reason why I should keep a termagant underfoot who antagonizes me for her own personal amusement?"

"I'll give you several reasons," Horatio generously offered. "The first reason is that you would sentence that lovely lass to a stint in jail for doing nothing more than protecting her virtue and honor before she escaped."

Donnovan became perfectly still, his startled gaze leaping back and forth between Fitz and Horatio. *"Escaped?"* he parroted.

"The day you hired Hannah, a patrol came knocking on our door while you were upstairs packing," Fitz reported. "Horatio and I decided to have the claim—that Hannah had committed a crime and was on the run—investigated by someone we trusted. We sent a message to Jeffrey Wilcott."

Donnovan knew Jeffrey well. The capable lieutenant had been in charge of reconnaissance and military intelligence for the militia unit. Jeffrey had a fascinating knack of discovering the enemy's intentions, enabling Donnovan and his men to strike hard and fast, and escape with few rebel casualties.

"And what did Jeffrey learn about our governess?" Donnovan wanted to know that very second.

"First of all, her name is Hannah Rothchild," Horatio informed him. "Jeffrey did some checking with the patrons at the bakery where Hannah has worked for the past ten years. Her no-account employer took advantage of Hannah's industriousness and her cheerful disposition that kept steady customers filing in and out the door. While Daniel Braxton, the owner of the shop, was in the army, Hannah ran the bakery and made the foundering business prosper. But Braxton didn't seem the least bit appreciative of her efforts on his behalf."

Donnovan tensed when the expression on Horatio's weathered features puckered in a resentful frown. He had the feeling he wasn't going to like what Horatio had to say next.

"After Hannah left, the business all but closed down. Everyone Jeffrey questioned told the same tale and empathized with

Hannah. Braxton had made several public attempts to have his way with her. God only knows what the woman has suffered behind closed doors. He regards her as his dutiful mistress and obligated servant."

Rage boiled through Donnovan's veins. The thought of Hannah being used and preyed upon by that lecherous scoundrel put a snarl on his lips. He well remembered what Hannah had said about women assuming tasks for men during the war and that the thanks she had received didn't measure up. Now he knew exactly what she meant.

"How could her family have allowed her to remain in such an intolerable situation?" Donnovan asked, bewildered.

Fitz released an audible sigh. "What was left of Hannah's family wasn't worth having. Jeffrey discovered that Hannah was taken in by a second cousin after her parents died. Her inheritance was squandered by her cousin. When the man couldn't afford another mouth to feed, he sold the child to Daniel Braxton."

"Sold?" Donnovan howled in disbelief. "Her own kin sold her into bondage?"

Horatio nodded grimly. "According to Jeffrey's report, Hannah's cousin was envious and resentful of her father's success. He must have decided to have his own fiendish revenge by reducing Hannah to the status of bondservant and paramour. As for Braxton, he had his own disgusting designs for his young servant. Fortunately for Hannah, the colony's call to arms prevented him from subjecting her to years of humiliation. But when Braxton returned from battle with a bottle of whiskey in his fist and lust on his mind, Hannah had to tolerate his drunken pursuits. 'Tis said she has taken her share of beatings during Daniel's drunken bouts. She has borne his marks several times since Daniel came marching home. Finally, when he tried to attack her on the floor of the bakery in broad daylight, she clubbed him with a rolling pin and fled."

Donnovan turned as peaked as a suntanned man could get. The thoughts of that lovely female being abused because she resisted her lecherous employer's advances sat on his stomach like an indigestible meal. Snarling, Donnovan shot toward the door with the speed of a discharging cannonball.

"Where are you going?" Horatio called after him.

"To Charles Town," Donnovan threw over his soggy shoulder. "You can inform Hannah that I've decided to keep her as Alicia's governess."

When the door slammed shut, Horatio and Fitz exchanged relieved glances.

"I didn't think the captain would send Hannah away or allow the injustice to go unpunished," Horatio murmured.

"I'll tell cook not to set a place for the captain at supper," Fitz said. "A pity we won't be on hand to watch Donnovan deliver Daniel Braxton's just deserts. No doubt, the drunken baker will wish he were eating raw dough rather than the Stone Dragon's doubled fist."

Three

Hannah chuckled as she playfully wrestled Alicia from her wet diaper. Giggling, Alicia wormed loose and scrambled off the bed situated in the far corner of the nursery. As had become the child's nightly ritual, she streaked naked across the room, expecting Hannah to give chase.

"Come back here!"

As usual, Alicia's reply was a squeal of delight. But a new element had been added to the nightly chase, Hannah soon found out. Alicia had learned to twist knobs and open doors. The child burst—buck naked—into Donnovan's bedchamber.

Aware that Donnovan had been absent all afternoon and evening, Hannah never gave a second thought to racing into the room to retrieve Alicia. Hannah came to a skidding halt when she realized Donnovan had not only returned from wherever he had been, but that he was lounging in the brass tub!

Hannah's captivated gaze settled on the hair-matted expanse of Donnovan's chest, and then drifted over the broad width of powerful shoulders and muscular arms. Hannah gulped air when the sight of raw masculine power sent jolts of awareness shooting through her.

Alicia, however, was oblivious of her uncle's predicament and her governess's stunned reaction. While Donnovan and Hannah stared at each other—Hannah's face aflame with color and Donnovan's expression betraying his amusement—Alicia scurried to the tub to splash her hands in the water.

"Is this, perchance, another facet of the unusual education

you're providing for my niece—or for yourself?" Donnovan inquired.

Hannah struggled to locate her tongue, fairly certain she had swallowed it. "I . . . d-didn't k-know y-you were h-home," she said, her voice reminiscent of a bleating lamb.

"A likely story, *Miss Roth.*"

Hannah's brows knitted at the unfamiliar tone in his voice. She could never be certain, but she sensed a hint of teasing humor. Indeed, there was something about Donnovan's demeanor that seemed less remote and standoffish than usual.

In helpless fascination Hannah's gaze roamed over Donnovan's well-sculpted physique . . . until she noticed the cuts on his right knuckle. "What happened? Have you been hurt?"

Donnovan lounged against the back of the tub while Alicia continued sloshing water on his chest—and the floor. "I got into a discussion this afternoon while I was in Charles Town," he said enigmatically. "It ended with a few blows."

"Someone attacked you?" she asked, alarmed.

"Not exactly."

"Well, what, then?" she demanded.

Donnovan shrugged those impossibly broad shoulders, and then reached for the bar of soap. "Perhaps you should whisk Alicia back to the nursery and put some clothes on her. I believe we both have had adequate lessons in human anatomy."

Hannah smiled mischievously when an inspiration struck her. 'Twas the perfect opportunity for her to strengthen the bond between Donnovan and his niece. Green eyes gleaming, Hannah sallied forth to scoop Alicia into her arms. Instead of wheeling toward the door, Hannah plunked Alicia on Donnovan's bare lap—and left her there.

"What the hell—" Donnovan slammed his mouth shut when the curse word that sprang from his lips landed on Alicia's tongue.

"Hell . . . hell . . . hell . . ." Giggle, splash.

Snickering at the stricken look on Donnovan's face, Hannah retrieved the bar of soap that had clattered to the floor. "After

you bathe your niece, Captain, perhaps you should take the time
to wash your mouth out with soap."

Feeling immensely pleased with herself, Hannah sauntered
from the room, leaving Donnovan to tend his playful niece. Seeing the pleasure Alicia took in bathing would surely erode the
stone barriers around Donnovan's heart, Hannah convinced herself. The man simply couldn't spend the next hour with Alicia
without being enchanted and amused by her lively spirit.

Donnovan stared down at the child who had been planted in
his lap. Tentatively, he glided his arm around Alicia's waist to
ensure she didn't fall facedown and swallow a tub full of bubbles
and water. He silently cursed the sensations trickling through
him as Alicia nestled against his chest, seemingly content in his
arms. He flinched when she tweaked the dark hair she found
there. When Alicia glanced up, wearing that devilishly innocent
little smile, Donnovan felt the first barrier of his defenses come
crashing down.

A blow as equally devastating as the one Donnovan had delivered to Daniel Braxton's jaw that afternoon thumped against
the inside of his chest. He had but to peer into Alicia's dark eyes
to see the striking resemblance to the brother he had lost at sea.

Alicia reminded him so much of Stephen that it nearly stole
Donnovan's breath. She also bore a strong likeness to Jessica,
Donnovan noted with a pang of sorrow. 'Twas in the way Alicia
smiled, the way her nose turned up at the end, the way her eyes
sparkled while she amused herself. Alicia was the stunning combination of her mother and father, and she was as spirited and
incorrigible as her new governess, who encouraged this child to
live every moment to its fullest.

"Hell . . . hell . . . hell!" Alicia jabbered as she splashed
water everywhere.

"That is quite enough of that, young lady," Donnovan said,
casting the child a stern glance.

With soap in hand, Donnovan bathed his niece, discovering

every ticklish patch of skin that made Alicia giggle and squirm. As hard as Donnovan tried to remain emotionally detached, he simply could not. Hannah's tactic of dropping Alicia in the tub and scurrying off forced Donnovan to hold his niece, forced him into close contact, forced him to realize how delightfully playful this little tyke could be.

Even as Donnovan dried Alicia and set her to her feet, he could feel another smile forming on his lips. When Alicia streaked across his bedroom to climb onto his bed, Donnovan's hearty chuckle rattled the empty shell of his chest, filling the vacuum with a warmth that had been drained from him an eternity ago. The affectionate bond he had tried to avoid had taken root, thanks to Hannah's shrewd tactics.

While Alicia jumped on his bed and flopped on his pillows, Donnovan pulled on his breeches. He ambled over to retrieve Alicia, but she scrambled off the opposite side of the bed and crawled into his wardrobe closet. Donnovan had one devil of a time getting her out. She tucked herself in the corner and then squirmed from his grasp before he could get a firm but painless grip on her.

"You have spent entirely too much time with that ornery governess of yours," Donnovan grumbled as he made another futile attempt to drag Alicia from the closet.

Finally, Donnovan rocked back on his bare heels, deciding to wait Alicia out. Within a few minutes Alicia tired of her game and poked her head from behind his boots. Donnovan quickly snatched her up. While Alicia kicked and bucked, he carried her to the nursery.

Hannah was nowhere to be found. Donnovan was not surprised. He did, however, find the clean diaper and nightgown that Hannah had laid out on the bed.

Wrestling Alicia into her clothes proved to be a major challenge. Dressing a squirming child took more patience and energy than he anticipated. He had nearly worked up a sweat by the time he had caught his escaping niece—twice—and restrained her while he fastened her into her diaper without drawing blood.

Donnovan didn't know how he was going to get Alicia to calm down and go to sleep. She was wound tighter than an eight-day clock. *Ordering* her to close her eyes and lie still was an exercise in futility. *Demanding* that she remain in her cradle didn't work either.

As a last resort, Donnovan toted the child back to his own room and lay down beside her on the bed. Since he didn't have Hannah's soothing voice, Donnovan simply lay there like a slug while Alicia crawled all over him.

Several minutes later Alicia, nestled against his shoulder, breathed a sigh and dropped off to sleep so fast that Donnovan was flabbergasted. How could such an energetic child become oblivious of the world so quickly? 'Twas an absolute marvel!

Gently scooping Alicia up, Donnovan retraced his steps to the nursery to tuck the child in her cradle. Then he set out to find the mischievous governess who had forced him to tend his niece. He expected to find Hannah in the garden—one of her favorite haunts—but she wasn't there.

The sound of hooves caught his attention. Curious, Donnovan followed the sound to see Hannah's shapely silhouette astraddle a steed, spotlighted by silvery moonbeams. When she reined toward the stables, Donnovan darted across the lawn like a soundless shadow to intercept her.

Hannah inhaled the refreshing fragrances of the night and smiled in contentment. The incident at the bathtub had been the situation needed to force Donnovan and Alicia together. Hannah had purposely made herself scarce so Donnovan would have to put Alicia to bed.

'Twas just what they both needed, Hannah assured herself. Even a man of stone could not be unaffected by Alicia's endearing bedtime rituals. Watching that little angel sleep would touch even the hardest of hearts.

With each passing day, Hannah promised herself, she would ensure that Alicia's contagious spirit rubbed off on Donnovan. The child would become such an integral part of his life that he couldn't help but accept her, love her.

"Are you proud of yourself, Miss Roth?"

Hannah was jerked back to reality when Donnovan's baritone voice broke the silence and he emerged from the shadows like a floating specter. He had certainly lived up to the legends of a mythical creature who appeared from nowhere to surprise and conquer his enemy.

"I thought you said you were willing to work the Sabbath and evenings," Donnovan reminded her. "Have you decided to become lax in your duties since I decided not to send you on your way today?"

Hannah stared down from atop the gray mare, her gaze focused on the wedge of bare flesh exposed by Donnovan's gaping shirt. Heightened arousal swirled through her when moonlight accentuated the trim fit of breeches that clung to the muscular columns of his thighs.

Odd, wasn't it, that she had spent her waking hours trying to avoid Daniel Braxton's hurtful touch, and now she secretly yearned for Donnovan's embrace. She wondered what it would be like to be held in those sinewy arms, to feel those sensuous lips slanting over hers.

When Donnovan had carried her from the river earlier that day, Hannah found herself wanting more than to be rescued. She had wanted . . .

"Dear Lord, Miss Roth, don't tell me I have rendered you speechless. I didn't realize the feat was possible. Ordinarily, you have a quick answer for everything."

Hannah mentally scrambled to rein in her wandering thoughts—ones scattered by the arresting sight of a man who'd come to mean a great deal to her. "I . . . um . . . forgot the question, Captain. . . ."

Her voice dried up when strong hands encircled her waist to pull her from the steed. Air rushed from Hannah's collapsing lungs as Donnovan slowly, provocatively, drew her down in front of him. Her breasts glided against his chest. Her hips brushed his thighs before he finally set her to her feet.

"I asked . . ." he prompted her, his lips only a hairbreadth from hers, "if you intended to become lax in your duties from here on out."

Hannah heard the husky whisper of his voice, as if it streamed through a long, winding tunnel. Desire hummed through every part of her being like a tuning fork. Her skin burned, branded in each place his hands touched. Her knees showed an alarming tendency to fold up like a tent as she stared into his shadowed face, mesmerized by those glowing amber eyes.

Hannah was struck by the unmistakable feeling that her *like* for the Stone Dragon had evolved into *love*. Why else would her longing gaze search him out each time he was within viewing distance? And why, she wondered shakily, would she be tormented by this insane urge to hurl herself into his arms and melt against him in wanton surrender? That had never happened before with any other man. It must surely be one of the outward symptoms that love had indeed taken hold of her heart and whispered through her soul.

"Oh, the hell with it. I'm tired of fighting. . . ."

Hannah had not the time or inclination to ask Donnovan what he meant by that remark. Her brain broke down the instant his mouth took masterful possession of hers. Hannah never even considered withdrawing as she instinctively did when Daniel Braxton tried to manhandle her. She simply responded to the extraordinary pleasure of being molded against Donnovan's powerful body.

Perhaps Donnovan hadn't meant for Hannah to feel so wanted and desired, but she did. 'Twas in the tender way he held her, the way he savored the taste of her while she absorbed the heady pleasure of love's magical kiss.

When his hands glided up the small of her back and then drifted along her rib cage, Hannah was instantly reminded of sparkling rainbows and blinding sunshine, of dreams coming true. Perhaps what she was experiencing and enjoying couldn't last forever, and perhaps the hunger in Donnovan's kiss was no more than the momentary appeasement of his male appetite, but Hannah knew this was the moment she would cherish forever. She was most definitely in love, and she was relishing every delicious second of it!

Without a moment's hesitation she pushed up on tiptoe and kissed him back, using the seductive techniques she had learned from him. She was rewarded by Donnovan's muffled groan, the quick contraction of his encompassing arms. He pressed his intensely masculine body into intimate contact with hers.

Whatever she had done must have been right, Hannah decided. Donnovan seemed to be enjoying their moonlight tryst as much as she was. If she'd had her way, this moment would have lasted forever. Loving him, touching him, brought a wondrous sense of elation. Hannah wanted to capture the sensations and hoard them like priceless treasures.

When his thumbs teased the throbbing peaks of her breasts, fire simmered in her blood, holding her utterly spellbound, making her ache for more of the delightful sensations. When his hands coasted down her hips to press her against the hard evidence of his arousal, Hannah feared she would swoon for the first time in her life.

Then his warm lips skimmed down her throat to hover over the fabric covering her nipples. His intimate touch turned her bones to mush and her flesh to steam. A gasp wobbled in her chest when his caressing fingertips skimmed her breasts, teasing her until she shivered uncontrollably.

"Dear God . . ." Hannah whispered as the world spun in dizzying circles. "Dear . . . God!"

Donnovan was vaguely aware of the sound of approaching footsteps, but his sensitized body was slow to react to the warning sent down by his brain. Somewhere between first kiss and most recent caress he had lost all remnants of the good sense he'd spent thirty years cultivating. He had succumbed to the temptation of tasting Hannah's dewy-soft lips and he'd become obsessed with her in the space of a heartbeat.

Fortunately for Donnovan, he had honed that sixth sense that alerted him to sounds that often indicated impending danger. The same sense of survival that had spared him from death saved him from embarrassment now. Before the groom wandered from the barn to check on Hannah—and found them clinging so tightly together that neither of them could breathe normally—Donnovan stepped back into his own space. His legs weren't as sturdy as he remembered. 'Twas not helping matters one whit that Hannah had become as limp in his shaking arms as Alicia had been when Donnovan placed her in her cradle.

Donnovan managed to put a respectable distance between himself and Hannah before the groom stepped outside. Hannah, Donnovan noted with wry amusement, had propped herself against the mare for support. Donnovan realized he was clinging to the top rail of the corral, suffering from the same lack of stability.

"I'll put the mare away for you—" The groom halted abruptly when he noticed Donnovan's shadowed silhouette. "Pardon, sir. I didn't realize you were out here."

"I'll see to the horse," Donnovan managed to say.

The groom shifted awkwardly. "I . . . a . . . didn't think you'd mind if the lass took one of your horses for a short ride. I—"

" 'Tis quite all right, Bently," Donnovan interrupted the stammering groom. "I'm sure Miss Roth wouldn't be reckless enough to place my livestock in unnecessary danger."

The groom nodded and then made a hasty retreat. Donnovan inhaled several cathartic breaths to collect himself. When he was capable of walking without tripping he strode over to grab the trailing reins.

Hannah, curse her, was still staring up at him in a way that tempted him to swallow her up in his arms and finish what had begun when his firm resolutions scattered to the four winds.

Even now Donnovan wasn't certain what had come over him.

He had simply cast all caution aside and yielded to the temptation he'd been fighting for two weeks. Once he had yielded, his unrestrained hunger had caused a momentary lapse of sanity. If Bently hadn't arrived upon the scene, 'twas no telling what might have happened.

For a man who almost never reacted emotionally, Donnovan had done quite a lot of it where Hannah was concerned. He was more vulnerable to her ample charms than he'd thought!

"It's late, Miss Roth," he said, striving for an impersonal tone to diffuse the tension in what had become an all-too-personal encounter in the moonlight. "Perhaps you should go upstairs to bed."

She looked up at him with those luminous green eyes that were the windows to her soul. Donnovan quickly rallied behind his self-restraint—or, rather, what was left of it, which wasn't much!

"I'm not at all sure I'll be able to sleep," she said in all honesty.

Donnovan doubted he could either. His body was aching in the most sensitive of places. He would not be able to sleep on his stomach for hours, and he expected to be visited by the most erotic fantasies imaginable.

The sad truth of the matter was that he hadn't *satisfied* the craving for this feisty, outspoken female, he had *intensified* it beyond measure!

Somehow Donnovan managed to lead the mare into the stable without doubling over and howling in pain. 'Twas a near-miss. Tantalizing memories hounded his every step. The moment he'd surrendered to forbidden temptation he'd leapt over the walls he'd erected between himself and Hannah.

He had felt her uninhibited responses as if they were his own. 'Twas as if those wondrous pleasures were the first of their kind. Damn, one would think it *was* the first time he'd kissed and caressed a woman!

Discovering what a tormented life Hannah had endured and confronting the despicable bastard who had bought her for his own lusty purposes had infuriated him to the extreme. *Bought her!* The very thought still consumed him with outrage. He'd taken one look at the drunken lecher in the bakery and his doubled fists had gone flying. Donnovan had knocked the baker flat on his back, sending the whiskey bottle he clutched in his hand rolling across the floor. Donnovan hadn't even realized what he'd done until the lopsided battle ended.

While Daniel Braxton lay there with his bloodshot eyes rolling around in his head, Donnovan had flung a handful of coins on the man's heaving chest, announcing that the debt of Hannah's indentureship had been paid in full, even if she had paid tenfold by mere association with the disgusting excuse for a man.

But 'twas not pity that provoked Donnovan to ignore the hard and fast rules he had established about Hannah, he reminded himself as he shut the mare in the stall. Pity didn't sear a man's body in flaming oblivion and leave him with the obsessive craving for the taste of the woman in his arms. Pity did not satisfactorily explain the intensity of need that burgeoned in the empty vacuum of his chest and filled it to overflowing.

Hannah Roth—*Rothchild,* Donnovan corrected himself—had gotten under his saddle like a cocklebur. She had become as addictive as the whiskey Braxton consumed. Now, how the sweet loving hell was he going to keep *his* hands to himself when he discovered the foretaste of pleasures he knew awaited him? Hannah was entirely too responsive to his touch. When she went up in flames she took him with her. Each unforgettable shiver that swept through her body had echoed through his . . . and lingered long after.

God, 'twas as if he had lived and breathed *through* her, *because* of her, for that spellbinding space out of time!

Hannah had no right to create such a devastating effect on a man who had vowed not to become emotionally involved with a woman, least of all his niece's governess. Donnovan didn't want to become so possessive and driven by emotion that he followed in his father's footsteps. If Donnovan let himself care for someone as vivacious and enchanting as Hannah, if he al-

lowed her into his heart and then lost her, he would be setting
himself up for heartache.

And, dammit, Donnovan was tired of losing those he cared
about. Each tragic loss had tormented him unbearably, making
him draw deeper into himself to protect what was left of his
shriveled soul. He simply could not risk the hurt, not again!

Donnovan had to fortify his defenses. The erotic encounter
beside the barn wouldn't happen again. Distance was the only
solution. If he had learned nothing else from the incident, he
discovered he was more susceptible and vulnerable than he'd
previously believed. Any situation that placed them in close contact was an engraved invitation for trouble. And he had better
not let himself forget that!

Hannah flung back the quilts and threw her legs over the side
of the bed when she heard a thump and wail in the nursery. It
didn't take her long to reach the cradle where Alicia flounced
about, tangled in her blanket.

Moonlight gleamed through the window, granting Hannah a
clear view of Alicia's miniature features. The child was gearing
herself up for a full-fledged squawk, probably because she had
knocked herself on the headboard.

'Twas time to train Ali to sleep in a regular bed rather than
being wedged in the cramped cradle. According to Horatio,
Stephen Maxwell had begun work on a new bed to accommodate
his growing daughter, but the bed remained as Stephen left it
when he and his wife set sail to the West Indies.

Something would have to be done soon, Hannah decided as
she scooped Ali up, hoping to prevent the child's wailing from
awakening the entire household. Soothingly, Hannah cuddled
Ali, singing a lullaby that she remembered from childhood.
'Twas the one her mother had sung to her so many years earlier.
Hannah summoned up the cloudy vision of her mother, hearing
the whisper of a song that had chased away her own nighttime
fears.

A smile tugged at Hannah's lips as she sang the enchanting melody. She felt Alicia relax. The child dropped her head against Hannah's shoulder and drifted into peaceful dreams.

Hannah placed Alicia in the cradle, then retrieved a blanket to tuck against the wooden headboard. She would have to insist that Donnovan finish the larger bed, and soon.

Hannah's gaze drifted to the door between the nursery and Donnovan's room. She found her footsteps taking her toward his bedchamber. Even though Donnovan had made no mention of the night she'd melted beneath his sensuous kisses, Hannah had thought of little else the past week.

'Twas difficult to be in love with a man and not know what to do about it. Should she come right out and tell him? Keeping her feelings to herself seemed dishonest, unnatural.

Hannah halted when she realized she had entered Donnovan's room. Once she was there, she couldn't force herself to retreat. Watching Donnovan from afar had become a whimsical preoccupation. She was inviting heartache and disappointment, she knew, but watching him sleep was as close as she could get to him these days without him finding an excuse to make himself scarce.

At least Donnovan had begun to let his guard down ever so slightly with Alicia. That endeared Hannah to him all the more. Donnovan wouldn't soften up overnight, of course. But he had shown more interest in the child—a fleeting touch now and then, a brief smile. In time Hannah hoped Donnovan would open up completely and let the child into his heart.

A tremulous sigh escaped Hannah's lips as she studied the shadowy outline of Donnovan's body beneath the quilt. She inched closer, longing to see his face in quiet repose, without that façade of calm indifference.

She stared down at him, smiling wryly. Would that she could press a kiss to his lips like some fairy princess, transforming him into her Prince Charming. Would that she could utter the heartfelt confession aching to be voiced. Perhaps she could say the words while he was asleep, then he wouldn't object or mistrust her intentions.

Adoringly, Hannah bent to brush the lightest breath of a kiss to his brow . . . and found herself tossed off balance.

She landed flat on her back in his bed—with Donnovan lying naked beside her!

"Never, ever sneak up on a veteran guerrilla fighter," Donnovan warned in a hushed voice.

"Sorry, Captain," she whispered.

"What the hell are you doing in here?"

Her head turned fractionally, staring at him with those lustrous green eyes. "I . . ."

She peered at him, unable to formulate a thought to save her life. Donnovan propped up on an elbow to study the very same face that haunted his dreams. How many times had he envisioned having Hannah right where she was? More than he cared to count. Now that she was there, he wondered if he could muster the willpower to let her go.

"What do you want, Hannah?" he asked, and then sorely wished he hadn't. Moonlight glimmered in her eyes and glowed on her pixielike features. The way she was gazing at him would have brought him to his knees had he been standing. The words she whispered the next moment were heaven and hell in one.

"I wanted you to know I love you. I can't help it, I just do. . . ."

When her hand lifted to trace the curve of his lips, Donnovan felt his resistance tumble like a landslide. He couldn't have sent her away if he tried—and he wasn't trying at all. The open honesty of her loving expression, the sincerity in her voice, went all through him, as had the soft lullaby she'd sung to Alicia. He'd heard every stirring note of her song and knew the instant she had entered his room.

He could have pretended sleep when she bent over him, but he hadn't wanted her to vanish into the night like so many of his dreams. God forgive him, but he had wanted her in his arms, in his bed.

A hungry groan rumbled in his chest when her sweet mouth feathered over his. Donnovan promised himself there and then that he would be as gentle with her as he knew how. She knew nothing of a man's tenderness, only abuse and impatience. For all the times Daniel Braxton had forced himself on her, Donnovan vowed to teach Hannah the difference between animal lust and skillful passion.

Not that he considered himself an expert on the subject, but he intended to treat them both to a new dimension of passion—with a slow, unhurried encounter that prolonged and intensified their desire until they were consumed by it.

To that dedicated end, Donnovan tunneled his fingers through the tangle of red-gold hair that curled around her face and drifted over his pillow like a wispy cloud. When he caressed her, he felt her body melt beneath his roaming fingertips. He marveled at her trembling response, the way she moved restlessly beneath his wandering hands.

Her quiet moans brought him immense satisfaction. He longed to hear his name on her lips, yearned to discover each place she liked to be touched. He ached to sensitize her feminine body with every pleasurable sensation imaginable.

With gentle care Donnovan eased her from her gown. He caught his breath at the essence of feminine perfection. Hannah was lovelier than he'd even imagined.

To think that lecherous bastard she'd worked for had abused her when he should have cherished her! For once she would know what it was like to be worshiped, Donnovan vowed as he kissed the hollow of her throat and felt her pulse drumming like thunder. He would pleasure her until she welcomed him into the depths of her silken body, and together they would burn down the night.

Just once, Donnovan promised himself, he was going to open his carefully guarded heart and unleash the emotion trapped there. For one night he was going to turn his forbidden dream into reality.

Donnovan dipped his head downward, his tongue flicking at the beaded crests that demanded his rapt attention. He took each pink bud into his mouth, sucking with the greatest of care, feeling her quiver in response. Exploring her delicious textures riddled his body with bulletlike sensations, urging him to take what he craved, but Donnovan was determined to make a slow, thorough study of Hannah.

His hand coasted down her ribs to swirl over the flat plane of her belly. She quivered in anticipation and his body clenched in helpless response. With a nudge of his elbow he eased open her thighs and felt the warm rain of her desire bathing his fingertips.

Fascinated, Donnovan traced her, aroused her by delicate degrees. When she all but came apart in his arms, whispering his name like a lullaby, Donnovan felt another hard throb of need pelting him. His penetrating fingertips glided and stroked her, drawing her wild, shimmering response. He felt her secret caresses sweeping over him like a storm across the sea. Her body was calling out to his, entrancing him, luring him ever closer.

Donnovan eased between her legs, vowing to be patient and gentle, wondering if that was possible when he was so hungry to feel her molten body burning around him.

Ardent desire strained like a spirited steed against its reins. Donnovan lifted her hips and thrust against her softest flesh. His body surged out of control as he sheathed himself completely . . . and penetrated a secret barrier he hadn't expected to encounter.

He froze, noting the tense lines that bracketed her kiss-swollen lips. Donnovan had presumed Daniel Braxton had had his way with Hannah on a number of occasions. He'd never dreamed she'd escaped unscathed, but the proof of her virginity clung to him, was stated in the discomforted expression on her face.

It may have been Donnovan's first time with a virgin, but he definitely knew the difference. Some things spoke for themselves. Donnovan didn't know if he was relieved or annoyed by the intimate knowledge, didn't know if he wanted to smile in satisfaction or curse in frustration. For sure and certain, a man couldn't retreat across a bridge that collapsed behind him. 'Twas *not* the new dimensions of passion he intended to explore when he surrendered to his forbidden fantasies.

"I'm sorry," she murmured, her fingers clenched in his forearms, battling the pain he had unknowingly forced on her. "I lack your expertise, Captain."

" 'Tis not the appropriate time to call me Captain," Donnovan said, giving way to a smile. "We're far too familiar with each other for that, don't you think?"

Hannah smiled in return, and he felt her stiffened body relax beneath him. "I'm sure there are others who could have pleased you more," she said, "but I'm trying very hard to—"

His index finger brushed her lips, shushing her. "You please me very well, but 'twould have been less painful for you had I known the truth." He regarded her for a long, pensive moment. *"Why,* Hannah?"

The look she gave him knocked his heart against his ribs and made it stick there. "Because I love you."

Crosscurrents of sensations warred inside him when she repeated the confession. "What do you expect in return for the gift that can never be given again?" He waited, gauging her expression, searching for hidden truths.

She smiled that dimpled smile again. Her hands glided up to frame his face, smoothing away his wary frown. "All I want," she said as she stirred sensuously beneath him, "is to find a cure for the fever that was burning like wildfire . . . until you stopped to question my motives."

His thick brow arched inquiringly. "No other demands or requests, Hannah?"

She nodded her head. 'Twas just as he thought. A trap—and he had stumbled headlong into it.

"Aye, now that you mention it, I do have one demand."

He came face-to-face with the consequences of his unruly desires for the woman who had bewitched him. "What might that be?" As if he didn't know.

If she thought she heard wedding bells, she was hallucinating. Donnovan Maxwell had played this game before, with women far more worldly and experienced than this innocent leprechaun. No one had ever been able to force Donnovan to do what he had no inclination to do. 'Twas his first rule of thumb.

Her gentle caresses trailed over the tendons of his back in a feather-light caress "I demand to know if this is all there is. If it is, I'm mightily disappointed. I had imagined—"

Donnovan did something he hadn't done since he couldn't remember when—he laughed out loud. "Then by all means let's cultivate your all-too-fertile imagination."

His lips slanted across hers, his tongue gliding inside her mouth the same instant his body took exquisite possession. He moved above her, teaching her the rhythmic cadence of passion, creating wondrous sensations that converged and then splintered like white-hot sparks.

He felt her fingers flex, digging into the muscles of his back, assuring him that they were both caught up in the same whirling vortex. Her heart pounded against his chest like hailstones, matching his frantic pulse. Her supple body moved perfectly with his, as if she were made for him, as if she were his vital other half.

Donnovan's thoughts spiraled away when Hannah shivered beneath him. He felt her letting go of her tight grasp on him, engulfed in the rapture of release. The cry she muffled against his chest followed her over the edge into splendor, taking him with her on the most intimate fall imaginable. Pulsation after helpless pulsation thrummed through Donnovan. He hadn't intended to surrender completely, but he was tumbling through space. He was overcome by such phenomenal pleasure that he couldn't remember what it felt like to be in control of his mind, body, and emotions—or why that had seemed so crucial.

Sometime later—'twas impossible for him to determine how

long, when he lost all sense of time and place—Donnovan summoned the strength to raise his ruffled head. And there it was again, that impish smile that constantly tugged at his heart, even when he tried to remain immune.

" 'Twas *I* who received a special gift," she murmured in a passion-drugged voice. " 'Twas worth fending off—"

He knew what she refused to say. Although Hannah had suffered heartaches, she looked on the bright side, never letting torment or disillusion get her down. She was an inspiration to his troubled soul. She made him look deeper than responsibility and dutiful existence. She made him want to believe in magic.

"Captain?"

"I thought I made it clear 'twas not the time for formality."

"Aye, but that was *during,* this is *after,*" she pointed out. "What I was going to say was that I expect nothing from you, though I'm sure you're leery of my ulterior purpose. But I was wondering if—"

Donnovan waited. Suspicions swarmed and cynical speculation warned him where this conversation was going to lead.

"Would you mind very much if—" She hesitated self-consciously and then tried again. "That is, if—"

"Quit beating around bushes and spit it out the way you usually do," he requested.

Hannah inhaled a deep breath and blurted out, "Do you think we could do that again without an interruption in the middle?"

Donnovan jerked up his head and gaped at her. Of all the things he expected her to say, that wasn't even on the list! *"Now?"* he croaked in astonishment.

"Is it taboo to ask to do it twice in the same night?" she asked in such a somber, curious tone that he laughed out loud—again.

"You, Hannah, are absolutely outrageous."

"Another of my failing graces."

"Besides being straightforward and outspoken."

"Aye." Her open sincerity never failed to undermine his defense. "But the thing is, I didn't have the chance to touch you when you made me forget everything except the pleasure of your touch."

"You would like to touch me?" he questioned, his voice hitting a husky pitch, his mind leaping in anticipation.

"Aye, very much. Would you mind?"

When she set her hands upon him, exploring him with a sense of wonder and the gentlest of care, Donnovan felt reality slipping from its moorings, sending him sailing on a sea that was domed with rainbows, and he didn't care if he ever navigated his way home.

In the past he'd eased his basic needs with a woman and then went on his way. Never had he permitted a woman the kind of intimate privileges he'd granted Hannah. But her adventurous caresses made him want things he'd never wanted before, made him cast aside every rule he applied. She made him feel wild, reckless, and uninhibited. Yet, when he came to her, shaking with fervent need, he vowed to treat her with a delicate care that superseded his own hungry impatience.

In her loving arms Donnovan found the contentment and peace that had escaped him so long ago. But with those extraordinary feelings of pleasure came that secret fear that caring too much would become his tormenting curse. Donnovan forced himself to tread softly with his heart, not to hope for too much, not to feel too strongly.

And then Hannah whispered her love for him like a hypnotic lullaby, making him forget everything he ever knew.

Four

During the days that followed, Hannah detected improvement in Donnovan's standoffish attitude. He was less restrained than before, more attentive toward her and Alicia.

Hannah liked to think that her willingness to be open and honest about her affection for Donnovan had changed his life. She wanted more than anything to see Donnovan let go of his troubled past and haunting memories so he could enjoy life rather than view it as a succession of duties and obligations.

Even Fitz and Horatio made mention of Donnovan's transformation. His smiles came readily, and occasional laughter graced the halls of Maxwell Plantation.

Hannah did everything possible to call attention to Alicia and her amusing antics, hoping, praying, that Donnovan would take that final step and emerge from behind his shell of self-restraint, becoming the substitute father Alicia needed. Hannah wondered if Donnovan's respect for his brother's memory was partially responsible for his reluctance to replace Stephen in Alicia's eyes. But the child was too young to understand anything except her need for love and acceptance.

Hannah deliberately pointed out each new sound Alicia made, each object she correctly identified. Fitz, Horatio, and the two men who served as cook and valet were lured beneath Alicia's enchanting spell. For sure, the child had acquired by her own charming techniques four honorary uncles. 'Twas only the father figure who remained just beyond the little girl's reach.

Donnovan was on the verge of completely letting go, Hannah

confidently encouraged herself. She had caught him breaking
into a smile the previous day, when Alicia had performed her
version of a somersault on the carpet in his office. His twinkling
golden eyes had darted from Alicia to Hannah, and she had
melted beneath the warmth she had seen burning there.

Ah, Donnovan, she had thought whimsically, *if only you
would let down your guard and love the both of us. 'Twould be
like capturing a glorious rainbow in my hand.*

The day she heard Donnovan chuckling at his rambunctious
niece while Alicia hung upside down on the porch railing like
a monkey assured Hannah that she was making headway. The
Stone Dragon was beginning to erode. Donnovan was gradually
adjusting to civilian life, burying the ghosts from his past. He
had also begun to treat Hannah as if she were an integral part
of the family, not a nuisance.

Hannah had made preparation to celebrate Alicia's first birthday with a grand flair, intent on marking another milestone in
Donnovan's life. She had suggested they attend the county fair
that was being held at the rural church two miles away. But the
pleasant outing was very nearly ruined by the unexpected intrusion of one of Donnovan's neighbors.

The tall, handsome blond man had followed Hannah around
for the better part of two hours. Everywhere she turned, Garrett
Grantham was a step away, flirting outrageously. He had leaned
unnecessarily close to tickle the underside of Alicia's chin while
she was clamped to Hannah's hip. Garrett's hand had brushed
the swell of Hannah's breasts, causing her to sidle away.

Garrett's rakish grin was the kind of overt warning Hannah
had learned to recognize while dodging the unwanted advances
of zealous men—Daniel Braxton in particular. She knew the
look on Garrett's face all too well. Problem was, Hannah wasn't
granted the privacy needed to tell Garrett where he could go and
what he could do with himself when he got there. The milling
crowd worked to Garrett's advantage, not Hannah's. She was but
a governess, a newcomer to the community, just as she had been

an indentured servant in Daniel's bakery, trapped by circumstances beyond her control.

The second time Garrett stepped uncomfortably close, he draped his arm familiarly around Hannah's waist. Hannah tensed in annoyance. When Garrett leaned down, his breath stirred against Hannah's neck, and the words he whispered were *not* meant for Alicia.

"Why don't you find another set of arms to hold the baby," he suggested in what Hannah presumed to be his most seductive voice. It fell short of the mark. Hannah preferred Donnovan's husky whisper to Garrett's lusty growl. "You and I can wander off to the woods. I know just the place where I could sample your sweet delights, luv."

Hannah retreated apace. Though her eyes flashed, she took care not to project her voice farther than Garrett's ears. "I am Alicia's governess, no more, no less. Take your disgusting proposition where it might be welcome, though I cannot imagine any woman eagerly participating in a tumble in the grass with you."

Garrett's smile vanished, replaced by the spiteful curl of lips. "Don't take that haughty tone with me, wench. I'm sure Maxwell has taken his pleasure with you. Women from your station in life are always looking to trap a wealthy planter and improve themselves, but you'll never be more than his convenient whore."

"Grantham, as usual you have allowed your tongue to outdistance that chunk of wood you call a brain."

Hannah winced when Donnovan's low, ominous voice came out of nowhere. He stepped up behind Garrett, a stony expression carved in his craggy features. Obviously, Garrett wasn't familiar with the warning signs Hannah had come to recognize at a glance. Although Donnovan appeared to be in perfect control, she could feel the formidable aura radiating from him. She attempted to diffuse the situation before Garrett succeeded in causing the kind of scene she'd tried to avoid. He wasn't the type who looked before he leapt, and he was every kind of fool if he thought he was Donnovan's match.

As bad luck would have it, Garrett opened his big mouth before Hannah could smooth over the situation.

"Come now, Maxwell, I wanted only what you're undoubtedly enjoying. 'Tis not as if you have honorable intentions toward a wench of her lowly status. If she's whoring for you, why not for me?"

Hannah could not believe the speed with which Donnovan struck. The force of his doubled fist sent Garrett spinning like a top. Clutching Alicia closer, Hannah retreated another step, still watching Donnovan with fascinated amazement.

Although cudgeling bouts were being held at the opposite end of the fairgrounds, spectators flocked toward the aisle between the craft booths when Garrett spouted a curse that offended everybody's ears.

"You asked for this, Maxwell," Garrett snarled as he wiped his bloody lip. "Remember that while you're scraping yourself off the dirt and counting the stars revolving around your head."

Hannah rather thought Garrett had overstated his abilities, considering he had squared off against the Stone Dragon. When Garrett ducked his head to ram into Donnovan, he found himself charging air. Donnovan had agilely sidestepped at the last possible second, leaving Garrett stumbling to regain his balance and looking like the clumsy clown he was.

Outraged, Garrett wheeled, swinging wildly. Hannah saw the misdirected fist coming and turned away to protect Alicia. Garrett's blow collided with Hannah's shoulder and she stumbled backward. When Donnovan darted forward to steady her, Garrett took unfair advantage. His blow caught Donnovan in the chin. All hell broke loose when the dragon roared. . . .

Although Hannah tried to comfort Alicia, the child burst into frightened tears. Patting Alicia, Hannah fixed her astounded gaze on Donnovan's impressive display of combative skills. Garrett had rattled the Stone Dragon's cage—and was in the process of paying for his mistake.

Donnovan's arm shot out like lightning bolts, leveling two quick punches to Garrett's jaw. The third blow—to Garrett's soft underbelly—doubled him over and claimed his breath. While Garrett sucked air, Alicia wailed at the top of her lungs. Donnovan delivered a hatchet chop to Garrett's neck, causing him to pitch forward. His chin skidded across the grass and his tongue fell out of his sagging mouth.

"And that is all I have to say on that subject," Donnovan told his downed foe. "While you're lying there, you can apologize for insulting the lady."

Garrett dragged himself up on hands and knees and raised his ruffled blond head to glower at Donnovan. Resentfully, he shot Hannah a quick glance. "I'm sorry," he wheezed.

"If you ever go near Miss Roth again," Donnovan continued in a quiet snarl, "you *won't* live to regret it. Do you understand me, Grantham?"

Flaming amber eyes burned down on Garrett, forcing him to admit that 'twas no idle threat, but a deadly promise. He nodded his downcast head.

"Now, get out of my sight before I decide not to be so generous as to give you a second chance. Perhaps you should try living up to the respectability your father exemplified. It should be a new experience for you."

By the time Alicia's wails had reduced themselves to shuddering sobs, Garrett had staggered to his feet and skulked off to nurse his wounds and his battered pride.

Still clutched in Hannah's protective arms, Alicia leaned out, her tear-filled eyes transfixed on Donnovan.

"Pa-pa . . ."

When Alicia raised her beseeching gaze to her uncle, the whole world came to a screeching halt. 'Twas obvious the alarmed child wanted very much to be held in Donnovan's arms. Hannah waited with the rest of the world, hoping beyond hope that Donnovan didn't disappoint the sobbing child who had accepted him as a worthy replacement for the father she had lost.

When Alicia overextended herself in an effort to reach Donnovan, she doubled over in the middle and hung there with her head dangling. Hannah saw the emotions swirling across Donnovan's rugged features. The last vestige of self-restraint crumbled. When Donnovan scooped Alicia up in his arms and cuddled her close, tears sprang to Hannah's eyes and her heart flipped in her chest.

" 'Tis all right, sweetheart," Donnovan murmured as he brushed his lips over Alicia's brow.

Alicia fastened her arms around Donnovan's neck and squeezed the stuffing out of him. Hannah swallowed the lump in her throat and assured herself that her tireless efforts to strengthen this much-needed bond had finally paid off. Donnovan had taken that final step and opened his heart, offering Alicia the affection she so desperately needed from him.

Fitz and Horatio were beaming like twin lighthouses as they watched. When both men nodded gratefully to Hannah, she was filled with a sense of accomplishment. She had achieved her mission. Alicia would not grow up as Hannah had. Donnovan's affection for his niece was obvious in the way he held her protectively to him, the way he murmured comforting words in her ear and smiled reassuringly at her.

"Shall we have a look at the toys in the booth, Ali?" Donnovan directed her attention to the row of dolls that lined a nearby counter. "What special gift would you like for your first birthday?"

When Donnovan strode off, Alicia's legs clamped around his waist, Hannah sighed in relief. Alicia had been granted the most precious gift a child could receive.

"Thank you," Horatio murmured to Hannah. "I knew you were just what the captain needed."

"With a little coaxing and nudging from you, the captain has put his past behind him and embraced life again," Fitz added with a pleased smile.

Hannah grinned as she watched Alicia snatch up not one but two china dolls and hug them to her chest. She jabbered nonstop as she tucked the dolls in the crook of Donnovan's elbow and then reached out to pluck up the wooden wagon that would transport the mud pies she was overly fond of making.

Shaking his head in wry amusement, Donnovan glanced back at Hannah, silently indicating he still held her responsible for Alicia's hoyden tendencies.

While Donnovan was maneuvering his niece and her gifts into one arm to retrieve money to purchase the toys, Hannah turned away. "Horatio, kindly inform the captain that I'm riding home to prepare the cookies and special treats I'm serving for Alicia's birthday party."

"Those melt-in-your-mouth strawberry tarts?" Horatio asked hopefully.

"Aye, in addition to the blueberry tarts for Fitz," she assured him.

"Ah, Hannah." Fitz sighed in anticipated pleasure. "You do know the way to my heart, don't you?"

She also knew where Donnovan's heart was, Hannah told herself as she ambled toward the picket line of horses tethered beside the fairgrounds. Although Donnovan had faith in his ability to provide and protect, he'd had no faith in his ability to love and be loved. Alicia taught him differently. She made it obvious that she cherished every scrap of his affection.

Perhaps one day Donnovan would even come to love Hannah the way she loved him. . . .

Hannah smothered the frivolous thought. 'Twas not the day for selfish wishes. Today was Alicia's special day, and Hannah intended to celebrate in grand style. She had pastries to bake before the men returned home.

In high spirits Hannah surged through the front door of the empty house. Since Donnovan had generously invited his employees to the county fair, Hannah had the place all to herself. Grabbing an apron, she set to work in the kitchen, humming a lighthearted tune while she performed the skills she had perfected in the bakery.

The unpleasant memories of her dealings with Garrett Grantham seemed to belong to another lifetime. She had taken her place here at Maxwell Plantation, caring for a child she adored, sharing the life of the man she loved with all her heart. If only Donnovan would . . .

Garrett Grantham's cruel words returned, causing her hand to stall in midair as she reached for the canister of flour. Garrett had claimed that a man of Donnovan's social prominence would never consider Hannah more than a convenient outlet for his sexual urges. She firmly reminded herself that she had wished for no more than the chance to love him, to be near him. 'Twas not his money or prestige that lured her to him, 'twas the man himself. She'd made no demands on him and refused to let him consider her one of his responsibilities. Besides, there was another reason she couldn't marry Donnovan even if he did ask. 'Twas the most important reason of all, and it had nothing whatsoever to do with the stigma that a cruel twist of fate had placed on her.

"Did you really think you could escape me, wench?"

The cold voice made Hannah freeze like a block of ice. She turned away from the table to see her worst nightmare glaring at her. Daniel Braxton's plain features twisted in a venomous scowl. His stubbled beard gave him a scraggly, ominous appearance, but 'twas nothing new for Daniel. He looked what he was—a worthless, slovenly excuse for a man.

His bloodshot eyes indicated he was suffering from the usual hangover, one that put him in the worst of all possible moods. He was just as she remembered him the day she escaped his lecherous pawing by cracking him over the head with a rolling pin.

The only difference was that now he held a pistol in his clenched fist instead of a whiskey bottle.

"I've been waiting to get you alone," he sneered. "You owe me a debt that's never been paid. You and that bastard employer of yours are going to pay dearly for what you've done to me."

Hannah frowned, baffled by the resentful comment. "Captain Maxwell has done nothing to deserve your wrath, and I had every right to protect myself from you. I kept your business afloat and tripled the profits while you were away. My thanks was your constant abuse. Despite what you prefer to think, I have already paid all too dearly while I was your bondservant."

"You sent that fire-breathing dragon to do what you couldn't do yourself," he accused her in a vicious tone.

Hannah blinked. "What are you ranting about? I never sent Captain Maxwell anywhere near you."

Daniel scoffed at her denial. "Didn't you? You set him on me and I damn well know it. He certainly knew where to find me and who I was when he served up several tastes of his meaty fists. I'm here to punish *you* for the trouble you've caused and to make *him* pay for it."

Hannah didn't have a clue how Donnovan had known where to find Braxton. She'd never mentioned Daniel or revealed much information about her past. And for good reason—the reason presently holding her at gunpoint.

When Daniel motioned her toward the kitchen door, Hannah had no choice but to go peacefully. She couldn't risk having Donnovan return with Alicia and become the target of Daniel's vengeful retaliation. 'Twas no telling what Daniel had in mind for him. If something happened to Donnovan, Hannah could never forgive herself. Alicia had just begun to bask in her uncle's affection. The poor child didn't deserve to lose the last of her family, and Hannah couldn't imagine a world without Donnovan in it somewhere.

When Daniel fished a crumpled note from his pocket and tossed it on the table, Hannah regarded him warily.

"A ransom note," he muttered in answer to the unspoken question. "That devil cost me my business. If he wants you back, then he can pay an expensive price."

Hannah winced when the pistol threatened to pry her ribs apart. Daniel's bulky arm snaked around her neck to ensure she didn't escape, as she had a month earlier. Hannah was half dragged, half carried past the garden to the river. She had the unshakable feeling she wasn't going to live long enough to determine if Donnovan planned to pay the ransom. Daniel would deal severely with her for the trouble he thought she'd heaped on him.

Her only recourse was to catch him off guard and flee. Hopefully, she could circle back to the fairgrounds to warn Donnovan.

The instant Daniel ducked beneath a low-hanging limb, Hannah hurled herself away, defying the loaded pistol. She had taken one step toward freedom when the pistol swerved toward her with deadly intent. Hannah dived toward the underbrush and rolled away as the pistol discharged. Searing pain shot through her chest and shoulder. She ignored it in her frantic effort to scramble to safety.

"I'll kill you, I swear I will!" Daniel snarled as he bounded after her, determined to do his worst.

Hannah swallowed down her pounding heart and leapt to her feet. Cradling her stinging arm to prevent leaving a trail of blood for Daniel to follow, Hannah ran for her life.

Donnovan sat atop his bay gelding while Alicia lay, fast asleep, sprawled on his lap. She had refused to release her grasp on the dolls and wooden wagon Donnovan had purchased for her. Even in sleep she retained her hold on her treasures.

A fond smile hovered on Donnovan's lips as he stared at his lovely niece. The afternoon had been one of unexpected pleasure, a new beginning. When Alicia had uplifted her arms and called him "Papa," Donnovan had been stricken with conflicting emotions. He didn't want to take Stephen's place in Alicia's eyes and heart because that special place belonged to Stephen.

And yet Donnovan could not have denied this lively child in that moment of reckoning any more than he could have sprouted wings and flown to the moon.

Hannah's tireless persistence had worn him down. That free-spirited, determined woman had refused to let him remain detached and distant. In the end he had demonstrated his secret affection for Alicia, and the child had responded in ways that healed his scarred heart.

Even now Donnovan could feel the surge of proud possessiveness, alerting him that he was going to be the most overprotective uncle on the face of the earth. Heaven help the young beaus waiting in Alicia's future. If any of them dared to treat this angel as despicably as Hannah had been treated, Donnovan would take the scoundrels apart with his bare hands.

He would probably smother this poor child with his protective affection, and she would resent his intrusion and interference in her personal life.

Donnovan Maxwell was an all-or-nothing kind of man. Garrett Grantham could now attest to that. Donnovan hadn't pulled any punches when Grantham insulted Hannah. Donnovan had become as possessive and protective of Hannah as he was of Alicia. Those who belonged to him would be closely guarded and kept from harm—because losing those near and dear to him was more than he could bear.

Once Donnovan surrendered to his vulnerability, he knew he could be hurt. Therefore, he would do all within his power to prevent that from happening. . . .

A speeding carriage clattered down the dirt path toward Maxwell Plantation, jostling Donnovan from his pensive musings.

"Who do you suppose that is?" Fitz questioned the world at large.

"I don't have a clue, but they seem to be in one devil of a hurry," Horatio noted.

Donnovan halted beside the arched gateway when Alicia stirred in his arms, awakened by the thunder of hooves and rattle of the coach. A muddled frown plowed his brow when he recognized his groom from the town house in Charles Town. The groom jerked back on the reins and stamped on the brake, causing dust to swirl like a whirlwind.

"Damnation, Hastings." Donnovan scowled, leaning forward to protect Alicia from the suffocating brown fog. " 'Tis a wonder the coach has any wheels left. What the blazes is the—"

His voice dried up when his long-lost brother and sister-in-law clambered down, looking bedraggled, exhausted, but very much alive.

The strawberry-blond, her clothes in tatters, dashed toward Donnovan. Jessica spilled a bucket of tears as she reached up to embrace her child.

Donnovan experienced another maelstrom of emotion when Jessica clutched Alicia to her and rained more tears on the drowsy child. He had let his guard down to welcome Alicia into his heart, intent on raising her as his own. . . .

And suddenly she was being whisked away from him.

Not that Donnovan wasn't relieved and grateful to have his family back—he most certainly was!—but, dammit, how was he supposed to function when his regimented world kept getting tossed upside down?

"We practically had to move heaven and earth to return to the colonies on Alicia's birthday," Stephen announced as he wrapped his wife and daughter in his arms. " 'Tis been one hell of a month."

Obviously, thought Donnovan. Stephen and Jessica were the worse for wear because of their trials. But praise the Lord that they had miraculously survived the storm that had sent their ship to the bottom of the sea!

"The five survivors in the rowboat with us were picked up by a French schooner bound for Martinique," Stephen explained. "I had to buy the damned schooner for our fleet, just to ensure Charles Town was the first port of entry."

Donnovan watched the reunion with a pang of remorse. To Alicia, Hannah and Donnovan had become her family. The child was clearly confused by the attention she was receiving from her long-lost parents.

"You've taken remarkable care of my baby," Jessica murmured through her tears. "Thank you, Donnovan. She looks wonderfully healthy and happy."

'Twas more Hannah's doing than his, Donnovan thought to himself. Hannah was going to have to make an adjustment too. Alicia had occupied most of her waking hours. But now Jessica

probably wouldn't let anyone else near her child for weeks—
perhaps months—to compensate for lost time.

There was also a strong possibility that Jessica would refuse
a governess. She'd made it clear months before that she intended
to raise and educate her child herself.

Donnovan's thoughts scattered like quail when a shot rang
out in the distance. Cold fear seized him, knowing Hannah was
alone in the house. Donnovan couldn't tell where the blast had
come from, but apprehension and instinct prompted him to dig
his heels into his steed's flanks. He had to locate Hannah, to
ensure she was safe. If she wasn't—

Donnovan tossed the grim thought aside and bounded from
the saddle, taking the steps two at a time. He made a beeline
toward the kitchen, only to find the crumpled note beside the
dough Hannah had rolled out on the table.

A second shot rang out, and desperation set in. Donnovan
barreled through the back door just as Fitz and Horatio burst
into the kitchen.

"What the hell—" Fitz muttered.

"Hannah," Donnovan threw over his shoulder. "That bastard
Braxton has her."

Alarm registered on both men's faces. They charged through
the kitchen to provide reinforcements. By the time they reached
the far end of the garden, Donnovan was a good fifty yards in
front of them. He was too frantic to wait, tormented by guilt. If
he hadn't yielded to the vindictive urge to track Braxton down
and return the abuse he doled out to Hannah, the bastard
wouldn't have known where to find her. She was suffering because of Donnovan's carelessness. He prayed Hannah would survive so he could apologize.

Hannah's wild scream spurred Donnovan into a faster pace.
She was still alive, he assured himself. For how long? He was
afraid to guess. But at least he knew the direction Braxton had
taken, thanks to Hannah's shriek.

Donnovan slowed his pace when he reached the moss-draped
trees and underbrush that lined the river. He'd practiced guerrilla

warfare too long not to revert to old habits. Pricking up his ears, he heard the thrashing and guttural growls that erupted from the weeds.

Motioning for Horatio and Fitz to surround the area, Donnovan crept closer, forcing himself to ignore Hannah's pained whimpers and concentrate on surprising his foe. But the rending of fabric was almost more than he could bear, knowing Braxton was intent on abusive molestation.

Very soon, Donnovan promised himself, Daniel Braxton was going to wish he'd never been born. . . .

"I'm going to enjoy using you for what I bought you for," Daniel sneered diabolically.

Donnovan pounced like a bloodthirsty tiger. Finding Braxton poised over Hannah—a pistol to her neck, her skirts riding high on her thighs—triggered murderous fury. Donnovan knocked Braxton sideways and then came up fighting. He delivered a series of punishing blows that rendered Braxton unconscious all too quickly. Donnovan had wanted the miserable son of a bitch to take his richly deserved beating—and remember every agonizing moment of it. Unfortunately, Braxton had done him the discourtesy of slumping on the ground, oblivious of the painful blows. The man couldn't bake appetizing pastries, and he sure as hell couldn't take a punch!

"I think you've overstated your point, Captain," Horatio insisted, grabbing Donnovan's cocked arm. "You knocked Braxton out cold—thrice."

Donnovan half twisted, his gaze leaping past Horatio to see Fitz hoisting Hannah from the weeds. The instant Donnovan noticed the bloodstains that soaked her shoulder and chest, he forgot his need for revenge.

Sweet mercy! If Hannah suffered a fatal wound, he couldn't live with himself!

"Fetch Dr. Fields from the fairgrounds and ask the constable to accompany you home," Donnovan ordered Fitz. "Horatio, drag Braxton to the barn and tie him in a stall."

When Donnovan scooped Hannah into his arms, the other

two men scurried off to do his bidding. He peered down into Hannah's ashen face, noting the bruises and welts that marred her cheeks. A lump the size of the Appalachians threatened to close his throat.

"I'm sorry," Donnovan whispered miserably. "I'm so terribly sorry, Hannah. 'Tis all my fault."

Green eyes glazed with pain momentarily focused on his face before her lashes fluttered shut. "I—"

When she slumped lifelessly in his arms, her head dropping against his shoulder, Donnovan felt the earth caving in beneath his feet. If he lost her . . .

He would not lose her, dammit! He had just begun to live again, *because* of Hannah.

"Hannah, listen to me. Fitz is on his way to fetch the physician you met at the fair. He's the gray-haired man with glasses and a paunch for a belly. Remember? He delivered me, you know. And Alicia too.

"Alicia is fine." He yammered on any topic that popped to mind, hoping to call Hannah back from the darkness that entrapped her. "Alicia is enjoying the best birthday a child could have. Stephen and Jessica survived. They arrived a few minutes ago. You'll like Jessica. I'm sure she'll want to thank you personally for taking such good care of Ali."

Donnovan glanced up when he realized he had reached the kitchen door—and didn't remember how the hell he'd gotten there. Stephen stood before him, gaping as if he'd encountered a raving lunatic, but Donnovan didn't care what his younger brother thought. Donnovan was a desperate man. If Hannah could hear him, Donnovan wanted her to know that he was with her every step of the way, that he wouldn't leave her, that he expected—nay, *demanded*—she return from the silent darkness.

"Stephen, fetch some bandages and hot water," Donnovan commanded, never taking his haunted gaze off Hannah. "That was Stephen. I'll properly introduce you to him when you're feeling better. And you *will* be feeling better in no time at all."

After Donnovan disappeared around the corner, still carrying on his one-sided conversation, Jessica entered the kitchen, cradling Alicia in her arms. "Is that the same Donnovan we left behind six weeks ago?"

Stephen shook his dark head and grinned. "I don't think so. The one we knew never became rattled in the face of crisis."

Jessica gave Alicia another hug—the hundredth—and chafed her cheeks with just as many kisses. "I wonder who the woman is?"

"The most important thing in Donnovan's life," Stephen speculated as he retrieved the medical supplies from the pantry. "I wonder if he even knows it yet."

"I don't believe he knows much of anything at the moment."

"Except that saving the young lady's life is his greatest wish and gravest concern," Stephen murmured as he followed in his brother's wake.

After what seemed a century-long nap, Hannah lifted heavily lidded eyes to find herself propped up in Donnovan's bed, her shoulder encased in bandages and a sling. Sweet fragrances permeated the room. Vases of colorful flowers were everywhere, camouflaging every stick of furniture except the bed, which was encircled with them.

For a moment Hannah thought she'd died and no one had bothered to tell her. From the look of the dimly lit room, she was the guest of honor at her own funeral.

Gingerly, she tried to ease onto her side, but pain lanced through her like a knife. She must still be alive—unless she was in hell, which certainly wasn't known for its comforts.

When she reached around a bouquet to grab the glass of water on the nightstand, a hand came from nowhere to lift the drink.

The devil? Wonderful! She had already clashed with a few of his close associates, so why not meet hell's dark prince while she was at it?

Hannah tried to focus her bleary gaze on the figure that emerged from the shadowed corner.

"Donnovan . . . ?"

The moment she whispered his name she realized she was mistaken. Though the man bore a striking resemblance to Donnovan, he definitely wasn't Donnovan Maxwell.

"Stephen," he corrected her as he urged her to take a sip of water.

Hannah swallowed dutifully and decided she *was* in the hereafter, united with those departed souls who had gone before her.

Stephen chuckled as he replaced the glass. "Despite what you're probably thinking, we have all survived calamity—you, me, and my wife, who is in the nursery watching Alicia sleep in that undersized cradle. My, how Alicia has grown!"

Stephen ambled around to the foot of the bed to peer at Hannah. "If you're feeling up to it, I'll summon my brother. Dr. Fields ordered him out of the room two hours ago because he was afraid Donnovan would wake you when you needed to rest."

Hannah's brows knitted in a frown, causing the bruises on her cheeks to throb in rhythm with her pulse. "I don't understand."

"Nay, probably not," he said, grinning. "Donnovan was consumed with the notion that if he kept talking, you wouldn't do something drastic—like die on him. He absolutely hates it when that happens. He favors our father in some respects, though not to such extremes—I hope."

Hannah still had no idea what Stephen meant. Bewildered, she watched the younger version of Donnovan amble away. She had just settled herself more comfortably on the pillows, when Donnovan burst into the room, looking as haggard and harried as she felt.

"Well, 'tis about damned time," he scowled at her.

His terse tone was not the greeting she'd hoped for. She opened her mouth to point out that he could be a bit more compassionate given her weakened condition, but he flung up his hand to forestall her.

"Don't you dare utter a word," he commanded. "You're supposed to be saving your strength. Dr. Fields reiterated that to me often enough before he left."

When Donnovan clasped his hand behind his back and paced the confines of the room like a caged beast, Hannah smiled in amusement. She'd never seen the calm, controlled Stone Dragon in such a nervous frenzy.

"I realize you probably want to read me the riot act for alerting Braxton to your whereabouts, but since you're recuperating, I'll do it for you."

"Capt—"

"I should never have sought Braxton out," Donnovan scowled at himself, not at Hannah. "I nearly got you killed." He wheeled to wear another path on the carpet. "I suffered all the torments of the damned, waiting to see if Dr. Fields could patch you up. You lost a lot of blood, thanks to me."

"I don't—" Hannah tried to interject a comment, but to no avail. Donnovan was hell-bent on beating himself black and blue in her behalf.

"Rest assured that Braxton is already behind bars and will remain there for years to come. And although Jessica still insists on raising Alicia by herself, I'll ensure that you have a place here. You needn't think you'll have to leave, because I'm responsible for you and I take my responsibilities quite seriously."

"Donno—"

"I want you to marry me, Hannah."

Hannah stared into his weary face, touched by the generous offer, knowing she couldn't accept—much as she would have liked to. "I can't."

Donnovan looked as if she'd stabbed him. "Why the hell not?"

"You know perfectly well why the hell not."

"I know nothing of the kind."

"I will *not* become one of your responsibilities, and I most certainly will not have your prestige and reputation threatened—"

"Oh, for crissake—"

Hannah employed his habit of interrupting in midsentence so she could finish what she was trying to say. "—because you feel obliged to wed a mere servant, to compensate for that fiasco with Daniel that you claim was all your fault—"

"It *was* my fault—"

"—Garrett Grantham spoke the truth when he said a man like you expects to take a wife who can match your social status."

"Hang Garrett Grantham!" Donnovan exploded in bad temper. "The man has the intelligence of a potted plant. I have never put stock in his opinions, and I sure as the devil don't intend to start now. What you *were* doesn't matter. What you *will be* does. And what you will be is my wife—as soon as possible."

And what *he* was, Hannah thought, was feeling sorry for her, because she had no particular place to go, no family to turn to. Misdirected sympathy and guilt were the last things Hannah wanted from Donnovan Maxwell. She had professed to love him, but that didn't mean she would allow him to do something he didn't really want to do. What she wanted from Donnovan—all she ever wanted from him—he had not offered. Until he freely spoke the magic words, there would be no marriage. And that was that!

"Go away, Donnovan," she said tiredly. "I need to rest."

"I'm not leaving without your answer."

"The answer is no."

"That is not the right answer," he blustered.

" 'Tis the only one you're going to get."

"Dammit, Hannah!" he blared. "You're stonewalling out of pure contrariness!"

"Be still," she hissed. "Alicia will hear you. You already taught her one curse word. 'Tis the one word she pronounces better than the rest."

"There will be a wedding as soon as you are up to snuff," he decreed.

"If you have your heart set on a wedding, find yourself another bride. 'Tis not going to be me."

Donnovan's shoulders slumped. His attempt to control this roiling turmoil of emotion had failed. He looked at Hannah— battered and bruised—and felt his heart contract. More than anything, he wished he'd been there to spare her the pain she'd suffered because of him. He wished he could magically wave his arms, erase her unpleasant past, and make her every dream come true. But he could do nothing if she didn't cooperate. Not for the first time he cursed her stubborn persistence.

"What must I do to persuade you?" he asked, at the end of his emotional rope. "I'll do my best to make you happy. I know I'm going to be impossibly overprotective and I'll probably smother you to death, because I won't want to let you out of my sight. But loving you the way I do, I can't imagine my life without you. I suffered nine kinds of hell, fearing I'd lost you today. 'Tis making me crazy already—"

"What did you say?" Hannah stared owlishly at him.

"I said you're making me crazy and 'tis bound to get worse."

"Nay, before that."

An amused smile quirked his lips when Hannah perked up like a withered flower that had finally been watered. He'd been talking around the truth for the past few minutes, wondering how he was going to tell her that she'd become the most important part of his life, his reason for being. In desperation he'd resorted to Hannah's tactic of blurting out thoughts and feelings without holding back. 'Twas awkward, to be sure, because he'd never offered the confession to any other woman. Never wanted to until now.

"I said I love you. Now, are you going to marry me or not, Hannah?" Dodging the maze of bouquets, he approached the bed, towering over her, waiting.

"You love me?" she repeated, dumbfounded. "When did you come to that profound conclusion?"

Donnovan sank down beside her, chuckling at her startled expression. "I believe 'twas the day you sauntered out on that limb and dared me to come get you if I wanted you. I wanted you then and I want you even more now. I walked out on a limb and risked my heart. Now that you forced me to become open and demonstrative in my affection, don't think you can stroll off, spouting a crock of malarkey about adhering to social protocol and conforming to conventionality. We both know you delight in breaking the rules other people make, Miss Roth*child*."

"And that's another thing," Hannah said, staring curiously at him. "How did you know—?"

"Now that Ali will be packed up and hauled back to Charles Town, I'm going to be lost without a child underfoot, amusing me with those hoyden antics you encourage. You insisted that I give my affection to Ali, and now look where I am—lost. I want children of my own, *our* children, the product of my love for you. Are you going to agree to marry me, or must I drag you, kicking and screaming, to the altar?"

Hannah peered up into those twinkling amber eyes and melted beneath his affectionate smile. Her heart burst wide open. Tears of joy spilled down her bruised cheeks, and Donnovan kissed them away, promising to love, cherish, and protect her all the days of their life together.

Hannah believed him, believed *in* him, had always believed in his potential, even when he had doubted himself. He had cast aside that restrictive shell and let his love blossom—like the effusive bouquets that filled the room.

"Hannah," he whispered a dozen kisses later. "Promise me you'll tell me if I smother you with too much love, if I hover over you like a protective mother hen and insist that you're at my side both night and day."

Hannah eagerly welcomed him when he stretched out beside her in bed, ever mindful of her injury. " 'Tis been a long time since anyone cared enough to smother me with affection. I seriously doubt you'll hear me complain."

He sighed in relief. " 'Tis nice to know. Does that mean we don't have to continue arguing about the wedding the rest of the night?"

She searched his face. "Are you sure you really want to marry me?"

Donnovan dropped another kiss to her lips. "I don't want it any other way, Hannah."

When he took her in his arms, whispering tender words like

a lullaby of love, Hannah saw rainbows arching across the darkened room and sunshine reflecting off silver-lined clouds. She had indeed found her destiny . . . and a love to last an eternity. . . .

And the children? There were three of them. Three free-spirited, green-eyed girls with curly raven hair—the bewitching combination of their parents. They were their cousin Alicia's dearest friends, their mother's pride and joy, and their father's cherished treasures. Donnovan demanded and provided nothing but the best for his beloved wife, his precious daughters, and his lovely niece, who always held a special place in his heart.

Donnovan Maxwell, however, was every prospective suitor's worst nightmare. Every young man who came to court his daughters and his niece was extensively interviewed and aggressively interrogated. Only the cream of the crop got past the Stone Dragon's front door, much to the amusement of his wife and, occasionally, to the embarrassed dismay of his daughters and his niece.

About the Author

Carol Finch lives with her family in Union City, Oklahoma. Her newest Zebra romance, *River Moon,* is currently available at bookstores everywhere. Carol loves hearing from her readers, and you may write to her c/o Zebra Books. Please include a self-addressed stamped envelope if you wish a response.

A Daughter for John

Phoebe Conn

One

Williamsburg, Virginia, Autumn 1763

"If we don't hurry, we'll be late for your sister's birthday celebration." John Cochrane held the door open for Stewart Parker as they left the Raleigh Tavern. The tavern's white weatherboards caught the bright glare of the afternoon sun, and after being inside for several hours, John had to tip his cocked hat to shield his eyes.

It was Saturday, and they threaded their way through the crowd sharing the walk, nimbly avoiding the women on their way home from Market Square carrying baskets heavy with produce. Stewart stuck by John's side with the same tenacity he had displayed during their billiard games, and John's only consolation was that it was Mary Beth's brother rather than her father who had demanded he declare his intentions.

Mary Beth was one of his sister Holly's best friends. Now that Holly and Sam Driscoll were married, John readily understood Mary Beth's yearning for more than the polite attention he had always shown her. In truth, there had been a time when he had believed Mary Beth would make him a fine wife. Her disposition was as sweet as her looks, and she would fill any man's home with warmth and charm.

But he had gradually become aware that he needed something more from a woman, an intangible quality he could not accurately describe even to himself, let alone to Stewart. His inability to express his desires had made for an extremely awkward afternoon. When they reached the shady spot where they had left their horses tethered, John quickly untied his mount's reins.

"Perhaps I'm simply not ready for marriage," he hedged, "and with Mary Beth turning eighteen today, she obviously is. I know I've not misled her though. I've not made any moonlight promises."

John was fair-haired with hazel eyes that frequently danced with a golden sparkle, but Stewart saw no trace of mirth in his friend's expression now. Instead, he observed an uncharacteristic wariness and feared he was to blame. He reached out to grasp John's shoulder in a brotherly clasp.

"No. I can't fault you for that. You love women just as I do and flatter them all shamelessly. It's just that I don't want to see my baby sister pining for someone she can never have."

Stewart's show of sympathy served only to increase John's discomfort. Mary Beth danced with a lively grace that made her one of his favorite partners. Perhaps every dance and playful jest they had ever shared had swelled her hopes for the future. With a shiver of dread, he wondered just how many other women he might have inadvertently misled.

He was suddenly distracted by a brightly painted wagon rumbling by on Duke of Gloucester Street. It had a blue body, dazzling red sideboards, and a stretched hempen cover. Pulled by a team of six dapple-gray horses wearing bells trimmed with ribbon streamers, it was a typical Conestoga wagon often seen on colonial roads hauling freight. But this was no ordinary load. Nearly a dozen people of all ages in colorful costumes leaned out the front and rear of the wagon to wave to passersby.

"My God," John gasped. "Are those Gypsies?"

Stewart laughed at his friend's mistake. "Not really, although I suppose they live the same carefree life. They're the Gilberts, a troupe of traveling musicians. We've hired them to entertain at tonight's party."

A young woman with long auburn hair appeared at the rear of the wagon, brushed a soft sun-kissed swirl from her brow, and waved to Stewart and John. John was startled by her low-cut gown and free-flowing hair, but he was completely captivated by the radiance of her smile. In the next instant she ducked back into the wagon and was lost from view.

John's breath caught in his throat. He didn't know whether to shout or cry, but one glimpse of the red-haired beauty had stirred him more deeply than all his dances with Mary Beth. He gaped like a witless fool until the wagon turned the corner and disappeared from view. "They're going the wrong way," he finally mumbled, "to arrive at your house for tonight's party."

Thoroughly disgusted with him, Stewart rested his hands on his hips. "I'll grant you she's lovely, but she sings in taverns and anywhere else they'll pay her family to perform. I don't know whether to be insulted or grateful that you've never looked at my sister with such open lust, but I'll warn you right now that comely wench will never satisfy it. I'm as good-looking as you any day, and she wouldn't give me more than that enticing smile you just saw. Come on. Let's be on our way."

Unable to deny the heated desire his friend had observed so clearly, John fumbled as he untied his horse's reins. Then he feared he might stumble as he mounted the handsome bay. Even if he couldn't argue with the accuracy of Stewart's observations, he knew he ought to say something, but his mouth had suddenly gone dry. It wasn't until after he had arrived home that he realized he had failed to ask Stewart the strikingly beautiful singer's name.

She had the most luscious shade of red hair he had ever seen, and he longed to wind his hands in the silken tresses and lose himself in the kisses Stewart had sworn he would never claim. He sank down on the side of his feather bed, then threw his arms wide and dropped back into it. He struggled to relive the brief moment when their eyes had met. He hadn't been able to discern the color of hers at that distance, but he cared little if they were blue or brown, or an exotic clear green.

With a confidence born of experience, he believed she would also be daydreaming of him. Now Mary Beth's birthday party was the only place he wished to be.

* * *

Melody Gilbert combed her daughter's curly red hair with her fingertips and then hugged her close to savor her plump sweetness. "I want you to be a good little girl for Mama Ruth tonight. Will you do that for me, precious?"

Meribelle squirmed down off her mother's lap, and ran to her grandmother. Ruth Gilbert scooped her up and cradled her on her ample hip. "Meribelle is the same irrepressible darling you were as a child," Ruth said with a lilting laugh, "and I've no hope she'll be good, but you needn't worry about her. I do hope the Parkers will provide a generous tip above what they're paying us tonight. Then maybe we'll be able to buy new toys for all the children. Would you like a new doll, baby?"

Content her daughter would be loved as well as entertained, Melody left the tent they had pitched beside the wagon and, taking her shears, stole into the Parkers' garden. The party was about to begin, and she needed a few rosebuds to add to her crown of yellow ribbons. She glanced toward the mansion, and satisfied all inside were too involved in the party preparations to notice her, she dipped beneath a trellis covered in fragrant wisteria and stepped out onto the brick path.

The Parkers maintained a lush garden replete with beautiful roses. Melody soon found enough buds to adorn her hair. As she turned away, she found the path blocked by a smiling stranger. He had powdered his own blond hair rather than wear a wig, and his almond-colored frock coat was heavily embroidered with gold thread, while his waistcoat, worn with plain oyster knee breeches, was decorated with a matching design. Even in the gathering dusk his linen shirt was sparkling white and his buttons and shoe buckles were unmistakably silver.

Melody had been surrounded by expensively clothed gentlemen her entire life, and wasn't in the least bit awed by him. But something about him struck her as familiar. She offered no excuse for helping herself to the handful of rosebuds she carried, raised her hem slightly, and took a step toward him.

"Excuse me, sir. I don't want to be late for the party."

Knowing he would have to be especially attentive to Mary Beth on her birthday, John had come early, hoping to speak with Miss Gilbert first. He had expected her voice to be a breathless soprano like his sister's, but she had spoken in a hushed, sultry tone that was as mysterious and exciting as her deep auburn hair. There was just enough light for him to tell her eyes were blue, providing a startling contrast. Up close, her features were simply elegant perfection and her skin as pale and smooth as cream.

"Forgive me if I startled you," he began softly, hoping to put her at ease. "I saw you in town today, and did not want to let the night pass without asking if I might see you on a night when I could provide the entertainment."

This is how it always begins, Melody mused silently. "Do you have a name?" she inquired.

"Yes, of course. I'm John Cochrane, and my family's plantation is not far from here."

"You must have a spectacular view of the river."

John was amused by her comment, and flashed an engaging grin. "Yes. We most certainly do. If you enjoy strolling along the banks of the James, I'll be happy to escort you at any time you choose. Now tell me your name."

A servant had left the house and begun lighting lanterns to illuminate the walks. Melody turned to watch his progress at the far end of the garden before replying. "I'm Melody Gilbert, and the Parkers own my time this evening."

"Yes. I understand, but what about tomorrow, or the next day?"

Melody now remembered seeing him in town, and looked down at the rosebuds clasped tightly in her hands. "You're very handsome, Mr. Cochrane, and bright and charming as well, but I've no time to spend with you."

John strained for even a hint of regret in her voice, but there was none. All he heard was a faint impatience, as though she had given the same excuse innumerable times. "Wait," he ordered as she took another step toward him. She was dressed in bronze satin that melted into the deepening shadows; the rich color was glorious with her hair.

"I realize it must strike you as ridiculous for me to seek you out before you perform, but frankly, I didn't want Mary Beth to feel slighted if I spoke with you during the party."

"Are you two betrothed?"

Crickets chirped all around them, and her voice had almost been lost on the night air. John hesitated a moment too long before denying her assumption. "No. We're merely friends."

"You ought to practice your lies," Melody scolded. "Then they'll roll off your tongue with more conviction." She stepped out on the grass and swept past him before he could stop her.

No one had ever called John Cochrane a liar before, and he was badly disappointed in the way his chance encounter with Melody had gone. He swore under his breath rather than pursue her.

Swiftly putting the incident behind her, Melody did not look back as she rejoined her family. She found Ruth's son, Henry, vainly attempting to revive Philander Hogue, who had apparently begun the party celebrations soon after they had arrived at the plantation. "Let him sleep," she advised. "We can make do with just Angus playing violin tonight."

"I'm tired of having to do all the work," Angus McClellan complained. Married to Ruth's daughter, Rose, he was a Scotsman with bright red curls that continually slipped out from under his hastily combed wig. He brandished his bow for emphasis. "If Henry isn't drunk, then Philander is, and I'm sick of it."

"I beg your pardon," Henry cajoled in a rolling baritone, "but I've not had a drink in ever so long." Philander had fallen asleep beside the wagon, and Henry nudged him in the ribs with his toe. "Perhaps Philander will be able to join us after he's had a little nap."

"He'd not wake even if you rolled the wagon over him," Angus cried. "This is absolutely disgusting. I am a fine musician, and I refuse to play with riffraff."

Angus's wife left the tent in time to hear her husband's testy tirade. "Nonsense, Angus. You'll play wherever you're paid and tonight it's here. Danny's cello gives us a full sound and Philander won't be missed."

Angus drew himself up to his full height, which wasn't much more than an inch or two above his wife's. "Don't you dare speak to me in that tone in front of the children."

Rose glanced around with a theatrical flourish. "I don't see a one of them, Angus. Now, stop arguing about poor old Philander. Let's just go over tonight's program."

Angus dropped his head and began to sulk. "I should be playing in England's finest concert halls rather than rural Virginia."

Danny had been tending the horses, and had to remove a straw from his mouth before he spoke. "We all know you're enormously talented, Angus, but England's a long way off, and the Parkers are right here." He dropped an arm around his sister Rose's shoulders. "You're lucky to have wed Angus, Rose, because he's given you such beautiful children, but I hope you'll choose a man who'll deign to care for our horses the next time you marry."

"Do you hear that, Angus?" Rose prodded. "It seems you're the one who's not doing his share of the work rather than Philander."

Melody sat down on an overturned barrel to weave the rosebuds into her hair ribbons. "Must we have the same wretched argument every night of the year? It doesn't matter in the slightest that Philander is overly fond of rum, when Mama Ruth loves him so. As for you, Angus, you'd be lucky to play for pennies on a street corner in London, so stop acting as though we're all beneath you. Hurry and get dressed, Danny, and we'll go on inside. We dare not anger the Parkers by forcing them to send someone out here to fetch us."

In the midst of a wild game of tag, Angus and Rose's three sons came tearing through their midst, and everyone was sufficiently distracted to follow Melody's suggestion and make their final preparations for the evening. She placed the floral crown on her head, put away her shears in the wagon, and then smoothed out the folds of her gown. She had found Virginia as lovely as Mama Ruth had promised it would be, but she had learned that it really didn't matter where they performed. Every audience was precisely the same.

John remained in the garden until most of the other guests arrived. He then circled the stately home and entered with several friends. Mary Beth looked especially pretty in a light blue gown that matched her eyes, but as soon as he had extended his best wishes, he stepped away to allow the next guest to greet her. When his sister and her husband found him, he was sipping his second glass of wine and was so envious of the adoring glances they exchanged, he could barely produce a faint smile.

"What's wrong with you tonight?" Holly asked.

"I should have known better than to attempt to hide anything from you," John replied, but he was reluctant to confide how quickly Melody Gilbert had brushed him aside. He had never been treated with such maddening indifference by a woman, and the muscles along his jaw tensed as he fought down the bitter-tasting memory.

"Will you excuse us a moment, Sam?" Holly took her brother's arm and steered him toward a secluded corner. The Parkers had removed the furniture from their parlor to create a ballroom, but until the dancing began, the room wouldn't be crowded. "You look furious, which isn't like you at all, brother dear. Now tell me what's the matter. Wilson Parker could not possibly have refused to consider you a suitable husband for his daughter."

John placed his back toward the room and whispered so he would not be overheard. "I have no intention of asking for Mary Beth's hand in marriage, tonight or ever. Please quash that rumor if you should hear it."

Holly raised her fan and tapped him on the chest. "Calm down. You know I never encourage gossip, and most especially not about my darling brother. Oh, look, the Parkers have found a new troupe of musicians. How wonderful."

John heard a chair scrape against the highly polished floor as the Gilberts took their seats on the far side of the room, but he did not want to turn around. He felt as though he had made a complete fool of himself in the garden, and feared Melody would laugh openly the instant she caught sight of him. He owed it to Mary Beth to stay the evening, but the party he had anticipated so eagerly now seemed a dreadful chore.

Holly studied her brother's deep frown and continued pursuing its cause. "Did you and Stewart quarrel?"

"Not exactly. Now, hurry back to Sam before he gets lonely."

Holly had not meant to neglect her husband. "Talk to me later," she begged, then breaking into a delighted smile at the thought of dancing with Sam, she left John to brood all alone.

Unwilling to stare at the pale green wall, John finally turned toward the room, where pairs were forming to dance the minuet. Dozens of candles lent the room a romantic glow, and brought a burnished sheen to the guests' satins and silks. He was relieved to see Mary Beth already had a partner, and finished the last of his wine before seeking out one of her friends.

While John did not want to see Mary Beth cry, he harbored a secret wish that the Gilberts' music would be dreadfully out of tune. But when they began to play, he was astonished by how polished their presentation truly was. A blond young man and woman who appeared to be brother and sister played the cello and harp with remarkable grace, while a red-haired man stroked his bow across his violin strings with the tenderness of a lover. The final member of the quartet was an older gentleman who played an ebony flute and produced a tone as pure as a nightingale's.

The men's suits were black and finely tailored. The young woman's gown was fashioned from the same lush bronze satin as Melody's. He had not expected such beautiful music from the exuberant group he had witnessed riding through town that afternoon, but he could not help but wonder where Melody was.

As the evening progressed, he was so distracted by thoughts of her, he barely recognized his partners. He replayed the garden scene in his mind, but could discern no errors on his part. He had certainly displayed his interest, but in a respectful manner while Melody had been aloof, no more interested in him than she had apparently been in Stewart.

Still stung by that insult, he was about to wander through the garden alone in an attempt to regain his usual good humor, when the flutist made a brief announcement. The man spoke with an actor's precise elocution as he promised continued entertainment from a singer with extraordinary talent. John hesitated at the doorway, still thinking he might be better off outside. Then after a polite scattering of applause, Melody entered and he could not bear to leave.

She was even more stunning in the flickering candlelight, and as she began to sing, her rich alto voice captivated John anew. She lent a rare magic to a familiar love ballad; a hush fell over the rest of the audience. Melody sang of a maiden's longing for a captain who had been lost at sea, and gave each line the rolling rhythm of the waves. She sang the poignant love song as though the story were her very own, and John was deeply touched. When the song crested in a bittersweet refrain, most of the women present began to blot away tears, while the gentlemen, equally moved, fought to maintain a stoic calm.

When she held the last note, allowing it to fade to a sigh, John did not know if he could bear to hear her sing another tune, but at the same time knew he would suffer a lifetime of regret if he did not. The applause that greeted the number echoed all around him, and as he saw Stewart moving toward him, he knew exactly what his friend was going to say. He held up his hand to plead for silence as Melody accepted a request from a guest and began to sing a lighthearted number.

Stewart stood at John's side as Melody began a playful exchange with the audience that required them to join in the lively refrain. She teased and flirted with the men standing closest, then coaxed the ladies to join her. John could not recall ever seeing such a diverting performance, and he could not understand how the cool young woman he had met in the garden could turn so warm with a crowd.

As Melody was rewarded with another hearty round of applause, Stewart leaned close to whisper, "Would you like me to introduce you? Frankly, I'd enjoy watching her rebuff whatever attempt you might make to impress her. She'd probably find an offer of a considerable sum the most enticing. Whores always do."

John turned on his heel and grabbed for Stewart's velvet lapels with such shocking speed, those standing close by bumped into each other in their haste to move out of his way. "Take that back."

Stewart's smile spread into a mocking grin. "Make me."

Alert to the mood of his guests, Wilson Parker noted the threat of a confrontation and signaled the musicians to begin playing another dance tune. He then rushed to his son's side. "Just what are you doing?" he demanded. "Tonight of all nights, I expect better from both of you."

John released Stewart with a shove, then strode from the room and left the house. At that moment he didn't care if he had caused a scene, insulted Mary Beth, or embarrassed Holly and Sam. He just knew he could not have listened to Stewart malign Melody without defending her honor with the proper vigor. Angry enough to walk home, he was about to dismiss his carriage and do so, when Melody suddenly appeared at his elbow.

"What happened in there?" she asked. "Were you so upset with me you'd start a fight just to make certain we weren't paid? You're obviously rich, but we need every penny we earn, and most of tonight's money is already spent."

John looked around to make certain none of the drivers of the long line of carriages drawn up in front of the Parker residence was within earshot. He then took Melody's hand and pulled her around to the side of the house, where they'd be hidden in shadow. He opened his mouth to deny her accusation,

then realized he would have to lie rather than repeat Stewart'
ugly insult.

"I merely took exception to something Stewart said," he ex
plained calmly. "I'd not intended to harm your family in an
way, and I didn't. The party's continuing with no more than
ripple of curiosity as to why I left. The incident will soon b
forgotten."

Melody quickly withdrew her hand from his and backed away
"I was mistaken, then," she apologized. Moonlight fell acros
his face, sculpting his even features in high relief, and for th
briefest of instants Melody wished they were lovers stealing
few private moments. She longed for the comfort of his arms
but just as promptly cast the dangerous thought aside.

"It's happened to us before, however. Then the people who'v
hired us have blamed us for the commotion and refused to pay
even if we've entertained for several hours before the trouble
began."

"I'm very sorry you've been treated so unfairly," John replied
"You sing beautifully. I can't imagine anyone causing a scene
while you're performing."

His words were as kind as his expression, and Melody regret
ted not having been more charitable earlier. Before entering the
ballroom, she had observed the party from the doors leading to
the garden. She had noticed him. Tall and lean, he was a fine
dancer, but he had not remained with Mary Beth Parker as she
had expected he would.

"Thank you, but you came very close to doing it yourself jus
now. I'm sorry, but I've forgotten your name."

Again stung by his failure to impress her, John gave a sligh
bow. "John Robert Cochrane, although you may call me by
whatever name you please."

A haunted light filled Melody's eyes. "No," she whispered
through a threat of tears. "All I'll say is good-bye."

She ran from him before he could catch her, but positive he
had detected a note of regret in her tone this time, John smiled
with renewed hope. The Gilberts were fine musicians, and he

was certain they would be hired to entertain at a great many parties. Fortunately, he was popular, and would be invited to them all. Now whistling the lively tune Melody had sung, he went to search out his driver. The party was over as far as he was concerned, but soon, he vowed, he would again be alone with Melody, and he would not waste a single moment by asking her to sing.

Two

John Robert Cochrane was not the only young man who approached Melody at the Parkers' party, but late that night, as she climbed into the wagon to sleep beside Meribelle, he was the only one she remembered. She was no longer a naive lass who could be easily taken in by a handsome appearance or the trappings of wealth, but during their second conversation she had been impressed by John's sincerity. At the time she had been relieved when he did not rejoin the guests, but as the evening progressed, his absence proved strangely unsettling.

It had been a long while since she had allowed a man to catch her notice. She knew just how foolhardy it was to daydream of an attachment that could not possibly last, but nestled in the folds of a blissfully soft Lemon Star quilt, she could not resist dwelling upon such a pleasurable diversion. When the morning could be counted upon to bring more than its share of troubling cares, surely the minutes before sleep could be devoted to a guiltless fantasy.

Meribelle stirred in her sleep, as though defending the need for a practical rather than fanciful outlook, and instantly chastened, Melody closed her eyes. A tear escaped her lashes and rolled down her cheek, but she could not still the silent longings of her heart as easily as she had quieted her wistful imagination. She had been raised to believe in love, and longed to celebrate it in her life as well as in song.

With a small child to support, and traveling with a band of musicians who were more contrary than harmonious, perhaps love would never find her, but such a bleak prospect was dreadfully hard to accept. She would never regret giving birth to Meribelle, but it had been at a cost she seemed destined to pay all her life. Knowing how quickly John Cochrane would lose interest in her should he learn the truth, she dried her eyes on the quilt, and still wishing dreams really did come true, fell into a fitful sleep.

John had not really expected to find the Gilberts at the Bruton Parish church on Sunday morning, but as his family greeted their friends after the service, he scanned the crowd. Noting his wandering glance, Holly drew him aside.

"I'll not embarrass you at dinner by asking about last night, but your early departure was most definitely noted. I don't believe Mary Beth cared much though. She's developed an avid interest in a rather dashing British officer. Of course, any man looks good in a splendid uniform, but I'll wager you could win her back without too much effort."

Holly was smiling knowingly, but John was not even tempted to accept her challenge. "I'm glad to hear Mary Beth enjoyed the party, but for all I care, the whole British regiment is welcome to her."

Holly's eyes widened in horror. "John Robert! How dare you say such a thing. Tell me the truth now. Someone else must have caught your eye, and if she wasn't at last night's party, then she can't be among our social set. Father will be nonplussed if you bring home a shopkeeper's daughter, but if one has enchanted you, he'll soon grow fond of her too."

While their parents had their favorites among the residents of Williamsburg, they never spoke ill of anyone, and John knew Holly was right. "And what of Mother dear?" he asked without revealing where his true interest lay.

Holly turned and waved to their parents, who appeared ready to depart for home. "Mother loves you too much to complain of your choice, no matter who she might be. Now, tell me. Do I know her? Does she work in one of the shops I frequent?"

"No, and no again," John replied. He slid his arm around his sister's waist and guided her into her husband's arms. "Please find an inventive way to distract Holly so I won't have to listen to any more of her incessant questions."

Sam flashed a wicked grin. "I'll do my best, but I'll have to wait until after we have dinner with your folks."

Holly blushed demurely, but her smile made it plain she was looking forward to spending the late afternoon in her husband's embrace.

John was also looking forward to the afternoon, but for an entirely different reason. He scarcely tasted the fine meal his mother served, and at his first opportunity announced he needed air and was going riding. He had expected the Gilberts to be camped on the outskirts of Williamsburg, but he had not seen their wagon on the way into town. Determined to find them, he followed the main road and kept a sharp eye out for signs of a wagon turning off into the bordering pine forest. When he at last found the ruts left by the wheels of a Conestoga wagon, he was elated he would soon see Melody again.

When he caught sight of the Gilberts' wagon and tent through the trees, he slowed his approach to their camp so as not to startle them. He heard the happy laughter of children as he dismounted and dropped his horse's reins to allow the bay to graze. He had recalled seeing children when the troupe had made their boisterous pass through town and hoped he had brought enough peppermints for them all.

John glimpsed Melody seated in the grass, intent upon building a fort out of sticks with three red-haired boys and a little girl, whom he assumed to be their baby sister. It was such a charming scene, he didn't want to call out and disturb their fun. Instead, he waited for Melody to glance up and notice him.

While he waited, he studied a white-haired woman seated near the wagon. She had not been at the Parkers' party, but he was amused by the fanciful gestures with which she punctuated her conversation with an elderly gentleman who was also a stranger. Perhaps she had been an actress in her youth, and had never lost her flair for the dramatic. As for the man, he was merely listening, but the remorseful way he hung his head made John curious as to the subject of their conversation.

The flutist lay napping in the shade, while a few yards away, the cellist was currying the horses. The man and woman who had played the violin and harp were nowhere to be seen. Standing in full view, John watched them all, thinking them a remarkable family indeed, even if he could not readily discern just how they were related. At last one of the boys saw him and gave Melody a nudge.

"Good afternoon," John called out as he walked toward them. "May I join you? I haven't built a fort in years."

John was dressed in dove gray, but there was nothing somber about his smile. Melody looked down at her own muslin gown, which had once been a bright emerald but had now faded to a pale green, and felt none of the confidence she had shown the previous evening. "I was just about to send the boys off to gather more twigs," she replied.

"All the better," John answered. He knelt by her side, and after gazing into her eyes a moment longer than was polite, he turned his attention to the fort she had been building. "Yes. It does look as though we'll need more twigs, but you boys must look for very straight ones we can stack like logs. Do you think you can find us some good ones?"

The brothers stumbled over each other as they got up off their knees. Then, with each shouting he could outdo the others, they raced off into the woods. The little girl, perfectly content to remain, leaned against John's knee and studied him with a rapt fascination.

"Aren't you a pretty little thing," John cooed softly. "I brought peppermints for the children. May I give her one?"

That John had taken the trouble to find them, when Melody knew it could not have been easy, had already given her a moment's pause. That he had been so thoughtful as to have brought candy for the children was completely overwhelming. "I'd rather you left it with me when you go," she replied. "I wouldn't want sweets to spoil her supper."

"Of course." Melody's averted glance made her embarrassment plain, but John regarded her unexpected shyness as utterly charming. "I've shocked you by coming here, haven't I?"

For a second Melody wished she could speak the truth and confess just how delighted she truly was to see him, but the impossibility of their situation made such an impetuous declaration absurd. Unaffected by her mother's torments, Meribelle had begun walking around John in her own private game. "I'll recover," Melody promised. "This is Meribelle," she added as the little girl passed by, and her daughter laughed at the sound of her name.

"I am so happy to meet you, Meribelle," John answered gallantly. "She's almost as pretty as you," he then whispered to Melody.

Melody held her breath, waiting for him to notice the striking similarity of their features, but the friendliness of his smile didn't waver. She knew she should have introduced Meribelle as her child, but before she could force the damning words over the knot in her throat, the boys came running back into camp, and she was robbed of the opportunity.

Deeply ashamed, she listened as John praised their efforts. He then added tactfully worded suggestions as to how to enlarge the fort. He glanced her way often, and by the clear light of day his hazel eyes reflected the verdant hues of the surrounding forest. She judged him to be in his late twenties.

Old enough to take a wife, but she had forfeited the right to be a respectable man's bride the night she had given herself to Meribelle's father. When Meribelle dropped into her lap and yawned widely, Melody immediately seized the excuse to get away. "It's time for her nap. I'll put her in the wagon."

John watched Melody rise and wondered where Meribelle's mother might be. "Where's your mother, boys?" he asked.

The brothers shrugged, then the eldest blurted out, "She likes to take long walks with Father on Sundays."

Readily understanding the couple's need for time away from the rest of the troupe, John looked up at Melody. "You'll come back to help us?"

He had assumed Meribelle was the boys' sister, but Melody again let the chance to explain their relationship slip by. Perhaps he would never return, and she would have only this one golden afternoon to remember. If that were the case, then there would be no reason to apologize for her past, and the pain of watching his eyes fill with hostile disillusionment could be avoided.

"Yes," she promised softly. "I won't be long."

John admired the graceful sway of her hips as she walked toward the wagon. Then one of the brothers could no longer contain his giggles and he realized the boys were observing him just as closely. He laughed with them. "Well, men, you have to admit that Melody is a beauty."

At being referred to as men, the boys' chests swelled with pride and John quickly distracted them by suggesting they construct a tower.

Once she had Meribelle curled up on the quilt, Melody rubbed her back lightly and sang her favorite lullaby. By the time she had repeated the chorus twice, Meribelle was sleeping soundly. There was no reason to remain with her baby then, but Melody tarried, uncertain as to how she wished the afternoon to proceed. Finally deciding not to show John more than polite friendliness, she climbed down out of the wagon.

Ruth Gilbert called to Melody the instant the toes of her worn slippers touched the grass. "Do you know what you're doing, darling?" she asked in a hushed whisper.

"Let her be," Philander scolded. "Can't no harm come to her with us watching."

Melody dropped a kiss on his weathered cheek. "He's right, Mama Ruth." The apprehensive glint in the older woman's gaze didn't fade, but Melody believed herself fully capable of talking to John without allowing it to become more than an amusing conversation. To conceal her excitement, she deliberately slowed her step as she rejoined him.

"The boys just told me that you're their tutor. Do you need any new books for them to read? I could bring you some especially interesting ones from my family's library."

"It's very kind of you to offer." Choosing to sit on the opposite side of the fort from him, Melody settled down on the grass. They had made considerable progress on the structure in her absence, and it was obvious John was far more proficient at directing the work than she. "Unfortunately, we would undoubtedly move on before we finished a single volume, and we can't afford to pay you for them."

"I meant them as a gift," John stressed. He handed a smooth stick to the youngest boy, who added it to the growing height of the tower.

Melody's hair framed her face in loose waves and spilled over her shoulders as she shook her head. "No. We can't accept charity."

John had not meant to wound her pride. "You mustn't consider it as such. You'd actually be doing us a favor. If you'd take a few of our books, it would make room on our shelves for some new ones."

Melody glanced toward the forest, where several noisy squirrels were playing tag through the treetops. Books were a luxury the Gilberts could seldom afford, and yet John Cochrane had so many, he apparently would never miss those he gave to her.

"I'm sorry, Mr. Cochrane, but we can't accept presents when we've nothing to give in return."

Convinced she would object to every offer he made, John broke into a good-natured chuckle. "Are you always so stubborn, Miss Gilbert?"

A bright sheen of anger sparked across Melody's eyes. "I'm not merely being stubborn. The Gilberts have made their way in the world for more years than you've been alive. We've never stooped to accepting charity, and we'll not begin now."

The brothers had ceased working on the fort to follow their argument, and John nodded toward the pile of twigs to encourage them to continue. "What if you had something you no longer needed but thought I might prize? If you offered to pass it along, I'd certainly not be insulted. I'd simply thank you, and, inspired by your benevolence, become more giving with others."

Positive such a ridiculous scenario would never occur, Melody responded with a brittle laugh. "We've the fine clothes we wear to perform, and the near rags we wear at other times. There's the wagon, of course, and our horses, which aren't nearly as fine as yours. Then there are the instruments, and a few household items: pots, pans, and such. Pray tell, Mr. Cochrane, what could we ever give you?"

She had innocently posed one of the most provocative questions John had ever been asked, and he was wise enough not to make light of the situation. "The very best things," he responded easily, "friendship, wise counsel, love"—he paused without glancing her way—"are intangible, and priceless."

Readily accepting the wisdom of his words, Melody had no wish to argue, but she could offer him none of the three. Any friendship between them would of necessity be built upon a lie, and how could she offer advice when her own life was so far from exemplary? As for love, that was the most difficult to preclude, but equally unimaginable between them.

Warned by her reticence to reply that he had overstepped his bounds, John quickly offered more suggestions to the boys rather than demand a response. Melody puzzled him though. He had not imagined she would have such a serious nature, although their conversations the previous evening had certainly been brief and to the point. Then he considered what her life must be, with constant travel followed by the strain of performing, and did not know how she could be otherwise.

"The boys are doing very well with the fort," he said. "Would you come with me for a short walk? I doubt we'll be missed."

Melody glanced toward Mama Ruth and Philander, but having someone to watch the boys wasn't really the problem. "Probably not, but we were all up quite late last night, and I'm rather tired."

"We could take my horse. He'll carry two with no trouble."

John's teasing grin was as enticing as his invitation, but again Melody refused. "If you're ready to leave, I'll walk you to your horse, but that's as far as I'll go."

The regret John had hoped to hear last night flavored her words, but he derived absolutely no satisfaction from it. Melody's stunning beauty had been all he had seen at first. Then he had heard her speak, and been entranced by the richness of her voice. She sang with an angel's grace, and the song he remembered now was the first one, so haunting in its sorrow.

"No," he assured her. "I'm not anywhere near ready to go. I'm sorry I didn't hear more than two of your songs last night. Your family was so popular, you must have been asked to perform at many other parties while you're here."

"Yes. We were, but people often make requests during the height of the merriment at a party and then fail to confirm them later. It will take several days to sort out the sincere offers from the frivolous."

John wished she were seated closer so that he could reach out and touch her fingertips. Believing she had chosen to keep the fort between them for a purpose, he took her reasoning a step further. "Have you found the same to be true of men?"

Melody found the way the sun brushed the boys' red curls with fiery highlights far easier to contemplate than John Cochrane's gently arched brow. She wanted to answer truthfully, but without sounding bitter. Forcing a smile, she replied with gentle humor. "Yes. Very much so. You must have heard a few rapturous lies from beautiful women yourself, haven't you?"

John laughed at how quickly she had turned the conversation back to him. "Women do tend to flatter me shamelessly. That's certainly true. But I make no promises under the moonlight that I'll not honor at noon."

He was again regarding her with a level gaze that invited trust, but Melody felt the conversation had just veered dangerously out of control. "That's commendable," she told him. "Now I'm afraid I really must excuse myself. It's my turn to cook tonight, and if I don't begin soon, our whole camp will ring with pitiful moans of hunger."

John got to his feet as Melody did. He wished she had invited him to remain for supper, but if their resources were as meager as she claimed, then he understood why she had not. "I shan't keep you, then. I would like to see you again. Will I find you all camped here tomorrow?"

With three pairs of eager eyes on them, Melody had to choose her words with care. "No. We'll be playing at Wetherburn's Tavern all week." She took a step toward John's horse to encourage him to go, and he followed. "I assume you know it?"

"Indeed I do," John confessed with obvious delight. "Will they give you free lodgings?"

"No, but we can keep our wagon close by and be comfortable enough."

John wondered if Melody ever slept in a feather bed, then realized the question was most improper, and caught himself before it slipped out. He leaned down to grab his mount's reins, and then faced her. "How long have you been living like this?"

Melody wasn't ashamed that her family traveled constantly and slept out under the stars. Nor did the fact they earned their livelihood by performing trouble her. "All my life," she answered simply. "It's all I know."

Unable to restrain himself, John raised his hand and caressed her cheek. Her skin was softer than rose petals, and held an intoxicating warmth that invited the kisses he dared not give with so many people watching their every move. "It's not the only way to live," he offered softly.

His touch was painfully sweet, but Melody took a step backward to break the contact between them. "For me it is," she assured him proudly, and turning her back, she started to walk away.

"Wait," John called, and he hurriedly overtook her. He pulled a sack from his pocket and handed it to her. "I forgot to give you the peppermints."

There was no veiled taunt in his glance, and Melody refused to regard a small gift of candy for the children as charity. "Thank you." Had she gazed up at him a moment longer, he would have seen the tears forming in her eyes, but as she again moved toward the wagon with a purposeful stride, her parting smile lingered in his mind.

Wetherburn's Tavern was located across Duke of Gloucester Street, but in the same block as the Raleigh Tavern, where John Cochrane usually met with his friends. Henry Wetherburn courted Williamsburg's wealthy with fine service and lavish appointments, which included serving dishes of solid silver. While it was not his favorite tavern, John was known there.

As he entered the Great Room, he caught the aroma of arrack punch mingled with the sharper scent of tobacco. Above them, a hint of the subtle herbs and spices used in the preparation of the tavern's sumptuous meals floated on the warm air. The room was beginning to fill, and John debated taking a seat near the front, then believing his interest in Melody would be too obvious, he chose one off to the side. The Gilberts would perform throughout the evening, but he had wanted to be there early, when they would be at their best.

He stretched out his legs to get comfortable and ordered an ale he intended to sip all evening. Melody was such an enchanting young woman, he did not want her allure dulled by alcohol. When Stewart Parker dropped into the seat beside his, he nearly blew out a mouthful of the golden brew. He recovered in time to save himself that embarrassment, but he wasn't pleased to find Stewart there.

"I knew you'd be here," Stewart vowed with a teasing chuckle. "I've never known you to be devoted to any particular troupe of musicians, so you have to be here to admire Miss Gilbert.

I'm really surprised at you, John. You've always had such excellent taste in women—until now."

John was sorely tempted to wallop Stewart across the face with his tankard, but in a supreme test of will he set it down on the table. "Shall we step outside?" he challenged.

Unfazed, Stewart sat back and steepled his fingers over his chest. "Calm down," he chided. "You'll see what she is soon enough."

What John had already seen of Melody Gilbert had convinced him she was a far more complex individual than Stewart Parker could ever appreciate. He had always liked Stewart, but when he reviewed their friendship, he realized it had continued from childhood out of mere habit. A week before he had not cared that they shared little other than the same circle of friends, but now Stewart struck him as unbelievably shallow.

"I'd much rather be alone than have to share this table with a disagreeable companion," John replied.

Stewart had just opened his mouth to respond, when the Gilberts entered and took their places. Philander Hogue had joined them that evening, creating a quartet with two violins, a cello, and flute. As they began to play a spirited drinking song, any comment Stewart might have wished to make was lost. He simply shrugged and smiled at John before turning his chair to improve his view of the musicians.

John certainly was not ashamed of his interest in Melody, but he had wanted to concentrate on her that night without the distraction of a companion, let alone one who had clearly come merely to annoy him. He considered moving to another table, but there were no places open that would guarantee him the privacy he desired, and Stewart would surely follow. He crossed his arms over his chest and regarded Stewart with a malevolent stare. Only the knowledge that Melody would soon sing kept him from giving his old friend precisely what he deserved for disturbing him.

* * *

Uncharacteristically nervous, Melody walked up and down behind the tavern. She was torn between a sinking dread that John Cochrane would be there, and the wretched fear that he would not. She crimped the sides of her crimson skirt with her fingertips, then tried to smooth out the wrinkles. The Gilberts had one repertoire for elegant private parties and another for taverns, featuring loud, bawdy numbers. While none of her lyrics were lewd, they were definitely suggestive and as she went over the first of her songs in her mind, she knew John would catch every double entendre.

What would he think of her then? she agonized, still uncertain if he was even there.

Mama Ruth had put Meribelle to bed, and could have gone to sleep herself, but she could not bear to watch Melody pace with a distracted stride, and soon joined her. "It isn't like you to be this nervous," she cautioned. "What makes this young man different from all the rest?"

Melody did not insult Mama Ruth by denying John Cochrane was the source of her anxiety. "His kindness," she posed, "although he is certainly splendid to look at."

Mama Ruth wiped her hands on her apron before resting them lightly on Melody's shoulders. "Don't let him touch your heart, darling. He'll only bring you pain."

"You needn't remind me," Melody countered, but she doubted it could be any worse than what she already felt. "I've not encouraged him, and if he's here tonight, I'll wish him no more than a polite good evening."

"They've begun the tune before yours," Mama Ruth noted. "Let me see you smile."

It was their old ritual, begun in the days when she had been little older than Meribelle and Henry had carried her out onstage. She hadn't understood the risqué meaning of the clever lyrics they had taught her, but she had sung them with a childish glee and adored the thunderous applause. After a tremulous smile she kissed Mama Ruth, then slipped through the back door.

She would give a polished performance as always, but the applause she would receive that night wasn't going to be nearly enough to soothe her aching heart.

Three

As Melody took her place beside the musicians, she was reluctant to scan the faces of the audience for John Cochrane's eager grin. She raised her glance slowly to mask her need to search, but when she did not find him among those seated at the first few tables, she was overcome with a perverse terror. It was a large room and he could be anywhere, but she had been certain he would take a seat in the front. *If he was there.*

Her first song was one of coy seduction, which she enhanced with the graceful artistry of her fan. Shyly peeking over its lacy folds between verses, she studied those seated close by. Several were young British officers, who were enjoying her performance as immensely as their kind always did. There were a great many other men too: shopkeepers with pinched faces, farmers with ample bellies. Toward the rear she noted a woman dining with an older gentleman who could have been either husband or father.

To widen her perusal of the crowd, she would have to move out among them, and to do so was to risk being grabbed and pulled down onto some sweaty individual's lap. The Wetherburn might cater to a wealthier clientele than most taverns, but that did not guarantee gentlemanly behavior. Melody dared not step away from the protective reach of the Gilbert musicians.

Still uncertain of John's presence, she pushed herself to sing the merry tune as though he were part of the appreciative crowd. She was rewarded with a noisy round of applause to which she gave a demure curtsy, then turned with a light dancing step and began her second tune. This was an old favorite she had sung for years, but until that night she had never allowed herself to dwell on the dismal prospect of repeating the lyrics in a succession of crowded taverns until she no longer had the necessary youth and beauty to make them convincing. The thought brought a painful wave of doubt, and when one of the British officers grabbed for her skirt and tossed out a ribald suggestion, she could not ignore it as she had equally crude offers on so many other nights.

She eluded his reach with a sidestep, but losing her concentration, she turned toward Henry and shook her head. He lowered his flute just an instant, nodded to dismiss her, and announced another musical number. His fellow musicians achieved the abrupt transition with remarkable aplomb, and the program continued without more than a momentary pause. Melody walked away with her head held high, but now she feared that John Cochrane might really be there, and have heard the officer's insulting invitation.

John had been following Melody's performance so closely, he had been completely unaware of the rest of the audience. He saw her glance toward the officers, and knew one must have spoken, but he was seated too far away to overhear. The horror of her reaction made it plain the remark had not been complimentary, and he was halfway out of his chair before she left the room.

Stewart Parker reached out to catch John's sleeve. "Sit down. She'd not be singing here if she had any honor to defend."

John sent Stewart a glance so filled with venom, the young man recoiled as though he had been struck. Knowing he could beat his one-time friend senseless whenever he chose, John turned his back on him and hurried after Melody. She had only stepped out the back door, and he would have sped right on past her had she not called his name.

"Are you all right?" he asked anxiously.

Appalled to discover John really had been in the audience, Melody remained in the shadows. She knew he had to be em-

barrassed not only for her, but for himself as well. Positive this
would be the last she would see of him, she provided a ready
excuse for a prompt farewell.

"I shouldn't have let such a shocking lack of manners disturb
me," she remarked. "I would have given that rude officer an
equally obnoxious reply, but I noticed at least one lady in the
crowd. Out of respect for her I held my tongue, but I don't want
you to believe I can't control an unruly audience. Lord knows,
I've seen more than my share."

Melody's voice had taken on a coarse edge, but John wasn't
fooled. She had been hurt as any lady would have, and he intended to make it up to her. "Can you describe the man who
insulted you? I couldn't see him from where I sat, but if you'll
point him out, I'll teach him some much-needed manners."

That John wished to be her champion was more than Melody
had any right to expect, and she quickly refused. "It would be
a wasted effort, Mr. Cochrane. His kind never learn, and there
are usually more than one in an audience. The later the hour
grows, the drunker they get and the louder the taunts become.
I know better than to walk out, but tonight—"

When she did not complete her thought, John reached out to
envelop her in a warm embrace. She resisted his touch momentarily, then relaxed against him, but she was trembling still.
Afraid he might crush her in his enthusiasm to offer comfort,
John took a deep, steadying breath.

Melody's willowy figure fit his muscular contours with the
easy familiarity of a longtime lover. He was convinced they had
been born to be together. Doubting she shared such a romantic
dream, he feared she would swiftly bolt, and cherished each
precious second of her closeness now. Laughter from the tavern's
back rooms and faint strains of the quartet's music swirled
around them. He would have asked Melody to dance, but the
scent of stale ale and rotting food thrown out for the dogs made
the scene anything but inviting.

John slid his fingertips down Melody's arms, then took her

hand to draw her along. "Come. Let's find somewhere more pleasant to talk."

Melody pulled away. "I would still have to come back here," she reminded him. She smoothed out her skirt and straightened her shoulders. "Wetherburn's paid for all of us, and I can't skip the rest of tonight's performance."

"Your sense of responsibility is commendable, but surely you deserve a few minutes to call your own."

"You don't understand." Melody would have reentered the tavern, but John had sensed her eagerness to escape him and moved to block the doorway.

"This is the first time we've been this far south, and Williamsburg has been good to us, but we're never certain from one day to the next which of us will be able to perform and how much money it will bring."

When John nodded as though he truly understood, Melody confided far more than she had meant to. "Henry's been sober for nearly a month, which is a very long time for him. When he's drinking heavily, he shakes so badly he can't play his flute at all. Philander is also fond of drink, but he can play his violin as long as he's conscious. He's an old man though, and it wouldn't surprise any of us if he simply didn't wake one morning.

"Angus dreams of playing for the crowned heads of Europe, but with a wife and children to support, he'll never stretch his meager talent that far. Rose should be playing her harp with a church choir rather than performing with us, and we excuse her whenever possible so that she can remain with Mama Ruth and the children. As for Danny, he's usually an indifferent cellist, although there have been occasions when he's been an inspiration to us all. Still, he's a young man, and restless for a better life."

Melody had begun to pace in front of John, and he was fascinated by her agile grace. He wished the shadows weren't so deep so that he could see her expression clearly. "So what do we really have here?" he asked. "Men who are overly fond of drink, or lacking in talent? A harpist with children to tend, a dear old grandmother, and a remarkably beautiful singer who is so devoted to her family, she'll not steal away for even a minute to follow her heart?"

Melody had paid dearly for believing in sweet promises of love, and refusing to listen to anything so dangerous ever again, she ignored John's questions. "In your entire life, have you ever lacked for anything?" she asked.

Believing the hunger in his gaze would provide the most eloquent answer, John simply stared at her for a moment. "I've already told you money won't buy the most precious things."

John Cochrane was the most determined man Melody had ever met, but she dared not let him touch her bruised emotions. "Well, for tonight I'm thankful Wetherburn has put food in our bellies. I've been away too long. Please tell me good night and go on home. Otherwise, you'll be sure to answer the next tasteless remark with your fists and Wetherburn will throw us out right along with you."

"I'll not cause you trouble," John swore, but he knew her prediction was likely to prove accurate. "I want to dance with you, but I can wait until you perform at another private party."

Melody laughed at such an absurd notion. "When you're entertained at a friend's home, do you usually dance with the servants?"

"No. Of course not, but you mustn't think of yourself as such."

Melody took a step closer. "Do not delude yourself, Mr. Cochrane. Musicians are often considered to be in a class below servants, and only the finest soloists are placed above them."

John raised his hand to caress her bare shoulder, then slid his fingers through her hair, separating the heavy auburn tresses into silken stands. "You are in a class by yourself, my dear," he whispered. He tilted his head to kiss her, but she allowed him only a faint taste of her lips before she escaped his grasp and disappeared into the tavern. John ached to follow, but knowing she would be more impressed if he were to respect her wishes, he did not. He had never encountered such an elusive woman, but the challenge she posed was not her only appeal.

"No, indeed." He chuckled to himself, and the next morning he returned to town leading a beautifully groomed black pony for the Gilbert children to ride. He had a tin canister of tea for Mama Ruth, a delicate piece of lace for Rose, and fine pipe tobacco for the men. He saved Melody's present until last, then handed her a tiny crystal bottle filled with French perfume.

The wagon was parked out behind the tavern's stable, and Melody had been seated upon a flour barrel planning their performance schedule with Henry while Meribelle played at her feet. Startled to see John, and amazed by his generosity, she set her calendar aside and opened the exquisite flask. It contained a heady floral scent that reminded her of the lush garden where they had met. Men were far more likely to toss coins at her feet than bring her expensive gifts, and she was at a loss for an appropriate way to respond.

"Just what is it you're trying to do, sir?" Danny asked. "Seduce the whole family?"

Philander laughed so hard at that question, he began to choke, and Henry had to whack him on the back to help him recover. Mama Ruth, who had been reverently tracing the design pressed into the sides of the tin tea canister, scolded Danny sharply, while Rose, admiring her lace, gave no indication she had even heard the question. Angus, meanwhile, was already filling his pipe with the new tobacco.

"I believe *impress* is a better word," John responded as soon as Philander stopped gasping for breath. "I enjoyed your music so much last night, I simply wanted to repay you with more than applause."

"Another stranger to the truth." Danny swore under his breath, and he walked away, but not before stuffing John's gift into his waistcoat pocket.

Stung by an insult that described her conduct more aptly than John's, Melody felt everyone's glance shift to her. The whole family was waiting for her response, but she was saved from having to be coherent, if not truthful, when Meribelle rushed to John, raised her chubby arms, and begged to be put on the pony. "She's really too small to ride alone," Melody warned him. She slipped the perfume bottle into her pocket and stepped between her baby and the pony.

John scooped up the pretty little girl and glanced toward Rose. "Peppercorn is as gentle as a lamb, and Meribelle will be all right if she rides with one of the boys. Do you mind if I lead them all on a tour of the town?"

With her sons clamoring for her consent, Rose hesitated only a second before looking to Melody. She understood the confusion in her eyes, and tried to ease it. "Thank you, sir. The boys would enjoy that. Why don't you go along with them, Melody? Mama Rose and I can take care of everything here."

As John turned toward Melody, the width of his smile convinced her that had been his intention all along. Rather than attempt to pry her away from her family, he was including her with the children. The boys often rode their horses, and with Meribelle riding double with one of them, Melody knew her little girl would be in no danger. She could not say the same for herself, however.

"We see so many towns," she hedged. "Could we go down Francis Street and just admire the houses?"

"That's a wonderful idea," John exclaimed, although the possibility Melody might be starved for such an ordinary scene touched him deeply. He quickly motioned for the eldest of the McClellan boys to hop upon Peppercorn. Once he was seated, John placed Meribelle in front of him. The little girl grabbed for the pony's glossy mane and giggled happily.

"All you boys will have plenty of time to ride," he promised, and after giving Peppercorn's reins a gentle tug, started his small parade toward Francis Street.

Melody kept a close eye on Meribelle for the first few paces, but then, assured of her daughter's safety, she relaxed a bit. "We seldom stay anyplace long," she remarked absently, "and everything is so well cared for here. The paint on the houses and fences looks fresh. The flowers are such vivid colors and the produce I've sampled is bursting with flavor."

John attempted to look at the town through Melody's eyes, but the neat little houses along Francis Street were very small compared to his family's estate. He knew better than to say so, when Melody's family lived out of a wagon, but it pained him to think she had so little. "Williamsburg is a most agreeable city. Do you think the Gilberts might be convinced to remain here?"

Flustered by the question, Melody quickly shook her head. "It's better for us to keep traveling. That way we're always welcome."

John laughed at her assumption. "Why do you suppose you'd swiftly become unwelcome here if you stayed?"

Melody glanced over her shoulder to make certain the boys couldn't overhear. She tried to find a believable answer for John's question, but a cold wave of panic encircled her heart. He continually pushed her in directions she had no wish to go, and yet he was such a likable man, she did not want to be rude.

"People would soon grow tired of our music, and then of us," she finally explained softly.

"I think you're very wrong. You're an excellent troupe and ought to be performing at the governor's mansion during Publick Times. The rest of the year you could give music lessons and play for private parties and celebrations. You'd not have to perform in taverns at all."

Melody waited while John stopped to give the next brother a chance to ride behind Meribelle. As they continued on down the street, she shrugged off his suggestion. "You think we're good simply because you haven't heard us play often. After you have, you'll begin to hear the mistakes, and wish for someone new."

She had said *someone* this time, and John was astonished to think she might actually believe he would ever tire of her. Then he recalled Danny's peculiar remark. "What was it Danny said about my being another stranger to the truth? Who's told you lies?"

The day was warm. The sky was gloriously blue and dotted with snowy puffs of clouds. The moment would have been blissfully serene had Melody not felt so uncomfortable about herself. "Who hasn't?" she replied flippantly. "That's the problem with moving as frequently as we do. No one has to keep his word for more than a few weeks."

A bee darted close to Meribelle, and when both Melody and John reached out to brush it away, their fingers touched. He would have liked to hold her hand while they strolled through the town, but she had chosen to walk on the opposite side of Peppercorn. She was always so careful to keep her distance that John wondered if she ever dared to flirt the way she did in her songs.

"I wish you'd flirt with me the way you do with an audience," he blurted out. "It's the only time you really seem happy."

"It's merely an act," Melody assured him.

"Oh, Melody. Aren't you ever happy?" John pulled Peppercorn to a halt, and the brothers thought it was time to change places again. The middle boy slid off the pony's back. The youngest quickly climbed into the saddle and grabbed hold of Meribelle.

Melody could remember being happy, and she missed those sweet, innocent days terribly. She had never told another man how she had come to be with the Gilberts, but John was getting too close, and she decided to reveal part of the truth to save herself from having to confess it all. After making certain Meribelle was still securely held, she crossed in front of the pony to walk at John's side.

"I was raised by the Gilberts," she told him, "but we aren't kin. I was just a babe who was left with them when I was no more than a few hours old. Mama Ruth says that my mother was a very beautiful young woman who refused to disgrace her family by raising her lover's child. I suppose she went on to make a fine marriage and never thinks of me, but Mama Ruth says I have her smile."

Melody heard John stifle a moan and couldn't bear to look up at him. "Now do you understand why it's best if no one ever knows us too well?"

Not in his wildest imaginings had John expected Melody to share such a shocking confidence. His first thought was of Stewart Parker's smirk, which filled him with shame. "I'm sorry," he mumbled.

Melody blinked away her tears. They continued their walk for another half hour, but the children's happy laughter was the only sound. In Melody's view, that she was a bastard was the least of her problems, but if that was scandal enough to send John Cochrane away, then she was glad she had told him. As soon as they returned to the wagon, she plucked Meribelle from Peppercorn's back and turned away.

"Wait," John called to her.

Doubting he would say more than good-bye, Melody turned slowly. "Yes?" She tried to focus her attention on his shiny silver buttons rather than on the sorrow she knew she would see in his eyes.

"My family's decided to host a party, and we want the Gilberts to entertain. I know you already have other commitments, but if you'll tell me when you're available, we'll have the party then."

Melody caught herself before she let her mouth fall agape. She had been distant. She had been cool to the point of being rude. She had even confided the pitiful story of her background, and still John Cochrane hadn't abandoned her. She drew in a deep breath and raised her glance to his. If he felt sorry for her, it certainly didn't show in the teasing light in his eyes. She cleared her throat and called to Henry.

"Please check the calendar for the list of dates. Work something out between you." She walked around the back of the wagon and leaned back against it. Meribelle wanted another ride on the pony and squirmed in her arms, but Melody wouldn't allow her to run back to John and gripped her firmly.

"Hush. There will be other days and other ponies," she promised, but she doubted they would ever meet another man like John. She did not know whether to be grateful or sad.

John took his place at the dining table for dinner, but he could barely remain silent while his father gave the blessing. Now that Holly was wed, there were just the three of them for meals, and while he and his parents usually had agreeable discussions, nothing of much consequence was ever said. "I think we should host a party," he announced in the same breath as the amen.

"A party?" Grace Cochrane repeated with delighted surprise. "Why, John, the servants are still sweeping out rose petals from Holly and Sam's reception."

"And I'm still paying for it," Michael Cochrane added. "If you want to entertain your friends, do it at the Raleigh."

"The party isn't for my friends," John explained. "I've met the most remarkable young woman, and it's the only way to lure her here."

Grace dropped her soup spoon to the table with a loud clatter. "Whatever do you mean? Who is she? Who are her people?"

Michael broke off a hunk of bread and gestured with it. "I don't care who she is. Why should you have to lure her here? We're among Williamsburg's finest families, and our invitations are never refused."

Thinking it was going to be a very long afternoon indeed, John sat back in his chair. His parents were a handsome pair, and even after nearly thirty years of marriage, they were completely devoted to each other. Now all he hoped was that they would remain equally devoted to him. "A man is known by his deeds as well as his family name," he began, "and surely a woman ought to be known by her devotion to others as well as for her beauty, charm, and grace."

Michael shook his head sadly. "Where did you meet this penniless paragon of virtue?"

John was relieved he didn't have to name a tavern. "She was

at the Parkers' party last Saturday. We spoke in the garden, and I've seen her a time or two since then."

"Thank God," Grace sighed. "You see, dearest. She's a friend of the Parkers and not penniless at all."

John waited a moment, but he couldn't mislead his parents any further. "Melody has the beauty of a princess, so it's obvious she is from a fine family, but her circumstances are far from ideal." A graduate of the College of William and Mary, he knew how to plot out an argument to stay ahead of an opponent and win a debate, but he had never been presented with a greater challenge than the one he now faced.

"I don't believe we can choose whom to love," John continued. "The magic, the sweetness, it's either there or it's not." As he began to describe Melody, he realized that whenever he saw her with her family, Meribelle was within easy reach. In fact, he had never seen the pretty child in Rose's arms.

With that disturbing realization, a sickening tightness filled his chest. He felt very foolish for beginning a conversation with his parents that he wasn't nearly ready to finish. Before they could argue that he did not know the beautiful singer nearly well enough to speak of love, he shoved his chair back and stood. "Forgive me, we'll have to discuss this later."

Grace watched her son leave the room, but waited until his footsteps had faded away to speak. She reached for her husband's hand and gave his fingers a fond squeeze. "He is so much like you, and while he's just confused me completely, I trust his choice of wife to be as wise as yours."

Michael had been ready to damn his son for being a fool, but he was so amused by his wife's comment, his anger dissolved in a hearty burst of laughter. "We'll have to pray that he is, beloved, hold our tongues, and wait."

"I don't think we'll have to wait long," Grace replied, for she had seen the glimmer of uncertainty enter her son's eyes. She knew that whatever its cause, he was not one to let it go unresolved.

Four

John returned to Wetherburn's Tavern Tuesday night and took a seat close to the front. When Melody came out to sing, he had to fight to keep the depth of his lingering dismay from darkening his expression. She sent him frequent smiles, and he nodded politely, but remained thoroughly confused. Despite the charm with which she imbued each performance, in private he had found her to be almost painfully shy. Now his impressions were blurred by dark suspicions, and he wondered if she wasn't simply a consummate actress rather than truly reserved.

"It's merely an act," she had admitted, but had she been referring only to the smile she wore for an audience? he wondered.

It was all happening too fast. He had wanted Melody at first glance, and begun pursuing her with an energy he had never shown another young woman. Now his doubts had forced him to step back and observe her more closely. Their morning stroll had put some color in her cheeks, and she was even more beautiful, but it was her character rather than her appearance that mattered most to him now.

Turning his attention to the rest of the audience, John saw the same lust that had once filled his gaze reflected in every other man's eyes. Far from being offended at such open desire, Melody's every gesture was designed to entice as clearly as her wickedly humorous lyrics. She knew precisely when to make a saucy turn, or avert her glance before coyly peering over her fan. The audience responded with a palpable hunger for more. She sang half a dozen songs before leaving the stage to the musicians, and found John waiting for her just outside the back door.

Melody stirred a cooling breeze with her fan. "Did it seem awfully warm in there to you?" she asked. She had been so excited to see him, she feared his presence alone had caused her discomfort.

"Very," John replied. Against the dank aromas behind the tavern, he caught the faint scent of the perfume he had given her, but that she had worn it failed to make him proud.

His voice had sounded flat, and Melody feared he had been offended by her performance. "You needn't worry that I'll sing the same tunes at your party," she rushed to explain. "We know the difference between what's preferable in a private home and what's acceptable in a tavern."

John had longed to have her look up at him with the touching uncertainty that now lit her gaze, but he stopped himself before again falling under her spell. "I'm going to be out of town for several days," he announced coldly. "I probably won't see you again until the night of our party."

Melody didn't have to ask if something was wrong. John's posture was rigid rather than relaxed, and his voice had lost the gentle timbre it had always held with her. Fearful that morning's confession had belatedly influenced his mood, she began to back away from the aloof stranger John had become.

"Have a good trip," she offered in a failed attempt to salvage her pride.

"Yes. I intend to." John left her standing in the shadows. He was nearly home before he realized walking away from Melody had merely increased his heartache rather than eased it.

As she had once pointed out, he had led a privileged life. He could not recall a single instance in which something he had desired had eluded him. Perhaps everything had come too easily, but the painful disappointment that had caused him to turn away from the one woman he might have loved was growing sharper by the hour.

The brief romantic interlude had been a tragic mistake. He

drew his mount to a halt and gazed up at the stars. The heavens shone with a perfection that was sadly lacking on earth. Cursing the loneliness that tore at his soul, he wished with all his heart that he could make it disappear.

Melody had more songs to sing, and after John had gone she paced the tavern's courtyard to compose herself before returning to the Great Room, but the gaiety she had displayed earlier had turned to melancholy. Rather than the naughty number she had planned, she sang the lament for the captain who had been lost at sea. When she brought it to an end, the applause was hearty, but she could no longer mask her sorrow behind lyrical rhymes. After a deep bow, she bade everyone a gracious good night.

When she reached the wagon, Rose and the children were already asleep, but Mama Ruth had waited up for her. "I'm afraid we've seen the last of John Cochrane," Melody greeted her. "It's a shame we'll receive no more presents."

Mama Ruth heard the painful catch in Melody's voice, but wasn't fooled by her flippant complaint. "Oh, darling, I'm sorry. Although I warned you not to risk your heart, I had hoped he would be a true gentleman and ask you to stay here with him."

Melody refused to blame John for her own failings. "The problem was not that John lacked manners, but that I lack the fine qualities a gentleman requires in a wife." Weary clear through, she sank down upon the barrel that served as one of their most comfortable chairs.

"I've done my best," Mama Ruth swore, "but you've not had an easy life. We have a little money set aside, and—"

"For the emergencies which befall us too often," Melody reminded her.

"Just listen to me a minute," Mama Ruth begged. "It's enough to give you a future. Leave Meribelle with me and go on down to Charleston, where you can make a new life as a respectable woman. You can marry some fine young man and have children you can raise as a proper family."

"Stop it right now," Melody scolded. "How can you even imagine that I'd abandon Meribelle to live such a selfish masquerade? Do you think I'm no better than my mother?" Overcome with tears, Melody raised her hands to muffle her sobs. She understood what Mama Ruth did not: Cunning lies would never cover a painful truth, no matter how thickly they were applied.

Worried about ruining her gown, Melody hurriedly wiped away her tears before they left ugly stains on the satin, and forced herself to stand. "John left a deposit with Henry. Someone at Wetherburn's will know where his family lives and I'll return it to him in the morning. That will save him the trouble of sending a servant with a letter to cancel. I know he can't want us to entertain his friends now."

Mama Ruth was about to suggest Danny run the errand instead, when she realized that would rob Melody of the opportunity to see John Cochrane a last time. Even if Melody had made up an excuse to do so, Mama Ruth readily understood why. "Yes. That's probably wise. Then we'll not have to worry about them canceling at the last minute and we'll be able to book another party in their place."

"Yes. I certainly hope so." If they were lucky, they would book several parties for the same evening so that she would be far too tired to miss John Cochrane when she fell asleep.

Melody doubted John really intended to leave town, but she left for his home early the next morning so as not to miss him if he truly had gone. She took Meribelle along with her, not to flaunt the child, but simply to give her precious daughter a pleasant outing.

They were just past the side road that turned off toward the Parkers' house, when they saw a rider coming their way. As soon as Melody recognized John Cochrane, she pulled her horse to a halt. Eager to continue, the dapple gray tossed his head to tug on the reins, but Melody held him in check.

When John drew near, Melody saw that he had no luggage tied behind his saddle. Having caught him in a lie, she felt no sense of triumph and extended an envelope in a trembling hand. "I've brought your deposit. After last night, I doubted you'd still want us to entertain at a party, and thought perhaps you might need the money on your trip." She stressed the last word, not even remotely curious as to where he had really been bound that morning.

John had endured a miserably restless night, but he was amused by her defiant gesture. A slow smile spread across his lips. He urged his bay alongside her mount, pushed the envelope back into her hands, and leaned over to scoop Meribelle from her lap.

"I've had a change of plan," he replied, "but it won't affect the party, so you must keep the money I gave Henry. Do you have time to ride with me down to the river?"

Meribelle had gone to John with a gleeful giggle, and was obviously content to ride with him rather than her mother. Embarrassed to have the money returned, Melody slipped it back into her pocket, but she didn't quite know how to respond. She had been prepared to dislike John thoroughly, or at least attempt to, but he was smiling as though they were still friends.

"I didn't mean to call on you unannounced," she murmured, her voice softening. "I simply intended to return your money."

After the way John had left the Wetherburn, he was astonished Melody would want to see him for any reason. She was the last person he had expected to meet on the road. Riding astride, dressed in pale green, her glorious red hair falling free, she resembled a goddess from the heart of the forest. Charmed by the sensual image, John could scarcely contain his joy.

"I'm sorry I was so curt with you last night. You'll always be welcome at my home, Melody. Didn't you know that?"

Melody didn't dare glance toward him, and instead kept her eyes trained on the road. She had expected him to snatch the envelope from her hand and turn away. She could have borne that insult, but she had never expected him to greet her with a smile and reach for Meribelle.

"I'd like to ride down by the river," she replied in a husky whisper, "but there's something more you ought to know before we go."

John turned his bay to lead the way. "We've not known each other long, Melody. You needn't reveal another secret until you're ready."

Melody wished that were true, but it wasn't fair to him to pretend to be someone she was not. "You are the kindest man I've ever met, and I'll not take advantage of you."

John had a firm grip on the back of Meribelle's smock to make certain she did not fall, but he was surprised by how delicate she was beneath all the ruffles. On the rare occasions upon which he had imagined himself having children, he had envisioned boys taking rough tumbles on the grass, but he could not deny how appealing little Meribelle was. "You could no more take advantage of me than you could fly," he replied.

Melody stole a peek at him, and his teasing smile warmed her clear through. "How can you be so certain? Perhaps I already have."

Twelve hours earlier, John had not been certain of anything, but after carefully sifting his memories, he had succeeded in separating what was real from what was merely artful pretense. It was only then that he had recognized Melody's touching vulnerability and been ashamed of how badly he had behaved. "If you did, I must have enjoyed it, so there was no damage done."

"No," Melody remarked absently. "It was enormous."

John wondered at the darkness of her mood, but kept his thoughts to himself as he led the way up a bluff overlooking the James River. He slid down from his saddle, with Meribelle cradled snugly in his arms, and turned to find Melody had also left her mount. She was gazing out toward the river, and the sadness in her face broke his heart.

"I used to ride up here when I was a child," he told her. "There was a time when I thought this was all there was to the world. Now I'm very glad that it isn't."

Melody's childhood memories were a blur of tiresome travel and noisy taverns, and she envied him this permanent haven. "This is your home. It's where your family lives, and all the people who matter."

The breeze off the river ruffled her hair and the soft folds of her gown. Her lashes were long and dark, but her pretty blue eyes were vast pools of sorrow. "Not all of them," he corrected her softly. "Not yet."

Melody had thought she understood all there was to know of the aching need for love, but fresh waves of longing welled up inside her now. She struggled to find the words to make the damning confession she felt sure would send him into a fit of bitter curses, but she had seen a sample of the dark side of John Cochrane's personality the night before, and did not want to coax forth another.

Sensing her distress, John shifted Meribelle to the crook of his left arm and slid his right hand around Melody's slender waist to draw her close. "You needn't tell me another of your secrets," he assured her. "Let's pretend they don't exist. I'd much rather hear about your dreams. What's your fondest wish for the future?"

Melody felt John's fingertips pressing lightly against her ribs and marveled at the tenderness of his touch. Savoring it, desperate to prolong it, she forced away her doubts and eagerly accepted his suggestion. More than willing to keep the secret of Meribelle's birth locked in her heart, she shyly raised her hand to cover his.

"I've not allowed myself to dream," she revealed hesitantly. "I'm afraid there will be too many disappointments if I look past today."

That she lacked any faith in a better future did not surprise John, but it troubled him greatly. Meribelle had begun to play with his hat, and he took her tiny hands in his and gave her an affectionate squeeze. "I'll give you until the night of our party to conjure up a dream," he told Melody. "It can be serious or silly, whatever you choose, but I want you to have at least one. Will you do that for me?"

"I can try" was all Melody would promise. "But what about you? I think you ought to conjure up one too."

Her expression had relaxed into a lovely smile, and John was relieved she had not been offended by his request. "I lead such an idyllic life, it will be difficult to think of something I don't already have, but I'll do my best to be creative. Now let's go on into town."

John held Melody's hand as they returned to the horses. "On our walk yesterday, I noticed a vacant house on Francis Street. I'd like to own some property in town and it might be a good one to purchase. I'd not want to live there, of course, but I'm sure I can find a family who'd put it to good use."

Melody didn't recall seeing the house, but took him at his word. "Yes. It shouldn't be too difficult to find someone who needs a home," she agreed.

"I don't suppose the Gilberts would be interested in renting a spacious residence while they're here?"

Melody laughed at his presumptuous question. "You really ought to wait until you own the house before you begin collecting rent on it, Mr. Cochrane. That seems the wisest course to me."

John waited until she had swung herself up on her horse and then placed Meribelle in her arms. "True, but I certainly don't want to make the mistake of buying a house that no one likes well enough to rent either."

"Yes, that is a point to consider." As they rode into town, Melody could scarcely believe how pleasant the morning had become. She had had no wish to perform at the home of a man who had grown bored with her, and would have taken great pleasure in canceling the date. That such a gesture had been unnecessary still amazed her. John's smiles were bright, and his conversation flavored with charm, so whatever problem had troubled him last night was clearly over.

He had dared her to indulge in dreams, and when they were together it was so easy to forget the past and believe in the magic of his smiles. If only every day could be as carefree as he had made this one, she would be content. John might think her foolish for wishing for something so simple, but in her mind it was the best of dreams.

John had had ample opportunity to learn Melody was not a woman who could be rushed into anything, let alone love. Setting a leisurely pace, he continued to bring treats for her family, but he took care not to be obvious with his attentions at other times. If he came to the Wetherburn, or another tavern where the Gilberts were performing, he sat off to the side and let the owner of the establishment punish any patrons who got unruly. At private parties he would send her a teasing wink rather than ask her to dance, but on more than one occasion he did meet with her in the garden and steal a light kiss.

Melody loved every minute of their chaste romance, but when the night at last arrived for the Gilberts to entertain at the Cochrane home, she still had no fanciful dream to share. She did have a growing dread that she and John would soon be parted.

She had expected him to live in a fine house, but the brick mansion overlooking the river was simply magnificent. She was dressed before the rest of the family, but John had seen the bronze satin gown on several occasions, and as she strolled through his family's well-tended garden, she wished she had something new to wear.

Then John joined her, dressed in the pale almond suit he had worn to the Parkers' party, and suddenly her bronze gown was the perfect choice to recreate the night they had met. He came close to add a gardenia to the pale pink roses she had already woven in her hair ribbons, then leaned down to kiss her cheek.

"Thank you," she whispered.

John gestured broadly. "We've a whole garden full of flowers. Do you want more?"

Melody turned away. "I wasn't referring to the gardenia, but to everything you've done for me, for us. I'll not forget these last few weeks, not ever."

John fell in step beside her. "Neither will I, but I'd much rather you remain here with me than merely exist in my memory."

Melody held her breath, not certain she hadn't simply dreamed the words she longed to hear. Then fear washed through her as she considered how different she was from the young woman he imagined her to be. It was that ideal woman he wanted, surely, not her.

"We ought to talk later," she urged fretfully, "or I'll not be able to sing for your guests."

John stopped in the middle of the walk and placed his hands on Melody's shoulders to turn her toward him. "No," he insisted firmly. "We'll talk now. We had a bargain, and you owe me a dream."

Melody stared up at him, but believed the loving light that filled his eyes was misplaced and she had to look away. "The time I've known you has been a remarkably pleasant dream," she finally answered. "When you've given me so much, I can't ask for more."

Rather than argue with her for not expecting a great deal more, John nodded slightly. "Thank you. Now I hope you'll feel obligated to make my dream come true in return." Melody shook her head slightly, but John tightened his hold on her to command her full attention.

"I bought the house on Francis Street for your family so they'll have a home whenever they tire of traveling, but I want you and Meribelle to stay here with me. I want to marry you and raise Meribelle as though she were my own dear child as well as yours."

John's voice was low and calm, each word chosen with deliberate care, but Melody was seized with a fierce panic. It took her a moment to catch her breath. She had been all too willing to put her last secret aside to preserve their friendship, but she had not imagined that John already knew it. She had to hold on to his arms to remain on her feet, but her heart was pounding so loudly in her ears, she feared it might burst.

John had expected ecstatic smiles and happy laughter, but when Melody went pale he was stunned. He swept her into his arms and carried her over to a wooden bench, where he could cradle her in his lap. He pressed her close and inhaled the floral perfume he now thought of as her own tantalizing scent. Despite her fiery beauty, she was every bit as delicate as the roses in her ribbon crown, and he loved her with a passion that grew stronger with each passing moment.

"There are several physicians among our guests," he assured her. "Shall I summon one?"

Melody shook her head and then rested her cheek upon his shoulder. That John knew Meribelle was her baby and wanted them both had simply astonished her, not made her ill, but she couldn't find her voice for several minutes. "I should have been the one to tell you about Meribelle," she finally murmured.

John spread a trail of light kisses from her damp lashes to her mouth. "No one had to tell me," he assured her. "None of your family betrayed your trust. It was simply something I saw for myself. Now, are you going to marry me? I've a houseful of wedding guests, and they're eager for us to get on with the ceremony."

Melody's lashes nearly swept her brows as she searched John's face for a telltale sign of the joke he surely had to be playing. "You can't mean that."

"What does it matter if my dream is a bit more elaborate than yours? It's the same. Now, I've waited a very long time to dance with you." He paused to nuzzle the hollow of her shoulder and drank in her resulting giggles. "You have a wonderful laugh. I'll never tire of hearing it. Let's hurry and have the wedding so that we can dance for hours and hours before we send everyone away."

The house was already ablaze with a thousand candles, and filled to every corner with guests, but Melody didn't want to leave the peace of the garden. "I can't believe your family agrees with your choice of bride, or your friends either."

John rested his forehead against hers. "As you may have noticed, I can be very determined when I want something. No one fought me on this, Melody, and if they had, why, I'd just have learned to play the violin and run away with you."

Certain he was teasing her now, Melody leaned back to study his expression, but he had never looked more serious. She raised her hands to frame his face and kissed him very gently. "There's just one more thing you ought to know," she whispered.

John stood and set her on her feet. He would never admit how sorry he was that she had ever believed she had to keep secrets from him, or how foolish he had once been to think anything that had happened in her past mattered now. "Whatever it is, it can wait," he insisted. Taking her hand, he started toward the house with a long, purposeful stride.

"But, John," Melody cried. "I can't dance!"

"What?" John halted abruptly, then erupted in deep, rumbling chuckles. "How can you not dance, when you've grown up surrounded by musicians?"

Melody shrugged helplessly. "That's just it. They were all too busy making music to provide me with a partner."

"Then I'll teach you how to dance myself," John assured her, "but my lessons will never compare with what you've taught me about love."

Before Melody could ask John to explain, they were surrounded by his friends and relatives, who were as excited as he to welcome her into their midst. After singing to please a crowd all her life, she was no stranger to such open adoration, but this was the first time it had come to her without having to perform. As John paused to pluck Meribelle from Mama Ruth's arms, she heard the Gilbert musicians begin the opening strains of a wedding march. Clearly she had been the only one among them to be left out of the wedding plans, but she was too thrilled to become John's bride to take offense.

"I love you with all my heart," John leaned down to whisper. "Welcome home."

Melody's love shone in the radiance of her smile. With John, she and Meribelle finally had a home—a home where the very best of dreams really did come true, and all the love songs were sweet.

About the Author

Phoebe Conn lives with her family in San Marino, California. Her newest Zebra historical romance, *Beloved Legacy,* will be published August 1996. Phoebe loves hearing from her readers, and you may write to her c/o Zebra Books. Please include a self-addressed stamped envelope if you wish a response.

Where Dreams Come True

Barbara Benedict

Where Dreams Come True

Barbara Benedict

One

"Our Meg can summon the Faerie Folk anytime she's of a mind to."

With a sigh, Margaret Mary McCleary set down a bucket to collect the drips from their leaky thatched roof, trying to ignore her young brother's boasting. At barely seven, Timothy thought his big sister could walk from here to London—atop the Irish Sea, to boot—and still be home in time to put dinner on the table. Meg wanted him to be proud of her, but these days she rarely had more than a crust to offer for each meal, nor much of a home for him either.

Ah, to be back in the cozy, sprawling farmhouse they'd lived in when Meg was Timothy's age. The McClearys had a fine home then, not some rock-strewn tenant farm for which Lord Gravesley charged outrageous rents. All before the Troubles, of course, when hard work reaped profits, before the English vultures began feeding off the dying carcass of Ireland. His Lordship should try breaking his back digging up rotting potatoes by day, and sleeping in this drafty hovel by night. Then they could see if he still considered it worth the ransom he charged them.

"Bah, Tim. Uncle Liam says your sister is full of the blarney."

Meg tried to like Paddy O'Neill, since he was Timothy's friend, but she found the boy as unpleasant as the stout, balding uncle he was forever quoting. But then, maybe her dislike for his uncle Liam had more to do with Liam being Lord Gravesley's bailiff, a position of which he took unfair advantage.

"Our Meg is not full of blarney!" Timothy's heated tone drew her gaze to the two boys, seated on the floor by the hearth. His red hair in need of cutting, his frame too thin for his age, Timothy seemed a neglected urchin next to the chubby Paddy. Resisting an urge to check her brother's head for fever, she wished she could have a fire blazing in the grate on such a damp, rainy day, wished they even had wood to burn in it.

She watched Paddy's pugnacious face twist in a sneer. "If she's so in tune with the Folk, then how is it she's gone past her twenty-first birthday without a mate? Uncle Liam says he'd think the first thing she'd be asking the faeries is to bring her a husband and children."

Grabbing the broom, Meg swept the dirt floor with short, hard strokes. Sure, and she wanted a family like everyone else. Her arms ached to hold a babe of her own, but with the rest of the McCleary clan lying in their graves, or off to America seeking their fortunes, she was all her little brother had standing between him and starvation.

"Yeah," Timothy said softly, "but could your uncle's sneering have aught to do with Meg's refusing him? Four times already, is it not?"

Meg smiled. He was her champion, that darling boy. A scrapper, like all McClearys, Timothy was forever bouncing back up to fight rather than staying downtrodden or glum—a lesson she should take to heart. Surely she could keep pretending to be stronger and wiser than she was for a wee while longer. Any day, their older brothers could be sending for them as promised, and they'd soon be off living the grand life in America.

"Meg!" Tim called to her. "Paddy here says you've never seen the Folk. Tell him about Prince Shane."

Meg looked away, hiding the sudden flush in her cheeks. The thing of it was, she'd stretched the truth when she'd told that story. Their grandda used to say it was a fine line to walk between weaving a yarn and telling a lie, with truth often in the eyes of the beholder. Most called her tales the gift of gab, or the art of embellishment, but the O'Neills, she feared, had little of the Irish sense of humor or imagination.

But it wasn't an outright lie, for she'd seen *someone* that night, standing alone in the mists rising off Shamorach Hill. From a distance, he'd seemed magical enough for the impressionable child she'd been, certainly interesting enough for a tale to be told later by a quiet winter fire.

And to be sure, she believed fervently in the Folk of the Middle Kingdom. Like all children in rural Ireland, she'd been bred on tales of otherworldly beings, creatures as real and mystical as the good Lord and his saints. In troubled times, both church and faerie realm were looked to for deliverance, so when Meg wasn't saying her prayers with the priest, she was out on the knolls, hoping to reach the ears of the hill-dwelling Folk. She cared little who answered her pleas, so long as she got Timmer to a warm, safe place with plenty to eat for dinner. Another winter like last one, and famine fever could well claim her poor little brother too.

"I can't be speaking of that night," she told him sternly, sweeping with extra vigor. "You know the Folk guard their privacy well. They won't be thanking me for blabbering about their affairs."

"Ah, Meg, it's only Paddy."

"Aye, today it's only Paddy, but he tells Tom, who talks to Eileen, who passes it on to Seamus, until it's the Folk themselves coming to me with a barely recognizable version. And none too pleased with my loose tongue, I might add. What then of our hopes they'll be helping us get to America?"

"Just tell us what Prince Shane looked like," Tim pleaded, his voice so young and hopeful, it was like to break her heart. "What can it hurt to be telling the color of his hair or eyes?"

She stopped sweeping. Telling the tale wasn't so much proving her claim to Paddy, she saw, but helping her brother. If Timothy needed to believe, what did it matter if she wove her yarn tighter? She'd rather be dragged the breadth of Ireland and back again than ever see that boy disillusioned.

"Perhaps you're right." Resting the broom against the wall, she settled cross-legged beside them on the floor. "To be sure, it can't be hurting anyone. But mind now, there'll be no repeating this in the village, either of you. It must stay our own little secret."

Both nodded eagerly. Behind her, rain dripped into the bucket, making the only other sound in the room.

"The Folk have their own special kingdom," she began solemnly. "Some think they're tiny, like the leprechaun, and in some places perhaps they are, but hereabouts they look so like you and me, they come and go between our worlds with nary a brow raised. I've heard it said they're fallen angels, forced to live in their narrow realm, never gaining heaven. Perhaps it's a need to atone, or merely to stop us from repeating their mistakes, but the Folk often involve themselves in our endeavors. In times of great strife they send their prince to live here, to guide and teach and even test us."

"Prince Shane!" Tim said breathlessly.

Meg nodded. "Aye, Prince Shane. He comes to show us humans we must never give up, that we must keep working and striving and fighting to make a better life, and he seeks out one brave, persevering soul to reward at the end of his visit. Now here's the magical part, because this gift is nothing you can see or hear or touch, yet everyone knows the one who's been blessed. Good luck seems to follow the lucky soul wherever he goes. As Grandda would say, he's reached the place where dreams come true."

Paddy snorted unattractively. "Uncle Liam says you've been spreading that blarney since the day you could talk. That you and your grandda made it up."

A good part of her need to go to America, Meg decided, was to get her brother away from the O'Neills. Liam had been working so long for Lord Gravesley, his entire family had begun thinking like the English.

"A lot you know," Timothy scoffed. "Tell him, Meg. Tell him about the night Prince Shane came to visit."

Trying not to squirm, Meg told herself again that it wasn't outright fabrication. "Keep in mind, now, that it was a night in late spring, the sort so alive with sound and scent and promise, you can't help believing in magic. The frogs were singing madly, the mists were on the hill, and the moon above was so bright and silver, it near hurt my eyes to gaze on it." She made wide, sweeping gestures with her hands, and like her grandda before her, used the twinkle in her wide green eyes to help weave her story.

"The times were bountiful and we McClearys owned acres of land and a barnyard of animals. Aye, I can almost hear the horses nickering in the paddocks now, the sheep bleating and cattle lowing in the pastures. Nature called out that night, not least of all to me in my bed."

"You went out," Tim prompted in a hushed tone.

Meg nodded. "Let me tell you now, the itching came over me so strong and fierce, it could well have been a Calling. I knew I'd catch the very devil for it in the morning, but it was a magical, anything-can-happen sort of night, and I was mad to be out and about in it. Creeping over the sill as quiet as you please, I streaked through the meadow—wild, free, and insanely happy. Lord knows how long I might have dashed about in such an unbridled state had I not been confronted by a sudden invisible force, as if a hand pushed at my chest. Standing still, scarce able to breathe, I looked up into the swirling mists of Shamorach Hill."

She waited a moment to heighten the anticipation, hearing the steady drip-drip behind her. Little Tim leaned forward, his blue eyes shining, while beside him, Paddy did his best not to seem eager.

"Aye," she went on, "and he seemed to rise out of the haze, glowing under the moonlight, tall and proud and pleasing to the eye. His hair was a soft red-brown, with golden highlights shining like a halo. His face could be that of an angel, strong, planed, each feature etched in perfect proportion." Close enough, she thought, for it was hard to recall an encounter of so long ago, and the last thing she'd expected that night was to find her dream man on what she'd considered her own private hill.

"What happened next? What did you do?"

She stood abruptly, not eager to admit that she'd run like a frightened rabbit. It was one thing to talk about the mystical prince, quite another to meet him face-to-face. "I can't be saying," she said evasively as she went for the broom. "I agreed only to tell you what he looked like. Anything else is disturbing the privacy the Folk guard so well. If you boys want more, you'll have to be asking Prince Shane himself."

"See," Tim said with ill-disguised satisfaction. "He did come to her. It *does* mean we've been chosen."

"Yeah?" Paddy rose also, his hands on his beefy hips as he surveyed their dreary shack. "And is this what you call being blessed with luck?"

Meg clasped her broom, fighting the urge to sweep the smirk right off his big pumpkin face. "It wasn't a true visitation that night. Prince Shane stays among us only in times of strife, remember. And before he arrives, there's always a sign."

"A sign?" the boys asked in unison.

"Aye, something out of the ordinary happens, something that makes you stand up and take notice. A change in the everyday course of life."

"You're making this up."

"No, Paddy, that I'm not." That much was true; Meg had heard the tale from her da, who'd heard it from his, and so on. "Your ma will tell you, as sure as I stand here, that Prince Shane is long overdue for a visit. If I were you, I'd keep my ears and eyes open to be ready when he appears."

"*I'll* be ready," Timothy said, shooting a glare at his friend.

"Aye, and I'm certain you will," she told him with a smile. "But now, with the rain letting up, it's time to be getting home to your family, Paddy O'Neill. You, Timmer, need to be getting washed up and into bed. Planting begins tomorrow and we've a long day ahead of us."

Both grumbled about the futility in planting potatoes that

would only rot, but Paddy eventually wandered home and Timothy went outside to wash, neither thinking to shut the door behind him. Ah, what of it? she decided. Fresh air wouldn't kill her. With the breeze blowing the storm away, it was likely damper *inside* the hut than out.

She continued tidying, determined to keep their surroundings clean and orderly. Poverty might be inescapable, her ma used to say, but no McCleary would ever succumb to filth and dirt.

Thinking of her mother, Meg felt a wave of grief wash over her. She fought the feeling, knowing there was no sense yearning for those she'd never again see. Famine fever had taken her mother and father and oldest brother; hopelessness had struck down her grandda. And poor Molly, in far-off Dublin, hadn't food or warmth enough to help survive the labors of childbirth. It haunted Meg that she'd been unable to reach her young sister, or her tiny nephew, now two months in their graves.

Liam O'Neill could scoff, but he had no idea how she longed for a family of her own to replace the loss, how she ached to fill the void her once-boisterous clan had left behind. Oh, yes, she wanted to find a man and fall in love, but these were secret, selfish wishes that must take second place to protecting her brother. Until she saw Timothy safely settled, she'd no time to waste with frivolous dreams of romance.

Aye, but she'd so dearly love a baby, a wee one like her dear departed nephew, Brian, to bring joy and hope back into their lives.

Leaning heavily on the broom, looking about the hovel in which they were forced to live, she sighed heavily. It seemed so endless, the work and worrying, only to have Liam O'Neill take all her hard-earned coins at the end of the month.

And this month, where would she find the money?

She glanced at the ceramic jar into which she'd been slipping every spare coin she could lay a hand on. Part of her longed to crack it open, to pay the rents and be done with the worry, but she'd long ago vowed that what went in that jar could not come out again. Meant for their emigration to America, it was their rainy-day nest egg and must stay where it was.

Even if they'd been having an overabundance of rainy days of late.

She looked to the half-open door. Valiantly breaking through the scattering clouds, the setting sun drew her toward its fading warmth and she stood in the doorway, gazing out over the green, rolling hills. It broke her heart to think of leaving this beautiful corner of the world, but Ireland was sick and dying and that was the way of it. She could cling to the Old Sod, perishing along with it, or she could work hard at finding her brother a home where he could hope and grow and dream.

"Give me a sign," she whispered to the powers that be. "Some indication I'm heading along the right path."

There was no answer, but then, she'd been alone with her struggles so long now, she hadn't truly expected one.

Turning back to finish her chores, she spied a slip of paper beneath the mat. She lifted it up to read the barely legible message. "Shamorach Hill," it read. "The far west side."

How odd—both the message and the means of delivery. There was something familiar about the handwriting, but try as she might, she could not place it. Was this some trick someone meant to play on her? Her gaze strayed to the dark, looming mound in the distance. Everyone knew she'd spent her childhood combing that hill for sign of the Folk. If dangling such hope before her was meant as a joke, it was a needlessly cruel one.

Then all at once a bright, gleaming rainbow streaked across the early evening sky, pointing straight to the west side of Shamorach Hill.

Logic might insist it was a natural phenomenon, common enough for their English landlord to be calling his estate Rainbow's End, but her heart told her otherwise. Surely it was too great a coincidence for that rainbow to materialize the very same moment Meg begged for a sign.

The McCleary optimism surged through her. If the man she'd seen that night *had* been Prince Shane, maybe it was too soon to be letting weariness get the best of her. Let Liam threaten eviction, let him say she was all blarney. Anyone looking at that rainbow, coming on the heels of the note, would know in his soul that magic thrived on that hill.

Imagine at long last finding the cave into the Faerie Folk realm. Would Liam O'Neill still be laughing once she and Timmer got the good-luck blessing? Or wouldn't he just turn green with envy, seeing them live and prosper in the land where dreams come true.

She had chores to finish. But once she swept up and tucked Timmer into bed, she'd be climbing up Shamorach Hill.

It would be dark by then, she realized uneasily, knowing the English curfew forbade Irishmen to be outside their homes between sunset and sunrise. Still, where was her choice? This was surely a Calling, and the Folk rarely extended their invitations twice.

Her heart skipped a beat at the possibility of once again encountering the handsome Prince Shane. After all these years of regret, of wishing she'd at least spoken to him, she could be getting a second chance. And this time, she vowed, she would not shame herself by running away.

Christian Alan Forrester sat in his father's oak-lined study, stretching his long, lean body in an overstuffed chair before the fire, savoring the vintage cognac he'd once taken for granted. With his auburn hair still damp from his bath, his stomach replete after a sumptuous dinner, he relished the luxury. Accustomed to the drab gray existence of the mean streets of London, he found the rich, warm hues of his current surroundings a balm to the soul. It was nearly enough to help him forget his five-year exile existed.

Until his cousin Gerald spoke beside him. "I need your help."

Of course, Kit thought cynically. Inevitable, that the deluxe accommodations would carry a cost. When dealing with Gerald

Forrester, the fifth Earl of Gravesley, Kit always had to pay, one way or another. "What is it you want this time, cuz?"

Sitting tall and straight on his high-backed chair, his thin dark hair cropped in a V at his forehead, Gerald frowned like a stern schoolmaster. "You're still bitter," he said, shaking his head. "But I'm not the one you should rage at. It was never my fault your father dallied with an Irish maid."

Apart from a tightened grip on his glass, Kit showed no sign the words had hit a nerve, a knack gleaned from his current acting career. Indeed, this could be his most challenging role to date, pretending that it mattered naught to him if his cousin now owned Gravesley Manor and all else he'd expected to inherit. "I hold no grudge," Kit said, nonchalantly waving a hand. "It was a blow at first, learning the truth at my father's deathbed, but all has worked out for the best. I'm too much the gadabout to settle in this stuffy old house. I prefer the grand adventure my life has been ever since."

Gerald played with his fine Irish linen cuffs, as if embarrassed by the bold-faced lie, but Kit doubted his cousin had the ability to guess the nightmare his life had become—the lice-infested bedding and inadequate food, the constant footpad dogging his heels to slit his throat.

Yet it wasn't the comforts, nor even the title Kit missed most, but rather the sense of knowing where he belonged in the world. His father's conscience might have been cleared by his deathbed confession, but it had yanked Kit's world out from under him, robbing him of his name, his home, his future. Overnight he'd gone from future earl to unwanted bastard—a social pariah to be ignored and deliberately forgotten.

Kit's sole remaining hope, the dream he clung to, was amassing enough cash to reach America. A man could buy land there, he'd been told. With hard work and ambition, he could yet carve out a future.

Getting to America was why he'd turned to an acting career, and why he'd returned to a home holding too many memories.

Kit hoped Gerald meant at last to honor his father's verbal dying bequest.

"If you crave adventure," his cousin was saying, "I might have one to offer. I've lost something. Perhaps you can find it for me."

Kit set down the glass. How typical. No display of a long-dormant conscience, no belated acknowledgment of the fourth earl's modest cash settlement. Kit had ridden halfway across England at his own expense to learn that nothing had changed, that Gerald still thought of his own needs first and foremost. "Sorry," Kit said, rising to leave, "but my troupe's to begin a Shakespearean tour of Scotland. I'll be playing Hamlet."

Not precisely accurate. The role *had* been his before his unexpected leave of absence. The stage manager's parting words, as Kit recalled, were that he'd be playing the Danish prince on the first frost in hell.

"I'll pay you." Gerald's knuckles gleamed white where they gripped the armrest. "Four thousand pounds."

Kit sat, reluctantly curious, for it was the exact sum his father had meant to leave him. More important, with what he'd already saved, it should get Kit to America, and perhaps buy a decent plot of land there.

Yet four thousand was a sizable sum and impulsive generosity was not in his cousin's nature. "I'm curious," Kit drawled. "What have you lost that can be worth that much to you?"

"Joanna."

It took all his acting ability to keep his face blank. Beautiful Joanna. It wasn't enough for Gerald to spirit her away the instant the title landed in his lap; he must call Joanna a *something,* an *it,* as though she were some trifling object he'd misplaced that morning.

Anger was futile, Kit knew, and completely unwarranted. A wiser man would have outgrown the habit of defending her years ago. What concern was it of his if pampered, willful Joanna Winston found marriage a disappointment? She had to have known Gerald was too selfish to make a suitable mate.

But then, it was the title she'd married, never the man.

"So you had some tiff and she ran away," Kit said with a shrug. "Why summon me?"

Gerald leaned forward. "You know Joanna better than anyone. As children, you were the one she would talk to, listen to. If you can't convince her to return to me, no one can."

"Provided she can be found. You must have a good dozen estates scattered about, and her family that many or more. With added friends and distant relations, I could well be off on the proverbial wild goose chase."

Gerald pounded the armrest with his fist. "You've got to find her!"

"Or what, Gerald?" Kit struggled for calm. "With what can you hope to coerce me? There is nothing left to take away."

Gerald looked away, into the fire. "You're right, of course, but it's been well over a month now, and I've grown frantic. You of all people must understand how miserable life can be without Joanna."

"You grow accustomed to it," Kit said dryly.

"Please, help me find her." Gerald rose to prowl about the room, pausing now and then to touch a marble bust, a Dresden figurine, seeking comfort from the treasures he'd amassed. "I can't endure another moment of this . . . this loneliness. Find her for me, Kit. Tell her I love her, that I'll do anything to have her here by my side."

Taken aback, Kit studied his cousin's distraught profile. He'd never guessed Gerald had it in him to love anyone, but then, Jo could charm even the hardest heart. "Aren't these things you should tell her yourself?"

"She won't listen to me." With a pained expression, Gerald faced the fire, speaking more to it than to Kit. "I forgot her birthday. She came to London in one of her snits and found me with a female. An innocent business meeting, but you know Joanna. Once she gets a bee in her bonnet, it's the very devil to dislodge it. For myself, I'd be happy to beg, but as the Earl of Gravesley, I can ill afford to be the subject of gossip."

"Instead, you will send me, your cousin? Won't everyone guess I'm acting as your agent? Including Joanna."

Gerald wheeled to face him. "I doubt anyone will recognize you. No one has seen you in years. With your long hair, those clothes—" He barely contained a shudder. "Besides, you're an actor, are you not, capable of assuming any identity you choose?"

"You expect me to don a disguise?"

"Not unless it proves necessary. Frown if you must, Kit, but even you must see this family can bear no further stain of scandal. Your own father would ask no less. He'd expect you to swear on your word of honor that you won't use the Gravesley title, or even the Forrester name."

It was a low blow, that reference to his father. An even lower one, appealing to his sense of honor. Gerald knew that Kit's word, once given, could never be retracted. "Have you thought this through?" he asked Gerald. "You are sending me in like some witless Cyrano, expecting me to woo your wife for you. What if I should opt to run off with Jo instead?"

"With what?" Gerald snorted. "You haven't a penny to prance on, cousin dear, and Joanna's tastes haven't changed. Indeed, I think you'll find her expectations higher than ever. Simply put, you can't afford her."

Having scored his point, Gerald flashed a thin smile. "The reward I offer can accomplish far more than running off with Joanna ever could. You can't tell me you won't welcome an extra four thousand pounds."

There had been a time when Kit considered the world well lost for love, but that was before suffering the loss of his world. Love was too fleeting and painful an emotion to base a life on, a lesson taught by Gerald and Jo themselves.

"Besides," Gerald went on, "you needn't contact her at all. Perhaps it would be best if you merely find her for me and leave me to do the rest."

Kit longed to throw his offer back at him, but he wanted the money owed him, *needed* it badly. Foolish, to let pride stand in the way of his future. Bringing Jo home was a job, nothing more, to be executed with a total lack of passion. His days of playing the hero were long since over.

"Very well," he said, rising from the comfortable chair. "I'll find your wife for you and I swear not to involve your precious name. Just make certain you put that four thousand in a separate account for me, for I'll be returning to collect it before the month is done."

Heading out of the room, he went to pack his meager belongings. Tomorrow he'd tell Gerald he was heading to Fox Hollow, Jo's family home in Kent, but in truth Kit would be traveling to Ireland.

For he knew better than anyone that it was there, at Rainbow's End, that Joanna Winston always went to think things over.

Keeping to the shadows as she made her way up Shamorach Hill, Meg noticed a light in the tower of Rainbow's End. In the past, it would have meant Joanna was in residence—since she alone stayed in the restored Celtic ruin—but Joanna was married now. Perhaps the light meant the earl, the well-despised Lord Gravesley, had come at last to inspect the estate.

English dog, Meg thought with a sneer. Like the rest of his race, the arrogant lout probably meant to breeze in, stir things up, and leave again at the first sign of trouble.

She reminded herself that it could as easily be Joanna in the tower. Funny, but Meg never used to think of her girlhood friend as English. Each summer she'd stayed here as a child, she and Meg had been inseparable, scouring the hills for sign of Prince Shane. Until the year they turned nine.

It was the guest Joanna had brought from England, that English boy in line for a title, who taught Meg the differences between them, traits that went deeper than nationality or social standing. Suddenly snubbed, ignored as if she no longer existed, Meg saw how little trust and loyalty meant to Joanna. It was her new English friend Joanna took searching for Prince Shane that summer. She'd given over Meg's secrets to the hateful usurper merely because Christian Forrester was the Gravesley heir.

Deceptively tenacious, Joanna had gotten her title, but Meg felt more pity than envy. She'd never met Christian Forrester, for Joanna had taken great pains to keep them apart, but a man who was so cruel to his tenants could scarce make a kinder husband.

And just what business is it of yours? she chided herself, hurrying past the estate. She had a purpose being out this night and hadn't a moment to dally. It wasn't her landlords she'd come looking for, but rather a sign of Prince Shane's upcoming visit.

Her gaze strayed to the spot where she'd seen him those years ago. With a wave of disappointment, she saw that no one stood there now. Perhaps the Calling was for something else. Gathering her shawl tight about her shoulders, she forced herself up the west side of the hill.

Aye, and it was no wonder she'd expected to see Prince Shane. It was an eerie, wind-whistling night, the sort that had one wondering where truth left off and imagination started. With the breeze dancing through her hair, she could almost hear the strains of distant music. Had the Folk taken to celebrating tonight? she wondered. If they drank like the McClearys, she must hope they weren't too deep in their cups to hear her petition.

She tilted her head to listen. The sound seemed less like music and more a keening. Chilled, thinking of the banshees said to prowl the more isolated hills and glens, she fought the urge to flee. Had she not braved this night to look for a sign? Ill spirits notwithstanding, she could not leave until she found it.

Clutching her shawl with nerveless fingers, she followed the sound, more a wailing now, to a shadowed section of the hill. All sorts of hideous creatures dwelled in the dark, she'd been told, breeding like rabbits in the underground caverns. With no light to guide her, she could well stumble into the worst of the lot and not even know until morning.

Still, she kept going, walking into the cave as if pulled by a string. "Come to Shamorach Hill," the note had beckoned, and having accepted the Calling, she was determined to see this through to the end.

Her diligence was rewarded by a faint glow, growing brighter with every step. Rounding a corner, she stumbled upon its source. Beside a flickering lantern, a tiny, wriggling bundle lay upon a bed of clean straw. It kicked at its covers, and as they parted, Meg gazed down on a red-faced baby boy, the most precious infant she'd ever seen.

And by far and away the loudest.

Dropping to her knees beside him, she lifted his chill little body into her arms. It warmed her heart how he quieted at once, his wails fading to halfhearted whimpers. Something squeezed in her chest at the feel and sound and scent of him, reminding her of the nephew she'd never held. Where was this one's mother that she could leave such a tiny babe here in this cold cavern? Had she, like Meg's sister Molly, lost her life in her struggle to bring her son into the world?

"There, there," she crooned, rising to rock him soothingly. "Aunt Meg will take care of you." Not that he looked deprived. The blanket he'd been wrapped in was of the softest, finest wool. As far as she could determine, his sole problem was a lack of food, which started her thinking. Recently widowed, her friend Mary had lost her babe to fever—maybe Mary could serve as a wet nurse. And Timothy's old cradle was still . . .

Meg stopped as she saw where her thoughts were headed. Did she truly need another wee one to think and worry about, to provide for? And the talk—merciful Lord, she could just imagine the questions the village would put before her.

But then the babe yawned, snuggling close to her chest. He needed her, this wee thing. Wherever his mother had gone, she'd seemed in no hurry to come back for him. It would be a sin, surely, to leave this baby here for the night scavengers to find.

Thinking ahead, she decided that should anyone ask, Meg would tell them this was Molly's babe, poor little Brian, whom she now had to raise. Brian, like the leprechaun, the king of laughter and magic.

Magical. Was it mere coincidence that the rainbow had appeared this evening, that a note had been on her doorstep, leading her right to this cave? Or could her wee little Brian be a gift from the Folk?

Perhaps not merely a gift. *Before Prince Shane could appear,* she remembered telling the boys, *something out of the ordinary must happen.* And nothing changed the course of everyday life more than a baby.

By faith and begorra, could Brian be her sign?

Two

Pulling her shawl tight about her shoulders, Meg glanced about as she slipped out of the cabin a week later. She hated to risk going out at night again, but she'd be seen in daylight, and then she'd be needing to explain her mission to the entire village. Everyone had accepted her tale that Brian was her sister's babe, and she saw no benefit in stirring things up.

Still, she had to find the blanket she must have dropped before rushing home from the cave. If Brian were from the Folk, they'd expect her to be taking better care of their gifts, especially a blanket of such fine wool.

Yet, to be honest, its retrieval wasn't the sole reason she risked climbing Shamorach Hill again. It wasn't precisely a Calling, like that night many years ago, but a certain restlessness had been tugging at her the week long. She'd tried telling herself she wasn't a child anymore, that she mustn't fall victim to yearnings and fancy, yet here she was, breaking the curfew and risking the penalty, because some vague instinct demanded it.

Stopping to catch her breath on the knoll before Rainbow's End, Meg eyed the estate sprawled before her, its ancient crumbling tower forming a dark, looming shadow against the moonlit sky. The villagers liked to fancy that it was haunted, that the keening within the turret walls was a banshee lurking to claim the unwary passerby, but Meg had been inside those gates and knew it was merely the wind, curling its way up Shamorach Hill.

Tonight no lamp glowed in the tower window. Someone must be in residence, however, since all would-be visitors continued to be turned away from the gate. Meg knew this, for she'd swallowed her pride yesterday to go begging an audience. With Brian, and now Mary, his wet nurse, to provide for, she needed Gravesley to be lowering her rents. Unfortunately, old friendship notwithstanding, Meg had been turned away like everyone else.

Shaking her head, she tried to put that hurt behind her. Always look about when a door slams in your face, Father Fitzhugh liked to say, for the good Lord is apt to offer another entrance. If those at the manor chose to ignore her, Meg would seek help somewhere else.

And even as the resolution formed in her brain, she saw the man on the path above her.

Heart pounding, she stopped to stare at the distant vision. He stood in the moonlight with the mists rising about him, legs astride and hands on hips as he stared off into the distance. There was no mistaking his height or the breadth of his shoulders, or the brown hair with reddish glints, the strong, planed face. His white shirt and baggy brown pants might be those of a simple farmer, but his proud stance was pure aristocracy.

Perhaps even that of a prince.

Her heart had now moved into her throat; but she forced herself to stay calm. She couldn't know for certain if he was Prince Shane, though to be sure, it seemed a great coincidence for the same man to be in the same place, and just now, when she was clamoring for a change in luck.

Yet the more Meg stared, the more substantial he seemed. He could as easily be a wanderer, whose travels simply brought him this way every few years or so. His appearance could be planned, expected, not supernatural at all. Only imagine the laughter Liam O'Neill could foster should she go blabbering this tale to the village.

A good part of her longed to bolt, for the very air seemed to crackle with uncertainty and danger, but the McClearys were a logical bunch, and reason insisted that she stay to learn what she could. She'd never discover who he was if she didn't speak to him, and she'd vowed this time she wouldn't turn coward. The good saints preserve her, but why did the mere sight of him take all her breath away?

Inhaling deeply, she forced herself up the hill.

Kit heaved a sigh of frustration. Now, too late, he realized how much he'd counted on a warm reception at Rainbow's End. Being turned away could prove disastrous, since he had no place to stay and few funds to squander on lodgings. His sole choice was to set up camp here, under the unpredictable Irish sky. Here, at least, he could keep watch on the estate. Jo had to venture out eventually, he reasoned; she'd never been one to remain long in one place.

He grimaced at the fog curling about his legs. It would be a damp and chilly night, but he'd slept in worse. At least here he needn't worry about lice.

Tossing his bag to the ground, he glanced about for fallen timber to build a fire. He was lifting up a sturdy branch, when he heard footfalls behind him. Accustomed to city dangers, he whirled, raising the limb over his head.

Relieved at first to find it was only a girl—a small, rather pretty one at that—he realized, belatedly, that she must think he was still threatening her with the branch. He lowered his makeshift weapon.

"My, but you startled me," she said, her voice rich with the local brogue. "I thought for certain you meant to be whacking me with that stick."

Kit tossed the branch aside. Reminding himself of his mission, he spoke with the same accent, practiced long and well on his journey to Ireland. "I came this close to hitting you," he said, holding his thumb and forefinger a hairbreadth apart. "Where I come from, a man protects himself first and worries over consequences later."

She tilted her head to study him, her eyes wide and curious. "And where might you be from?"

Where, indeed? "Here, there, everywhere. You see before you

stage actor," he told her with a courtly bow. "Out of work for he moment, but hopeful, ever hopeful."

"So it's just as I was thinking."

"Am I truly so ungifted, you can tell at a glance I'm unemployed?"

"No, I mean I can tell you're an actor. By your looks. You're . . . that is, none of the lads hereabouts have your—" She hesitated, looking up at his face, her blush visible even in the moonlight. "Your drama."

Stifling a grin, he fought the urge to pursue this further. "Well, I'm sorry for frightening you, but I've learned it's not wise to let strangers come up behind me."

Her smile seemed to light her face. "But we can remedy that, I'm thinking, for we won't be strangers once we know each other's name. Mine is Margaret Mary McCleary, but everyone calls me Meg."

As she stepped forward to offer her hand, Kit could feel the warmth of her welcome radiating from every inch of her. *Why, she's lovely,* he thought in a daze. Odd, but she didn't seem one whit aware of it.

He took the hand she offered, finding it as warm as her smile. Meg. Her name suited her, he decided, for she couldn't have been any more Irish, from her soft, lilting voice to the wealth of silky black hair. In daylight, he'd wager, he'd find a smattering of freckles across the bridge of her nose. "Good evening to you, Meg," he said, casting about in his mind for a fine Irish name to claim as his own. "Call me Shane," he said, recalling the imaginary prince he and Jo had once spent the summer seeking.

"Shane?" she asked with a catch in her voice. "Just Shane?"

"My family name is Woodsman." Woodsman, Forrester—he couldn't help but be amused by the play on words.

Once again she tilted her head to study him. "Then it's pleased I am to be making your acquaintance, Shane Woodsman. Forgive my prying, but you can't truly be meaning to spend the night here? You'll be catching your death of a cold exposing yourself like this to the elements."

Not knowing how to respond, for it had been some time since anyone had shown any concern for his well-being, Kit let the actor in him take over. "Ah, but what elements," he said, gesturing with his hands. "A wide starry sky, an emerald carpet, the magical murmurings of Shamorach Hill."

"It is magical, isn't it?" she asked in a hushed voice. "At times it feels as if I need merely make the wish for all my dreams to come true."

Kit more than heard the longing in her voice—he felt it. Standing there in her rags, gazing up at the heavens, she seemed so small and frail, so in need of protection.

"Yes, well," he said sharply, dismissing such thoughts. "I shall be fine. It's not as if I'll find better lodgings in yonder town. Not for the piddling amount lining these poor pockets."

"But the curfew." Her pretty face wrinkled with worry. "A fine Irishman like yourself can't be wanting to risk deportation?"

Kit had heard of the unjust curfew. "Don't you be fretting over me. I have connections." Gerald would intercede in his behalf, if only to spare scandal to the Forrester name, but then, why would Kit be arrested? He was far from a "fine Irishman."

Though he saw no benefit in admitting this to Meg. "What of yourself?" he asked. "Aren't you wary of running afoul of the law?"

She looked anxiously over her shoulder. "You're right, of course, and I must be getting back, but it doesn't seem right for you to be out in the cold and damp, when you could as easily be spending the night in our woodshed. Granted, it's not much, but it's empty and dry, and can serve as a roof over your head. I'd offer you a bed in our shack, but I can't see how it could be to your liking, what with that baby keeping all odd hours and refusing to sleep through the night."

Baby? Kit ignored the wave of disappointment. What could it matter to him if this girl was married? "It's nice of you to offer," he said stiffly, "but I'd think *Mr.* McCleary might be objecting to an unexpected guest."

"Mr. McCleary? But Da and . . . oh, my! You thought Brian was *my* baby?" She gazed up at him, searching his eyes. "Brian's my sister's babe. Poor Molly died giving birth to him."

She watched him, studied him, as if expecting to catch a flicker of recognition in his gaze. "I'm sorry to hear of your loss," Kit said, uncertain what she wanted of him. "I'm sure the last thing you want is a total stranger intruding on your grief."

Shaking her head, she reached out to cover his hands with her own. Once again he felt the warmth of her, clear down into his bones. "You're not intruding," she said, "so you can lose that notion this instant. Nor are you a total stranger, for I've seen you before. Standing here, not seven years ago, on this very hill."

Seven years ago? It must have been the night he'd been saying good-bye to Ireland. He'd come to Shamorach Hill, craving the magic he and Jo had once shared. During that last visit Jo had been more interested in flirting and dancing than in roaming the hills with him. How wistful his farewell had been, knowing their carefree childhood days were over.

And now here he was, not a guest this time, but on a mission for his cousin that required discretion. He'd a job to do, he mustn't forget, and a salary to collect for doing it. "Yes, well, I travel about quite a bit," he told Meg. "One of my favorite stops has always been Shamorach Hill."

She nodded, as if accepting his story. "Aye, maybe, but you haven't been to the McCleary place, I'm thinking. Stay with us, Shane Woodsman, and you'll soon be marking us as your first choice to visit."

"I couldn't—"

"Of course you can. My little brother would love a man about the place, I'm certain, and I sure wouldn't be minding a bit of adult conversation myself."

She made him feel as if he truly would be a welcome addition to their household, a powerful lure to someone not welcomed anywhere for a very long time. Gazing at her, Kit found himself resenting the shapeless peasant dress and work-roughened hands. What she needed was someone to spoil her, to sweep her off her feet and treat her like a princess.

A tempting fantasy, but he stopped before he embroiled himself in it. For one thing, he'd met the girl mere minutes ago, and he knew from sad experience that females rarely lived up to first impressions. And for another, as his cousin would quickly point out, Kit hadn't the means to be spoiling anyone. Five years earlier, as the Gravesley heir, he could have pampered Meg rotten, but today, as a penniless bastard, he could serve the girl better by leaving her alone.

She tugged at his arm. "Come along with you now, before we start attracting the attention of Gravesley's bailiff. Whatever your connections might be, rest assured Liam O'Neill will be in no hurry to check them. Spending the night in the tower dungeon is what he calls his *cure* for trespassing on His Lordship's lands, a remedy he takes great pleasure in administering. You'll be far more comfortable in our shed, I'm thinking."

Instinct might scream at him to run, to escape before this girl involved him in her problems, but for all Kit's cynicism, he'd never been able to resist the sparkle of fun and mischief in a co-conspirator's eye.

He could tell himself that it made sense to avoid this Liam O'Neill, that her shed *would* be an improvement on the damp, cold ground, but deep down he knew that logic had little to do with his response to Meg McCleary. The invitation she'd put into her grin had brought him back to his boyhood days at Rainbow's End, to the breathless moment he'd first sensed a door opening into a magical existence. Here in this secluded land of legend and magic, a man could forget what a nasty place the outside world could be. Here he could ignore that there was always someone, somewhere, ready to prove that dreams never come true.

Perhaps he could stay one night, he told himself as he followed her down the hill.

But any more, and he could be courting disaster.

* * *

Meg lay on her cot, fretting over her guest in the woodshed. he'd given him the best blanket and their only pillow, but still, e must find the floor uncomfortable. Perhaps she should have ffered her straw mattress.

Sure, and just where would you be sleeping then? she asked erself sternly. Heat flooded her body as the obvious answer ame to mind.

Enough of such nonsense. A girl couldn't be having such noughts about Prince Shane. It was improper, unfeasible . . .

And all too sadly true.

Even now she squirmed on her mattress as she relived the nelting fashion with which he'd gazed in her eyes. She was no tranger to such displays of male hunger—Liam O'Neill had een ogling her for years—but this time she'd been fairly stirred p herself. One glance, and Shane made her feel queer all over, et wonderful at the same time. Had he but asked, she'd have issed him right there on the spot.

Sheer folly, of course, for what in truth did she know about ne man?

She squirmed again, but now with uneasiness. Perhaps she'd een too eager to believe him Prince Shane. What if it were mere vishful thinking on her part?

Wanting and being were two separate things, her da had trilled into her. This Shane Woodsman might be the epitome of very dream she'd ever spun about their mysterious benefactor, ut he could be no more than he claimed. To her knowledge, he Folk didn't age, yet Shane had matured since his visit seven ears before. And wasn't it odd that he hadn't known about 3rian? One would hope he'd know which gift his own folk were ,ranting, even if he were not directly responsible for giving the aby to her himself.

Too, he didn't seem particularly gifted in the magical arts. Iandsome, yes—good Lord, almost too much so for her feeble eart—but Faerie Folk should have no need to be sleeping on the ground, or in their miserable woodshed. Not when with one quick enchantment he could have a ransom of gold coins in his hands.

Oh, he might have the eyes of a fallen angel, she thought with eyes so lost and lonely and needy, she'd wanted to hold and soothe him, but the more she added up the facts, the less likely it seemed he could be their mystical prince.

By inviting a stranger into her home, she could be asking for trouble.

For herself, she thought it well worth the risk, but she had Tim, and now Brian, and she'd no right to be taking chances with their future. There were men, she knew, monsters with angelic faces, who preyed on lonely women, using their caring and generosity to rob them of their meager possessions.

Yet when she considered turning Shane out, the prospect caused a physical pain.

What if he *were* Prince Shane, testing her? What would it hurt to proceed with caution, keeping her emotions tightly in check? If he were the prince, all well and good, but if he proved some ne'er-do-well, there merely to steal their hard-won savings, she'd be alert and ready to stop him.

Rolling over onto her side, seeing the cradle, she remembered too late that in all the excitement of meeting Shane, she'd once again forgotten Brian's blanket.

Three

The next morning Meg bustled about the shack, trying to make breakfast seem fancier, though there was little she could do with stale bread and a watered-down omelet. Their last six eggs for it, too, and Lord alone knew what they'd eat for dinner. Still, if the man turned out to be Prince Shane, she couldn't be stinting on hospitality.

You wouldn't be showing off your housekeeping skills, would you? asked a tiny voice inside her.

Luckily, Tim suddenly bounded in the door to divert her attention. "I hear we won't be planting today," he said, his gaze scanning the room. "Mary says we've a guest. A *real* guest, not some silly baby."

Too long the wee one in the family, the boy found it hard to relinquish his place to some squawking newcomer who kept him awake all night. Hoping to cheer her brother, Meg toyed with the idea of confiding that their guest might be Prince Shane, but she dared not trust his loose tongue. In the excitement of finding Brian, she'd told Tim the baby was a gift from the Folk, and in the blink of a lash he was heading out the door to tell Paddy. Since the last person she wanted spreading the tale about the village was Liam O'Neill, she'd done some clever backtracking to convince Tim she'd merely been teasing.

"We do indeed have a guest," she told him now, keeping her true suspicions to herself. "He goes by the name of Shane Woodsman. He's an actor, just passing through."

Tim frowned as his gaze settled on the cradle. "Maybe he'll be doing us all a favor by taking that baby with him when he goes."

Meg might understand her brother's jealousy, but she had to put a stop to it. "Brian is not going anywhere," she told him firmly. "He's family now, so we might as well be getting used to the fact."

"But it'd be so much better if he truly were a gift from the faeries."

She sighed. "That was mere wishful thinking on my part, a folly I don't want blabbered about. Can you picture the ruckus our lives would become if the village imagined we have a foundling living in this shack?"

"I know." Momentarily contrite, Tim looked up at her with his little-boy appeal. "But, Meg, if I thought we'd the favor of the Folk, that our luck would soon be changing, it wouldn't be as hard listening to all his wailing."

On cue, Brian began to whimper. Stifling a groan, Meg hoped he wasn't hungry again. Poor Mary had been playing wet nurse night and day for a week and was off on a well-deserved visit to the village.

Settle back down to sleep, Meg pleaded silently, but of course Brian did no such thing. "Tim, please, go pick up your cousin and comfort him."

Her brother eyed her as if she'd just suggested kissing a toad. "He'll just cry louder. I don't like him and he don't like me."

"Very well, you watch this pan," she said, hurrying over to inspect the baby.

Brian seemed dry enough, and appeared neither too hot nor cold. Snuggling him against her chest, crooning the lullaby her ma had once sung to her, she realized his tiny fingers clung to her dress long after his sobs subsided. "Look at you," she said, patting his little back. "I'll wager your hunger comes less from a need for food, and more from the need to be loved."

Hearing a noise just then, she turned to find Shane in the doorway.

* * *

It wasn't until he entered the shack and saw her bright smile that Kit realized how eagerly he'd been anticipating his next encounter with Meg McCleary. What he hadn't expected was to find her holding a baby.

He'd seen a hundred paintings of the Madonna with child, by both amateurs and the great masters, yet not one had captured the essence of maternal love Meg offered her sister's son. Standing together, they seemed so natural, so right—one would think she'd given birth to the baby herself.

If possible, she appeared even lovelier in the light of day, her face flushed and soft with pleasure, her luminous eyes the same shimmering green of the hills outside, her parted lips glistening like a mist-kissed Irish rose. "And if it isn't our guest himself, walking in the door." Soft and lilting, her words were aimed at the red-haired boy by the fire. "Shane, this little scamp is my brother Timothy, who we've taken to calling Timmer."

Kit pulled his gaze from Meg to the boy. Though small and scrawny, he nonetheless assumed a protective stance beside his sister, every bit the man of the house. Amused and no little impressed by his behavior, Kit hunkered down to face him. "It's beholden I am to your hospitality, Tim McCleary," he said in a fair imitation of their brogue, "and I'm hoping not to be a burden to you. If there's aught I can do to help you or your sister, you need only to call out my name."

Shaking his hand solemnly, Tim surprised him by asking, "Do you know your name's the same as the prince of the Faerie Folk?"

Uneasy under the boy's close scrutiny—as well as that of his sister beside him—Kit rose to his feet. "My sainted mother, God rest her soul, was given to flights of fancy." Her greatest fancy, Kit thought bitterly, had been in believing his father would marry a penniless maid.

"Well, I find it odd that you should appear now," Tim pressed, "just when Meg's been saying times can't be getting any harder."

"Timmer!" The look passing between sister and brother proved that for all her gentle manner, Meg still ruled the roost with a firm hand. "Where have you put your manners that you can be badgering a guest so? And why aren't you watching that pan?"

Grumbling, the boy returned to the fire, but Kit knew his questions would resume later. He made a mental note to stay on his toes around Tim.

"Do me a favor," Meg whispered, offering her bundle to him. "Please hold Brian?"

Kit took a step backward, palms extended.

"It's for Tim," she said quietly. "If he were to see you, a grown man, he'll know there's nothing to fear from holding a baby." Giving Kit no chance to argue, she thrust the infant in his arms.

The baby began to cry. He was nobody's fool, Kit realized; Brian knew the ideal spot was in Meg's tender grasp. Why accept an awkward male substitute, especially one who'd never held a baby before and hadn't the least idea how to stop him from bawling?

"He's not an egg, he won't break," Meg said softly. "Go on, snuggle him close. All he wants is to feel safe and secure and loved." She smiled as the baby settled in Kit's arms, his cries fading to sniffles. "It's a rare joy, putting that smile on his face. Doesn't it make a part of you glow?"

Kit might feel a certain satisfaction in soothing the infant's woes, but he saw no reason to make a practice of it. He wanted to hand back the baby, but oblivious, Meg continued to coo over Brian, her soft-scented hair close to Kit's face. Any glow he felt, he thought sardonically, came from his heated response to her nearness.

"Meg," Tim called out suddenly, "should the pan be smoking?"

With a squeal, she went running to her brother. "Saint Peter and all the apostles," she muttered as she yanked the skillet from the fire. "So busy making gibberish over that baby, and look what I've done. What will I serve for breakfast, will you answer me that?"

The little boy looked ready to cry. "I watched that pan, truly I did."

Biting her lip, she squatted down next to him. "Ah, Timmer, it's not you I'm angry at. It's me. This was the last of our eggs and bread."

She stood, looking about, her lower lip beginning to quiver. Following her gaze, Kit found no shelves of foodstuffs, no pantry or cupboard hiding surprises. As he realized the extent of her loss, his struggles of the last few years seemed mild in comparison. Battling lice was a mere nuisance compared to fighting starvation.

He watched Meg determinedly hold up her chin as she scraped the encrusted black mass from the pan. Trapped in poverty though she was, Meg didn't drown in tears of self-pity. She kept working, fighting against the odds to make a life for her small family.

Kit could feel the gold coin in his pocket as if it burned a hole there. It was all he had left between him and his own starvation, but he was not blind to the difference it could make to this house.

Cursing softly to himself, he crossed the room and thrust the baby in Meg's arms. "If you'll excuse us, Tim and I have an errand to run."

Although clearly confused, she took the baby without argument. It was Tim who asked, "What errand?"

"It's men's work to forage up the makings for a meal, and since I'm new to the area, I'm hoping you'll be kind enough to direct me to the nearest market."

"A trip to town?" The boy's face lit with excitement. "Can I ride on your shoulders?"

"You don't need—" Meg began to say at the same time, but Kit held up a hand to stop her.

"I'd be going to the village anyway." Eventually, he'd have to write to Gerald, so he'd need to scout out the nearest posting location. Striking a grin, he turned to Tim. "Maybe it's better that we both walk there, so you can show me the way. Though I might be coerced to do some carrying on the trip home."

"Ah, Shane, you haven't the money—"

He stopped Meg by placing a finger on her lips—a mistake. Touching her soft warmth set off alarming tremors in his body, the wide eyes drinking him in set off visions of how it would feel to hold her against him.

He stepped back quickly, knowing this a dangerous path to take. With her needs, and his dubious background, all they could ever create was heartache.

"I've enough for food," he threw over his shoulder as he went to the door, hoping his gold coin would be accepted at the local market.

Hurrying Tim outdoors, he worked hard to dispel all visions of quivering lips and fathomless eyes. Distance was the only cure for what ailed him, he told himself as he strode off, and if he couldn't maintain it, then he'd just have to leave. After all, it was Joanna he'd come to find. Joanna, who had taught where all that yearning could lead, a painful lesson he saw no need to repeat.

Touching Meg McCleary in any capacity was a pleasure he must take great pains to avoid.

Returning from the fields later that afternoon, Meg had a different view of things. To her, touching seemed a highly desirable pastime, and she wished Shane were less reluctant to indulge in it. He and Timothy had come home with a basket piled high with food, but Shane couldn't be talked into staying for breakfast. Muttering some nonsense about chores to be done, he couldn't have been in more of a hurry to leave the shack. Had she scared him, thrusting Brian in his arms without warning? Or did he feel the same odd fluttering in his insides each time their gazes met? Lord knew, the sudden lack of control frightened her silly.

"You should have seen the surprise on Liam's face when Shane handed him that gold coin," her brother was gushing beside her. "Imagine paying with *gold,* Meg. Especially considering his name *is* Shane."

Jolted out of her thoughts, Meg realized where Tim was headed with this. "Watch how that tongue of yours wanders, Mr. McCleary. Have you never stopped to consider that if Shane were the prince, he might prefer to keep his identity secret? Think on it. Why else would he be staying with us? He can choose from a hundred grander homesteads, even Rainbow's End, so why bed down in our humble woodshed?"

Tim's grin turned sly. "Could be he's taken a fancy to you."

She turned away, not wanting her brother to see her blush, nor the obvious pleasure the words brought her. "Go on with your nonsense," she told him with a shooing motion. "Stop teasing your sister and go visit with Paddy. But mind you be home for dinner," she shouted after him as he scampered off to the O'Neill cottage.

She wished she could be as certain as Tim that the coin proved Shane's identity. The Folk were famous for their gold, but a man who traveled frequently could be carrying coins as well. All it proved was that for once, the McClearys would be having a decent meal.

And in truth, did it matter if Shane were the prince or not? Wasn't it treat enough to be having such a man about the house?

She had her answer as she rounded the bed and saw Shane chopping wood in front of the shed. Naked to the waist, back muscles glistening with the sweat of his labors, he made for a grand sight indeed. Watching him, Meg felt her bones go limp and liquid. From his broad shoulders to his long, powerful legs, he was what her ma would have termed a fine, strapping specimen of manhood.

He turned, displaying the front of him, an even more impressive view. Meg knew she should look away, for a maid shouldn't be staring so openly at a man's unclad torso, but she found his bare chest fascinating. And the Lord alone knew when she'd be gifted with such a sight again.

"Ah, here you are." Putting down the ax, he reached for his shirt. "I was wondering where you'd gotten to."

"Tim and I were out planting the potatoes, though I can't see how it's worth the effort. I fear the blight will be worse than last year." Grimacing, she held out the basket. "I found a few small ones still in the ground. Not much to look at, but pared and cubed they should help stretch the soup I've been stewing from your chicken."

"That scrawny fowl?" He shuddered into his shirt. "It will be a miracle if you find anything worth eating among all those bones."

"In troubled times we learn to make do." She pointed to the pile of wood. "I must say, it's been a good long while since we've had a stack like that. There's not too much timber left to be gathered hereabout, save for the grounds of . . ." As she realized where he'd gotten the wood, she felt suddenly frightened for him. "Oh, Shane, you can't be caught taking anything from Rainbow's End. It's a punishable offense."

"Pilfering a few branches may yet be the least of my crimes," he said with a cheerful grin, "considering that I'm hungry enough to hunt down and eat His Lordship's horse. If you can indeed work miracles with a fowl, I suggest you do so post-haste."

It made her laugh, the thought of him gnawing away on Gravesley livestock, unbeknownst to the hated earl in faraway London. Apparently, Shane thought it humorous too, until their gazes met and locked. No sooner did the fluttering begin in her gut than he was looking away, marching over to stack the logs by the shed.

She'd done it again, she realized, scared him off as she'd done when she handed him Brian. Sick at heart, she muttered something inane about needing to cook her soup. He merely nodded, giving her no choice but to go inside the shack.

Preoccupied with thoughts of Shane, she was halfway across

the room before realizing that Mary sat at the table. Next to her, perched like a king on his throne, sat the obnoxious Liam O'Neill.

"Meg," Mary began, rising to her feet like a thief caught in the act. "We were just . . . I was just . . ."

"You've no call to be apologizing," Liam all but barked at her, keeping his seat. "Meg's not your mother, to be taking exception to your suitor."

Suitor? Meg had guessed Mary must be lonely, but to turn to the tightfisted Liam O'Neill, she had to be desperate indeed.

Still, since she'd made it plain that as a new part of their family this was as much Mary's home as hers, she could scarce be making objections as to how her friend spent her free time. "Don't mind me," she said with false cheeriness. "I'm just here to prepare dinner. You go on with your visit."

Rising, hat in hand, Liam fixed her with his beady gaze. "Actually, it's you I need to speak with, Meg. We've unfinished business to settle."

From sorry experience, Meg knew his "business" likely included badgering her about the rents. "No, you two go on with your chatting," she said with a shake of the head. "I'll go outside and wash my potatoes." Turning, she ran for the door, holding the basket like a shield in front of her.

Trust Liam to follow, and catch up with her before she reached the stream. He grabbed for her roughly, causing her to drop the basket. Potatoes went rolling in all directions. "Liam O'Neill," she huffed, spinning to face him, "whatever can you be thinking of, mauling me this way?"

"You know what I'm thinking." His voice was low, menacing. "Dammit, Meg, I'm always thinking of you."

"While paying court to Mary?"

"A man gets lonely." He hadn't the grace to be ashamed, shrugging off Meg's remark with not the slightest twinge of conscience. "It's a good sign, though, that the thought of me stepping out with her makes you jealous."

The conceit of the man. "Are you trifling with Mary? You'd best take care how you treat my friends, Liam, or—"

"Or what?" His grip tightened. "We're no longer children, Meg, so there'll be no more playing our games by your rules. I hold the cards now. You'll play my way, or you won't play at all."

Years ago, the village children had all thought Liam a whiner, easily dismissed and discounted. A mistake, she could see now, for at heart he'd always been a bully. He just needed size and a wee bit of power to show what a fine monster he truly could be.

Momentarily loosening his hold, he softened his tone. "Ah, Meg, my darlin', you're too lovely to be rotting in this hovel. Say but the word and you can be living the life of a queen."

"I'll be building my own palace, thank you all the same. Just as soon as I get to America."

"You and your dreams." He spat at the ground. "Do you think your older brothers are working to buy your passage? Colin is likely at the local pub, imbibing his last penny of ale, while Sean is wasting his coins, strutting his wares for the ladies."

Plagued by such worry, Meg lashed out defensively. "I plan to be paying my own way to America, don't you know, and I've a good part of it saved already." She didn't need his narrowed gaze to see her mistake; she knew she shouldn't have admitted to that extra cash the moment the words left her mouth.

"Do you now? Then maybe it's time I was talking to His Lordship about raising your rents."

Meg resorted to bravado. "You think to force me to the altar by driving me from my home? Don't bestir yourself. I'd not have the likes of you, Liam O'Neill, if you were the last man standing."

"Aye, and I suppose it's your fancy-man actor you're preferring." He pulled her closer until his mouth, ripe with the scent of stale beer and old potatoes, hovered inches from her lips. "Tell me, can he give you this?"

His kiss was a cold, wet, unrelenting assault. "Can your precious Shane Woodsman make you shiver like this?" he rasped when he at last pulled away, oblivious of her struggles to get free before retching in his face. "Is he man enough to show you what you truly want?"

"I'd say that remains to be seen," said a familiar deep voice.

With a flood of relief Meg looked up to see Shane standing behind Liam with his arms crossed at his chest. Though his smile was pleasant, his rock-hard gaze made him appear every inch her avenging angel.

"But I can assure you," he went on coldly, "that I'm more than man enough to land *you* on your boorish arse. I suggest you unhand Miss McCleary at once."

"This is between her and me," Liam blustered, but his grasp went slack enough for Meg to break free and rush to Shane's side.

"Indeed? It would seem the lady feels otherwise."

"Meg, a lady?" Liam's sneer went from her to her protector. He snorted, as if he'd taken Shane's measure and found it lacking. "And what would the likes of you know about true ladies?"

"I've enough experience with the aristocracy to know a true gentleman never forces his attentions where they're not welcomed. I'd wager your Lord Gravesley will be appalled to hear you've been using his rents to coerce his tenants to do your bidding."

Liam's sneer merely deepened. "You'd lose that bet. His Lordship cares only about getting his money. How I collect it doesn't concern him in the least."

Shane stiffened, and his voice went icily calm. "Nonetheless, your boorish behavior toward Miss McCleary must come to an end."

"And who will be stopping me?"

"I will." Shane stepped forward, putting Meg behind him. "Touch one hair on her head without her permission, and I'll make certain you'll wish you'd kept your hands to yourself."

As he eyed his opponent, Liam's courage visibly crumbled as he saw how Shane towered over him. "Yeah, well," Liam blustered even as he backed away, "don't be forgetting she's behind in her rents. She knows the consequences if I'm not paid, one way or another, by the end of the month."

"You'll get your payment," Shane said through gritted teeth. "One way or another."

"Don't you be thinking this is the last you'll be hearing from me," Liam flung out as he stomped away.

Meg watched Shane scowl at Liam's retreating figure. "I'm sorry," she said softly. "You didn't need to get involved in my mess."

"No, I didn't, did I?" He turned to face her. "It was far from my best performance. Rather cheap melodrama, at best."

"It was only too real, I'm afraid. That Liam has a mean streak. He won't like knowing you bested him, and he'll be looking for ways to get even."

"But at least then he'll be leaving you alone."

Warmth spread through her chest. "That was nice, what you did. No one has ever rushed to my rescue before."

"It wasn't much of a rescue."

"You can't know how awful it felt, having him . . ." Suddenly flustered, she remembered how Liam had compared his kiss to Shane's.

As if sharing her thoughts, Shane's gaze focused on her lips. Meg held her breath, waiting, hoping, but his hand alone approached her, reaching out to brush the hair from her face. She could see the light in his gaze, the hunger. Responding to it, she leaned closer, unconsciously moistening her lips.

"Meg?" Mary cried out from the house. "Are you all right?"

Shane took a quick step back, the light in his eyes extinguished. Partly embarrassed, but more disappointed, Meg watched him pointedly look away. "I'm fine," she lied, calling back to Mary. "I'll be in to explain in a minute."

Explain what? That she ached for a man who couldn't wait to be quit of her? She still trembled with desire, while he wore regret like a coat of armor. And no wonder. A fine-looking man like Shane would be wary of women who clung to his coattails.

Take another step near him, she feared, and he'd be making a dash for the woods.

Determined to prevent his flight, she leaned down for her basket. "I'd best be cooking dinner," she said, keeping her tone deliberately light as she gathered the scattered potatoes. "We're in trouble enough with Liam without you eating His Lordship's horse."

Her reward was a faint grin.

When the last potato sat in the basket, she nodded at the shack. "Don't look for miracles, but I'll do my best to have food on the table by dark."

"Don't hurry on my account," he said absently. "I might not even be there for dinner."

"You're not leaving?" Heaven help her, but she couldn't stop from blurting that out, though she might have managed to sound less desperate.

He frowned. "I mean to walk for a bit. Up in the hills, to clear my head. Go on and eat without me. I'll be along presently."

Watching him walk off, she told herself he'd at least be returning; she must be content with that. As long as he stayed, there was always a chance she might convince him to stay longer, though not by pleading and crying and making demands.

Since the way to a man's heart inevitably involved the taste buds, perhaps dinner was as good a place as any to start. Clutching her basket, she made her way to the shack. Tonight, she swore, she'd make certain Shane Woodsman had a meal fit for a king.

Or, perhaps more appropriately, a prince.

Kit watched Meg scurry off, wondering what had come over him. "Seeing red" had always seemed a silly term, yet coming upon Liam O'Neill mauling her, blood-red was the only color he'd noticed. So easily, he could have murdered that pompous pig. It was only her wide eyes pleading with him that had brought him slowly back to see reason.

And a good deal more as well.

Kit was far from the poetic sort, but damned if he hadn't found the wealth of Ireland in the depths of her emerald eyes. He'd let himself be swallowed up by all that gratitude, that caring, until he'd become lost to good sense. What had he been thinking, offering himself up as her protector, knowing he stayed on a temporary basis? In a matter of days he'd be gone, and then what would happen to Meg and her family?

Bad enough to put unrealistic notions in the impressionable girl's head, but to compound his crime with a kiss? He recognized the signs. He'd known what had flared between them, but he knew also that what he had to offer could only break the girl's heart.

An honorable man would walk away, and he liked to think himself as a man of honor.

Gerald would call him a fool, tell him to quit his soul-searching and take his pleasure. Lord knew, there had been a time when Kit and his London cronies had seduced girls like Meg with careless ease, thinking a shilling payment enough for the tumble. Why must his conscience put in an appearance now?

Because she was Margaret Mary McCleary. She had loyalty and integrity, all tangled up in dreams he had no wish to be squashing, which was the least he'd be doing if he stayed too long around her. It was too late for him to be laying his heart out where anyone could stomp upon it, yet such a commitment was what Meg required, what she deserved.

If he had any sense, he'd take his cue from her and return to the easy banter that kept the boundaries between them. Better, he should put distance, physical distance, between them, by moving out of her woodshed. He had a job to do, and kissing lovely Meg McCleary was not part of it. He might not be a hero, but he wasn't a cruel enough cad to raise hopes he had neither the intention nor means of fulfilling.

As he'd told her, she was indeed a treasure worth protecting,

ut he should have added that he was not, nor ever would be the
nan to do it.

Better he leave, and as soon as possible. In all, it was the
onorable—the only thing to do.

Marching home, Liam O'Neill could scarce contain his fury.
God save the world from swaggering pretty-boys like that Shane
Woodsman. How unjust, after all Liam's scheming and plotting,
hat the man should turn up now to stand between him and Meg
McCleary.

Liam knew it was a sickness inside him, his lust for that girl,
nd he would not be well again until he appeased it. He should
ape her and be done with it, but he wanted to own her, a goal
e'd have accomplished already had Shane Woodsman not ap-
eared with gold in his pocket.

Odd, that. With ever an eye for profit, Liam rarely looked
wice at those he took money from, but he found himself wondering where an out-of-work actor would find gold, or how he'd
icked up the poise and affectations of his betters. Was it boast-
ng, his claim to know aristocracy, or had he actually mingled
vith society? There was more than met the eye to this stranger,
Liam was thinking, and wouldn't it be splendid to find that one
vee lie to discredit him in Meg's vision?

Yet how did one investigate a rogue? Quite probably, it would
ake more cash than Liam cared to part with, not to mention a
wealth of well-placed connections. His sole link to England
vas . . .

Gravesley!

With growing excitement Liam thought of contacting his employer. Liam hadn't intended to tell the earl that his wife was
iding here, feeling his allegiance belonged to the Winston fam-
ly first, but perhaps it was time to reconsider. After all,
Gravesley should be grateful to learn of his wife's whereabouts,
perhaps even grateful enough to return the favor.

And while he was writing to his lordship, Liam thought with

malicious glee, perhaps he'd suggest a much-needed raise in the rents.

He chuckled as he thought of Meg's inevitable capitulation. As he'd warned, today's fiasco wasn't the last she'd be hearing of Liam O'Neill.

Oh, no, not the last indeed.

Four

As she passed through the grand entrance of Rainbow's End, Meg chewed at her lip. The long-awaited summons, coming so close upon the incident with Liam, held an ominous note. Too well, Meg could imagine the odious Lord Gravesley glaring down from his throne, demanding an impossible increase in rent. Why else would she be called there, if not for some retribution? Else, surely the matter could wait for the light of day.

If the butler were still the amiable Seamus O'Brien, she could ask him the whys and wherefores, but Lord Gravesley had replaced Seamus with a stranger from London, whose gaunt, forbidding features revealed nothing as he ushered Meg into a room at the end of the hall. The ballroom, from the size and length of it—though tonight it held a far from festive air.

A brace of flickering candles worked to dispel the gloom, as did a feeble fire in the great hearth, yet the room remained sunk in shadows. Covered by dusty white shrouds, furniture huddled in the corners like uneasy spirits in the dark. Stains bled across the faded Persian carpet, long rents slashed the worn velvet drapes, and everywhere mildew spread like a nameless plague. Once people had laughed and danced there, but tonight the place was as empty and silent and cold as a tomb.

Not quite empty. A faint cough sounded at the far end of the room. As a young woman rose from the bench behind the grand piano, all Meg's notions of meeting the stern, avenging Gravesley evaporated into the damp air. Clad in a flowing white gown and looking for all the world like a banshee, the woman leaned against the instrument as if its sole purpose were to help her remain erect. "Meg McCleary," she said on a sigh. "Dear, trustworthy Meg. Why am I not surprised to find you've grown into such a beautiful woman?"

It was the smile, weak as it was, that brought recognition. Joanna Winston always grinned so when she talked blarney. As children, they might have argued over whom Prince Shane would choose, but both knew that with her hair of spun gold, her eyes the melting brown of a doe, and her graceful frame like a willow, Joanna could pass for faerie royalty herself. Meg's own looks were common in comparison, and far too inclined to freckling to attract any prince.

Yet the years had not been kind to Joanna. Her delicate pallor had deepened, grown waxen. In contrast, dark circles now hollowed her eyes, making her seem either desperately unhappy or deathly ill.

Meg stepped forward with some vague notion of offering comfort, but Joanna squared her shoulders to assume a businesslike air. "I imagine you're wondering why I've asked you here," she said, dissolving the illusion of friendship resumed after a long, reluctant separation.

Meg stopped where she stood, the ugly scene with Liam flashing across her mind. This girl was no longer her fun-loving partner in adventure, she must remember, but, rather, the haughty Lady Gravesley.

"I need help." Joanna waved a weary hand about the cavernous room. "I can't spend a moment more in this pigsty. With the chimneys too clogged with soot, I can't light a decent fire. I shall soon be knee deep in mold and mildew, a situation my doctors insist must cease at once."

Doctors? Meg wondered.

"I can't summon my servants from London," Joanna went on, "and I trust none of the locals save you. Do say you'll help me, Meg."

How very English of Joanna, appealing to friendship when all she wanted was a maid. *McClearys are farmers, not lackeys,*

Meg wanted to shout, but times being what they were, she couldn't afford to alienate her landlord's wife. "I'd like to help, truly," she said, striving for diplomacy, "but I've a farm to keep up, a family to raise, and a mountain of chores to be doing at home."

"Yes, I hear you've a baby," Joanna said softly, leaning slightly forward. Noticing the gleam in Joanna's eyes, Meg wondered if her ailments included a fever. "Your sister's child, I'm told. Poor Meg, it must be a hardship for you."

"Hardship? You should be seeing our wee Brian." Meg stopped her prattle, knowing she might better guard the truth, or her old friend would be running straight to her English earl with the secret. And were Gravesley to guess Brian to be a gift from the faeries, it would be the last the McCleary household would ever see of him.

"Babies require a great deal of attention," Meg went on, hoping to divert her. "Even with my friend Mary helping out, I can't be taking care of Brian, and Timmer, and cleaning your house, too."

"Bring them with you." Two spots of color rose in Joanna's cheeks. "My nurse will watch over the baby while you and Mary clean, and perhaps your Timmer can help with the heavier work."

Meg couldn't picture her brother hauling trash and moving furniture, but Shane needed employment. Why, a house this size would take days to clean, which would mean he'd be needing to stay around longer.

Around Joanna, a snide little voice reminded her.

Ashamed by her sudden jealousy, Meg told herself that the proud Lady Gravesley would hardly be interested in the hired help. Still and all, Joanna's offer now held even less appeal.

"Of course," Joanna added, "I'm quite prepared to pay handsomely."

She named a sum that made Meg swoon, a more-than-handsome wage only a fool would refuse. With that much cash, Meg might yet purchase their passage to America. She needn't heed Liam's threats, or wait for a letter from her brothers.

Joanna suddenly coughed, a sound she tried to subdue by covering her mouth, but her shoulders shook betrayingly. "You won't need to start until the end of the week," she said abruptly, haughtily, as if to dispel all notion of weakness. "I have business in Dublin and won't return until Friday."

"Is it business you're attending?" It might be rude to pry—downright unwise if she hoped to be hired on—but Meg didn't appreciate being lied to. "Or is it those doctors you're meaning to visit?"

Joanna gestured ineffectually, only to be overtaken by another spasm. "As you can see," she said as the cough subsided, "my health is not what it should be."

"Then should you be traveling to Dublin alone?" Concerned, Meg couldn't help asking, "Can't Lord Gravesley go with you?"

"What, and tear himself away from counting his coins in London?" Joanna looked away, her lips tightening. "No, Meg, this is none of his affair. None of it."

"None of what?"

Joanna stiffened, again using her position to hide behind. It had always been thus; Meg's curiosity could never get past that British reserve. As children, she'd suspected the Winstons ignored their only daughter, but she could never get Joanna to talk about her parents' neglect.

"You can report to my butler Friday morning," Joanna ordered, ignoring that Meg had yet to accept the position. "He shall direct you and your entourage to the proper locations."

She began coughing again, no ladylike throat-clearing, but violent spasms over which she had no control. Once again Meg stepped forward, only to be pushed aside by a large, burly woman, pushing past to Joanna. Eyeing her stiff white clothing, Meg assumed she must be the aforementioned nurse.

Supporting Joanna's shoulders, the woman glared at Meg as if she were the root of her patient's suffering. "You must go now," she said coldly. "You've exhausted Lady Gravesley."

While Meg hated to leave her old friend in such a state and

with such a stern female, it was clear she'd been dismissed. And in truth she could not see how her presence was helping anyone.

Meg turned and was halfway through the door when Joanna called out. "You will come Friday, Meg?" the frail voice coaxed, her anxiousness echoing across the room. "You will bring your family?"

Poor Joanna, so tiny and alone in her huge, empty house. Nothing had changed; it had always been thus too. Joanna made her pretty plea, and Meg hadn't the heart to refuse her.

But all the way back to the shack, Meg fought a growing dread. Was it intuition or merely her own insecurities that had her regretting her decision? She couldn't quite shake the feeling that going back to Rainbow's End would prove a terrible mistake.

Kit paced the floor, eyeing the door, wondering just when Meg McCleary planned to come home. For all he knew, she could be anywhere—dead in a ditch, helpless in O'Neill's clutches, or having a grand time with some light-o-love he knew nothing about. And all while he spent the night wondering what to do with her sister's baby.

It was far from how he'd pictured the evening. Tears, he'd expected, or perhaps a few sighs of regret, but his noble decision to leave in the morning lost momentum with each second Meg failed to appear.

Her friend Mary hadn't been much help. She'd claimed to have no idea where Meg had gotten herself off to, which posed quite the dilemma, since Mary herself needed to step out a wee while. Telling Kit that his stew was warming on the fire and that Timmer and the baby were tucked into bed, she'd slipped out the door before he'd fully realized that she'd left him alone to watch over the boys.

And the moment she'd gone, Brian began to holler.

Having spent an hour walking with the infant, crooning to him, Kit was now relieved to see the little eyes drifting shut. Gingerly, he leaned down to set the baby back in his cradle, only to have the crying pipe up again. "Tyrant," he growled. "Is there no one you haven't got jumping through hoops to please you?"

Tiny fingers curled around his own, causing a pang in his chest. *This little boy needs me,* he thought. *Me, who's never been needed by anyone.*

Seeing no hope for it, he resumed his rocking.

It was this place, he thought resentfully as he paced with Brian. The scent of wildflowers and fresh baked bread, the stew bubbling on the fire, the riotous flowers in a jar on the table—all those homey touches seduced him, made him lose perspective. He wasn't there to babble like some infatuated fool over a drooling infant. He had to find Joanna, collect the money Gerald owed him, and be on his way across the Atlantic.

Only, where was Meg?

Anger shifted into dread as he thought of O'Neill's threat. What if he were right, what if they hadn't heard the last of him? The brute could have cornered Meg in some dark, empty lane where no one could hear her cries for help.

Pacing the floor with the infant, his mind building upon this gruesome scene, Kit was primed to slay a hundred dragons by the time the door burst open. He was not, however, prepared to watch Meg breeze in, safe and intact and lovelier than life itself, her flushed face leaving him to wonder if she'd just been kissed silly.

Jealousy spiked through him. "Where the hell have you been?" He rounded on her, furious that he'd worried where there was no real cause.

She tilted her head, clearly puzzled. "I was summoned up to the manor," she began hesitantly. As her gaze dropped to the baby in his arms, the color drained from her face. "Dear Mother of us all, what's happened to Brian?"

"He's fine." Kit stepped forward, thrusting the baby in her arms. "Take care with him, for it took me forever to stop his bawling. My limited talents do not include playing nanny."

"Where is Mary?" Bewildered, she glanced around the empty room. "She said she'd stay with the boys."

Kit shrugged. "She stepped out for a moment. We expected you home long before now."

"She'd better be back before your night feeding," she told Brian as she crossed the room to settle him in bed. "Heaven help us all if you must wait too long for your next meal." Softly, she began to sing.

"He's partial to Brahms," Kit suggested.

Meg smiled, an expression so fresh and guileless, it could well be a warning arrow aimed at his heart. She made him feel things, this gentle woman, embroiled him in emotions he had no business entertaining. Getting to America was his sole goal, and he was too close now to be distracted.

What did it matter if Brian quieted when Kit sang to him? What did he gain by having Tim gaze up at him with adoration and Meg with trust? Only a fool would risk the future on such fleeting emotions, a lesson he should have learned at his father's deathbed.

"Meg," he said quietly, clearing his throat.

She tensed, a nearly imperceptible motion he would not have noticed had he not been watching her every breath. He was reminded of a doe, alert and wary of the hunter creeping ever closer.

"I'll be leaving in the morning," he said bluntly.

"The morning?" She rose slowly, the tension more visible now. "And why so soon?"

"I think it best that I find other lodgings."

"Do you now? And what has you thinking that?"

"I can't be imposing on your generosity," he lied, trying hard not to focus on her lips. "I can never repay your hospitality."

"And who's mentioned payment?" He might have suggested killing the pope, from her reaction. "As if a McCleary expects a return on their hospitality. Do you know what I'm thinking, Shane Woodsman? That maybe you're too proud by half, and overconcerned with money."

"Meg—"

"Don't you 'Meg' me. We wouldn't be eating today if not for

your basket of food. And here you are, watching out for the wee ones while Mary takes it in her head to be gallivanting off. It's me who can never repay *your* generosity, I'm thinking. Me who's beholden to you."

She was so fervent, so incredibly lovely in her need to reassure him, it was all he could do not to relent. "Dammit, Meg, I don't want you beholden to me," he ground out brutally. "I'm a wanderer. I can't be tied to any one person or place. I breeze into a different village each week and stay long enough only to earn what I need for my travels."

"And what if I could offer employ—"

"I have to go, Meg," he told her firmly, turning to leave, meaning to cut off any further opportunity for protest.

He received unwitting help from Mary, who burst through the door as he reached it, looking flushed and excited. A swelling about the lips proved she, indeed, had been kissed silly.

Brushing past, Kit made his escape. As he shut the door behind him, he told himself, *There, now that is that,* but he felt no real satisfaction, no sense of accomplishing what he'd set out to do.

He left feeling empty and hollow instead.

Meg longed to go running after Kit, but she had Brian and Timmer to consider. She must first make certain that this time Mary would remain with them. "You're home to stay, I hope," she asked the woman more sharply than she'd intended. "You won't be stepping out again?"

Mary, who'd been bending over to unlace her shoes, looked up in surprise. "Will ya listen to you, now? What has your young man done to put you in such a bother?"

"I am not in a bother, and he's not my young man."

"You'd know best, of course." Mary grinned knowingly. "Still, since your gaze hasn't left that door since he stepped through it, why not just go out and talk to him as you're so clearly burning to do?"

"I'm not the one burning," Meg said indignantly, fearing Mary must have been out with Liam again. "I have business to discuss with Shane."

"Do you now?" Mary chuckled. "Ah, lass, why be in such a hurry to deny your feelings? Why cheat yourself of the best life has to offer?"

"What am I being offered? He's leaving in the morning." Meg was horrified to hear how flat her voice sounded.

"Then all the more reason to go now and talk him out of it. I promise, I'll be here for the wee ones if that's what's giving you pause."

Biting her lip, Meg eyed the door. "If you're sure . . . well, maybe for just a moment . . . it is important, after all."

"Aye, that it is."

Meg paid no heed to the teasing note in Mary's voice, preoccupied with what she'd say to Shane. Going to the door, she hesitated at the threshold. "Mary, how is it . . . I mean, with a man . . . how do you know when he's meaning to kiss you?"

Mary gave her a dreamy smile. "Ah, lass, you can't be mistaking it. He gets that look in his eye, the one that makes you swear you're the only thing existing, and you find yourself breathless and warm all over. It's a rare pleasure, your first kiss, and let me tell you, you can't ask for a more perfect night to be getting it. So you go on outside and talk to your young man, Meg, and I'll sit in here, hoping the best for you."

Too sorely tempted, Meg slipped out the door. As she made her way to the shed, she saw that it *was* a perfect night, the air warm and balmy, the sky etched with a thousand constellations.

Though coming out here had nothing to do with romance, she insisted to herself. It mattered little how gently Shane held the baby, or how he made Timmer laugh, and good heavens, she'd more vital concerns occupying her mind than whether or not the man meant to kiss her.

Knowing all this, however, didn't stop the rush of emotion when she saw him standing outside the shed. Tall and gloriously handsome, he dominated the moonlit landscape with his solitary figure. She sensed an overwhelming sadness about him, could feel his pain in the pit of her stomach.

He didn't see her at first, so she should have had time to recover, yet gazing at his profile made the ache in her tighten. She longed to touch him, shield him, hold his loneliness at bay.

Stunned by the depths of her feelings, she realized Mary had been right. There was no use pretending she felt otherwise; somehow, despite the brief span of time, this mysterious stranger had become an integral part of her life. It no longer mattered if he was Prince Shane or just a roving actor, someone had to fill up the emptiness she saw in him.

He turned suddenly, his unguarded gaze linking with hers. "Go back to the house, Meg," he said softly, as if recognizing a few hard truths of his own. "Please, don't make this harder."

"You want to be moving on and I'd be a poor friend indeed to stand in your way." She plunged right in, speaking too fast to be interrupted, ignoring her own fears in the face of his need. "But before you go, you might want to consider this. If it's cold hard cash you're after, and you're not afraid to dirty your hands, we've been offered a job, you and me, up at the manor. Cleaning's not the best work, I'll grant you, but the pay is substantial and we can consider it a rare privilege to be let in the gates of Rainbow's End."

His stance altered, became alert and wary. "Rainbow's End?"

"Aye, His Lordship's estate, the one you were gazing at the night I found you. I wouldn't suggest this post had Lord Gravesley hired us, but I've known Lady Joanna since we were children and we can trust her to treat us fairly."

"This Lady Joanna—you saw her? Spoke to her?"

Did he think she'd lie to him? "Aye, that's where I was tonight. I feared Liam had brought about the summons, but no, it was Jo—Lady Joanna asking us to come clean the place for her."

"She asked for *me?*"

She'd expected a yes-or-no answer, not this untoward interest in her one-time friend. Her jealousy stirred once more, Meg resorted to petulance. "Now, how could she be asking for you when she's never met you?"

"Quite so." He forced a laugh. "Well, I must say, it sounds a marvelous opportunity. Do we start in the morning?"

Her heart leapt at his use of the plural pronoun. "Not until Friday," she told him. "Her Ladyship has business in Dublin till then. Though, of course, you're welcome to sleep in our shed in the meantime."

He looked behind him, then back to her, clearly weighing things in his mind. Ah, but to know what those "things" entailed.

"I'll stay only," he said at last, "if I can earn my keep. Come tomorrow, I'll start gathering wood to fill the shed for winter."

Alarmed, she reached for his arm. "Oh, but you mustn't be caught taking timber from His Lordship's lands. You could land yourself in prison."

He glanced at her hand with a frown. She removed it quickly, telling herself that touching Shane did queer things to her insides anyway.

"Lord Gravesley can't be that much a tyrant," he said stiffly. "All that wood lying around unused. Why not let his tenants take it?"

"Oh, we can take it," she rattled on, grateful to get past that uneasy moment, "if we're willing to have a hefty fee tacked onto our rents. Which, I might add, already far surpass the property's value."

"But the man is a nobleman. He must have a sense of justice."

"British justice," she said bitterly, "has one set of laws for the Irish, and quite another for those born in England. Traveling as you do, maybe you don't know how it's been for us farmers since the famine began, but let me assure you, our fine English landlords have no intention of sharing the burden of a failing potato crop. On the contrary, the more we lose, the more they wish to take."

"You must be exaggerating."

"Must I?" She told him how her folks had been forced from their home, how her grandfather sickened and died of heartache.

"Look around and tell me I've reason to trust anything British. All the starving babies and still they take our few remaining crops to sell for a profit elsewhere."

"But to let innocent children suffer? There must be a reason."

She shrugged. "Perhaps it's greed, or mere contempt, even hatred for our people. Sometimes, I think the English won't be happy until every last Irishman gives up the fight and leaves for America."

"But not you, Meg," Shane said quietly. "I bet you'll stay until the fight's knocked out of you."

She shook her head sadly. "That's something I can't afford to do, not with Timmer, and now Brian, to look after. In truth, I'm merely waiting to hear from my brothers, right now on American soil, looking for a farm we can afford. The very minute they find one, they'll be sending for us. My hopes are on Sean, for he's less likely than Colin to be wasting his coins on ale, but just in case, I'm taking any odd job that comes along. I might not be much of a maid, but I can't afford to turn down this position at Rainbow's End."

"Nor can I, I suppose." His thoughtful expression focused on her face. "Although I can't claim my motives are as unselfish. Tim and Brian are two lucky lads."

She blushed, warmed all over, but she couldn't accept his praise. "It's what family does, Shane. We're supposed to look out for each other."

"It was never thus in mine. Perhaps had I someone like you behind me while I was growing up, it might have made a difference."

Wanting only to banish the hurt in his voice, she stepped closer. "Ah, but I am behind you, Shane. I'm your friend now, and I won't be letting any harm come to you either."

He grunted. "You have enough on your plate without heaping a lost cause like me onto it."

"Don't we all have our burdens? It's only by sharing them that we make them lighter."

"Nothing gets you down, does it? How can you remain such an optimist?"

She grinned. "Isn't it odd? My ma used to call me a pessimist, for I was forever grumbling about the rain as a girl. Shaking her head, she'd say I could waste my day complaining about things I couldn't change, or I could skip outside and have fun looking for rainbows. Nowadays, each time I see that sweet, blessed miracle of light arc across the sky, I understand what Ma meant. It's the hope of a rainbow, Shane, that makes the rain endurable."

As she spoke, she unconsciously reached out to touch his arm again, to offer her reassurance, but instead of frowning, he stared so deeply into her eyes, she felt as if her very soul had been bared to him. And then there it was, the look that made her swear she was the only thing existing, and an intensity that near took her breath away as his lips brushed her own.

Mary was right about this too, she thought. Kissing was a rare pleasure, indeed.

Warm and sweet, his lips moved over hers, gently at first, but increasingly hungry and demanding. Lost to all thought, swept up in a current of overwhelming sensation, she leaned into him, wanting more. As his arms encircled her waist, pulling her closer yet, she melted against him, no longer knowing where she ended and he began. No longer caring.

It was Shane who drew the distinction, pulling away with an abruptness that left her stunned. "I shouldn't have done that," he said, his voice terse and rasping.

She had to bite her lip to keep it from trembling. That kiss had been the most glorious experience of her life, the culmination of years of yearning, and he spoke of regret? "Well, you did do it," she said, forcing herself to sound calm and composed and far more reasonable than she felt, "so there's not much sense in wishing otherwise. For my part, I found it far more pleasant than I expected, given my experience with Liam."

"Meg—"

She held up a hand to stop him—she couldn't bear an apology. "You've no cause to fear I'll be following you about like a mooning calf, for I've a hundred and a half chores to better occupy my time. I'm not saying that I didn't enjoy that kiss, mind you, or that I'd be reluctant to try again, but rest assured, I won't be pulling at your sleeve or getting teary-eyed when you decide it's time to go. I'm not making claims on your life, Shane. I'm just offering you a job."

"Yes, at Rainbow's End." He looked away, his voice flat. "I should just leave, Meg, as I intended. Trust me, you'll be better served if I do."

"You'll be leaving soon enough, I'm thinking, but in the meantime, we can still be a friend to you, Timmer and I. Stay and be part of our family for just a wee while longer," she finished off, touching him gently on the shoulder. "What can be the harm in that?"

She left him then, knowing there was little more she could say. He would either be there in the morning when she woke, or he would not.

It didn't stop her from saying a little prayer though—to the good Lord, and, for good measure, another to the Faerie Folk of Shamorach Hill.

Kit watched Meg leave him, not daring to speak. In truth, what could he tell her? That he didn't deserve her friendship, that he meant to use her to get to Joanna? Soon enough the sorry details would be out. Meg would discover that he was English, and part of the despicable Forrester family—an illegitimate part at that—and she'd turn from him in disgust.

God help him, but he wished he could have found her sooner. Had she happened earlier in his life, they might have stood a chance, before hard experience taught him to be jaded and cynical.

Rainbows.

How easy she made it sound. Listening to Meg, kissing her, he'd had a taste of what it could be like, a future filled with hope and love. Holding her in his arms had been like going back to his childhood, to the days when he'd roamed these hills with Joanna, her tales of mythical creatures bringing his imagination blazing to life. Meg, with her own special brand of magic, made him wonder that if a man worked hard enough and didn't give up, could any dream—even his own—indeed come true?

Reality snapped him back into focus.

They came from vastly different worlds, he must never forget, with a mountain of hatred between them. Hearing her rattle off her accusations against his countrymen, he'd seen little hope of mending fences. Nothing could change the fact that he was English and she Irish. Meg might kiss Shane Woodsman, but she'd promptly toss Kit Forrester out on his ear.

Yet he was tempted to stay. Too sorely tempted.

It would only get him in trouble, pretending to be what he was not, but she'd thrown out the most irresistible lure of all. *Stay and be part of our family,* she'd tempted. *What can be the harm in that?*

A few short days, he promised himself, just a small, brief time of playing the role of his life. Come Friday, Meg would see him with Joanna, and learning the truth, she'd come to hate him soon enough.

But until that time, didn't even a bastard deserve a few days of pretending he had a true family? That he too could be loved?

Gerald Forrester, fifth Earl of Gravesley, stared at the fourth earl's portrait with a now-familiar twinge of inadequacy. Uncle Edward had never recognized his genius, ever preferring the bastard he'd sired. No doubt he wished his precious Kit stood in Gerald's shoes that very moment.

God bless the British rigid rules of entailment as well as his uncle's stiff conscience. Up until the end, Gerald had feared Uncle Edward would try to pass Kit off as the legal heir, an eventuality he'd schemed and plotted a lifetime to prevent. Armed with evidence, Gerald could have taken Kit to court and won, but he was just as glad his uncle had in the end listened to reason.

Gerald had no wish to drag the Forrester name through the scandal. If he'd learned nothing else from Uncle Edward, he knew that to hold one's own in society, the family reputation must be zealously upheld.

He frowned as his gaze went to the table, to the letter from Ireland. Had he known Joanna would cause such trouble, he'd never have married the silly bitch, despite the pleasure he'd derived by taking her from Kit. Did she truly think she could hide from his wrath at Rainbow's End? By now she should have realized that her husband had his spies everywhere.

Gerald smiled as he imagined Kit chasing from one corner of England to another. The decent thing would be to call off the search now that the wayward bride had been found, but decency had never been his strong suit. He'd far rather ignore Kit's existence, as he'd done so successfully these past five years.

Besides, his gallant cousin might insist upon accompanying him to Ireland. Gerald didn't need Kit at the tearful reunion, or learning the real reason Joanna had left him. Kit, with his lamentably keen sense of honor, could well ruin his careful plans. All that righteous anger could stir up more trouble than Gerald could currently handle.

No, he must prevent Kit from learning anything, by whatever means necessary. And as the Earl of Gravesley, he had a good many means at his disposal.

Kit wished to leave England—perhaps Gerald could help his cousin along, have him shanghaied. That should prevent any unpleasant scene or nasty revelation, as well as all unwanted stains upon the Forrester name. It would be a shame should Kit die in captivity, but then, it would mean one less nuisance with which Gerald would need to deal.

Yes, once he punished Joanna, he'd dispose of his cousin.

All rather neat, actually. Crumbling the missive and tossing it into the fire, he barked for his valet. No time to lose. He would travel to Ireland on the morning tide.

Five

"But, Meg," Tim begged two nights later at the dinner table. "You promised if I helped with the planting, you'd tell one of your tales tonight."

Kit saw the harried expression she tried to hide from her brother.

"Aye, that I will," she said cheerfully enough, "but first I've got the dishes to wash and sweeping to do, and with Mary off to visit with Liam again, I've got to see Brian settled in bed."

Tim made a face at the cradle. "That baby always comes first."

Seeing her shoulders sag, Kit intervened. "That's because Brian's too small to do for himself. Maybe there's something we men can do to help your sister."

With a grin, Meg nodded toward Brian. "Well now, his nappies need changing."

As Kit groaned inwardly, Tim rose indignantly to his feet. "That's women's work! Paddy says—"

"I'm aware of the nonsense his family spouts." Meg rose beside him, green eyes glittering with her own indignation. "Michael O'Neill preens over siring ten lusty babes on his poor Eileen, yet what effort did he put into it save strutting about the village the day they were born and drinking himself into a stupor? Had he bothered to change a nappy now and then, or stay up pacing to calm the babes' colic, Eileen might have survived past the eleventh year of their marriage. A man who takes his pleasure and then shuns his responsibility, I'm thinking, is no real man at all."

Just so, Kit thought, remembering the kiss he had taken from her.

"And just what," Tim asked, "has pleasure to do with siring babies?"

Helplessly, Meg glanced from her brother to Kit. It was time, clearly, for the boy to learn how babies were made, but this was something a father should relate, not a sister. Even had Meg the knowledge or experience to carry it off, she had worries enough without having this thrust upon her too.

Kit rose reluctantly to his feet. "Come along, Tim. Let Meg finish the dishes and we can muddle through this nappy business. While we're at it, perhaps there's a thing or two about babies you and I can discuss."

It was a rash offer when he hadn't the least idea how to proceed, yet he would make it a hundred times over to see the lift in her shoulders.

Or so he thought until he stood in the corner by the cradle, struggling to make sense of the cloth Meg had handed him. Fold and twist though he might, he could not get it to adequately cover the baby's bottom. "What do you think?" he asked Tim, holding up the nappy.

But the boy showed less interest in covering that part of Brian's anatomy than he had in cleaning it. "You said we'd talk about siring babies," Tim urged, prompting a soft chuckle from his sister.

It was his own fault for volunteering, Kit thought with a reluctant grin. Figuring it was a case of in for a penny, in for a pound, he laid the cloth out for a fresh fold as he plunged into his explanation.

Sweeping under the table, Meg strained to listen as Shane spoke to her brother. From the sound of their struggles, she'd need to fix the nappy later, but how could she quibble when

Shane set such a fine example for Tim? And when he relieved her of the duty of this man-to-man talk.

"They do *what?*" she heard her brother cry out, clearly appalled.

"It's the way of it, Tim. Men and women are like pieces of a puzzle, meant to come together."

Looking over to the corner, she saw Tim shake his head thoughtfully. "I've seen horses and cows, of course, but I can't say they seemed to be taking much pleasure in it."

"Ah, but there's a certain magic between a man and his woman. A lure exists, drawing their souls together, so their mating becomes a thing of beauty and a force too hard to resist. Some say it's God's way of making families, since their joining, like as not, results in a baby."

Tim was quiet a moment, as if digesting the information. "Is it like that between you and Meg?" he asked, his tone thoughtful. "Do you feel the lure when you're around her?"

Horrified, Meg turned back to her sweeping, pretending to be too busy to hear them, though she strained to catch Shane's reply.

He spoke slowly, carefully. "The thing of it is, Tim, your sister and I can never be more than friends."

"But I saw you standing up to Liam O'Neill for her. And you're always looking at her as if she were a stick of candy."

"Am I now?" Shane gave a short, bitter laugh. "That's because Meg's a real pleasure to look at, and one of the sweetest souls I've ever known. But the sad fact is, I'm not the marrying sort, and that's the *least* your sister deserves."

Meg let out her breath. A lot of pretty words in that statement, but the result cut her hopes dead.

Yes, but just what had she been expecting? That a fine-looking man like Shane Woodsman would leave his career and devil-may-care lifestyle for the likes of her? He'd made it clear from the start that the instant he earned enough to fill his pockets, he'd be taking his leave without looking back.

Her throat tightened at the prospect of his departure. Gazing at his profile, drinking in the sight of him as if it might be her last, she felt a fierce, hot need sweep through her. It was shameful, perhaps even sinful, but she craved to be in Shane's arms. Surely that was where she belonged, experiencing all the joys a man could give to a woman.

No, there was no sense denying the lure was there. The question was, what did she hope to do about it?

"Meg?" Tim said suddenly, drawing her gaze to their corner of the room. "We've put Brian to bed. Can we have our tale now?"

Flustered by her thoughts, Meg started to mutter about her unfinished chores, until Shane stepped forward to take the broom from her hands.

"Can't you clean later?" he asked, resting his hands over hers on the handle. "For now, come sit and enjoy the fire."

She found it impossible to breathe, much less speak, with Shane standing so near and her mind tumbling with needs and desires. *He shouldn't be looking at me this way* was all she could think, fighting an urge to throw her arms about his neck. If his hunger were as deep and commanding as his eyes suggested, then he should forget all else and just kiss her.

"C'mon, Meg, and tell us about the Faerie Folk of Shamorach Hill," Tim said, startling them both and causing Shane to remove his hands from hers. "Tell us about the night you first met the prince of the Faerie Folk."

"Go on with you," she said shakily, stepping away from Shane's overwhelming presence. "Who'd want to be hearing that tired old tale?"

"I would," Shane said all too steadily. "Come sit with us, Meg, and let's hear your story."

She envied his ability to act as if they hadn't just shared a breathless moment. But then, considering what he'd just said to Tim, perhaps the breathlessness was all on her part, the sharing only in her imagination.

Removing her apron, she told herself she'd spin her yarn and that would be that. But she'd barely gotten to the part where she'd climbed Shamorach Hill, when Mary breezed in the door, humming softly, wearing the air of a woman who'd been recently loved. Distracted from her story, Meg battled envy. Just once she wanted to look like that, feel like that.

She glanced up at the one man who could make it happen and found Shane watching her.

I *must have him,* she thought desperately, *even if for only one night.*

It was wicked of her, she knew, and quite likely mad. The last thing she needed now was to be pregnant, but Shane could be gone tomorrow and then her yearning would never cease. Wasn't it better to have one night of bliss and suffer the consequences than spend the rest of her life wondering what might have been?

The prospect alternately thrilled and terrified her. It was a risk, surely, for what if he laughed at her—or worse, smiled indulgently as he shooed her away? And even if he did kiss her, would she know what to do next? She'd been raised on a farm, true, but as he'd told Tim, it was different with animals. By impulsively rushing into this, she could well make a mess of everything.

But then Shane smiled, encouraging her to go on with her story, and his tender expression warmed its way to the core of her heart.

Aye, she would take the risk, for she was brimming over with love for this man. And there was a chance, however small and tenuous, that he might come to realize that one blissful evening was not enough. That there were worse things than staying in one place, with one woman.

Rapidly winding up the story, hushing Tim's protests that she'd left parts of it out, she asked Shane to settle her brother in bed while she had a few words with Mary. She had a special place in mind, a magical place, and she wanted Mary to watch the boys while she and Shane visited it.

One way or another, she meant to prove to Shane that the "lure" existed. Then she'd wait and see what *he* meant to do about it.

* * *

Kit was thinking about Tim's words as he strolled beside Meg in the moonlight. How daunting, that his longings could be so obvious when he gazed at this woman. Had everyone seen his need but him?

Useless, now, to deny his feelings, or to pretend he could control them. Indeed, he was finding it easier to understand why O'Neill made such a pest of himself. Being near Meg and playing the gentleman grew more difficult every day. Each time she'd laugh, or gaze up with her soft emerald eyes, Kit would think back to their kiss. It was all he could do not to snatch her up and carry her off. All in all, he had no business being alone with her on this soft, balmy night.

Only a proper cad would start something with so many lies between them. He should not imply promises he could never keep; he had nothing to offer. He was a loner, the bastard son of a British earl, an out-of-work actor who could barely support himself. Even were he crazy enough to suggest taking Meg and her brood to America, where would he find sufficient funds to transport them? Worse, he'd need that money before morning, for it would be too late once they walked through the gates of Rainbow's End.

He could imagine Meg's reaction when Jo called out his true name. Meg loathed the Forrester clan with a hatred she had every right to nurture. Once she learned Kit was Gravesley's cousin— worse, that he'd lied to her, using her goodness and generosity to contact Joanna—Meg's trusting gazes would chill with disdain. In her eyes Kit would have proved no better than Gerald. At long last he'd have his funds for going to America, but there would be no taking the McCleary brood with him.

Meg interrupted his thoughts, pointing at the trees ahead. "There it is, my favorite spot. On the other side of the stream there's a glade where you can see clear to the top of Shamorach Hill. As a girl, I'd come out here many a summer night to watch the stars. It's a magical place, you know, an altogether too perfect spot for spinning dreams in your head."

Taking his hand, she led him through the trees and over the stream. Kit knew he should go back to the house, but something about the glade drew him closer. Meg might have termed it a Calling, but he was far more apt to blame the allure of the woman tugging him forward.

She stopped in the middle of the clearing on a bed of soft moss. Ancient, towering oaks formed a circle around them, guarding it, keeping the rest of the world from intruding. A soft breeze whispered in the leaves overhead, adding to the sense of seclusion. A child would feel safe here; anyone would.

"My, but isn't this a glorious night," Meg said in an awed tone as she twirled before him, gazing up at the sky. "My grandda used to say the stars are sparkling diamonds that the Folk sprinkle across the heavens. Every so often, he claimed, a gem will drop, so it's the wise traveler who keeps his eyes and hands open. I used to watch the sky every night, hoping to catch one to help my family with our failing finances, yet fretting over how it would affect the Folk. I thought it must be a hardship for them, having us mortals depleting their treasure."

"I would think, being magical folk, they'd have taken such losses into account and more than made up for them."

She grinned. "That's what Grandda said. He insisted that diamonds are just rocks, after all. Helping others is the true source of happiness."

Kit found himself wishing he could have met this grandfather.

"Aye, and on a night like tonight," Meg went on, gazing upward, "I can't help but think the Folk must be feeling extraordinarily happy and generous. I ask you, have you ever seen so many stars?"

"Yours is most definitely a unique way of viewing the world. Do you and your grandfather have a tale for every occasion?"

She laughed easily. "Living among these rolling hills, how can you *not* believe in the mysterious and uncanny? Up there on Shamorach Hill, in among the outcroppings and underground caves, I swear you can actually feel the magic beneath your toes. I'm convinced, though I've yet to be able to prove it, that that's where the Faerie Folk dwell."

Shamorach Hill, Kit thought with a wistful smile. "As a boy, I had a friend who lived and breathed such legends. I found it contagious. I wanted to believe in faeries too."

"Funny, I did the same to my friend." Staring up at the hill as if she could see herself playing there, she drew her shawl tighter about her shoulders. "At first I had to coerce her to go roaming the slopes with me to find Prince Shane. Folks thought it odd for us to be such friends, she being so timid, and rich, and English, to boot. It baffled them how I led her to share and perhaps even surpass my obsession, but thinking back, I suppose she was just looking for love. Considering how her parents ignored her, poor Joanna must have been terribly lonely."

"Joanna? Not the Lady Joanna we'll work for tomorrow?"

She nodded, clearly surprised by his sudden interest.

Odd, not to have realized they could be childhood friends. Thinking back, he could see Meg's touch in all the stories Jo told him, though Jo's renditions now seemed pale in comparison.

For that matter, everything about Jo seemed to fade in the light of this woman's vitality and warmth.

"She's married now, of course," Meg added quickly, "so perhaps she has found someone to love her."

What she'd found, Kit thought, was his cousin Gerald. "Even married," he said aloud, "she must be happy to have a friend like you."

"Ah, but we stopped being close long ago." Smiling sadly, she gestured at the moss, then took a seat. "It sounds silly and childish, I suppose, but she lied to me and I've not been able to forgive her for it."

Kit sat beside her, sinking into the moss, his body more comfortable than his mind. No, Meg would not take kindly to deception. "What did she do?" he prompted, hoping Jo's crime would make his own seem harmless.

She shrugged. "We had this sacred pact, you see. We solemnly swore to work hard, the two of us alone, until we found Prince Shane and his magical kingdom together. Though sorely tempted, I made sure to limit my searching to when she came each year for her summer visit. Imagine my dismay when one year she came to Rainbow's End without warning and I was turned away from her gate like some dirty beggar."

Kit knew the feeling. He'd felt as if he'd been punched in the gut the day Jo told him she was marrying his cousin.

"I doubt she'd even have spoken to me had I not stumbled upon her in the village," Meg went on. "What a stranger she'd become, cold and hard, demanding I stop pestering her. She had a new best friend, she told me, a boy brought here from England, and she didn't want me near him. His name was Christian Forrester, but she called him Kit, purring the name like he was some overstuffed cat and I was a disease from which he needed protection. She announced that *he* would help her find Prince Shane, so if I didn't want me and my family arrested, I'd best be keeping myself away from Shamorach Hill."

"She could hardly make good on such a threat."

"She's English, is she not? And her family owned half the county. Oh, I did my searching at night, when they were to bed, but let me tell you, my bitterness festered. Her precious *Kit* was everything I despised most, rich and arrogant and spoiled beyond good sense. My brother Colin worked in the Winston stables, and he told me how His Lordship pitched a fit when his horse wasn't there waiting for him, no matter how unexpected his appearance. It made me furious to think Joanna was sharing my tales, my adventures, with such a lime-livered English brat."

"Actually, I've met your Christian Forrester. In London, doing a play there." A foolish ploy, perhaps, but Kit felt compelled to defend himself. "He was a regular enough chap, though given the circumstances, I suppose he might once have been a trifle arrogant. Boys of his station are raised to value their own consequence, you realize. It's expected of them."

She made a most unladylike snort.

"Yes, well," Kit went on, adding to his defense, "perhaps it will help to know he's had his comeuppance. On his deathbed his father made it clear that he was illegitimate and unworthy of any consequence at all. The title passed on to a cousin, as did the Gravesley estates, so that by the time I met Kit Forrester, he had nothing but the shirt on his back. Overnight he'd lost everything. Friends, future—even his own family shunned him."

"That can't be true." She seemed puzzled. "He was quite good-looking, my brother said. Surely, there was a woman who loved him."

"One would have thought." Hard to keep the bitterness from his tone. "He was courting your Lady Joanna at the time. They were madly in love, and planning to marry, but since he no longer had a name to offer, he had to stand aside while she married his cousin instead."

"His cousin? But I don't understand. If she loved him, what should it matter what side of the blanket he'd been born on?"

"Few women want the father of their children to be a bastard, Meg."

"Bah!" She rose up to her knees, facing him, her body a study of indignation. "You're talking about a few lines on a piece of paper. Love and caring is what makes a man a father. Titles can't change what he is underneath. You know what I'm thinking? She can't have loved him very much to have given up so readily."

No, but then, there had been no room for grand passion in the ordered world he and Jo had shared. How could love conquer all, when each emotion remained stored in the proper compartment, to be trotted out only when the occasion called for it?

Meg would never grasp such a stilted relationship. For her, love should be like the wildflowers blanketing her verdant hills, meant to blossom with glorious abandon, a gift of nature to be given and taken freely.

"If I loved a man, I wouldn't care what the world called him," she told him solemnly, her steady gaze twisting his heart. "I would stand firm beside him, no matter what."

He reached out to touch her face. It was all he dared do, for the cynic in him found it hard to believe her. Oh, she might want to love him, but the faith he now saw in her eyes would collapse like a wounded soldier when faced with the truth.

"What if he'd lied to you, Meg?" he probed. "What if he'd deliberately let you believe things about him that weren't true?"

She tilted her head, studying him for a moment. "I would imagine he had his reasons. And I'd be happy to hear him explain them to me."

"Ah, Meg—"

She reached out to put a finger on his lips. "Some things are just meant to be, Shane. The hardships, the misunderstandings, they're just obstacles to be gotten over in life. A man and woman can work out most anything if they truly desire to be together."

She held hope out to him like a dangling, dazzling thread. It was at that moment that he realized he loved her.

"Just tell me, do you feel it, Shane?" she whispered, her eyes drinking him in. "The lure, is it pulling at you too?"

Taking her hand, he kissed each finger, unable to stop his lips from trailing up her slender arm. "You're so damned beautiful, Meg," he ground out hoarsely. "How is any mortal man supposed to resist?"

"Don't. It's meant to be, you and I. Listen, feel. Can't you sense the magic?"

And indeed he could. Gazing into her eyes, finding all he sought and more within the emerald depths, he surrendered his battered heart into her care.

Threading his fingers into her hair, he pulled her face to his. As his lips touched her trembling mouth, he could swear he heard the breeze whisper its encouragement. The earth he lowered them to seemed to pulse with a similar energy, the same primitive need that throbbed in his veins. And as he rolled with Meg in the soft bed of moss, his brain hummed with a primitive rhythm, chanting over and over that this was his woman. And here was his one slender chance to prove that whatever obstacles lay between them, she was meant to be his.

Slowly removing each article of clothing, he revered each inch of her body, glorying in the sweet, blossoming miracle of

Meg McCleary, from her lean white thighs, to the luscious, creamy breasts she offered so freely. Licking her budding nipples, taking each breast into his hungry mouth, he made certain she would never forget his touch. Every moan from her lips was a vindication, an invitation, and he went half mad with wanting more.

He kept repeating her name, over and over with each new part of her body he tasted, until it became an intonation, an unconscious pleading with the powers that be. For he knew, even in the driving force of desire, that this was but the start of his need for this woman. There had to be more than just one night together. Running his hands possessively down the length of her body, he swore he would take her, brand her, make certain she remained his forever.

And he would do it now.

Ripping at his trousers, his shirt, it was not until he knelt poised between her legs ready to thrust into her that he saw her wide, frightened eyes. He'd forgotten, in light of her eagerness, that this would be her first time at loving. He cursed himself for a thoughtless beast.

But when he would move away, she reached for his hand and set a kiss upon it. "It's meant to be," she repeated, placing his hand on her breast. "Can't you feel my heart beating for you? My entire body quickening? I want this, Shane. I want you to be part of me."

With a groan he slipped into her, taking care to be gentle, crooning endearments into her ear as he eased past her resistance. After that it was no easy thing to maintain control, for Meg was wet and hot and welcoming, meeting his every thrust with one of her own. He could feel his heart thunder in his chest, beating faster, louder, as they soared together toward an impossible peak. He stroked her, kissed her, craving all of her at once.

His greedy lips were on hers when he felt her first startled gasp, and her telltale tightening about him. His arms gripped her waist as she began to shudder, moaning into his mouth, until he too exploded with a mad burst of color. A rainbow of clear, sparkling color.

Pouring his seed into her, his very heart and soul, he clutched Meg tightly against him, making certain they would not draw apart on the slow, spiraling descent to reality.

Yet the magic could not shield them forever. Rolling off her, lying at her side, he grew steadily aware of the enormity of his actions.

"Oh, my," she said after a moment of silence.

Oh, my, indeed.

Lying on her back, gazing up at the heavens, Meg wondered if she would ever breathe normally again. In all her wildest imaginings, she could never have anticipated this delicious, fluttery feeling. It was amazing, incredible—dear, sweet Lord, but she loved this man with all her being.

She turned on to her side to see Shane better, to touch him and make certain that what they'd just done and felt was altogether real.

He faced her, reaching out to trace her cheekbone, his touch light and tender. "Ah, Meg," he said, sighing as if the weight of the world lay upon his shoulders. "I should never have let myself do that."

"Excuse me for thinking so, but to my recollection there were two of us involved in the act, were there not?"

"Most assuredly." He grinned reluctantly.

"There you have it, then. Don't be putting yourself in a hair shirt, Shane. It was the lure, plain and simple, insisting we come together."

He rolled onto his back. "But it's not plain or simple, Meg. We've got to consider the consequences." He pushed up from the ground and rose to his feet. Grabbing his trousers, he shrugged into them.

Meg sat up, watching him gather up their clothing. "Like as not, we'll have but this one night together," she said, not liking the quiver in her voice. "I for one want to savor every moment. There'll be plenty of time in the future for dealing for what life throws our way."

He tossed her dress on her lap. "You could well have a child."

You could have a child, not *we*. Foolish, to feel disappointment. Shane had never pretended to be the settling-down sort.

Nonetheless hurt, she let the dress lie unheeded in her lap. Considering her cycle, it wasn't likely she'd be having a baby, but she wouldn't be shunning her responsibilities if she did. It would mean further hardship and sacrifice, but the child would be part of her, and part of Shane, and she could not bring herself to regret it. "Don't worry," she told him. "I've got money saved in my jar in the kitchen to tide me over."

"Meg—"

"I'd care for that babe just as I do for Brian and Timmer, and every day I'd be blessing my lucky stars for having that little bit of you still with me. No matter what you say or do, I won't ever be sorry we came together. Look at me, Shane, and tell me you don't feel the same."

He gazed down at her with all the love and longing she could hope for. "Ah, dammit, Meg, a man could get lost in the depths of your eyes."

"Go on with you now. That's the pessimist talking. An optimist would be thinking he might find himself there instead."

He turned abruptly, pulling his gaze away. "No, I'm being realistic. It's an ugly world out there. There's so much you don't know about it."

Reaching for her dress and slipping into it, she waited to hear what was truly bothering him. As each second ticked by, she realized he meant to withdraw into himself, shutting her out. "Maybe that's true," she told him firmly, "but is that any reason to stop striving to make your dreams come true? I still say that for every storm there's always a rainbow."

"You and your rainbows." Sighing, he straightened his shoulders. "I wish I had your faith, Meg, but it's a bit late for me to be trusting in faeries and magic."

She strove for the right words to convince him. If only she could gather up the charm of this glen and wrap its special aura around them, form a protective shell against the ugly realities of the outside world. Sighing, she found herself staring up at Shamorach Hill.

Bathed in moonlight, it gave off a golden, otherworldly glow, seeming more than ever the shimmering oasis of enchantment. *Come,* she could almost hear it beckon.

The cave, she thought instantly, remembering the rainbow that led her to Brian—and ultimately to Shane.

Rushing to his side, she knew she must take him there and explain how she knew they were meant to be together. "If you can spare the time," she told him, linking her arm through his, "I'd like to show you that dreams truly can come true."

Walking beside Meg up the slope, Kit battled his conscience. Sweet, generous Meg had left the path clear for him to leave in the morning. It would be best this way, making the break neatly and cleanly.

Yet there was the hope she'd offered him, a slim thread of possibility, that left him wondering if he shouldn't take the chance and confess the truth. Hearing the truth from his lips might soften her sense of betrayal.

She lied to me, she'd said of Joanna, *and I've not been able to forgive her since.*

"I have a confession to make," she said suddenly, stopping before a dark, yawning cave. Her words so nearly echoed his own thoughts, she could have been reading his mind.

Something was troubling her, he could see by her solemn expression. So he listened as she told him about the rainbow that had lured her up there. How when she'd stumbled upon him, she'd thought him to be Prince Shane. "You looked so like his earlier visitation, you see," she explained sheepishly.

Kit realized that she must have seen him on his last visit to Ireland. It made a perfect opening for his own confession, but

Meg went on quickly. "The signs were there, even the extraordinary occurrence. I was altogether certain you'd come to take us to the land where dreams come true."

"But now you're not?"

"Aye, well, you said it yourself that the lure happens only between a man and a woman. And there's no denying that was a flesh-and-blood man who taught me the mysteries of love this evening."

He fought the hot, pulsing bolt of desire. Tell her, his conscience demanded. Confess the truth now, logic insisted and there might yet be a prayer for them.

Once again, she spoke first. "More important, tonight helped me realize that I don't need a visitation, that you are my blessing. You and . . . better yet, come, let me show you." Giving him no chance to argue, she slipped inside the cave.

"It's pitch black in here," he protested, though too curious by now not to follow. "How can you know where we're going?"

"It's just a wee bit farther. Don't worry, I've been here before."

He had to trust her—until she suddenly released his hand. "Meg?"

"It's all right. Just wait while I find the light . . . ah, here it is."

He heard a rasp, and then Meg stood before him, holding a flickering lantern, gesturing about the cavern in which they now stood. "This is where I found my first true gift from the faeries."

At their feet, Kit now noticed, lay a rumpled bed of straw. A very tiny bed.

Meg made a noise, then scrambled over to a soft yellow bundle by the wall. "I always meant to come back for this, but one thing after another got in my way. I was out seeking this the night I met you, Shane. It's what drew us together."

"A blanket, Meg?"

"Not just any blanket." She held it against her cheek, rubbing her face against it. "See how softly woven it is, clearly crafted by loving hands. Look at it, touch it. Have you ever seen wool so fine?"

Taking it, Kit felt a sudden chill. Oh, yes, he'd seen such wool. He knew the special weave, recognized the "G" embroidered on the satin border. He himself had once been cuddled in such a blanket.

His mind raced, adding up the possibilities, coming up with a solution that made his blood run cold. "Who does this belong to, Meg?"

She gazed at him as if he'd lost the better half of his brain. "Why, Brian, of course. He's our gift from the faeries. Our blessing."

He gripped the blanket with nerveless fingers. "You found him here, in this cave? I thought he was your sister's child."

"I wanted to still the talk in the village. I feared that if Lord Gravesley learned how special Brian was, he'd want him for himself."

It was all he could do not to groan. Kit might now be the Forrester bastard, but his sense of family duty remained. A duty that demanded he go to Gerald with this.

For unless he was very much mistaken in his calculations, young Brian could well be the Gravesley heir.

Gerald stepped off the quay in Dublin, glancing about for his bailiff. He should have anticipated that O'Neill would be late. His cronies at the club warned him against hiring the Irish, calling them dull-witted and lazy, but until now it had suited Gerald to have this fool running things at Rainbow's End. While he needed his Gravesley estates to flourish, those Joanna had brought to their marriage were ripe for the picking. For five years Rainbow's End had kept him in gambling funds, but now that it was nearly sucked dry, it could well fall to rack and ruin.

But not, he amended, until he got his hands on his wife.

"Lord Gravesley?"

Brushing past, Gerald barely glanced at his plump overseer. "You're late," he sneered, seeing no reason to hide his disdain as he strode to the waiting carriage.

"Yes, well, it was Her Ladyship that detained me," the fool blubbered, stumbling in his wake. "Has the whole house in disarray."

Gerald spun on a heel, fixing him with his stoniest glare; "And who pays your wages?"

"Aye, and sure enough you do, Your Lordship, but with her health not being what it should be, and her just returning from Dublin, and this stranger sniffing around at the gates—"

Gerald's patience, nearly worn thin with the idiot's prattle, snapped at the thought of a male stranger in his home. "And who is this man you've allowed near my wife?"

"Didn't you get my letter, asking about him?"

Gerald shook his head irritably.

"He's tall, with auburn hair and blue eyes, and goes by the name of Shane Woodsman, though I'd not be surprised to learn it's a fake. Usually is with those actor gents."

"Actor? That must be my cousin," Gerald blurted out, appalled. "Trust Kit to use such a twist on the family name. Damn him, why isn't he in England?"

Too late, he saw the knowing gleam in his bailiff's eyes. So much for keeping Kit's involvement a secret. Never one to regret his impulses, Gerald moved on to the next order of business. He had to get rid of Kit; he wanted no well-meaning witnesses when he dealt with his errant wife.

"You, bailiff," he barked, unable to recall the fat oaf's name. "Hire a horse and ride on ahead. Warn anyone visiting my wife that if they are still inside when I reach there, they shall be considered a trespasser and dealt with accordingly, to the full extent of the law. Do I make myself clear?"

A smile spread across his bailiff's jowls. "Aye, that you do, Your Lordship. Warning your wife's guests will be my utmost pleasure."

Gerald stared after the man as he hurried off to the stables. He realized that he and his bailiff had something in common. As he anticipated the possible confrontations ahead, he too could not stop a slow, spreading grin of satisfaction.

Six

Early the next morning Meg sang to herself as she made her way to the woodshed, her heart near to bursting with joy and love. Now that she'd told Shane the truth about Brian, she felt as if a weight had lifted from her shoulders. True he'd seemed a bit preoccupied as they'd walked down the hill, but then, it would take time for a cynic like Shane to get used to the magic. Though, heaven knew, they'd made a good start on it last night.

Warmed by thoughts of their lovemaking, she stepped into the shed, eager to see him again, to wake him with a kiss. But to her surprise and increasing dismay, there was nary a soul in the shed.

He must be gathering wood, she thought, going out to look about the yard. He wouldn't leave without word or warning. Yet the more she searched, the more uneasiness blossomed into dread. His tender kiss as they'd parted last night took on a new, more dire meaning.

She hurried to the shack, praying she'd find him waiting for breakfast. What a big fake she was, saying it didn't matter if they had but one night together. Already her heart ached so, she feared it might snap in half.

Shane was not in the shack either. She wanted to cry, but one glance at her sleeping brother warned her to hide her pain. Poor Tim had grown fond of Shane. He'd be missing him enough without her long face to look at.

Biting her lip to keep it from trembling, she reminded herself that until she took care of the boys and their future, it was not for her to entertain romantic notions. She'd let Shane distract her, but now it was time to be going to Rainbow's End. That was her goal—getting the boys to America. Without Shane there to claim a share of the earnings, and with what she'd saved in the jar, there might be enough for their passage.

Yet when her eyes sought the jar, needing the reassurance it always gave her, she found it lying on its side. Stifling a gasp, she ran to lift it up. A single tuppence fell to the floor.

Shaken, Meg flopped back in a chair, remembering how she'd told Shane about her savings. He wouldn't have taken her money, she protested silently, he couldn't have. Leaving was one thing, as roving was in his nature, but to steal her hard-earned pennies—no, she couldn't believe he could be so petty and selfish and stunningly cruel.

Shaking Tim awake gently, she asked if he'd been playing with the jar. From his bewildered expression, she had to believe his protests that he'd never touched it. She'd have asked Mary next, but she discovered her friend had apparently left the shack. More confusing still, she seemed to have taken Brian with her. Staring at the empty cradle, Meg had the ugliest sensation that her life had spun out of control.

She ordered Tim to get dressed and took him out searching for Mary, but the woman wasn't gossiping with the neighbors, nor doing laundry at the stream. In the village, Terence Kelly told them he'd seen Mary earlier, on her way up to His Lordship's manor. Yes, she was carrying a bundle, but whether or not it was a baby, Terence couldn't say.

Meg tried to find reassurance in this. In general, Mary was an early riser; perhaps she'd wanted to get a head start on their work. Yet, as they stood before Rainbow's End, Meg couldn't shake the feeling that something was very, very wrong.

Nor did it help to be halted at the gate by Liam O'Neill, charging up on a lathered horse. "Where is he, your pretty boy?" he barked out as he slid from the saddle. "The one who calls himself Shane Woodsman?"

Sheltering Tim as she moved them away from the skittish animal, Meg shook her head. "He's gone. Left this morning."

Liam laughed noisily. "Must have gotten wind of His Lordship's visit. So much for his fancy ways and pretty speeches. Gravesley comes to town and he bolts like a frightened rabbit."

Was that truly why Shane left so abruptly, why he'd felt compelled to take her money? But what threat could Gravesley possibly pose?

She must have asked the question aloud, for Liam answered gleefully. "What a sham, calling himself Shane Woodsman. I just learned from His Lordship himself that he's in truth the earl's cousin, Christian Forrester. Was real close with Her Ladyship years back, it's said in the village. What do you wager he's been playing a game with the likes of you, while doing his true entertaining here at the manor?"

Meg went instantly cold. Her Shane, a Forrester? The so very English *Kit* Forrester?

Liam grabbed her, spinning her to face him. "You're better off without him. Can't you see I'm by far the better man for you?"

She pushed free, conscious of Tim's wide, bewildered gaze. "What I'm seeing, Liam O'Neill, is that you're standing in our way. Lady Gravesley is waiting for us, so if you'll move aside, we'll be going in that gate."

His face grew dark with anger. "You hope to skip off to America with your wages? There will be no job for you, Meg McCleary. Not if I have aught to do with it."

"That's Jo—Her Ladyship's decision, not yours." Grabbing Tim's hand, she pushed through the gate. "We're going inside, Liam, and you can't stop us."

"Maybe not," he called out behind them, "but Lord Gravesley will be barreling down that road any minute, and he'll be stopping you soon enough. You go and enjoy your visit, Meg, though it be of short duration. And in the meantime, you start thinking about how you'll be paying your rents."

Ignoring his nasty laughter, she hurried through the door,

dragging poor Tim behind her as she fought a rising desperation. With her rainy-day savings stolen, and Liam threatening to stop her wages, where would she find the funds for her and the boys to survive?

"Don't worry," Tim said gently by her side. "Shane will help us."

There is no Shane, she wanted to shout, alternately hurt, then angry at his betrayal. His true name was Kit, an actor who played his part to perfection, save for the wistful note when speaking of his lost love. What if Liam were right about why he'd come to their village? What if, all along, Kit had been after Joanna?

She felt sick to think how he must have laughed at the silly Irish girl who fawned over him, snickering at the humble poverty of her home and family. Gazing down at her sweet, trusting brother, she cursed the man she'd loved so completely a short time ago. Bad enough to deceive her, but he'd used Tim, and Brian too, and for that she could never forgive him.

Not waiting for the butler, she barged in the house, seeking Mary and the baby. She was eager to have her family gathered safely around her.

She found her friend in the hallway, twisting her apron with nervous fingers. "Was that Liam I heard?" Mary asked eagerly. "Is he home at last?"

"Never mind Liam," Meg snapped, good and truly alarmed to find the woman alone. "What have you done with Brian?"

"Weren't me. It was him, that Shane." With a nervous glance backward, Mary pointed up the stairs. "He's up there with Lady Joanna."

Stunned by the news, Meg could barely react. Part of her longed to rush to him in overwhelming relief that he hadn't left after all, but a more logical part pointed out that he was with Joanna. Her mind played out the scene last night, her heart protesting his innocence as she remembered his plea for understanding. Surely, he'd his reasons for what he'd done, and it would take a mighty poor spirit indeed not to listen to them.

If only he hadn't run straight to his beloved Joanna.

Old insecurities surfaced. How could she hope to compete with the rich and beautiful Lady Gravesley? On the other hand, why should Meg bestir herself? Kit Forrester was a liar, a traitor, a thieving . . .

It struck her then, the true extent of his treachery. While she lay sleeping, he had crept into her house and taken Brian.

Telling Tim to wait with Mary, she turned for the stairs, not much liking the implications behind why he'd brought the baby there. One look at his face, she promised herself, and the argument could rest in her head. One glance at the pair of them, and she'd know the cold, hard truth.

Kit gazed down at the woman he'd once loved, feeling nothing but pity. Bundled in her shawl, dwarfed by the huge, stuffed chair, Jo looked more the aging dowager than the reigning beauty of London.

"Just tell me, is he yours?" he asked, his very tone an accusation as he held Brian out. "Is this poor, helpless infant my cousin's heir?"

She looked away, nodding slowly.

"Was a baby too great an inconvenience," Kit exploded, "too much the drain on your social life, that you could feel justified in abandoning him in some cold, dark cave?"

"I didn't abandon him," Jo cried out. "I waited there, shivering in the shadows until I saw Meg take him away. Until I knew he'd have a home."

Ah, so there was life in her. If only he could goad her into showing a conscience. "But he already had a home. Gerald can certainly better provide for the Gravesley heir than some penniless Irish peasant."

"Provide what? Wealth, title, connections? Tell me, Kit, in the end, what good did any of that do for you?"

"The direct cut," he drawled, stung. "It was ever your specialty. But tell me, Jo, are you saying this baby is a bastard too?"

"I suppose I deserved that, but no, I was faithful to Gerald.

He made certain of it." She shuddered. "But can't you see why I want more than position and money for my son? I know Meg, how big her heart can stretch, and I know she'll love him like one of her own."

"How? Can't you see she's a breath away from the poor-house?"

"I meant to provide money," Jo said defensively. "With her stiff pride, I knew Meg wouldn't take charity, so I offered her a job here. Besides, whatever hardships he'll face with Meg, my baby will be safe and loved. Which is a damn sight more than I can say if he stays with his father."

"This is your flesh and blood," he said angrily. "Not some pawn to force your husband into compliance."

"You don't—" Her angry outburst dissolved into a spasm of coughing.

Kit took a step forward. "Good Lord, Jo, what's wrong with you?"

She waved a hand, dismissing her attack as of no import. "What did he tell you?" she asked in a measured tone. "That this was some silly snit?"

"He mentioned you'd caught him with another woman."

"How inventive he's grown, but then, he's had practice. Gerald's quite clever at divining what you want to hear. Lord knows I listened heedlessly enough. Until after we were married."

"Come now, we played together as children. You knew his shortcomings as well as I."

"Yes, you did try to warn me, but not even you guessed the depth of his cruelty. He beat me senseless, and often. Not because I was faithless or disobedient, but just for the sheer pleasure of it. It helped relieve his ennui, he claimed."

Seeing her hopeless expression, Kit tightened his arms instinctively around Brian. If Gerald could do such things to a grown woman, what would he do to a helpless baby?

"Quite so," she said, noticing his reaction. "I know you think me selfish and shallow, but I swear, this one time I was not thinking of myself. You can have no conception of how empty it makes me feel, giving up my son." She looked up at him, eyes glistening, pleading. "I don't suppose, one last time, I could hold my baby?"

Kit could remember the many times she'd wheedled her way around him, yet he found far more in her yearning expression than a spoiled young miss wanting her way. It was a mother's love for her son he now saw, and he hadn't the heart to deny her.

She smiled tremulously as he set the baby in her arms. "He's a beautiful babe, isn't he?" she asked as she hugged Brian close. "The one truly fine thing I've done in my life. I can't let Gerald get his hands on this boy, ruining him as he has all else he's ever touched."

"Wasn't leaving him in a cave a bit drastic? Wouldn't it be simpler to take him away somewhere?"

"I won't have the chance." She wouldn't look at him. "Our last set-to, Gerald was especially rough. He broke my rib. I thought it healed, but during . . ." She grimaced, gazing down at the baby. "It was a hard birth and the doctors think I've torn up a lung. They don't offer much hope."

"My God, are you saying you're dying?" Kit felt pummeled. "Why didn't you come to me? You must know I'd have helped you."

She smiled gently. "I hadn't the nerve, after how I treated you. Besides, you've always had more of a conscience than any of us. I feared you'd see it your duty to report to Gerald."

Grimly, Kit thought of the letter he'd meant to send to England.

"But of course, that's why you're here, isn't it?" Her eyes narrowed as she gazed at him. "What did he promise you to find me?"

She made it sound like blood money, which, in light of what she'd told him, perhaps it was. "Four thousand pounds," he told her. "The money my father promised me."

"I take it Gerald didn't reveal the full terms of Edward's will."

Puzzled, Kit shook his head. "We both know I'm the last one Gerald would ever confide in."

"Yes, well, I myself might not have known had I not gone out on my own one night and suffered a carriage accident. A minor one, but Gerald was in a rage when I got home, ranting about me risking the life of our unborn child. That I was eight months along didn't stop him from beating me, however, and while he did, he shrieked out why a son was so vital to him. Your father gave Gerald precisely five years to produce an heir or the bulk of the Forrester fortune must be given to a distant cousin. Come November, Gerald will be a virtual pauper. He'll have the title and Gravesley Hall, but barely a penny to sustain them."

Kit gazed down at Brian. "But he has an heir."

"Gerald's son died of childbirth complications," Jo said with a small, secretive smile. "I filed the death certificate two days ago in Dublin."

"It's quite an elaborate hoax, Jo—"

She held up a hand to stop him. "It has to be. Look what he's done to me, Kit. Do you honestly think he'll be better with his son once the fortune is safely in his hands? Promise you'll say nothing of this to Gerald. To anyone. It could mean my baby's life."

She began coughing again. With Joanna it could well be a ploy—save for the deathly pallor and the way she clung to the baby.

She reached for his hand. "Gerald will come after me, and he will be desperate. Meg must be gone with the baby before he does."

"She'll never take Brian away from his rightful father." He paused, seeing that look in her eye. "Surely you mean to tell her."

"You said yourself, she'd never take my child if she knew the truth. Nor does she know Gerald like we do. He'll practice his charm on her and she'll think him the grieving father. It would be his word against ours."

And his own word, Kit feared, would hold little value for Meg once she learned his true identity.

"Please, Kit," Jo begged between coughs. "I need you . . . to help me . . . protect my son."

"Ah, Jo—"

"I beg you. Swear . . . you'll stand by me." She tugged at his hand. "On your word of honor . . . you'll say nothing to Gerald . . . or Meg."

"Shh, Jo." Appalled by her spasms, he kneeled beside her, sliding a comforting arm about her shoulders. "It's all right, I'm not going anywhere. I'll stay by you. You have my word."

It was no small thing, that promise, but feeling the tension leave her frail body, seeing the gratitude in her tear-filled eyes, he considered it well worth any sacrifice he might have to make.

Until he glanced up and saw Meg in the doorway.

It was hard to miss her anger, but what pierced his heart was the hurt she strove so hard to hide. Cursing under his breath, he removed his arm from Jo's shoulder and rose to his feet. He would not leave her side, however. He couldn't, not after giving his word.

"Aye now," Meg spat out as she marched toward them, "and if this isn't a touching scene. I should warn that Her Ladyship's husband will be coming down the road any moment."

Stiffening, Jo looked up to Kit. If he had any remaining doubts about her story, they fled in light of the panic he saw in her eyes.

"I imagine," Meg went on, "he'll be wanting to know what his cousin is doing here in the bedroom with his wife."

"Kit and I, er, were talking about old times."

Meg's tight smile proved that she wasn't believing any of it. "What you're up to is none of my affair, but I can't see how it has aught to do with my wee Brian. If you don't mind, I'll be taking him with me now."

She stepped up, holding out her hands. For a moment it seemed Jo might deny her and cling to the baby with her last breath, but with a sigh Jo gave Brian over into Meg's care. Though her smile was warm and her tone light, her rigid posture betrayed what the surrender cost her. He knew then how much poor Jo must love her son.

"He's a beautiful baby, Meg," she said, gathering her shawl about her. "You take care of him, now. Keep him . . . safe."

A look passed between the two women. Kit saw Meg's eyes widen, as if she realized why Jo had been so reluctant to part with the boy. "That I will, now," she said, hugging Brian to her chest. "And I won't be letting anyone"—she stared straight at Kit—"not anyone, take him away."

She could have slapped him, so directly did he feel the cut. Hours ago he'd held this woman in his arms, letting himself be tempted by her hopes and dreams for the future. So much for her undying faith in him.

"Yes, well," Jo said beside him, "I'm concerned about His Lordship's arrival. With your financial woes and his harsh practices, I fear you might soon find yourself without a roof over your head."

"We'll manage." How like Meg to toss back her head and thrust back her shoulders.

"I've no doubt you will, but you might better manage in America." Jo dug in the bag beside her chair and offered a wad of bills. "Here, I have some money set aside." She shook her head when Meg tried to protest. "It's just a loan, Meg. You can repay me once you're back on your feet."

He watched hope flare in Meg's eyes, then saw the stiff McCleary pride dampen it. "A loan, is it?" she asked bitterly. "And what possible reason could Her Ladyship have for offering a loan to the likes of me?"

Jo stared her straight in the eye. "I treated you badly when we were children and want to make up for it. It's my fault we never found the faerie treasure. I owe you this chance to make your dreams come true."

"Come now, we both know there's more to it, isn't there?" Meg asked Joanna, though she looked directly at Kit. "I'm not stupid, you know. I can see it's the child you're protecting. You can't have His Lordship learning about him, or who his true father must be."

She glared at him. Could she truly think Brian was his, that he was capable of abandoning his son in a cave? Stung by her lack of faith, he nearly protested, but Jo shot a warning glance his way. His promise, and her tightly controlled coughing, was enough to force him to silence.

Meg turned to Jo. "It was you who left me the note, wasn't it? You knew I'd be taken in by all that nonsense about rainbows and faeries."

"Just go, Meg," Jo gasped out, thrusting the money into her hands.

"Aye, I'll go, but from this day on this precious little boy will be known as Brian McCleary. I won't have a soul in this world even guessing he's an unwanted by-blow, so don't either of you come near us again."

"Meg—"

"Let her go, Kit." Jo grabbed for his hand even as they heard the loud commotion downstairs, the too-familiar voice bellowing for his servants. Eyes wide, she looked to the door. "My God, Gerald is here already. Quick, Meg, go out the back stairs."

"Aye, I'll go," Meg lashed out, once more glaring at Kit. "I was wrong to think you knew aught about rainbows and magic. You wouldn't know a dream if it stepped up to bite you in the face." Hugging Brian, she swept from the room.

She didn't know how wrong she was. He was intimately aware of what a dream could be, and his was now marching out of his life forever. Meg was his salvation, and if he didn't explain now, he'd lose all that was good and right and worth fighting for in his life.

Yet gazing into Jo's ravaged face, hearing her husband rage down below them, he knew he couldn't reveal her secret and live with himself after. He'd given his word to remain silent, to stand by Jo while she faced his monster of a cousin. His word of honor.

And in truth, what good would his explanations do save salve his guilty conscience and delay Meg's safe departure? Keeping silent would be a selfless act, the honorable thing.

And all things considered, his honor was all he had left.

* * *

Holding Brian, Meg waited on the quay before the boat that would take them to America, refusing to shed a tear. Crying would accomplish nothing. Shane's silence as she left him told her he had found his true love at last, and it was with Joanna he meant to stay.

Nonetheless, when she heard the horse come thundering up behind her, she turned to greet him, her heart tripping madly.

Disappointment flooded her when she saw it was a female, but it swiftly transformed to shock when she recognized Mary.

"I sure hope this ship is ready to sail," Mary said between gasps as she dismounted and secured the animal. "Liam is combing all the ports, determined to stop you."

"We sail within the hour. But how did you find me when he did not?"

Mary smiled. "I kept asking for a woman with a squawking infant. I figured by now wee Brian would be demanding his dinner."

Meg grinned. "I've tried giving him goat's milk, but you know that boy. I hope this means you'll be coming with us to America?"

Mary winced. "I'm not deserving of your friendship, Meg. Not after taking your rainy-day savings from your jar."

"You took my money?" Foolish, to feel such relief that it wasn't Shane. "But why?"

"Liam asked me to. He said it would encourage you to marry your Shane, so him and me could then be together. His rage when you left showed me it was you he truly wanted, that he'd been lying to me. Lying to everyone, it seems. He's been charged with embezzling His Lordship's funds and is now on the run from the law." She sighed. "I was a fool, Meg. I only hope that someday you can find it in your heart to forgive me."

Touched by the apology and grateful that Mary could at last see Liam for what he was, Meg smiled warmly at her friend.

"Of course I can forgive you. You're like a sister to me. Part of the family."

Mary wiped at the telltale moisture in her eyes. "Aye, and it's missing you all sorely I'll soon be doing."

"Nonsense. You're coming with us. America is a grand place, I'm told, and if you don't mind traveling steerage, I've just enough here to pay your passage. Someone must feed this screaming baby, Mary, or there'll be no rest for us all on the voyage."

This time Mary didn't bother to hide the tears. "You're a saint, Meg McCleary, and there's no disputing it." Blinking swiftly, she reached into her pocket. "But there's no need to be offering more when I still have the funds from your jar. And there's yonder horse I can be selling. I'll be happy to let them add that nag to the list Liam's embezzled from Rainbow's End."

"Hurry, then," Meg said with a grin. "The boys will be devastated if we must sail without you."

"Where is young Timmer?"

Meg gestured behind her. "Running about the ship, making friends with the sailors. A good thing too, since he had not taken well to parting with that lying, conniving Shane."

Mary frowned. "If you can forgive me, maybe you should do the same for your young man. There's more to that story than meets the eye, I'm thinking. I certainly got that impression from Lady Joanna when she asked me to deliver this letter." She handed over a sealed missive. "It will do you no good to hide from the truth. Face it, my girl. You love that man and will do so until you die."

Mary strode off, leaving both that bombshell and the letter behind her. Clutching the paper in her hand, Meg feared her friend was right. It would be no easy thing, forgetting her Shane.

Well, she had to, she thought determinedly. Tucking the letter into the baby's bunting, she refused to read it, wanting no more of Joanna's machinations. She felt foolish enough over that first missive, exploiting her silly, naive faith in rainbows and faeries. It was time to leave Ireland and her fantasies behind. Rainbows might be wondrous, and glorious to behold, but still and all, when their magic faded, you were left standing alone in the dark.

Marching onto the ship, she swore she would go to America with her eyes wide open. And from then on, there would be no looking back.

Kit stood at the gates of Rainbow's End, missing Meg with all his being. How accustomed he'd grown to her smiles, to her lilting voice and sunny disposition. It seemed it hadn't stopped raining since the day she had left.

And what a dreary day it was, an apt scene for Gerald's departure, with the constable's carriage waiting like a tumbrel before the guillotine, the horses dancing in impatience, the prisoner making his slow, hesitant march.

"That's that, then," the Forrester family lawyer said beside him. Watching Gerald climb into the carriage that would take him to jail, the man shook his gray, balding head. "Not much more I can do for him until the trial."

Perhaps Gerald had asked for such an end, so freely giving vent to his greed and senseless rages, but Kit still felt sickened. Who could have known, when they'd played together as children, that he would one day watch Gerald go to jail for Jo's murder?

"It pains me to say this, but as the earl's representative, I must order the estate vacated. Normally, it would be his bailiff's duty to evict you, but since the embezzling O'Neill has long since been sent packing, I fear I must take on the unpleasant task."

Kit smiled ruefully. "Fret not, Simpkins. I have little desire to spend another moment under that roof."

The lawyer nodded. "Be grateful your cousin had you removed from the premises on the night in question. Had you not been locked tight in the local jail, Gravesley would be using his connections to have *you* charged with the murder of his wife."

Kit glanced back at the house, enraged that in the end he'd been unable to help Jo after all. It haunted him, the way she'd smiled as the constables dragged him off. "You've been a good friend, Kit," she'd told him softly. "Go to America. That's where your future lies."

There were no tears, just peaceful resignation, as if she'd known she wouldn't live to greet the morning. As if she'd had no need, no intention, of living through the night.

"What will happen to him?" Kit nodded at the departing carriage.

Simpkins shrugged. "I might manage to spare him the gallows by claiming he went mad with grief over the death of his son, but even so, I can't prevent the stain on the title. Your cousin is ruined both socially and financially. You did know the terms of your father's will, did you not?"

"Barely. Joanna mentioned that the bulk of the fortune will revert to a distant cousin if an heir is not produced."

"Not all that distant a cousin," Simpkins said dryly. "In point of fact, you stand to inherit a tidy sum of money in the next few months."

"Me?" Stunned, Kit nearly protested. It was one thing to think some unknown relative might take Brian's birthright, but quite another to take it himself.

Yet what could be served by telling the truth now? The heir was presumed dead, and it was Jo's dying wish that he remain so. In this small way he could keep his promise to help her. He would take the money and use it to build a better life for Brian.

In America. With Meg.

The rush of elation swiftly died as he remembered her last words to him. How Meg wanted him nowhere near her or the baby.

"I do hope you're not feeling awkward about taking the money," Simpkins said, interrupting his thoughts. "Rest assured, it's what your father wanted. He felt duty bound to give the rightful heir a chance, but he always felt you were worth ten of your cousin, that you would succeed where he would fail."

How typical, that his father would speak of his pride to his lawyer, but never to his son. How sad, when it would have en-

riched them both if just once before he died his father had re
vealed his emotions. Kit was tired of shielding his heart so wel
it grew cold and hard from disuse. His one true regret was th
he'd never told Meg how much he loved her.

"What are your plans?" Simpkins asked. "Will you sett
here in Ireland?"

"Actually, I plan to leave tomorrow." Kit found himself grir
ning ear to ear. Why had he ever doubted he'd be going to Ame
ica? That was where he belonged, with his family. There was s
much he could teach the boys, so much he wanted to give t
Meg.

True, she'd fight him, for she was proud and stubborn an
unjustly hurt. It would take all his power of persuasion to cor
vince her, but she was the heart of his hopes and dreams an
his reason for living, and he would fight to the death to be wit
her.

Gazing at Shamorach Hill, remembering her tale, he though
it likely that he'd been the one singled out for Prince Shane
blessing. Since meeting Meg, his luck had certainly changed fc
the better. "I'll be heading across the Atlantic," he told the law
yer.

To America, he added silently, and one Margaret Mar
McCleary.

Seven

"Please, Meg," Tim begged, standing by the sole window of their rented room, rocking Brian's cradle with his foot. "It's only here, with you and Mary out working all the time. I miss hearing your tales. Can't you spare a moment to talk about Prince Shane?"

Rushing about trying to tidy up the place before leaving for work, a harried Meg failed to hear his wistful note. "Aye, and I can just hear McGivney's reaction should he hear me. They don't believe in faeries here in America, Timmer, and they show nothing but scorn for those that do."

"Have you stopped believing, Meg?"

The question made her pause, coming as it did with a quiver in his voice. Truth was, she'd had little time to think about *what* she believed. In the two months since they'd come here, life had proved every bit the struggle for survival it had been in Ireland. Working day and night with little to show for it, she'd had few moments to search for Colin and Sean, or the farm that by now her brothers should have managed to buy for them.

Edward McGivney, their greedy, grasping Irish landlord who made Gravesley seem a saint, loved to point out the foolishness of such hopes. Big and bustling New York was but a small part of an even vaster America, making the odds of her finding her brothers next to nothing. There was no pretty farm waiting for her and her boys, he'd add with a nasty chuckle, so maybe she'd best stop complaining about her lodgings.

"Did I stop believing?" she asked Tim, her tone stretched and

thin. "Tell me, what has my dreaming accomplished? Th
squalid one-bedroom flat, with its peeling paint and crackir
plaster? Neighbors who can hear our every whisper when the
cease their fighting and screaming? All I see is gray building
and muddy streets and poverty everywhere I turn. I'm thinkir
I made a mistake dragging us here. That maybe the land of m
dreams is a nightmare."

Sighing heavily, Tim turned to stare out the grimy windov
his lonely stance tugging at her heartstrings. How hard it mu
be for him, a mere lad stuck each day in this rat-infested ho
with a baby to care for, no longer able to run free across th
green, dew-kissed hills of Ireland. She was a selfish beast, blur
ing out her bitterness and ill feelings, when more than ever Tir
needed the hope Prince Shane would come to their rescue.

"But I want to believe," she told her brother, striding over t
put an arm about his frail shoulders. "It's just hard to imagin
the Folk making an appearance in this huge, busy city. I thin
we must buy our farm in the country if we ever expect to se
Prince Shane."

Tim nodded. "I think we're more likely to see the other Shan
first."

She froze, feeling the anguish the mere thought of him pro
voked. "If you're talking about Kit Forrester, be careful of rais
ing false hopes, Tim. I told you. The man chose to stay behin
with Lady Joanna."

"He didn't want to stay. I know it." He turned to look at he
his expression wiser than his years. "But that's not what's both
ering you. You think it's your fault he stays away because yo
told him never to come near Brian. That's what has you feeling
hopeless."

At times the boy could be *too* perceptive. Having rea
Joanna's letter at last, Meg now knew Brian's real father, an
the reason Kit needed to protect him. It didn't help, knowing
the man wasn't as evil as she'd wanted to paint him. It just mad
losing him more unbearable.

"He'll come for us." Tim's tone was soft and gentle, but no ess firm for it. "He's part of the family now."

She shook her head sadly. "Ah, but I said dreadful things to :hat man. With just cause, mind you, but even should he choose :o ignore them, you heard Mr. McGivney. It's a big city and an even bigger country. How can anyone hope to find us?"

"Someone told me as long as there's hope, there's always a way."

"Timothy McCleary, are you casting my words back in my face?"

He grinned sheepishly. "When life rains down woes on us, you said, we'd better start looking for rainbows. It's such a gloomy place, Meg. If we keep hoping, maybe we can get a spot of color back into our lives."

"Are you nine, young man, or fifty-nine?" Hugging him, she could see his point. Maybe no one could make certain her dreams came true, but she could sure guarantee they wouldn't if she gave up and stopped dreaming them. And in truth, what could it hurt to once again be making entreaties to the Middle Kingdom?

"I must get to work," she told Tim, squeezing him before turning to gather her coat and hat, "but when I get back, we can talk about Prince Shane, and plan how we'll entice him to come visit this dismal city."

Tim grinned ear to ear, all little boy once more. "In the meantime, we must look for a sign. The proof that he's coming to offer his blessing."

Slipping into her threadbare coat, she went to the doorway, pausing to place a hand on her chest. "From this moment on, I'll be keeping my eyes and ears and heart wide open. I was wrong to lose sight of the magic. As Ma always said—"

"Want to bet you'll go outside now and find a rainbow?"

"That's one tale I've told too often, from the looks of it." No doubt about it, that boy knew how to make her beam.

"I like it better when you smile, Meg. That's my idea of a rainbow."

Aye, and he brought her close to tears too, with his sweet
youthful wisdom. In truth, she had much to be glad about. The
were still together, her and the boys, and someday, if they didn'
give up, they might yet find their brothers. Blowing Tim a kis
and hurrying down the four flights of stairs to the street, she
vowed never again to lose sight of what was truly important.

Hope, like love, wasn't a prize you snatched and held tight
to yourself, but rather a gift you gave to others. Passed on from
one to another, the act became contagious, and if enough people
proved generous, why, even the streets of New York could be
filled with color.

As if to prove this theory, the rain was letting up as she stepped
outside. Grinning, she wondered if this was one of Tim's signs
proof of sunnier times ahead. Scanning the sky hopefully, she
found it—gossamer thin at first, but growing in color and bril-
liance as the sun broke through the clouds.

"A rainbow," she breathed out in quiet awe. A sure sign, indeed.

Whimsically, she thought of the leprechaun legend, of the pot
of gold reported to lie at the end of every rainbow. To be sure
they could be using a treasure now to bail them out of their
troubles.

But as her eyes followed the arc of light to the end of the
street, she found a far greater treasure than gold.

He stood much as he had the first time she'd seen him, legs
astride, his auburn hair glinting as his classically etched profile
sought out the house numbers. Was it a coincidence that he'd
come to her street? Wouldn't Gravesley's cousin seek finer lodgings for himself?

It did no good to warn herself to be logical. Tim had planted
the hope in her heart and there it continued to blossom. Her
mind might question such good fortune, but her feet took her
steadily forward.

She knew, the very instant his eyes met hers, that she was the
reason he'd come here. "Meg?" he said, running over to sweep
her up in his arms. "Please tell me I'm not dreaming, and it's

truly you. That you'll still be smiling when I set you down on your feet."

"Tim said you'd come." To her shame, she heard the tears in her voice even before she felt them drip down her cheeks.

Kissing them away, he made everything in the world seem good and right. "Ah, Meg, it's been an eternity," he said as he set her back down. "I've searched everywhere. I found your brothers—"

"Colin and Sean? Where?"

"They're waiting in my hotel room. They've a lot to tell you, as do I. We'd all begun to fear we'd never see you again."

Patting her hair, she managed a shaky laugh. "And here I am, looking a sore sight indeed."

He reached out with one hand to tilt up her chin, his gaze locked on hers. "I don't think I've ever in my life seen anything quite so beautiful."

He kissed her again, slow and tenderly, and when he was done, he pulled her tight to his chest as if he daren't let her go. "Do you remember the night in the glade, Meg? You said if your man lied to you, you'd wait and listen to his explanation. Well, I'm here to explain, if you'll let me."

"Aye, that I will. I don't doubt we've issues aplenty to resolve between us, but the truth of it is, I'm too well acquainted with the rarity of miracles to waste time talking. I just want to drink in the sight of you, for as long as you mean to stay in the city."

He looked away. "Well now, that's the crux of it. I must leave in two days, to make the last payment on my farm in Pennsylvania."

"Two days?" Meg felt as if the world had dropped out from beneath her feet. "You'll be gone in forty-eight hours?"

"Not much time for wooing a bride, is it? For proving I can be a good husband and father for the boys."

"Kit Forrester, are you asking me to marry you?"

He smiled, warming her inside and out. "That I am, Meg. And be warned, if you won't come with me now, I'll be back, again, and again until I wear down your resistance. I mean to start a new life, Meg, and you have to be part of it."

In the face of such a demand, she couldn't help but tease him. "Well, I don't know. How big is your farm?"

He grinned. "Big enough for sheep and chickens and ponies for the boys, as well as a few unruly brothers. Marry me, Meg. Don't make me face the future without you. Can't you see I love you with all my heart?"

She could see indeed, and better yet, he made her feel it, kissing her long and hard and not at all suitably for standing in the middle of the street.

And when they were done, she reached up to touch his face in wonder. "Ah, Kit, I don't think I could bear to lose you again. You once said you wandered so you could find the magic in life. What if you learn you can't settle down?"

"You have my word, I'll stay by you till the day I die," he told her solemnly. "Why would I leave? You are my magic, Meg. My place where dreams come true."

About the Author

Barbara Benedict lives with her family in Tustin, California. She is the author of three Zebra historical romances: *A Taste of Heaven, Destiny,* and *Always.* She is currently working on her next Zebra historical romance, *Enchantress,* which will be published in December 1996. Barbara loves hearing from her readers, and you may write to her c/o Zebra Books. Please include a self-addressed stamped envelope if you wish a response.

Wanted: A Husband and Father

Jane Kidder

One

"I'm sorry, ma'am, but your husband is dead."

Sarah Clarke clutched her three-month-old daughter to her breast and stared down at the lifeless body that only a few minutes before had been her beloved John. "He can't be dead," she announced flatly. "The bullet hit him in the shoulder. People don't die from shoulder wounds."

The stagecoach driver who had delivered the ominous news dug the toe of his well-worn boot into the dust. "I'm afraid, ma'am, that the bullet hit him lower than we first thought."

"He's not dead!" Sarah repeated desperately, thrusting the wailing baby into the driver's arms and dropping to her knees next to the still form. "John! John, open your eyes!"

"Mrs. Clarke," the driver entreated, "please! Your husband is gone. It ain't gonna do any good to yell at him."

Sarah lifted tear-filled blue eyes, her expression beseeching. "But he can't be dead! We have to get to Fort Laramie. John had orders from General Grant himself to report there tomorrow. They have a house all ready for us. If John doesn't show up, they won't let me stay, and where will I go? What will happen to my baby? Don't you see? He can't be dead. Everything will be ruined if he is!"

The stagecoach driver again shifted his feet, not knowing how to deal with this sudden, unexpected outburst. A minute before, the lady had been so calm. Looking around as if hoping to find someone who would intervene, the driver settled his gaze on the tall, dark-haired soldier who had been the only other occupant of the stagecoach at the time of the robbery. "Captain," he blurted out, holding out the baby, "could you hold this child while I—"

"Certainly not," the captain interrupted. "I'll help Mrs. Clarke." Leaning down, the handsome blue-eyed man cupped his hand under Sarah's elbow. "Come on now, ma'am," he said quietly. "Let's go sit down under this tree over here. There's nothing more you can do, and your baby needs you." Plucking the screaming baby out of the much-relieved driver's arms, the soldier handed the infant to her mother, then gently guided Sarah over to a nearby oak. "Just lean your head back here and relax. The driver and I need to . . ."

"Dig the grave," Sarah finished dully. "I know."

Captain Ethan Grant looked down at the fragile little woman slumped against the tree and felt his heart wrench. Never through all the years of death and destruction that he'd witnessed during the recent war had he ever seen a more pathetic sight than Sarah Clarke and her tiny child. She seemed so defenseless . . . so abandoned. Ethan knew well how desolate and alone she was feeling, and it was all he could do to maintain his composure while saying what he knew he must.

"I'm sorry that we can't give your husband a proper funeral, ma'am, but we have to bury him as quickly as possible and move on. The officers at the fort need to know about what happened here so they can start tracking the outlaws who attacked us."

Sarah, who was bent over, cooing to her daughter, nodded without looking up. "I understand," she whispered, "and a funeral doesn't matter. There's no one to grieve anyway."

Ethan swallowed hard. "Then I'll be about helping the driver." Tipping his hat, he quickly retreated, grabbing a shovel from the boot of the stagecoach and heading off to join the driver, who was already beginning the tedious task of digging the six-foot-long trench.

Despite the oppressive July heat, the two men completed the difficult task in less than an hour. Sarah produced a beautiful flower garden quilt from one of her trunks and, with Ethan's help, carefully wrapped John's body in it. Then the two men laid the body in the grave and after one short hymn and a couple of whispered prayers, left Colonel John Clarke, late of the Ohio First Volunteer Cavalry Unit, to his eternal slumber.

Ethan helped Sarah and the baby back into the stagecoach, then shouted to the driver, who flapped the long reins over the horses' backs, sending them lumbering down the well-worn track heading west.

An hour passed without a word being spoken. Sarah sat with her head back against the seat, rocking the fussy baby as tears trickled unheeded down her cheeks. Ethan sat across from her, trying hard to afford her what little privacy he could by keeping his eyes averted.

"Why do you suppose we got robbed?" Sarah asked suddenly.

"Somebody must have known we were carrying a payroll."

Sarah shook her head. "John should have just let them have it. I don't know why he thought he had to get out of the coach. It wasn't his money. He should have just stayed inside, as you suggested."

Ethan shrugged. "I was thinking that if we both stayed inside the coach, we could get a shot off from in here. I guess your husband thought that confronting the outlaws would be more effective."

Sarah bit her lip and squeezed her eyes shut. "Well, he was wrong, wasn't he? It was typical of him though. He always had to try to do the heroic thing. It was just his nature. He never gave a thought to his safety, not during the war, not ever."

"He was a very brave soldier," Ethan said quietly. "Everyone has heard of Colonel John Clarke. You should be very proud of him, ma'am."

"Proud!" Sarah blurted out. "A lot of good being proud is going to do me. Because of his foolishness my child has no home and I have no bro—husband."

"I don't think the situation is as hopeless as you seem to believe, Mrs. Clarke. Once the army finds out what happened,

I'm sure they'll provide some sort of temporary quarters for you—at least until you can travel back to your family."

"You don't understand!" Sarah gritted out. "There is no one to go back to. My father was killed early in the war and my mother died last year."

"Still," Ethan insisted, "as the widow of a war hero, the army is going to feel some responsibility to care for you. You'll receive a pension or something, I'm sure of it."

"No," Sarah despaired, lowering her head so that her tears dripped onto the baby's soft blanket. "There isn't going to be any pension."

"Sure there is. Your husband was killed in the line of duty. The army takes care of widows."

Sarah raised her head, her face a mask of misery. "John wasn't my husband," she whispered. "We just said that so I could go with him to Wyoming."

Ethan drew in a startled breath, his gaze unconsciously dropping to the baby sleeping in Sarah's lap. "I see," he said slowly.

Sarah noticed where Ethan's gaze had strayed, and her face hardened. "No, you don't see, sir. John Clarke wasn't my husband. He . . . he was my brother."

Ethan shook his head, confused by the distraught woman's disjointed story. "What? Colonel Clarke was your brother?"

"Yes. My husband was killed eight months ago."

"In the war?"

"Yes."

"Then you're still a war veteran's widow."

Sarah sighed heavily. "My husband was a Confederate, Captain. Do you understand now? There aren't any widows' pensions for Confederate soldiers' wives." She lowered her head as tears once again began to stream down her face. "Dear God, what am I going to do?"

Ethan stared at the beautiful weeping woman for a moment, wishing desperately that he could help her. She was like so many other innocent victims of the war: alone, homeless, without family or resources. With all the hardships southern women had already had to endure, it seemed so unfair that even now that the war was over, they were still suffering.

Slowly Sarah lifted her head. "You're wondering how the sister of the famous Colonel John Clarke could be married to a Reb, aren't you?"

"It's none of my business," Ethan responded quickly.

Sarah didn't seem to hear his answer. Instead, she closed her eyes, allowing her mind to drift backward. A small smile curved her lips. "I was at school in Virginia when the war started. I fell in love with a young soldier who was training nearby and we were secretly married the week after the hostilities began. When his company was called up, I returned home to Ohio. My parents were furious about the marriage, of course, but I loved Marcus Hollings and I didn't care what side he fought on. We saw each other only a few times during the war, when he'd be granted a pass. The last time I saw him was just a few months before the fighting ended." She looked down at the baby, a fresh rush of tears coursing down her cheeks. "Four months before Anne was born, I got the news that Marcus had been killed. He never even knew about his daughter."

"Mrs. Hollings, you don't need to tell me any more," Ethan said quietly.

Sarah sniffed, valiantly attempting a smile. "But I want to." She paused, not even sure herself why she was telling her story to this stranger, but, somehow, now that she'd started, she couldn't seem to stem the flow of words that poured forth. "Just a few weeks after Marcus was killed, my mother took ill with smallpox and died. Then the war ended and I stayed on in Ohio at my parents' home until John returned. After Anne was born, John got word that he was being sent to the western front. He felt responsible for me since both my parents and my husband were dead, so he and I came up with the idea that I would pose as his wife in order to be allowed to go to Fort Laramie with him."

She stopped, drawing a deep, shuddering breath. "You know the rest."

Ethan looked at Sarah thoughtfully. "You two really thought that you could convince everyone you were married?"

Sarah's chin rose a notch. "You believed it, didn't you?"

"Well, yes, but I was with you for only two days. It's not hard to pull the wool over somebody's eyes for that length of time, but permanently? I think that would be awfully difficult."

"It wouldn't have been permanent," Sarah argued. "John had only one more year left on this tour of duty, and he wasn't planning on reenlisting."

"I see."

Sarah again tipped her head back, closing her eyes. "But you're right, Captain. Pretending to be married was a pretty desperate idea, but it was all we could come up with. Besides, it doesn't really matter now whether it would have worked or not. John's gone and Lord only knows what's going to happen to us."

Ethan considered this last statement for a few moments, then said, "Maybe during the time you're at the fort, you should try to find yourself a husband for real."

Sarah's large blue eyes snapped open. "Surely you're joking. What am I supposed to do? Post a notice somewhere that says WANTED: A HUSBAND AND FATHER?"

Ethan shrugged. "It would probably solve your problems."

"Well," Sarah sputtered out, "I suppose it would solve some of them, but it would also give me a whole new set. Besides, I would never marry another soldier." She bit her lip, determined to stem another onrush of tears. "If I ever marry again, it's going to be to a schoolmaster or storekeeper or farmer. Someone who lives a dull, predictable, *safe* life."

"I don't think you're going to find many farmers at Fort Laramie," Ethan said dryly, "but you will find several hundred soldiers, any number of whom would probably be more than happy to marry you right on the spot."

"I don't want another husband. I just want—" She paused, studying Ethan closely for a moment. "What I need is the *appearance* of a husband. Just for a little while—until I figure out what to do."

Ethan's brow furrowed. "I'm sorry, I don't understand what you mean."

Sarah's eyes narrowed as the idea flitting through her mind formed into a full-fledged plan. "If the commander at the fort thinks I'm married to an officer, he'd let me stay, right?"

"I suppose," Ethan returned warily. "But how are you going to find an officer willing to pose as your husband—even if it's just for a little while? Especially when you'll need one by tomorrow, when we arrive at the fort."

Sarah drew a deep, bolstering breath. "You're an officer, aren't you, Captain?" As soon as her brazen words were out of her mouth, her heart started pounding so hard, she was sure he could hear it.

Ethan stared at her, dumbfounded for a moment, then shook his head. "Oh, no," he said, holding up his hands as if to defend himself, "I know what you're thinking, and the answer is definitely no."

Sarah let out a breath she didn't even realize she was holding. "Captain Grant, please, just hear me out."

"You're wasting your time, ma'am," he interrupted. "Even if I were willing to go along with your scheme—which I can assure you I'm not—we'd never get away with it. You were posing as Colonel Clarke's wife. How would you explain arriving as mine?"

Sarah shrugged. "That's simple. Since the commander doesn't know I'm even coming, what difference does it make whom I arrive with? John told me that any officer posted to Fort Laramie is allowed to bring his wife. In fact, he said the army encourages it. They're hoping that once the officers are mustered out, they and their families will decide to settle in the area. They're even offering free land as an incentive for people to stay."

Ethan shifted uncomfortably on the stagecoach's hard seat, disturbed by how much knowledge the innocent-looking woman across from him seemed to have. "Mrs. Hollings," he began slowly, "I appreciate the predicament you're in and I wish there

were some way I could help you. But I will not defraud th
United States government by telling my commanding office
that you are my wife. Period."

Sarah's face fell and her shoulders slumped in dejection. "
understand," she murmured. "Well, thank you for at least listen
ing to me. I guess I'll just have to think of something else."

Ethan nodded, then quickly turned away, annoyed by the fac
that he was fighting a nearly overpowering urge to cross to th
other side of the coach and gather the beautiful woman into hi
arms. She was so pretty, so delicate, so vulnerable and alone
As he sat surreptitiously looking at her, he realized that at
different time and in another place, Sarah Clarke Hollings migh
be exactly the type of woman he'd like to court—maybe eve
marry. But not here, not now, and not under the outrageous cir
cumstances she was suggesting. He'd worked too long and to
hard to reach his current prestigious rank to throw it all away i
a fleeting moment of pity for a destitute woman and her baby.

And yet, with a woman as needy as the one sitting acros
from him, might it not be worth the risk, if for no other reaso
than to see if they could actually get away with it? And wh
knew what might develop between them if they actually set u
housekeeping together?

Emitting an annoyed little grunt at his own wayward thoughts
Ethan pulled the brim of his hat down over his eyes and crosse
his arms over his chest, determined to clear his mind and coo
the sudden unbidden tightening in his loins.

Don't even consider it, he silently berated himself. She's no
your problem. He squeezed his eyes more tightly shut, willing
himself to go to sleep. But even with his eyes closed he coul
still see the image of Sarah's face—weary and tear-stained, bu
still pristine in its beauty. And worse yet, he could still hear he
lilting voice as her challenging words floated through his mind

You're an officer, aren't you, Captain?

Two

"Fort Laramie's right up ahead, folks."

The stagecoach driver's trumpeting call caused both Ethan and Sarah to immediately straighten in their seats. Ethan tipped his head out the stage's open window, a grin lighting his face. "He's right," he confirmed, drawing his head back inside. "We're almost there now."

"Thank goodness," Sarah sighed, absently patting the fussy baby's bottom. "Poor little Anne is so wet and hungry, she's just miserable."

Ethan threw a fleeting glance at the baby, privately thinking that if the past four hours were any measure of the child's temperament, wet or dry, hungry or full, didn't seem to make much difference. She cried all the time.

As the stage neared the fort's main gate, the driver bellowed something to the guards and the huge doors swung open without the stage even having to slow down.

"Pretty poor security," Ethan mumbled. "Looks like all you have to do is yell your name and they open the place right up."

"They must know this driver," Sarah commented. "It probably isn't that easy to gain admittance if you're a stranger."

Ethan nodded, his expression dubious. "I'd like to think that's the case. Otherwise, I've got a lot of work to do."

Sarah looked at him quizzically. "What sort of work do you do, Captain Grant?"

"I deal in security," he answered evasively.

Before Sarah had time to question him further, the stagecoach

rumbled to a stop. Wistfully, Sarah peered out the window, getting her first good look at what was to have been her new home.
The fort was everything she'd hoped it would be—clean, orderly
and secure. And she wasn't going to be allowed to stay.

Her brother had told her that in the thirty years that Fort
Laramie had stood sentinel on the flat prairie land of southeast-
ern Wyoming, it had been in a constant state of growth and
improvement. Built originally in 1834 as a privately owned fur
trading post, it had languished in the early '40s until the army
acquired it late in that decade for use as a temporary refuge and
reprovisioning post for thousands of westward-bound immi-
grants. Even after the great western migration slowed, the fort
had continued to expand and flourish. Now, in 1866, the primitive outpost had become an established settlement complete with
neat rows of houses and barracks, stores, a school, and even a
church.

As Sarah scanned the area she could see out the window, her
gaze settled on a row of small, identical houses.

"Officers' housing," Ethan commented, noting the direction
in which her eyes strayed.

Sarah nodded mournfully. One of those houses was supposed
to have been hers and John's. One of those tiny wooden struc-
tures had held the promise of a real home for little Anne and a
new beginning for the war-weary soldier and his beleaguered
sister.

Now, thanks to her brother's misguided heroics, she and her
baby would never be allowed to join the other families enjoying
safe and happy residency in the tidy little cottages. Instead, as
soon as the commanding officer found out that Colonel John
Clarke was dead, she would be sent back to Ohio. And there was
not a single person in the world who cared that she had no
money, no family, and nowhere to go once she got there.

Sarah's pensive reverie was suddenly shattered by an eager
young private who unexpectedly wrenched the stagecoach door
open.

"Captain Grant?" he inquired, saluting Ethan smartly.

Ethan nodded in silent response.

"Welcome to Fort Laramie," the young man announced. "We've been expecting you. I'm Private Wesley Shores, sir, at your service." The private's eyes quickly assessed Sarah and the baby, then he stepped aside as Ethan rose to exit the coach.

Sarah continued to sit where she was, not really sure what to do, but her decision was quickly made as Ethan turned back toward her and extended his gloved hand. Holding the baby close, she accepted the proffered hand and lightly stepped out into the hot summer sunshine.

"Where will I find your commanding officer, Private?" Ethan asked once Sarah was safely on the ground. "The stage was robbed a ways back and, unfortunately, Colonel John Clarke, who was also a passenger, was killed. I need to make an immediate report."

The private's eyes widened in astonishment. "Oh, my God!" Quickly, he threw an apologetic look in Sarah's direction. "Pardon me, Mrs. . . ."

Sarah flicked a quick look at Ethan, then squared her shoulders and said, "Grant, sir. Mrs. Grant." She heard Ethan's sharp intake of breath, but steadfastly continued to stare at the smiling private, refusing to meet the captain's eyes as she waited to see if he would betray her.

To her profound relief, Ethan remained silent.

Private Shores nodded. "Of course. Mrs. Grant." Turning his attention back to Ethan, he pointed to a small square building near the fort's main gate. "The general's office is in that building, sir. Would you like me to accompany you?"

"No," Ethan answered, shaking his head. "I can find it myself."

"Yes, sir. Then, if you'll come with me, ma'am, I'll show you to your quarters."

Sarah quickly stepped away from Ethan, grateful to put some distance between herself and the man. It was obvious from his rigid posture that he was furious with her, and she wanted to make a quick getaway before he changed his mind and exposed her for the liar she was.

Private Shores politely offered her his arm, and as she took it, she chanced a quick backward look at Ethan, but he was already striding off toward the general's office and she couldn't see his face.

Silently, the private guided her toward the row of houses, pausing in front of one of the small dwellings to usher her up the steps. "All officers' housing comes furnished," he announced as he pushed open the door, "but we weren't aware that Captain Grant was bringing a wife and baby, so I'm afraid these quarters may be a little cramped for the three of you. Maybe the general will be able to do something about finding you a larger house, and in the meantime I'll try to round up a cradle for your baby. There might be one over in the provisions shed."

Sarah took a quick look around at the house, her heart sinking. The dwelling was indeed tiny, consisting only of a front room that included a table for eating and a minute kitchen area. Off to the back she spied a single door, undoubtedly leading to a solitary bedroom.

Only one bedroom, she thought dismally. If Anne and I take that, where is Captain Grant going to sleep? Looking around again, she spotted a narrow settee pushed up against one wall. She smiled, feeling better. It might not be the most comfortable of beds, but at least the captain wouldn't have to sleep on the floor. And since he was obviously a hardened soldier used to sleeping in tents or even on the bare ground, he surely wouldn't mind.

Turning back to Private Shores, Sarah graced him with a shy smile. "I'm sure Captain Grant and I will be quite comfortable here, Private. And as for a cradle, perhaps there is another family who might have one they're not using that we could borrow."

As if on cue, there was a sharp rap at the door. Sarah looked around to find a plump, rosy-cheeked woman in her mid-thirties standing in the open portal.

"Hello! I'm Rita Bryant, Major Dorsett Bryant's wife. I understand you're to be my new neighbor."

"Yes, I guess I am," Sarah returned, pleased by the other woman's friendly overture. "I'm Sarah Cl—Grant."

Rita shook Sarah's hand warmly. "We heard that Captain Grant was arriving today, but none of us knew he was bringing a wife." She looked absently around the tiny cottage. "I'm sure if General Martin had known you were accompanying your husband, he would have tried to secure larger quarters for you."

Sarah laughed a bit nervously. "That's what Private Shores here said, but, really, this is just fine, Mrs. Bryant. I'm sure we'll have plenty of room."

Rita looked around again doubtfully, her eyes suddenly lighting on the baby whom Sarah had placed on the settee. "You have a baby?"

"Yes," Sarah answered, hurrying over to move the baby to a more secure position. "This is my daughter, Anne."

Rita beamed down at the pretty blond infant. "What a darling little girl."

Private Shores cleared his throat, then smiled self-consciously as both women turned to look at him. "If there's nothing else you'll be needing, ma'am, I'll be returning to my duties."

"I'm fine, Private," Sarah responded. "Please feel free to go, and thank you for your assistance."

The young man grinned, thrilled to be the object of the pretty woman's praise, then hurried out of the house.

As soon as the door closed behind him, Rita turned her attention back to the sleeping baby. "I was going to ask if you and the captain were newlyweds, seeing as none of us knew about him having a wife, but now I see that's obviously not the case."

Sarah quickly shook her head. "No . . . we're not . . . newlyweds." Her voice trailed off lamely.

Rita studied her for a moment and then nodded. "Did you bring a cradle for the baby? I didn't see one when Sam was unloading your belongings."

"No . . ." Sarah stammered. "It was my understanding that all our furniture would be supplied."

"It is," Rita nodded, "but a baby's cradle isn't standard issue unless the provisions officer knows that a baby is coming. Don't worry about it though. I have a cradle that you're welcome to use. My youngest, Beatrice, is four now, so I certainly don't need it anymore."

Sarah smiled gratefully. "Thank you, Mrs. Bryant. I'd appreciate that if you're sure you don't mind."

"Heavens, no!" Rita laughed. "I've been wanting to get that thing out of the house before Dorsett gets any ideas about wanting to fill it again." She chuckled and turned toward the door. "I'll go get it right now. That way you can put the little darling down for a proper nap." With a gay wave she opened the door, almost bumping into Ethan as he entered from the other side, carrying several heavy valises.

"Oh, Captain, excuse me! I was just greeting your wife. I'm Mrs. Bryant. Perhaps you know my husband, Major Bryant."

Ethan's cold gaze raked over Sarah for a moment, then he turned to Rita and nodded. "Yes, ma'am, I just met him." Setting the valises down, he pulled off his hat and held out his hand. "It's a pleasure to make your acquaintance, Mrs. Bryant."

"Likewise." Rita beamed. "I'll be back in a few minutes with that cradle," she added before disappearing out onto the porch.

The front door had barely closed behind her before Ethan turned to Sarah, his expression furious. "Okay, lady, we need to talk."

Sarah immediately whirled away from his icy glare, heading toward the bedroom at the back of the house. "Could our conversation wait for a bit, please? I really would like to take advantage of Anne being asleep to start getting settled."

"Get settled!" Ethan thundered, then threw a wary glance over at the baby, who suddenly stirred. Guiltily, he lowered his voice. "What do you mean, get settled? Do you really think that little trick of yours outside is going to work? That I'm going to allow you to stay here?"

"Captain, please . . ."

Ethan's deep voice rose again. "No! I told you on the stage that I wouldn't go along with this ridiculous scheme of yours, and I meant it."

Sarah pressed her fingertips against her forehead, her face a mask of anguish. "You're right," she said quietly. "What I did was wrong. But please try to understand. I have no place to go. Besides, even if I did, I can't leave today. The stage has already gone. I heard it. So, I guess that means I have to stay at least until another stage comes and, since I'm here, I might as well make myself useful and help you get settled." Turning, she again headed for the bedroom.

"Now, you listen to me," Ethan roared, following the fleeing woman into the bedroom. "I don't want you to help me do anything. I just want you out of here and gone."

It was these words that Rita Bryant heard through the open bedroom window as she returned with the cradle. Stopping dead in her tracks on the short walkway up to the house, she cocked her head, incredulous. Had Captain Grant really just told his wife that he wanted her gone, or had she somehow heard him wrong? Unsure of whether to interrupt the arguing couple, she stayed where she was, then drew a stunned breath as Sarah's next words floated out the window.

"Please, I'm beseeching you. Let me stay here for just a little while. I promise I won't bother you. You'll hardly know I'm here. You wouldn't really turn Anne and me out with nowhere to sleep tonight, would you?"

"I'm sure that won't be a problem. I'll find somewhere for you to stay until the next stage comes."

"But where?"

"I don't know where. Anywhere but here."

"Oh, please don't do this to me," Sarah entreated. "I don't think I could bear the humiliation if you make me stay somewhere else."

"Your humiliation is not my concern," Ethan flared. "I didn't agree to you being here, and I refuse to accept responsibility for you or that baby."

Rita Bryant gasped with shocked dismay. Not his responsibility! What kind of man was Captain Grant to say such a thing about his wife and daughter?

"All right," Sarah sighed. "I know you don't want me here, and I was wrong to force my presence on you, but if you'll just let me stay here tonight, I promise that I'll try to find another situation for Anne and me tomorrow."

This statement was followed by a long silence, then Rita heard Ethan mutter, "All right. One night, but that's it. You can sleep on the settee."

"The settee!" Sarah gasped.

"Yes. The settee. Just like the rest of this house, the bedroom is mine. And, for God's sake, try to keep that baby quiet tonight. I have a busy day ahead of me tomorrow, and I need some rest."

Rita's mouth thinned in fury. Imagine! That poor, sweet girl being forced to beg for a night's lodging—and from her own husband! Captain Grant's behavior was absolutely unconscionable!

Oh, just *wait* until she got her hands on General Martin. Wouldn't she give him an earful about the quality of officers he was allowing at the fort! It was an outrage. She'd speak to the general immediately—this very afternoon. But first she'd enlist the support of several other of the higher-ranking officers' wives. After all, she was not unaware of how important it was to the general that families settle at the fort and eventually in the town blossoming outside the fort's gates. If the officers' wives banded together in protest, he'd have to listen. And if she had her way, by the time she got done telling the general all she'd just heard, that awful Captain Grant was going to find himself in more trouble than he could imagine. If that man thought he was going to chuck his pretty wife and precious baby out into the cold, then Rita intended to see that he would get chucked out right along with them.

Marching forward, Rita slammed the cradle down on the

porch, then turned and strode off toward Mavis Williams's house. Humphrey Williams was second in command only to Andrew Martin, and Mavis was the first ally she intended to garner.

Rita smiled determinedly. If Captain Ethan Grant thought the war was over, he was in for a very big surprise. This battle was just beginning. And, decorated hero or not, this was one fight that the captain was going to lose.

She'd see to it.

Three

"Have a seat, Captain Grant. I appreciate you coming to see me on such short notice."

Ethan lowered himself into a hard, armless chair and looked warily at his commanding officer, General Andrew Martin, who was seated on the opposite side of his massive desk. "Is there a problem with something, sir?"

"Not really, Captain. But there are a couple of things I want to talk to you about. First off, what can you tell me about the stagecoach robbery?"

"Unfortunately, not much," Ethan sighed. "It happened very quickly. There were three bandits, all wearing masks. They obviously had been lying in wait for us, because there was no chase involved. They just came out of the bushes and stopped the stage, demanding the strongbox. The second Colonel Clarke realized what was happening, he drew his gun and jumped out to confront them. I don't think he realized how many of them there were, and he thought he could surprise them. He got off one shot before they killed him."

"Did he hit any of them?"

Ethan shook his head. "No, but I did, I think. At least I saw one of them slumped over in his saddle when they took off."

"And you stayed in the coach with your wife and daughter?"

Ethan hesitated a moment, then nodded. "Yes. I thought I'd stand a better chance against the outlaws by staying inside."

General Martin nodded thoughtfully. "Did they see you?"

"I'm sure they did. I was leaning pretty far out of the window when I fired."

"And how about your wife? Did they see her too?"

Again Ethan hesitated. "No," he said slowly. "She and the baby were on the floor. They might have heard the baby crying, but they couldn't see anything."

"Well, that's good news, at least."

Ethan remained silent.

"And the guard, Sergeant Willis," Martin prompted. "Did he put up any resistance?"

"None that I could see. Like I said, it all happened very fast. I think, though, that when Willis saw the bandits with their guns trained on him, he knew it was useless to resist, so he just gave up the box."

Andrew Martin frowned. "That disturbs me a great deal, Captain. A soldier assigned to guard a payroll is expected to lay down his life, if necessary, to protect that strongbox. If Willis just threw it down to the outlaws without so much as a token resistance, then he's obviously failing in his duties."

"Have you spoken to him?" Ethan questioned.

"Yes. His explanation is simply that he froze."

Ethan shrugged. "That's possible. As I said, there were three men and they were heavily armed."

"That didn't stop either you or Colonel Clarke from mustering a defense, did it?"

"No," Ethan conceded, "but both the colonel and I are battle-hardened by the war. You know that after serving that long in combat it's almost second nature to retaliate."

Andrew Martin nodded in agreement. "I do understand that, and it's an admirable quality. Unfortunately, in this case, John Clarke retaliated too quickly. If he'd thought his position out a little more carefully, he'd have realized that he had a better chance of mounting a defense by taking the same course of action you did and staying in the coach."

"Perhaps, but Colonel Clarke was a man well known for his daring heroics."

"Yes, but ultimately those 'daring heroics,' as you call them got him killed."

Ethan averted his gaze, uncomfortable with talking about John Clarke for fear he would inadvertently let something slip about Sarah. Although he had every intention of seeing that she vacated his house as soon as his meeting was over, for some reason he didn't fully understand, he just couldn't bring himself to mention her deceit to the general. Regardless of how angry he was over the lies she had told the previous day, in his heart of hearts he felt she had endured enough pain already without having the wrath of the commanding officer brought down on her head. Better that he personally see to her leavetaking and then come up with a plausible story that would save both of them from the embarrassment of confessing their perfidy.

A moment passed in silence, leading Ethan to believe that the audience was over. Slowly he began to rise from his chair. "Is that all, General?"

Andrew Martin blew out a long breath. "Not quite. There is one more situation which we need to discuss."

A little ripple of apprehension skittered down Ethan's spine. Careful to keep his face impassive, he again sank into the chair "Yes, sir?"

"I don't know any other way to broach this, Captain, except to get right to the point. It's about your wife."

Ethan's heart slammed against his ribs. "My wife?"

General Martin sat back, steepling his fingers and tapping them against his lips. "First of all, I want you to know that I don't believe in interfering with any man's marriage. As far as I'm concerned, as long as a man's work is not affected, what goes on behind closed doors between a husband and wife is strictly their business."

Ethan nodded slowly.

"However," Martin continued, "the community that has sprung up here at the fort has forced me into a position of interceding in situations where I normally wouldn't."

"I'm afraid I don't understand what you mean, sir."

"Let me explain. As you know, now that we have the Indian situation pretty well in hand, our superiors in Washington are very eager to settle this area. In an attempt to encourage families to put down roots here, I have been charged with the task of making sure that the ladies who are living here at the fort are content with their surroundings. In that regard, I have encouraged the officers' wives who have been here for a while to feel free to come to me with any complaints or concerns they might have about various matters. That includes letting me know if any soldier at the fort is, in their opinion, behaving . . . inappropriately."

Ethan remained silent, a puzzled expression on his face. "Are you telling me that I've done something to offend one of the ladies at the fort?"

Martin sighed wearily. "Indirectly, yes."

Ethan's brow furrowed, and he ran his hand across his chin in bewilderment. "I can't imagine how, sir. I've hardly even spoken to anyone."

"I know that, Captain, but apparently, one of the ladies overheard you and Mrs. Grant having a rather, ah, heated argument yesterday afternoon."

Ethan's bemused expression immediately dissolved into one of outrage. "Are you telling me, sir, that one of these women was eavesdropping on a conversation between myself and . . . my wife?"

General Martin nodded. "Something like that."

Ethan's lips tightened into a thin line. "I'm sorry, sir, but in my opinion, eavesdropping is also 'inappropriate behavior.' "

"I agree, Captain, but you know how women are, and, unfortunately, with the directives that I am currently under, I have to take note of the ladies' complaints and do something to rectify them."

Ethan shifted in his chair, his body rigid with anger. "Let me get this straight, sir. What you're telling me is that some old biddy came in here and said that she was eavesdropping on a

conversation I was having with Sarah and because she didn'
like what I was saying, I'm being taken to task for it?"

General Martin straightened in his chair, his face now betraying his own anger. "You're way out of line here, Captain Grant
I assure you, the lady who spoke to me, or, more accurately, the
ladies who spoke to me are not 'biddies.' They were simply
concerned because they heard you tell your wife that you fel
no responsibility toward her or your daughter since you hadn'
wanted them to accompany you to this post. Further, they said
that you ordered your wife to leave your house immediately,
even though you knew she had nowhere to stay until she could
return to Ohio."

Martin paused, drilling Ethan with a hard stare. "Are these
accusations true, Captain?"

Ethan swallowed back the bitter retort that rose in his throat
and said simply, "It was something like that, yes."

"And is that really the way you feel toward your family? Do
you not believe that you should be responsible for the well-being
of your wife and child?"

Ethan lashed out with a retort before he could stop himself.
"That woman is not—" Choking his rash words back, he halted
in mid-sentence.

General Martin eyed him closely. "She's not what, Captain?"

Ethan exhaled slowly, trying to calm his rampaging temper.
"Sarah's not . . . easy to get along with, and I—"

The general held up a hand, interrupting Ethan. "Try, Captain.
Try very hard to get along with her. As important as you are to
this fort, I cannot risk upsetting the families who have already
settled here. A peaceful, permanent community is one of my top
priorities, and if you cannot fit into that community, then I will
have no choice but to request reassignment for you."

"Reassignment!" Ethan exploded. "That's ridiculous!" Leaping up from his chair, he strode over to the window, raking his
hands through his hair in frustration.

Tell him! a little voice deep inside raged. *Tell him she isn't
your wife. Tell him she's actually John Clarke's sister and a Reb's*

widow. What do you care if she's disgraced and humiliated? What do you care if she's banished without a penny? She deserves whatever she gets!

"Captain! Sit down!"

Ethan turned back toward the general, his expression chagrined. Never in all his years of military service had he ever shown such disrespect toward a superior officer, and he was appalled by his own actions. Damn the woman! She was making him act like as much of a lunatic as the general suspected him of being.

Quickly, he returned to his seat and sat down, shaking his head in self-disgust as he realized that regardless of how justified he would be in betraying Sarah Clarke, his conscience wasn't going to allow him to do it.

"My apologies, General Martin," he said sincerely. "I had no right to lose my temper with you."

Andrew Martin nodded grimly. "Your apology is accepted, Captain, but you would be well advised to learn to control that temper. And, in that vein, I would like an answer from you now."

"Yes, sir?"

"Are you willing to try to reconcile your differences with your wife and make a serious attempt to fit into our community here, or would you prefer that I request reassignment for you?"

Ethan stared out the window for a moment, then swung his gaze back to his commanding officer, his expression grimly determined. "There's no need for a reassignment request, General. Ever since the war ended, I have hoped for a position on the western frontier, and now that I've been granted one, I'll not jeopardize it."

The general nodded slowly. "So, do I have your word that there will be no further complaints about your behavior?"

"Yes, sir, you have my word."

Andrew Martin smiled in relief. "Very good. That's what I was hoping you'd say. And now, sir, we are finished and you are dismissed."

With a curt salute of acknowledgment, Ethan rose from his chair and strode out of the general's office, heading for his small neat cottage to tell his "wife" that she could unpack her bags. For the time being, at least, she had won.

Four

Sarah was setting her valises next to the front door when Ethan walked in.

"Were you able to find someplace for me to stay?" she asked, hurrying over to scoop the fretful Anne out of her cradle.

Ethan threw his hat and gloves down on the table. "Yeah," he muttered. "You're staying here."

"Here! But I thought you said . . ."

"I know what I said," he barked, pinning her with an icy glare. "But General Martin has other ideas, thanks to your new battalion of allies."

Anne burped loudly as her mother patted her on the back, causing Sarah to smile at her in approval. "I'm sorry, Captain Grant, but I don't have any idea what you're talking about."

Ethan blew out a long breath and shook his head. "Apparently, some busybody neighbor woman found out that I wanted you to leave and ran to General Martin, complaining that I was mistreating you."

Sarah's mouth dropped open in shock. "Surely you don't believe that I had anything to do with that . . ."

"No," Ethan admitted. "I don't. Not that I'd put it past you, considering your penchant for deceit, but you haven't been out of my sight long enough to spread any tales."

Sarah's eyes narrowed angrily. "I have already apologized for saying I was your wife yesterday and, as you can see——" She paused, making a sweeping gesture at the luggage piled by the front door. "I was prepared to leave for whatever hovel you decided to stick me in. I really don't know what else I can do to make amends, unless, of course, you expect me to go to General Martin and tell him the truth about everything."

"The truth," Ethan drawled sarcastically. "Now, there's a novel idea."

By now Sarah was so furious that she began agitatedly bouncing little Anne up and down, causing the baby to wail in protest.

"Doesn't that baby ever stop crying?" Ethan snapped.

"I'm doing the best I can to keep her quiet, Captain. Perhaps you'd like to hold her for a while and see if you can do better."

"No thanks! And don't call me Captain. My name is Ethan."

"I know what your name is, *Captain,* but I'm not in the habit of calling men I intensely dislike by their first names."

For some reason he couldn't fathom, Sarah's words cut Ethan to the quick. Whirling around, he aggressively stepped up in front of her, his face so close that she could feel his warm breath against her cheek. "Well, you'd better learn, lady, because everyone here thinks we're married, and you're going to blow your cover if you persist in being so formal with me."

The baby, frightened by the loud, angry voice, let loose with an ear-splitting scream, waving her arms and kicking her legs so hard that Sarah feared she might drop her.

"Stop shouting," Sarah hissed, taking a quick step backward. "You're scaring poor little Anne to death."

"Oh, here, give her to me!" Ethan thundered, reaching out and plucking the baby out of Sarah's arms. "It's probably you bouncing her around like she's a rubber ball that's scaring her."

As if to validate his accusation, Anne immediately stopped struggling and looked up into Ethan's chiseled face with curious blue eyes.

Ethan stared down at the baby in astonishment, then a slow smile spread across his handsome features. "See?" he murmured, his voice suddenly soft and crooning. "There's nothing wrong with you, is there, little girl?" Looking up at Sarah, he said, "What did you say her name is?"

"Anne," Sarah replied softly, mesmerized by the vision of the huge dark-clad soldier and the delicate blond baby. "Her name is Anne."

Again Ethan gazed down at the baby in his arms. "Well, little Annie, it looks to me like you just wanted a change of scenery. Do you enjoy being held by someone other than your mama?"

"She probably thinks you're my brother," Sarah suggested. "John used to hold her a lot, and she always loved it when he did. Oftentimes she'd go to sleep right in his arms."

Ethan's eyes widened at this bit of information and, hurriedly, he thrust the baby back at her. "I don't have time to stand around and hold babies. I have work to do. I just stopped by to tell you that you can stay here until the stage returns."

"I understand," Sarah murmured, reclaiming the baby and swaying back and forth in a gentle rocking motion. "And I want you to know that I appreciate your hospitality."

"It's not hospitality," Ethan retorted. "It was an order." Walking over to the narrow board that served as a kitchen counter, he picked an apple out of a bowl and bit into it, careful to keep his back turned.

"Then the general knows?"

"Knows what?" His voice was muffled by the apple filling his mouth.

"Knows that we're not married."

With a sigh, he turned back to face her. "No, he doesn't. I just told you, everyone here thinks we're married. That includes the general."

"Why didn't you tell him the truth?" Sarah questioned softly.

Ethan's gaze fled. "It would just make things more complicated. If I tell Martin we're not married, then he'll know that we both lied yesterday and my credibility as an officer would be shot all to hell."

Sarah's eyebrows arched in offense at Ethan's profanity, but he didn't apologize. "So, what do you suggest we do?" she asked.

"I suggest that when we're out in public, we try to act like a typical married couple."

Sarah drew in a startled breath. "You mean be affectionate with each other?"

Ethan's return glance was equally startled. "Not at all. I mean, be cordial. Act like we get along, like we're reasonably happy with each other."

"All right." Sarah nodded. "I think I can do that. And what about when we're here?"

Ethan tossed the apple core into a small box of trash sitting next to the sink. "When we're here, I think we should try our best to just stay out of each other's way."

Sarah looked around the tiny room in which they stood. "That's no easy task considering the size of this house."

Ethan shrugged. "All we can do is try. I shouldn't be here that much anyway, except to sleep."

Sarah squared her shoulders and before she lost her nerve, said what was uppermost in her mind. "You can't expect Anne and me to sleep out here on the settee every night."

"Why not?"

"Well," she blustered, "because Anne needs a quiet place to nap and I . . . I need my privacy."

Ethan stared at her for a moment, then sighed. "I suppose you're right. I guess we'll just have to share the bedroom."

"What?"

"The bed is big enough for two."

"Captain Grant, I cannot believe you think so little of me that you'd even suggest such a thing. Share the bed, indeed! What kind of woman do you think I am?"

Ethan ran his eyes slowly down Sarah's body, then back up again. "Don't flatter yourself, Mrs. Hollings. I'm no more interested in you than you are in me."

It was a lie, and he knew it. Despite all this woman had done to annoy him in the last twenty-four hours, what he felt for her was a far cry from disinterest. Even now, in the heat of yet another argument, he couldn't stop thinking about how beautiful Sarah was. Blond, blue-eyed, petite—just the kind of woman he'd always favored. And with a spirit to match her beauty, which was an attribute he rarely found in young, pampered girls, especially wealthy ones who had been educated in the South.

"I'm relieved to hear that you find me so singularly unattractive," Sarah retorted. "It'll make things much easier for both of us."

Ethan smiled mirthlessly. "I'm sure it will. But let's get one thing straight. I might have been forced to agree to let you stay here, but I'm not going to sleep on that hard, little settee every night. So I'm giving you a choice. Either you and the baby sleep out here, or we share the bed in the bedroom."

"That's my choice?"

"Yup. That's it."

"That's no choice at all. You're putting me in an impossible situation."

Ethan swept his hat and gloves off the table and walked toward the door. "Impossible or not, that's the way it is. Just let me know what you've decided, so I'll know how many clothes to take off when I get ready for bed."

Sarah gasped in outrage, then turned her back to hide her flaming cheeks. "You're despicable, do you know that?"

Ethan shrugged. "I like you a lot too. Don't worry about fixing me supper. I'll eat at the officers' mess."

Before Sarah could think of an appropriate set-down to this latest presumption on Ethan's part, he was out the door.

Sarah flew to the window, watching him as he disappeared around the corner of the house. "What an awful man," she muttered angrily. "He's rude, crude, and insulting beyond belief." She paused a moment, then a small, unbidden smile quirked the corners of her mouth. "Too bad he's also the most handsome creature God ever put on this earth."

Turning away from the window, she sank down on the settee, looking around the barren little room and wondering what she was going to do to occupy herself for the rest of the day.

* * *

She didn't have to wonder long. Ethan had been gone less than a half hour when there was a knock on the door, followed by Rita Bryant's voice calling a greeting.

With a pleased smile Sarah threw down the book she was reading and opened the door. "Hello, Mrs. Bryant! Won't you come in?"

Rita Bryant sailed into the house, looking around with approval when she saw how much Sarah had already settled in. "Just call me Rita, dear. Now, I know you're probably busy, so I'm not going to keep you, but I wanted to invite you and Captain Grant to our house next Wednesday night for supper. I'm having a few of the other officers and their wives, so you'll have a chance to meet everyone. After all, this is your home now and you'll want to get acquainted."

Sarah hesitated, not knowing how to respond to the unexpected invitation. Her first instinct was to accept, but she wasn't sure she dared, considering her relationship with Ethan. What if she said yes and then he refused to go out with her in public? Or, worse still, what if she accepted the invitation and then the stagecoach returned so that she wasn't even there to attend a party being given in her honor? As much as she disliked Ethan, she still couldn't bring herself to leave him with the task of having to explain their rather bizarre relationship to the good ladies of Fort Laramie.

"Can you tell me how often the stagecoach comes to the fort?" she asked.

Rita looked at her in surprise, clearly taken aback by her question. "Are you planning on going somewhere when it does?"

"Possibly," Sarah demurred.

"Well, you needn't worry about it as far as my party is concerned. The stage comes only once every two weeks."

"Oh, well, then . . ." Sarah's voice trailed off, then suddenly a new excuse came to her. "My baby," she said hopefully, "what would I do with Anne? I have no one to leave her with, and she's so fussy all the time that bringing her along would probably ruin the evening for everyone."

Rita waved a dismissive hand. "I'll have my oldest girl, Nola, come stay with her for the evening. Nola's sixteen, and with five younger brothers and sisters, she's used to taking care of little ones. Your baby will be just fine."

"That's very nice of you to offer," Sarah said, trying hard to keep the disappointment out of her voice.

"So you'll come, then?"

Taking a deep breath, Sarah made her decision. "Of course I'll have to ask Cap—Ethan, but unless he has, er, duty that night or something, we'd love to come." There, she thought with satisfaction. If Ethan refused to attend the dinner, at least she'd given them a reasonable out. She could just say that he had to work.

However, her delight at her quick thinking was abruptly shattered by Rita's next words. "That won't be a problem either. General Martin and his wife will be there, and I know he's eager to meet you. No doubt he'll keep Captain Grant's schedule clear that night."

"I see," Sarah murmured, her heart sinking. "Well, then, I guess you can count on us."

"Wonderful! We'll see you then. Seven o'clock. Oh, and if there's anything you need before that, Sarah, even if it's just another woman to talk to, feel free to call on me."

Sarah looked at Rita quizzically for a moment, then nodded. "Thank you."

Rita moved toward the front door, pausing a moment to look down at Anne, who was now fussing in her cradle. "Fretful little thing, isn't she?"

Sarah sighed. "Yes, she seems to have a problem with gas on her stomach."

Rita looked down at the grimacing baby thoughtfully, then nodded. "Colic, undoubtedly." Opening the front door, she looked back at Sarah and added, "Put a tiny drop of peppermint in her water bottle. That should help to put her in a better mood."

Sarah's eyes widened. "Really? Oh, thank you. I'll try that."

After Rita made her departure, Sarah immediately went to her small medicine case and began rummaging through it. Finding a small bottle of peppermint extract, she held it up, smiling.

So, just a drop will put her in a better mood, will it? she mused. Maybe I should try adding some to Ethan's water glass too!

Five

"Captain, may I speak to you for a moment?"

Ethan looked up from the pile of papers he was perusing and gestured to Lieutenant Caleb Ashbrook to enter. "Good to see you, Lieutenant," he said shortly. "Do you have anything to report?"

Lieutenant Ashbrook lowered his lanky frame into the chair opposite Ethan's desk and nodded. "The investigation into the robbery is proceeding at an excellent pace, sir. In fact, my staff and I are quite sure that we know the identity of the perpetrators of the crime."

Ethan gazed at the lieutenant with interest. "Really! Well, then, please accept my congratulations to both you and your staff. Has an arrest been made?"

"No, sir, not yet. Although we are convinced that Abel Ritter is the mastermind behind the crime, we do not yet have enough hard evidence to arrest him." Seeing Ethan's expression darken with disappointment, he quickly added, "It's only a matter of time though, sir. Ritter has been bragging to his cronies that he's made a big score and that he's set for life."

Ethan leaned back in his chair and crossed his hands over his lean stomach. "Just who is Abel Ritter, Lieutenant?"

"He's a corporal here at the fort, sir."

"What?" Ethan shot to his feet, his eyes ablaze with furious disbelief. "Here at the fort! You mean this crime was committed by one of our own men?"

Lieutenant Ashbrook swallowed. "It appears that way, sir."

"Has this man been in trouble before?"

"Yes, but minor infractions only. We've been watching him for some time though, because we suspected he might be up to something."

"Obviously, you weren't watching him closely enough, Lieutenant, or this wouldn't have happened."

Caleb shifted uncomfortably in his seat. "Actually, sir, he's a bit hard to keep track of."

"Oh? And why is that?"

"Because he's a scout and therefore he's not at the fort most of the time."

"A scout! What kind of scout?"

"We have a small battalion of men who ride out daily to check the surrounding area for renegade Indians or other miscreants."

Ethan's mouth dropped open in astonishment. "And just who the hell assigned this paragon of virtue to a post like that?"

The lieutenant shrugged nervously. "I don't know, sir. He was in that position when I arrived here."

"Well, I want him out. Now."

It was a moment before Caleb spoke again. Finally, in a hesitant voice, he said, "Yes, sir. If you really think that's best."

"You don't?"

"Actually, I think it's wiser to leave Ritter where he is for the time being. That way he won't be alerted that we're on to him. If he's suddenly reassigned to some unimportant duty, he's bound to get suspicious and we may lose whatever chance we have of pinning him to the robbery."

Ethan sighed and sat down, running his hand distractedly through his thick, dark hair. "I suppose you have a point. All right. Leave him where he is. But I want someone to watch him every minute. Assign him a partner and make sure it's someone we can trust. Instruct the man to be friendly to Ritter so that he'll take him into his confidence. Maybe, that way, we'll get a confession out of him."

"Yes, sir," Caleb nodded quickly, jotting down a few notes in a small notebook. "I'll take care of it." He rose to his feet.

"Just one more thing, Lieutenant," Ethan said. "I want you to report back to me tonight on whom you have chosen and what the plan of action is."

"Yes, sir. What time tonight would you like to see me?"

Ethan hesitated a minute, then grimaced as a thought struck him. "I just remembered, I can't see you tonight. I have an engagement."

The lieutenant smiled. "Ah, yes, the dinner at Major Bryant's house. I heard."

"What do you mean, you heard?"

Caleb had the good grace to look chagrined. "You have to understand, sir. Fort Laramie is a small place, and when something as unusual as a dinner party for all the top officers is being held, it's bound to be talked about."

Ethan nodded in resignation. "I suppose. Okay, then, let's plan to meet tomorrow morning at ten."

Lieutenant Ashbrook saluted. "Yes, sir. Ten o'clock tomorrow. Have a pleasant time this evening, sir."

Ethan watched as the young officer exited his office, then leaned back in his chair and gazed absently out the window. *A pleasant time.* There were any number of phrases he could think of to describe how he felt about the party this evening, but "pleasant" was definitely not one of them.

In the week since he and Sarah had arrived at the fort, they had managed to coexist relatively successfully. Even baby Anne hadn't been as much of an annoyance as Ethan had thought she'd be. After the first couple of days she had seemed to cry less and be more content. Ethan didn't know what had caused the change in the cranky baby's disposition and he hadn't asked, but whatever the reason, he was extremely grateful.

As he had known she wouldn't, Sarah had not taken him up on his offer to share his bed. Rather, she quietly spread her sheets and blankets on the settee every night, placing Anne's cradle on the floor next to her before she stretched out on its short, hard surface.

Ethan had felt a twinge of guilt the first night as he'd surreptitiously watched Sarah toss restlessly on the lumpy sofa in an attempt to get comfortable, but he'd assuaged his guilt by reminding himself that after all, he *had* offered to share the bed. If she elected not to avail herself of his generosity, that was her problem, not his.

Still, he couldn't help but feel sorry for her. The mauve shadows under her eyes were testament to the fact that she wasn't sleeping well. Several times, he had come close to offering to switch places with her, knowing that his battle-hardened body could rest on any surface, regardless of how inhospitable, but every time he'd opened his mouth to do so, he'd stopped himself. If she wanted to suffer on the uncomfortable sofa, then let her.

Other than their disagreement over sleeping arrangements, though, the week had passed surprisingly peacefully. They had even shared dinner together on several occasions. And despite Ethan's vow to ignore Sarah when he was at home, he found himself strangely drawn to her. The past two nights he'd actually joined her out on the porch, sitting next to her on the double swing and chatting for a few minutes before he retired to the bedroom.

Although he had enjoyed those quiet moments spent in her company, they had led to uncomfortable nights. Far into the wee hours of the morning, he had found himself lying in his big, comfortable bed, wondering what it might be like to be married to a woman such as Sarah. To hold her curvy little body in his arms every night as he fell asleep and to see her beautiful face smiling at him every morning when he woke up.

A loud sound outside his office door jerked him back to reality. *Stop this,* he told himself irritably, picking up a sheaf of dispatches. *You're acting like a horny kid. Just concentrate on getting through this damned dinner party tonight without making a fool of yourself. In another week she'll be gone and life will get back to normal.*

Normal, he thought, again gazing out the window. Could he ever again settle for the loneliness of "normal" now that he'd had Sarah Hollings in his life?

"Of course you can," he growled, staring balefully at the dispatches. "You're a soldier and an officer. That's the only thing that's important."

Now, if he could just make himself believe that.

"Are you ready to go?"

Sarah walked out of the bedroom, carrying Anne and talking to Nola Bryant. Seeing Ethan standing by the front door, she immediately planted a welcoming smile on her face. "Yes, dear, all ready."

Ethan blinked in surprise at Sarah's unexpected endearment, then noticed the young girl. Pasting on an equally happy grin, he took a quick step toward Sarah, bending over the baby and chucking the infant under the chin. "How's my little girl? Have you been a good baby today?"

"She's been just wonderful," Sarah informed him. "Ever since I took Nola's mother's advice and started putting a drop of peppermint in her water, she's like a new person."

"Peppermint?" Ethan asked, looking up at Sarah quizzically.

"Yes. Don't you remember? I told you about Mrs. Bryant suggesting that a bit of peppermint in Anne's water bottle might help her stomach."

"Oh, yes, I guess I do remember, now that you mention it," Ethan said lamely.

Sarah turned toward Nola and rolled her eyes. "Men . . ." she sighed dramatically. "They *never* listen."

Nola giggled, her dark eyes bright with excitement. Unbeknownst to either Ethan or Sarah, all the young girls at the fort had spent the last week rhapsodizing endlessly about the handsome new captain. Nola had been ecstatic when her mother had told her that she'd offered her services to stay with the Grants' baby, knowing that the other girls would be pea green with envy when they heard that she'd actually been in the gorgeous man's house and seen him up close.

"We better get going," Ethan said. "We don't want to be late."

Sarah nodded, and after giving Nola several last-minute instructions, allowed Ethan to usher her out of the house.

"We'll be home early," she called back through the open door.

"Take your time," Nola answered. "We'll be fine."

As they turned on to the lane in front of the cottage, Sarah cast a covert look at Ethan. "I don't think we'll have to stay very long tonight," she murmured. When he didn't answer, she added, "I'm sure that after dinner I can make our excuses and we can leave. I'll just say that I have to get back for Anne's late night feeding."

"Whatever," Ethan muttered. "Let's just see how things go. We don't want it to look like we're in an obvious rush to get away."

"I know that," Sarah snapped. "I just thought that the baby would serve as a good excuse for us not to have to linger after dinner.

"Like I said, let's just see how it goes. I'm sure everything will be fine."

Sarah gritted her teeth in annoyance. "I'm sure everything will be fine too, Captain."

Ethan threw up his hands in exasperation. "For God's sake, don't call me Captain!"

"I won't! Will you please quit worrying about that?"

Ethan took Sarah's elbow and turned up a walkway leading to another house. "Okay, we're here. Now, smile and pretend you adore me."

Sarah cast him a jaundiced look, then, drawing a deep, bracing breath, she forced a wide smile. Ethan did the same, and together they climbed the steps to the Bryants' home and knocked on the door.

Six

Despite her trepidation about spending an evening in public with Ethan, Sarah couldn't help but feel a ripple of excitement as they stepped into the Bryants' large, welcoming home. It had been so long since she had been to an actual party, so long since she'd worn a pretty dress and sat at a table laden with rich, well-prepared food. So long since she'd had a handsome man at her side.

She was surprised when Ethan helped her off with her shawl, handing it to Rita and then placing an arm affectionately around Sarah's waist as they strolled into the parlor to join the other guests. If she closed her eyes and let her mind drift, she could almost imagine that the handsome man accompanying her actually cared for her comfort. She smiled up at him as he seated her on a little wooden chair with a needlepoint cushion, and to her delight, the smile he returned was the most genuine she'd ever seen on his usually stern visage.

Ethan and Sarah were introduced to the three other couples present, then drinks and canapes were served. Sarah smiled with delight as she was handed a small stemmed glass filled with sherry, remembering fondly the many evenings in Virginia when she had sipped this same elegant wine while soft-voiced servants prepared the evening's meal in the kitchen.

Her sense of well-being soon disappeared, however, as once the entire gathering was comfortably settled, a barrage of questions began.

"So, tell us, Mrs. Grant, where were you and the captain posted before coming to Fort Laramie?"

Sarah shot a wary glance at Ethan before turning toward Mavis Williams. "Actually, we weren't together," she said hesitantly. "Ethan was in Washington and I was in Ohio."

"Ohio," Colonel Williams echoed. "I didn't know you were from Ohio, Grant."

"I'm not," Ethan said smoothly, "but Sarah has relatives there, and she stayed with them while I was in Washington."

"So you're from Ohio?" Mavis prodded, turning her bright, birdlike eyes on Sarah.

"Yes," Sarah replied, "although I lived for several years in Virginia." She glanced up, noticing the slight lift of Mavis's eyebrows as Sarah's obvious connection to the South sank in.

"I assume you and Captain Grant met during the war?" Mavis said.

"Yes," Ethan answered quickly. "I was posted outside Richmond for a while."

Carrie Alexander, a young woman with merrily dancing blond ringlets, suddenly chimed in. "I think it's so romantic when you hear about couples who met during the war—especially when they were on opposite sides of the conflict. It's heartwarming to know that despite the differences of opinion between the North and South, people were able to put aside their prejudices and fall in love."

Ethan smiled, somewhat amused by Carrie's reference to the great war as a "difference of opinion." "It does occasionally happen," he remarked wryly.

"Well, you certainly did keep it a secret, Grant," Will Alexander interjected. "None of us had an inkling that you were married with a child. When that stagecoach arrived last week, we were all expecting a bachelor."

To Sarah's astonishment, Ethan reached over and picked up her hand, brushing her knuckles with a gentle kiss. "Some things are just too personal to talk about," he said softly.

Several of the ladies sighed at Ethan's unprecedented gesture, then shot chastising frowns at their own husbands as if silently reproving them for their romantic shortcomings.

"My, my," Rita tittered, fanning herself with a small, dimpled hand. "I was terribly worried that your little cottage wouldn't be big enough for you, but it looks as though the two of you could live quite happily in one room."

Sarah drew her eyes away from Ethan's lingering gaze. "Please don't trouble yourself about our quarters, Mrs. Bryant. They're fine."

"Yes," Ethan added. "We're very comfortable."

"And obviously very cozy," General Martin added with a chuckle.

The embarrassingly personal conversation finally came to a halt as a small gray-haired woman stepped through the parlor doorway and nodded at Rita. Immediately, their hostess rose to her feet. "If you've all finished your drinks, we can proceed into the dining room now."

Everyone set down their glasses and stood up, the men taking their wives' arms as they moved into the dining room. Again Ethan slipped his arm around Sarah's waist.

"You're doing a very good job at making them believe we're blissfully married," she whispered.

"Thank you."

"I thought you said we needed only to be cordial, not affectionate."

"I *am* being cordial."

Sarah shot him a startled look. Never in all the time she had been married to Marcus had he ever kissed her hand the way Ethan had just then. If this was what Ethan considered being cordial, what must he be like when he was being affectionate? A little shiver ran down Sarah's spine at the very thought.

Dinner progressed without incident, although Sarah could hardly eat a bite, so unnerved was she at the way Ethan doted on her. Several times he offered her a tidbit from his plate, and once he even went so far as to feed her a particularly succulent bite of roast beef right off his fork.

Even though she knew he was dancing attendance on her purely to diffuse any notions the women in the room might have about the state of their "marriage," it was still disconcerting to have the handsome man treating her with such blatant intimacy.

Clearly, the other ladies at the table were entranced by his performance, audibly sighing and smiling every time he touched her. And touch her he did—stroking the back of her hand as she reached for her soup spoon, reaching over to tidy an errant curl that slipped out of its pins, even brushing a crumb away from the corner of her mouth with his napkin.

Sarah truly did not know what to make of Ethan's actions. Could the cold, austere soldier she'd lived with for the past week really be the same man who was now treating her so charmingly? Was anyone that good an actor, or was it possible that maybe Ethan wasn't acting? That somehow, in the course of the last few days spent together, he'd developed an affection for her?

Sarah smiled to herself at the thought of that possibility. They *had* spent several pleasant evenings together, sitting on the porch swing and talking about inconsequential matters. One night Ethan had leaned so close to her that for a moment Sarah had even thought he might be planning to kiss her. But he hadn't, and she'd been annoyed with herself for feeling disappointed. Since then, she'd been careful to keep her distance, fearful that he might notice her growing attraction for him.

Even tonight, as easy as it would be to allow herself to believe that this gorgeous, virile man was sincere in his attentions, she carefully reminded herself that Ethan's behavior was nothing more than a masterfully orchestrated ruse.

The thought saddened her.

It's just because you're lonely, she told herself firmly, determined to pull herself out of her sudden morose mood. You're lonely and vulnerable and unloved—and looking for anyone who might show you the slightest bit of attention.

Ethan was indeed doing that. Even after dinner, when the company again retired to the parlor for little cakes and port,

e continued to treat her like the well-loved bride they hoped
everyone would think she was.

By the time they finally left, near midnight, there was no
doubt in Sarah's mind that whichever lady had overheard their
argument the day of their arrival, if she had been there that night
and witness to Ethan's stunning performance, she must now believe that she had misunderstood their entire confrontation.

As he had all evening, Ethan placed his arm around Sarah's
waist as they exited the Bryants' home and headed for their own
small cottage. Even after they were well out of sight of the Bryants' porch, he didn't move his hand. Rather, he left it lightly
resting against her back for the entire duration of their trip home,
removing it only to open the front door and see her through.

Much to Sarah's relief, Nola announced that Anne had been
"just a little darling" the whole time they were gone and that
she was now fast asleep.

"How wonderful," Sarah laughed, "and how unlike her!
Maybe you should look after Anne all the time, Nola. She seems
to behave much better with you than she does with me."

"Mama says that little children always behave better with
strangers than they do with their own mothers," Nola informed
her. "But Anne was a perfect angel and I would love to take care
of her anytime you and the captain want to go out."

Sarah smiled her gratitude and walked over to the sugar bowl,
where she kept her small stash of money.

"Don't bother, darling," Ethan said, seeing where Sarah was
headed and guessing her intent, "I'll take care of paying Nola."
Before Sarah could protest, he reached into his pocket and extracted a silver dollar, pressing it into the stunned girl's hand.

"Captain Grant, this is much too much!" Nola protested.

"Take it," he insisted, flashing a grin that made the girl's knees
go weak. "You deserve it. I know what a handful our little Annie
can be."

Nola opened her mouth to protest again, but before she could
get a word out, Sarah suddenly said, "By the way, where is
Anne?"

"She's asleep in the bedroom," Nola announced. "I know you had her cradle out here next to the settee, but I figured you mus' move it into the bedroom when you put her down for the night so I just went ahead and did it. I thought that way, you wouldn' have to wake her up to move her once you got home."

Noting how Sarah started at this bit of information, Nola threw her a stricken look. "Did I do something wrong, ma'am?"

"You did exactly the right thing," Ethan interjected smoothly "Of course the baby doesn't sleep out here alone at night, and it was very thoughtful of you to put her in the bedroom. Now if you're ready, I'll be happy to walk you home."

"Oh, that isn't necessary, Captain," Nola giggled. "It's just a few houses down. I'll be perfectly safe."

"I wouldn't hear of you walking home unescorted," Ethan said, the commanding tone in his voice brooking no further argument. He opened the door, then turned to look at Nola expectantly. For her part, she was so thrilled by the thought of the glamorous captain escorting her home that she was nearly speechless.

"Well, th-thank you again for having me, Mrs. Grant," she stammered. Sarah nodded. Then, with a last little giggle, Nola shot by the waiting Ethan and out onto the porch.

"I'll be back in a couple of minutes," he said, casting Sarah a searching look. "Leave the door unlocked."

Again Sarah nodded, curious as to what the look had meant.

Once Ethan and Nola were gone, Sarah flew into the bedroom, quickly shrugging out of her dress and donning a light nightgown and a silk wrapper. After washing her face, she pulled the pins out of her hair, ran a brush through its thick blond length, then turned toward the sleeping baby's cradle, biting her lip as she contemplated what to do.

"Just leave her," rumbled a deep voice from behind her. "Don't wake her up."

Sarah nearly jumped out of her skin. Whirling around, she slammed her hand against her mouth to squelch the little shriek of startled surprise that threatened. "I didn't hear you come in," she blurted out. At the sudden loud sound of Sarah's voice, Anne moved restlessly in her cradle.

"I didn't want to disturb the baby," Ethan whispered, his eyes feasting on the sight of Sarah, lit only by the flickering glow of a single candle and clad in her nightgown. Without a thought as to what he was doing, he reached out and took her hand, gently pulling her back out into the front room.

"How did you come in so quietly?" Sarah asked as he closed the bedroom door behind them.

"I took my boots off outside."

She looked down at his bare feet. They were beautiful, just like the rest of him.

Embarrassed that Ethan was going to notice her ogling his feet, she quickly lifted her head and looked into his eyes, and found the same searching expression that she had seen before. Abruptly, she pulled her hand out of his and backed up a step. "I have to move Anne's cradle. She can't sleep in the bedroom when I'm sleeping out here. She might need me during the night."

"Don't move her," Ethan murmured, his gaze never wavering from hers. "Just leave her where she is."

"But . . ." Sarah began.

Again Ethan closed the distance between them, effectively cutting off the rest of Sarah's protest as he buried his hand in her hair and bent his head toward her. "Don't worry about the baby, Sarah. She's fine."

And before Sarah could gather her wits enough to make another protest, his mouth closed over hers. His lips were soft, warm, and seductive, covering her mouth in a long, drugging kiss.

Instinctively, Sarah parted her lips, moaning softly as she felt Ethan's warm tongue tangle with her own. Relishing the heady sensation, she tipped her head back farther, inviting him to caress her neck.

Ethan readily accepted, running his fingertips around the shell of her small ear, then downward across the fluttering pulse in her throat. Pulling his mouth away from hers, he untied the sash on her robe and released several buttons on her nightgown, exposing her generous, rosy-tipped breasts to his hungry gaze.

His eyes darkened with burgeoning passion as he ran a gentle fingertip across her aroused nipple and heard her catch her breath. "You're so beautiful," he rasped, sweeping his tongue intimately across the pebbly little bud. "The most beautiful woman I've ever seen."

Sarah felt as if she couldn't breathe. Desperately she clutched Ethan's broad shoulders, fearful that her knees might buckle if she let go. Her gaze drifted downward and she drank in the arousing sight of his black hair against her alabaster skin. "I want to touch you," she whispered, her voice breathless.

Ethan lifted his head and smiled at her. "I'm all yours."

With shaking fingers Sarah unbuttoned the blouse of his starched military uniform and spread it open, uncovering the wide planes of his chest. She reached out a shaking hand, running it lightly across the broad expanse of muscle, then leaned forward and kissed him.

Ethan gasped as her lips brushed across his flat nipples. Throwing his head back, he skimmed his hands down her back, cupping her bottom and pressing her hips against his.

Sarah drew in a shuddering breath as she felt his hot, hard arousal pressing intimately against her. Slowly, she raised her eyes to meet his. Seeing the unashamed need raging deep in their dark depths, she emitted a trembling sigh and lowered her hands to his waist to unbuckle his belt.

The thick leather band fell away. Without hesitating, Sarah continued her erotic quest, reaching intimately inside Ethan's waistband to unbutton his trousers.

Ethan stood perfectly still, fearful that if he moved to assist her in any way, she might stop.

But Sarah was in no mood to stop nor did she need assistance. Hooking her thumbs into the loosened waistband of his trousers, she shimmied them down his lean thighs until they dropped in a heap at his feet. Quickly, he stepped free of the cumbersome clothing.

As if finally realizing what she was committing to, Sarah lifted her eyes to meet those of the nearly naked man before her. Their gazes locked for a moment, then Ethan stepped forward, gathering her into his arms and kissing her again. "I want to make love to you, Sarah," he whispered, his lips still touching hers as he spoke.

"And I want you to," she whispered back.

It was all the encouragement Ethan needed.

Gently, he pushed her wrapper off her shoulders, leaving her clad in nothing but her thin, gaping nightgown. He bent down, gathering its folds and slithering it up her hips, past her breasts, and over her head. As the soft material floated to the floor, Ethan took a step back, hungrily drinking in the exquisite sight of the nude Sarah. Her body was perfect—her breasts round and thrusting, her waist gently curving, and her legs long and lithesome.

Ethan swallowed, staring in unabashed awe at the beautiful woman before him. Then, to his astonished delight, Sarah reached forward and divested him of his shirt, her eyes feasting as greedily on the magnificence of his naked body as his were on hers.

Without a word Ethan scooped her into his arms, walking over to the little settee and laying her carefully on its hard surface.

"Don't you want to go to the bedroom?" she whispered.

He shook his head. "We might wake the baby, and as much as I'd like the comfort of the bed, I don't want to take the chance of being disturbed."

Sarah nodded, agreeing with his logic. In the next second, however, all logical thought fled her mind as Ethan lowered himself on top of her, nestling his throbbing arousal between her slender thighs.

Sarah moaned, reveling in the sensation of Ethan's hot, hard shaft pressing so intimately against the core of her womanhood. Slowly, she reached down and closed her hand around him.

Ethan emitted a long moan of pleasure and raised himself above her, an anticipatory shudder rippling through him as he gazed into the fathomless blue depths of her eyes. "Do you know how gorgeous you looked tonight?" he whispered. "You should always wear blue. It sets off your eyes . . . your beautiful, beautiful eyes."

His voice trailed off, and again he lowered his head, kissing her breasts, then moving down her stomach. He paused a moment, and Sarah lifted her hips, enticing him to move lower still. When his mouth touched the fleecy down at the juncture of her thighs, he paused again, his warm breath causing her to shiver involuntarily. Glancing up at her face, he noticed the tightening around her mouth as she braced herself for the first waves of climactic pleasure and, without hesitation, plunged his tongue deep inside her.

Sarah let out a little cry as she surrendered to this new and shocking intimacy. "Ethan," she cried, burying her fingers in his ebony hair as wave after wave of pleasure crashed over her. "Oh, Ethan, what are you doing?"

"Making love to you, sweetheart," he answered simply.

Sarah closed her eyes, so stunned by the orgasmic pleasure she'd just experienced that she could barely form a coherent thought. "This is not like any lovemaking I've ever known," she sighed.

"There are lots of different ways to make love," Ethan whispered, rising to his hands and knees and looking down at her.

Sarah smiled sublimely. "Do you know another that we might try?"

"As a matter of fact, I do," he rasped, his breathing shallow and ragged.

"Will you show me?"

And with a primitive growl that spoke far more eloquently than any words could have, Ethan lowered himself between Sarah's thighs and slowly, exquisitely, entered her.

Although she was more than ready for him, he moved carefully, giving her time to adjust to his presence within her.

But Sarah was having none of it. Highly stimulated by the climax she'd just experienced, she was hot and eager for him. Hooking her heels behind his thighs, she moved downward on the settee, driving him so deeply within her that she was sure he was touching her very soul.

Ethan set a gentle rhythm at first, but the feeling of Sarah's warm, welcoming body surrounding him, coupled with many months of celibacy, conspired against him. Very quickly his pace increased, his hard, deep thrusts coming faster and faster. Suddenly, he felt Sarah's womanhood begin to pulse around him and knew that she was again reaching for the pinnacle of passion. He, too, was at the very brink of his control, but he waited until he felt her hurtle over the precipice before he let himself go, pouring his hot, potent seed deep within her.

When their shattering climax finally subsided, they collapsed together, still intimately joined. Moments passed as their breathing and heart rates returned to normal. Then Ethan kissed Sarah one last time and moved away to lie next to her on the narrow sofa. "Are you cold?" he whispered, feeling her shiver.

"A little," she confessed, "but I don't want to get up."

Ethan smiled his understanding and pulled an afghan that was thrown across the back of the settee over them.

Sarah cuddled against him, nestling herself in the crook of his arm. "Ethan?"

"Yes?"

"Were you . . . were you planning on our making love tonight while we were at the party?"

Ethan sighed, a long, tortured sound that made Sarah look up at him quizzically. Ethan saw her tilt her face up to stare at him, and was relieved that the darkness of the room concealed the naked pain he knew must be apparent in his eyes.

"No, Sarah, I wasn't planning anything. I was just enjoying being with you. Then, when I saw you standing there in the candlelight with just your nightgown on and your hair down, making love to you somehow seemed very natural."

Softly, Sarah kissed him just beneath his ear. "I'm glad it did."

Ethan squeezed his eyes shut, trying desperately to think of a suitable response to Sarah's heartfelt declaration. There were so many emotions careening through his exhausted mind that he couldn't seem to grasp any one of them long enough to analyze it.

But one thing was certain—he definitely did not feel glad about what had just happened. Rather, he suspected that he had probably just made the biggest mistake of his life.

Seven

When Sarah woke the next morning, she was surprised to find herself in Ethan's bed. Quickly, she looked over at the pillow next to her, but it bore no trace of an imprint. Obviously, Ethan had not slept with her.

Confused, and feeling suddenly apprehensive, Sarah threw back the blankets and stood up, grimacing as she felt a telltale tenderness between her thighs.

She gazed down at herself, shocked to see that she was still naked. Ethan must have carried her into the bedroom and put her in his bed. But when? She didn't have the slightest recollection of him moving her from the settee. The last thing she remembered was cuddling up to his big, warm body and blissfully falling asleep.

Sarah walked over to the commode and poured water into a small basin, catching sight of herself in the mirror as she set the pitcher down. She gasped, appalled by the image that stared back at her. Her hair was a tangled mess, her eyes heavy, her lips swollen. "You look like a whore," she accused the face in the mirror. Quickly, she turned away, realizing with awful clarity that that was also exactly how she felt.

Desperately, she gazed about the room, hoping to find her nightgown and wrapper. As she did so, her eyes swept across Anne's cradle. It was empty.

With a little cry of horror Sarah grabbed the first garment she saw—one of Ethan's military blouses—and threw it on, quickly buttoning it around her as she flew through the bedroom door and out into the front room.

"Good morning, Mrs. Grant."

Sarah stopped in her tracks, her mouth dropping open in astonishment at the sight of Nola Bryant sitting on the settee holding Anne.

"Nola! What are you doing here?"

Nola gaped openmouthed at the sight of Sarah's scanty garb and then hurriedly got to her feet. "Captain Grant came over to our house early this morning and asked me to look after the baby for a while. He said that you hadn't slept well and he wanted to let you rest."

Sarah felt hot color scorch her cheeks. What must Nola think of her? Even a girl of sixteen couldn't miss the obvious signs of a night spent in wanton passion. The tousled hair, the well-kissed lips—anyone who looked at her would undoubtedly know why she hadn't "slept well."

Plucking the baby out of Nola's arms, Sarah held Anne close for a moment, struggling to gather her wits. Then she turned away from the girl's curious gaze and said, "Do you happen to know where Captain Grant went this morning?"

Nola's face registered her surprise. "I'm not sure," she said slowly, "but I suppose he went to his office."

"To his office? So early?"

"It's not really early, Mrs. Grant. It's after ten."

"What?" Sarah whirled around, looking with horror at the clock on the mantel. Sure enough, the hands pointed to 10:20. "Oh, this is terrible! You shouldn't have let me sleep so long. Why, poor little Anne must be starving!"

Nola's face fell at Sarah's unexpected attack on her judgment. "I'm sorry, ma'am. The captain said not to disturb you. I gave Anne some sugar water, and that seemed to satisfy her, although I'm sure she's ready to be fed."

Seeing the girl's crestfallen face, Sarah quickly apologized. "I'm sorry I snapped at you, dear. I know you were only following the captain's instructions. I appreciate you coming over his morning." Quickly, she walked over to the sugar bowl. "Let me pay you something for your trouble."

"Oh, no," Nola demurred. "Captain Grant was so generous last night, I couldn't possibly take any more money from you."

Sarah hesitated a moment, then nodded. "Well, then, thank you very much."

"Anytime, Mrs. Grant." Nola smiled, heading for the door. "I just love your baby."

Sarah smiled and reached out to pat the girl's shoulder. "Give my best to your mother, and please thank her again for the lovely party last night."

After Nola left, Sarah quickly went into the bedroom and fed the baby, then put her down for her morning nap. She had just finished dressing and pinning up her hair, when she heard the front door open. Ethan was back.

Sarah drew in a shuddering breath, not sure whether she wanted to run into his arms or stay in the bedroom and hide. How was he feeling toward her this morning after their passionate night together?

"There's only one way to find out," she muttered, squaring her shoulders determinedly and opening the bedroom door.

He was there, standing at the tiny kitchen counter drinking a glass of milk. Sarah's heart leapt into her throat at the sight of him. "Good morning, Ethan," she said, furious with herself when she heard her voice shake.

Slowly, Ethan turned to face her, his expression inscrutable. "Good morning, Sarah. Did you sleep well?"

"Ye-yes," she stammered. "The bed is . . . very comfortable."

Ethan nodded. "I just came by to let you know we got word this morning that the stage is going to be back in three days."

Sarah's fluttering heart suddenly dropped into her stomach. "Oh?" she said, trying desperately to sound nonchalant. "It's coming back early?"

"Yes. They're veering away from the normal schedule to try to avoid any more confrontations with robbers." Setting the half-drunk glass of milk down on the counter, he drew a deep breath, as if girding himself for his next statement. "That informati⟨ is confidential, Sarah, but I thought I should tell you so th⟨ you're ready to leave when the stage gets here."

With a quick, jerky movement, Sarah grabbed on to the ba⟨ of a chair, feeling as if she might faint. "Thank you," she sa⟨ in a strangled voice. "I . . . I appreciate your letting me kno⟨ and I promise, I won't tell anyone."

Ethan stared at her for a moment, as if wanting to say som⟨ thing more, but he didn't. Instead, he pulled on his gloves a⟨ turned toward the door. "That's all I wanted to tell you. I'll s⟨ you later."

Sarah nodded miserably, then quickly turned away before ⟨ saw the tears filling her eyes. She didn't turn back until s⟨ heard the soft click of the door closing. Then she sank into t⟨ chair and buried her head in her hands, letting the tears f⟨ unchecked.

"Well, what did you expect?" she asked herself furious⟨ "You act like a whore, you get treated like a whore!" But s⟨ wasn't a whore, and despite the self-loathing she was mome⟨ tarily feeling, she knew it. Before Ethan, she'd been with on⟨ one man in her entire life, and he had been her husband. S⟨ why, *why*, had she succumbed last night?

"Because you're in love with him!" As the words tumbl⟨ out of her mouth, she lifted her head, gazing out the windo⟨ as she struggled to come to terms with what she'd just adm⟨ ted. It was true. She was in love with Ethan Grant. She couldr⟨ deny it any longer. Somehow, sometime, in the last ten da⟨ spent in his company, she'd fallen in love with him. S⟨ couldn't name an exact moment or a single event that h⟨ precipitated her feelings, but she knew it was true. And la⟨ night, when Ethan had pulled her into his arms and kissed h⟨ so passionately, it had seemed like the most natural thing ⟨ the world to respond.

Sarah shook her head, shocked and appalled by her ov⟨ thoughts. And worse still, she realized that even though Etha⟨ obviously didn't return her feelings, if he walked into the hou⟨

ght that minute and kissed her the way he had last night, she'd
espond in exactly the same way.

"Maybe you are a whore after all," she said aloud. Rising,
ne brushed the tears off her cheeks and walked slowly into the
itchen to throw what was left of Ethan's milk into the sink.
icking up the glass, she stared at it morosely. "But even if you
ren't a whore, Sarah Hollings, one thing is for sure. You're a
tupid, gullible fool."

Ethan didn't come home until late that night. Sarah, who was
gain sleeping on the settee, heard him come in, but she said
othing. Instead, she watched him carefully take his boots off
nd set them next to the door, then saw him approach the settee
s if to check on her. Quickly, she closed her eyes.

But not quickly enough.

"I know you're awake," he said softly into the darkness. "We
eed to talk."

"Go away," she whispered, the very sound of his voice causing
painful lump to form in her throat. "You're going to wake the
aby."

Ethan shot a look over at the sleeping Anne, then said, "Come
n the bedroom with me, then."

"No."

"Please, Sarah. I need to talk to you."

"You said quite enough this morning. Now, go away."

Ethan's lips thinned. "I'm not going away," he said, his voice
ntentionally louder, "and if you won't come into the bedroom
nd talk, then we'll do it right here and that'll wake Annie for
ure."

Sarah clenched her fists, incensed at the man's high-
andedness. "Don't call my daughter Annie," she blazed,
hrowing back the afghan and getting to her feet. "Her name is
Anne."

Ethan, who had spent a torturous day trying to make the biggest decision of his life, sighed heavily. "All right. *Anne.* Now, pleas⟨ come with me. What I have to say will take only a minute."

Reluctantly, Sarah followed him into the bedroom, casti⟨ him an arch look when he closed the door behind them. "If y⟨ think you're going to entice me into your bed again, Captai⟨ you're very wrong."

Ethan raked his fingers through his hair. "I suppose I deser⟨ that, but I can assure you, making love is the last thing on m⟨ mind."

His words of rejection hit Sarah like a blow, but she continu⟨ to gaze at him squarely, unwilling to let him see how much sh⟨ was hurting. "What *do* you want, then?"

Ethan hesitated for a moment, then walked over to the windo⟨ and braced the heels of his hands against the sill. "I want . ⟨ to apologize. What happened last night was a mistake and I wa⟨ you to know how much I regret it."

Sarah didn't know what she had been expecting him to sa⟨ but hearing him tell her that making love to her was a mistak⟨ that he regretted hurt more than anything she could imagin⟨ When she again spoke, her voice was as glacial as the icy blu⟨ of her eyes. "You don't need to concern yourself, Captain. ⟨ allowed you to take advantage of me, so what happened is ⟨ much my fault as yours."

"I didn't take advantage of you, dammit!" Ethan flared, spi⟨ ning around and taking an aggressive step toward her. "It wasn⟨ like that, and you know it!"

"Oh, really? Then, what was it like?"

"It was like, well . . . *dammit,* Sarah, I don't know how ⟨ describe it! You're a beautiful, fascinating woman and I . . . I'v⟨ fallen in love with you."

Sarah's eyes widened incredulously. "You have?" sh⟨ breathed.

Ethan balled his fists at his sides as if angry at his own ad⟨ mission. "Yes, I have, but that doesn't make any difference, be⟨ cause there can never be a future between us."

"Why not?" Sarah asked quietly, feeling something die deep within herself.

"Because of what I am. What I've worked ten long, hard years to become."

"And what exactly is that, Ethan?"

"I'm an intelligence officer," he said quietly, "and the work I do is very dangerous. Men in my position can't be married."

"Do you mean it's a regulation?"

"No, it's not a regulation, it's just good sense. Every day when I walk out the door, there's a chance I won't come back. Sometimes I have to be gone for days or even weeks on secret assignments. They're always dangerous and I can't be distracted by thinking about a wife and a bunch of kids at home, much less expect any woman to spend her time sitting around worrying about me."

Sarah studied him carefully for a moment. "What if a woman wanted to marry you despite the danger of your work?"

Ethan stepped forward, taking both of Sarah's hands in his and lifting them to his lips. He gazed at her for a moment, his eyes filled with naked yearning. "It wouldn't work, sweetheart," he said softly. "You deserve much more than I can give you. You deserve a man who's always there, a man whose every thought is about loving you for all the things you are. And little Anne deserves a full-time father—someone who's around to help her take her first steps and tell her how pretty she looks in her first party dress. I care far too much for both of you to expect you to settle for anything less than that."

Sarah yanked her hands out of Ethan's warm grasp and turned away. "A man to love me for all the things I am," she spat out. "Do you mean like lying, deceitful, manipulative? Aren't those the words you use most often to describe me?"

Ethan walked up behind her, wrapping his arms tightly around her waist and kissing the back of her neck. "I know I used those words and I'm sorry. I understand now that what I thought was deceit was merely desperation. And when you lied and told everyone you were my wife, I know that it was the only way you

could think of to put a roof over your baby's head. I've learne
a lot about you in the past days, Sarah, and I want you to hav
the life you deserve." He hesitated a moment, then delivered th
final blow. "But I also know that life is not with me."

Slowly Sarah unwrapped Ethan's strong arms from aroun
her and stepped away. "I understand, Captain, and you needn
worry. I'll be on the stage Monday and out of your life." Sh
drew a tremulous breath and pressed two fingers against he
forehead as if to massage away an ache. "I guess the only thin
left is for you and me to figure out what we do until then."

"I've already taken care of that," he said quickly. "I'll bun
with my men."

"Don't you think that will raise a lot of questions?"

Ethan shrugged. "So what? There are going to be question
anyway as soon as you leave. I'll think of some way to handl
them."

They stood in silence for a while, then with a heavy sig
Ethan turned and quietly walked toward the door. "Good-bye
Sarah Hollings. I wish you every happiness."

Sarah nodded, but she didn't answer. She couldn't. She wa
far too busy trying to hold together the splintering pieces of he
heart.

Eight

It was very late Sunday night when Sarah finally snapped her overstuffed valise closed. "There," she sighed. "That's everything." Mournfully, she stared at the heavy satchel, wondering where she would be the next time it was unpacked.

It was then that she heard the noise. She cocked her head, listening carefully—and heard it again.

Someone was moving about the front room, very close to where Anne lay asleep in her cradle.

Her heart pounding in fear, Sarah crept silently over to the bedroom door, opening it a crack and peering into the darkness.

A crescent moon that had spent most of the evening playing tag with the clouds suddenly shot a stream of dim, silvery light through the window, illuminating the brass buttons on a dark blue military blouse. Sarah narrowed her eyes, trying to focus on the intruder's face. Then, as recognition suddenly dawned, she drew an infuriated breath and yanked the door open. Rushing into the front room, she demanded, "What in heaven's name are you doing sneaking around out here in the dark?"

Ethan looked up from where he sat on the settee, holding the sleeping baby. "Hi," he said simply.

"What are you doing here?" Sarah repeated. "You nearly scared me out of my wits! I thought you were a prowler."

Ethan had the good grace to look abashed at her accusation. "I'm sorry, I didn't mean to scare you. I just thought I'd come and check on you, and when I saw Annie out here alone, I decided to take a minute to say good-bye to her."

Sarah bit her lip as she stared at the heartwrenching sight of the man she loved cuddling her baby. "I thought you didn't like babies," she accused, her voice catching as she fought back the tears that threatened.

"I thought I didn't either," Ethan said quietly. "But that was before I got to know this one." Standing up, he bent his head and gently kissed the baby's velvety cheek, then returned her to her cradle. "She's very special." He smiled, adding wryly, "Cranky, but special." Slowly, he walked toward Sarah, picking up her hand and placing a soft kiss in her palm. "Just like her mother"

"Oh, Ethan," Sarah breathed as the tears she could no longer contain began to stream down her cheeks. "I wish things could be different between us."

Ethan closed his eyes for a moment, then reached out and wrapped his arm around Sarah's waist, pulling her close. "I know, sweetheart," he rasped, burying his face in her soft hair. "God, this is so hard!"

Sarah turned her face toward his and, suddenly his mouth closed over hers, kissing her with a passion that sent both their senses reeling.

The kiss was endless, drugging, and desperate. Finally Ethan pulled away, his eyes clouded with regret and his voice, when he spoke, thick with misery. "Godspeed, Sarah."

Then he was gone.

The stage arrived the next morning. As Sarah stepped out of the cottage, carrying Anne in one arm and her valise in the other, she was surprised to see Rita Bryant and Mavis Williams standing near the coach, waiting for her.

"We're going to miss you so much," Rita cried, running up to hug Sarah.

"We certainly are," Mavis chorused, "and we hope that your sister will be much better soon so that you can come back."

"My sister?" Sarah said dumbly.

"Of course, your sister," Mavis said, looking at Sarah in bewilderment. "Captain Grant told us about her illness and how you have to go back to Ohio to care for her."

"Oh . . . oh, yes. I do." Quickly Sarah turned away from the two women, hoping her shocked expression didn't betray Ethan's lie. "Thank you both very much for coming to see me off."

"We were happy to," Rita said, craning her neck so she could see the officers' barracks. "I can't imagine why your husband isn't here though."

Sarah swallowed, trying desperately to think of a plausible excuse for Ethan's absence. "I asked him not to come," she improvised quickly. "I . . . I didn't want to cry in front of anyone." She smiled tremulously, realizing that much at least was true.

Rita looked at her pityingly. "I understand, dear. I know how hard it is for young married couples to be apart."

"We gotta be goin', lady," the stagecoach driver suddenly called. "If you're comin', you better get in."

With a flurry of petticoats, Sarah quickly climbed into the coach and settled Anne on her lap. She waved at her friends as the coach lurched forward, then turned tear-filled eyes to cast one last, longing look at the cottage.

The stage rumbled out of the fort's gates and Sarah faced forward again, never noticing the solitary man who stood on the ramparts, sadly staring down at her as she made her departure.

The wild-eyed, disheveled sergeant burst into Ethan's office without even knocking. "Captain!" he shouted. "You gotta come quick!"

Ethan lunged to his feet, nearly tipping over his desk chair. "What's the matter, Sergeant? What's happened?"

"It's the stage, sir. It's been robbed again!"

Only one thought leapt to Ethan's mind as the shocking announcement slammed into him: *Sarah and the baby are on that stage.*

Through sheer will, Ethan fought the immediate surge of panic that rose within him. "Was anyone hurt?"

"I don't know, sir. When the patrol rode in shouting that the stage had been robbed again, I didn't wait for any details. I just ran straight over here because I knew your wife and daughter were passengers."

By now Ethan was already heading out his office door, the overweight sergeant puffing along behind him.

"Saddle my horse," he shouted, "and tell my men to get mounted. We're riding out immediately."

Ten minutes later Ethan and his highly trained, heavily armed company of eight men galloped through the fort's gates, heading down the road that the stage had taken that morning.

They'd traveled about five miles, when Lieutenant Ashbrook rode up alongside Ethan. "Captain, you've got to slow down a little. At the rate we're going, we're going to run these horses to ground before we ever reach the stage."

Ethan shot a furious look over at the lieutenant, but knowing the man was right, sawed back on the reins and slowed his winded horse to a trot.

Caleb Ashbrook nodded approvingly. "We've also got to come up with some sort of plan, sir, before we just charge into their midst."

Ethan drew a deep, calming breath, then turned around and signaled his men to break ranks and join him.

"Have you seen any sign of the rest of the patrol?" he asked one of the soldiers as he rode up.

"I think that's them coming now." All eyes turned in the direction that Lieutenant Ashbrook was pointing.

Sure enough, two soldiers rode over a rise off to the east, spurring their horses to greater speed when they saw Ethan and his men advancing toward them.

"Captain," one of the men called as they rode up, "I'm glad you're here. We've found them."

"Found who?" Ethan asked, his voice tight.

"Abel Ritter."

"Is anyone with him?"

"Yes," the soldier said, carefully avoiding Ethan's eyes. "He has your wife and daughter."

Ethan felt as if he'd just had the wind knocked out of him, but with the well-disciplined reactions of a trained soldier, he showed no sign of his agitation. "What about the driver? Where is he?"

"Dead," the soldier answered, shaking his head. "And the guard too. Looks like they got Ritter's cohorts though, since we found two other bodies at the scene."

Ethan nodded slowly. "Where is Ritter now?"

"About three miles north of here. I don't think he's going to make a run for it. He's hiding in a cottonwood grove by the river."

"Then he should be easy to pick off," Lieutenant Ashbrook interjected.

Ethan shot him a quelling look. "No one is going to pick anyone off, Lieutenant. At least not until Sarah and the baby are safe."

"Yes, sir," Caleb responded, embarrassed by his rash words. "Of course you're right. Do you have a plan?"

Ethan nodded. "I'm going in alone."

"But, Captain, you can't do that. It would be suicide!"

Ethan didn't so much as blink. "That's a chance I'll have to take. Lieutenant, you and the other men will circle around from behind, and when I give the signal, move in."

"And what will that signal be, sir?"

"I'm going to let Ritter capture me. He's obviously looking for a hostage, since he took Sarah. I'm sure he'd be willing to trade her for me. As soon as I've gotten him far enough away from her and the baby to get them out of harm's way, you move in."

"But what if Ritter refuses to give your wife up, sir?"

"He'll give her up," Ethan said coldly. "Just do as I tell you and make sure Mrs. . . . Grant and the baby don't get hurt."

"Yes, sir," Caleb replied, saluting smartly.

Ethan shifted around in his saddle to address the small group of men clustered around him. "All right, men, you know what to do. Let's move."

It was barely a half hour later when they heard the sounds of a baby crying. Ethan smiled grimly when he heard the persistent high-pitched wail coming from deep within a grove of cottonwoods. Thank God for Anne's demanding personality. Now he knew exactly where Ritter was hiding.

Signaling his men to fan out, Ethan dismounted and crept stealthily among the trees until he came to a small clearing. His knees nearly buckled with relief when he saw Sarah seated on a fallen tree trunk, vainly trying to hush the screaming baby.

Ethan pulled his gun and stepped into the clearing. "All right, Ritter, I'm here," he announced. "Let the woman go."

Abel Ritter looked up at Ethan with startled eyes, then lunged toward Sarah, nearly knocking her off the log as he wrapped his arm around her throat and pressed the blade of a long-handled knife against her throat. " 'Afternoon, Captain," he said, smirking, "I thought you might be joinin' our little party here."

"Let the woman and the baby go, Ritter," Ethan repeated.

"Oh, now, Captain, I don't think I can do that. See, I figure that once your wife is free, you're gonna signal your men to swoop in here and kill me, so if it's all the same to you, I think I'll just keep my arm around the little lady till you and I come to some sort of agreement about things."

"I don't have any men with me, Ritter," Ethan lied. "I came alone."

"Do you really expect me to believe that?"

Ethan threw his hands wide. "Think about it. If I had a company of men with me, don't you think I would have 'swooped' in on you already?"

Abel loosened his hold around Sarah's neck a fraction as he pondered this. "So, what d'ya figure's gonna happen here, Captain? D'ya think I'm just gonna hand over your little wife and expect that you're gonna let me walk away?"

"No, Abel, but I figured you'd probably be willing to exchange her for me."

"Why? So she can go back and round up a posse?"

"She's not going to do that, Ritter. You see, she doesn't particularly care whether I live or die."

Sarah looked up in astonishment at this statement, but she remained silent.

Abel's eyes narrowed in bewilderment. "She's your wife, ain't she?"

Ethan smiled, realizing that Abel had just given him a brilliant idea. "No, Abel, actually she's not."

"Whatd'ya mean, she's not? Everybody knows this here is your wife and your kid. I seen ya livin' at the fort together."

"Yes," Ethan admitted. "That's right. We were living together at the fort, but we aren't married. Never have been. My relationship with this lady was purely one of—how should I say it—momentary pleasure? But the moment is over. That's why I had sent her packing."

Abel Ritter felt Sarah's quick intake of breath. Bending forward, he squinted at her malevolently. "He tellin' the truth, girlie? Are you really just his fancy woman?"

"It's true, I'm not his wife," Sarah blurted out, tears springing to her eyes. "My name is Mrs. Marcus Hollings, and my husband is a deceased veteran of the Confederate Army."

To her mortification, Abel started to laugh. "Well, what d'ya know? I didn't think the stiff-necked bastard had it in him to keep a woman." Then he turned back toward Ethan, shouting, "Guess you're a better man than I thought, Captain." Suddenly, all traces of humor fled his homely face as a thought occurred to him. "Wait a minute here. If this girl don't mean nothin' to ya, why are you willin' to change places with her?"

Ethan thought fast. "Because I'm a soldier, Ritter, just like you. And no soldier worth his salt would let a woman die for him. Now, let her go and I'll come with you. But we better move fast. Even though I got away alone, they're bound to send a platoon out after you soon."

"Maybe not," Ritter chortled. "They never did before. All them officers back at that fort think they're so smart, but they ain't. They're dumber than shit, and that's the God's truth. Three jobs I've pulled and none of 'em been bright enough to figure out it's me doin' it."

"Yes, but things are different now," Ethan said carefully. "This time your partners got killed. Now that they know who they are, how long do you think it'll be before they figure out who they were working with? I figured it out fast enough and found you without much trouble. They will too. So I say, if we're going, then let's get the hell out of here before we both get killed."

For a moment Abel seemed to mull over what Ethan had just said. " 'Spect you're right, Captain. You are a lot more valuable to the army than this woman here. Guess I would be better off havin' you with me. That way, once we get clear of the area, you can write the brass a letter sayin' that if they want to see you again in one piece, they better call off their dogs."

"They'll do it too, Ritter," Ethan said confidently. "I'm important enough to them that they'll let you go to get me back."

Abel laughed, a hoarse, braying sound that made Sarah wince. "You surely are a conceited one, Captain. Yes, indeed, you surely are."

Ethan smiled blandly, then turned to glance at Sarah, desperately wishing that he could give her some sign of reassurance. But he couldn't. Not with Abel draped over her shoulder. "Come on, Ritter. Let's make the exchange." Slowly, Ethan set down his gun, knowing that in Sarah's present precarious position there was no way he could hazard getting a clear shot off.

Abel thought a moment more, then nodded, standing up and hauling Sarah to her feet in front of him. With measured steps he and Ethan approached each other, finally meeting in the center of the clearing. With a hard push Abel shoved Sarah away from him, nearly sending her to her knees.

Reaching out, Ethan grabbed her arm to keep her from falling, whispering "Run!" into her ear before she lurched away from him. Sarah tore off into the trees, quickly disappearing among the low-hanging branches.

"Now!" Ethan bellowed, hitting the dirt and rolling toward his gun.

Suddenly the clearing was filled with a cacophony of noise as horses and men descended on the unsuspecting robber. In a matter of seconds Ritter was restrained and handcuffed, cursing roundly as he glared at Ethan with belligerent eyes.

Ethan didn't even notice him, so eager was he to find Sarah. It took him only a few moments to locate her, kneeling in a thick pile of leaves beneath a low-hanging tree, crying pitiably as she held Anne close to her.

"Sarah," he murmured, dropping to his knees in front of her. "Sarah, sweetheart, it's okay." Pulling her into his strong embrace, he stroked her hair soothingly. "It's okay, baby, you're safe now. It's over."

To his astonishment, Sarah looked up at him through narrowed, hate-filled eyes. "You're right about that, Captain," she cried, pushing him away and struggling to her feet. "It's over, all right. Get away from me! I never want to see you again!"

Nine

Sarah walked into the cottage, looking around dismally at the small room she had so recently vacated. "I certainly didn't think when I left here this morning that I'd be back this afternoon," she muttered.

Ethan walked in the door behind her, frowning. "You have to stay somewhere until the next stage comes. It might as well be here."

Sarah nodded shortly, refusing to look at him. Ethan had escorted her back to the fort after her terrible ordeal with Abel Ritter, but during the entire trip they hadn't exchanged a single word. Even now that they were back inside the cozy little cottage where just a few days before they had shared such intimacies, they were treating each other more like polite strangers than recent lovers.

"Where are *you* going to stay?" Sarah asked quietly.

"I'll continue to bunk in with my men."

She sighed heavily. "Before you go, there's something I want to say."

Ethan looked at her, a glimmer of hope lighting his dark eyes. "There's something I want to say to you too, but you go first."

Sarah gazed down at Anne for a moment, then back up at the handsome man standing before her. "I just wanted to thank you for rescuing Anne and me today. You saved our lives and I'm . . . very grateful."

Ethan blew out a long, disappointed breath. He didn't know

what he had expected Sarah to say, but a stilted, polite apology was not what he had been hoping for.

Sarah looked up at him, her blue eyes clouded to a dull gray. "What did you want to say to me, Captain?"

"I just want you to know—" Ethan paused, struggling to express what was in his heart.

Sarah continued to gaze at him. "Yes?"

Suddenly his jaw clenched and he turned angrily toward the door. "Never mind. Just forget it." Sweeping his hat off the table, he clapped it on his head. "I'll be back later to pick up my things."

And wrenching the door open, he rushed out of the house, slamming the flimsy little portal so hard behind him that the windows rattled.

"What do you mean, they're not married?"

Carrie Alexander looked at Mavis Williams and nodded solemnly. "Will told me he heard it with his very own ears. Captain Grant told Abel Ritter that Sarah meant nothing more to him than a"—she paused, embarrassed to repeat what her husband had told her—"than a momentary pleasure."

Mavis glared at Carrie angrily. "I don't believe it. And I won't believe it until I've heard it from Captain Grant myself. Sarah's such a lovely young woman . . . why, she'd never agree to an arrangement like that! I just know she wouldn't, and I'm an excellent judge of character."

"What are you going to do?" Carrie asked, watching with wide eyes as Mavis picked up her hat and angrily pinned it to her tightly wound bun.

"I'm going to go talk to Captain Grant. Do you know where he is?"

"I think he's at his office. I saw him headed that way when I was walking over here."

"Good. Then I won't have to waste any time finding him. I

intend to get to the bottom of this ridiculous situation immediately before any more horrid gossip spreads."

"But what if it's true?" Carrie whispered. "What if they aren't
married?"

Mavis whirled on her, her eyes blazing with outraged indignation. "Then by tomorrow night at this time, if I have my say,
they will be. And, I assure you, my dear, I *always* have my say."

It was after eleven that night when Sarah heard a knock [at]
the door. She took a quick look in the mirror, patted a wayward
strand of hair into place, then hurried to answer the summons.

"I'm sorry I'm so late," Ethan announced, stepping into the
house without so much as a greeting. "I got . . . busy tonight."

"That's all right," Sarah murmured, stepping out of his way
as he walked toward the bedroom. "I laid some of your things
out on the bed."

Ethan paused, his hand on the bedroom doorknob. The
thought of Sarah laying his clothes out for him was almost more
than he could bear. "By the way," he said, forcing a casualness
into his voice that he was far from feeling, "I found out the next
stage will be here on Wednesday morning."

Sarah drew in a startled breath. "Really? So soon?"

Ethan nodded. "And Colonel and Mrs. Williams have invited
us to their house tomorrow night for a formal farewell dinner."

Sarah's eyes widened with disbelief. "You're not serious!"

"I'm absolutely serious."

"Well, I'm not going."

Ethan released the doorknob and took a step toward her.
"Why not?"

"Why not? I can't believe you have to ask me that! After what
you said about me this morning in front of all those men? Now
that they all know the truth, or think they do, you actually expect
me to go and socialize with them and their wives? Are you
crazy?"

"No, I'm not crazy, and yes, I do expect you to go. As you

ist said, I saved your life today and you owe me. Consider this my repayment."

"I can't believe this!" Sarah fumed. "I never dreamed that even you could be so arrogant and unfeeling. These men all think I'm your—what did you call it?—your fancy woman?"

"Ritter called you that, not I."

Sarah laughed mirthlessly. "Oh, yes, I forgot. You merely said I was a 'momentary pleasure.' "

Ethan drew a deep breath, knowing that the next words he uttered could be some of the most important of his life. "Sarah, about that—"

"No, Ethan," she interrupted, holding up a staying hand. "Don't say anything more. I know now how you really feel, and let's just leave it at that. The day after tomorrow I'll be gone, and we'll never see each other again. Let's not have our last few moments together spent in another pointless argument."

"We're not going to have an argument," Ethan said, quickly traversing the space between them and wrapping a possessive arm around Sarah's waist. "But I am going to say what's on my mind and you are going to listen to me whether you want to or not."

Sarah looked up at him, her face darkening with anger. But the naked entreaty in Ethan's eyes quickly cooled her flaring temper, and slowly she nodded her head. "All right. What do you want to tell me?"

"Just this," he said quietly. "The only reason I said what I did to Ritter was so he'd let you go. I figured that if he thought I didn't care about you, he'd have no reason to keep you. I realize now what a humiliating position I put you in in front of my men but, honest to God, it was the only thing I could think to say at the moment."

Sarah remained silent, and taking that as a good omen, Ethan plunged on. "The reason I want you to go to the Williamses tomorrow night is so that they can see that what everyone is saying about us isn't true. Please go, Sarah. It's important to me."

Sarah remained absolutely still as Ethan's words trailed o Then, in a quiet voice, she asked, "Why is it important?"

Ethan gazed down at her, his expression earnest and solem "Because I love you," he rasped, his voice hoarse with emotio "You and that beautiful little girl over there in the cradle. I to you before that I loved you, Sarah, but I thought I could get ov you. I guess it took almost losing you this morning for me finally realize that I don't want to get over you. I don't ever wa to be without you again."

Sarah looked up at him for a moment, the clouds of pain her eyes gradually clearing. There were a thousand things sh wanted to say, a thousand questions she wanted to ask. But whe she opened her mouth, she said simply, "Will you give me kiss?"

Ethan was more than happy to comply. With a groan of long ing, he bent his head and covered Sarah's waiting mouth wi his own, kissing her with all the love and desire he felt for he

When they finally broke apart, Sarah was breathless an flushed. "I guess maybe you do love me," she gasped.

Ethan laughed and held her close, burying his face in her sof thick hair. "More than you can possibly imagine." He paused moment, then said softly, "Marry me, Sarah."

Sarah threw her head back, staring up at him with incredulou eyes. "Do you mean that?"

"With all my heart."

"But your job. What about your position? You told me you'v worked ten years to get it."

"It doesn't matter anymore," Ethan said, shaking his hea "Nothing matters except that you and Annie are with me."

"Her name is Anne," Sarah reminded him, smiling so wide that her cheeks ached.

Ethan stretched out a finger and tapped Sarah playfully o the nose. "In my book, her name is Annie, and if I'm going t be her papa, then that's what I'm going to call her."

Sarah sighed happily and buried her head in Ethan's nec "All right, Annie it is."

Gently, Ethan lifted Sarah's chin until she was looking deep
to his eyes. "You haven't answered my question yet. Will you
arry me, Sarah? Will you stay here with me and be my wife?"

"Yes," Sarah nodded. "Oh, yes, Ethan, I will. I love you so.
could hardly bear it when I left this morning."

"I could hardly bear it either," Ethan admitted, "and then,
hen you were so angry at me this afternoon, I thought that—"

"I know what you thought," Sarah whispered, raising a finger
ad placing it across his lips. "Let's not talk about it anymore."
eaching up, she brushed her lips across his.

"Good idea," he murmured. "I can think of something I'd
auch rather do than talk."

Sarah threw him a saucy smile. "Oh? And what's that, Cap-
ain?"

With a broad wink the captain took her by the hand, led her
ato the bedroom, and showed her.

The following evening at eight o'clock Sarah and Ethan
valked up the front steps of Colonel and Mrs. Williams's home.

"I'm still not sure about coming here tonight," Sarah whis-
ered as Ethan knocked on the door. "I think we should have
vaited until we were married before I faced these people again."

"Don't worry about it," Ethan admonished quietly. "We'll be
aarried soon enough."

Suddenly the front door of the Williams' home swung open
nd a cascade of summer flowers showered down on the unsus-
ecting couple's heads. "Come in, darlings!" Mavis beamed,
shering them into the foyer.

There, to Sarah's shocked astonishment, stood Rita and
Dorsett Bryant, General Martin, Carrie and Will Alexander, and
Caleb Ashbrook. Even young Nola hovered on the periphery of
he smiling group, flushed and breathless from the exertion of
unning to her parents' house with Anne.

"Oh, Mrs. Williams," Sarah said, looking around apprehen-

sively. "I had no idea this was going to be such a large par[
And why in the world is Anne here?"

"Anne's here for the same reason that everyone is, my dear
Mavis gushed. "Where else would your friends and family [
on your wedding day?"

"My wedding day!" Sarah squeaked, whirling around to fac
the grinning Ethan. "Did you know about this?"

"Yes, I knew about it," he laughed. "After I explained o
situation to Mrs. Williams, we agreed that you and I should g
married as soon as possible. That's why I was so late last nigh
We were busy making plans."

"That's right," Mavis nodded. "I went to speak with the ca[
tain yesterday about . . . another matter . . . and he confided th
he was going to propose to you last night." With a pleased smi
she gestured at the flower-bedecked house and sumptuous
laid-out table. "He said he wanted to get married quickly, so w
ladies spent the day getting this ready."

"It's wonderful," Sarah murmured, nearly speechless wit
surprise. "I don't know how I can ever thank you." Turning bac
to Ethan, she threw him an arch look. "You were that sure th;
I'd accept your proposal?"

Ethan grinned. "I was that hopeful." Walking over to wher
Nola stood, he took Anne in one arm, then returned to Sara[
offering her his other. "I know it's short notice, sweetheart, b
I didn't want to wait even one more day to make you my wif
Will you marry me tonight? Right now?"

"Oh, yes!" Sarah cried, her eyes shining with love. And to
gether, Sarah and Ethan, along with the precious baby who ha
brought them together in the first place, stepped into the parl
and into a new life, filled with happiness and love everlasting

About the Author

Jane Kidder lives with her family in Scottsdale, Arizona. Her newest Zebra historical romance, *Passion's Kiss,* is currently available in bookstores everywhere. Jane loves hearing from her readers, and you may write to her c/o Zebra Books. Please include a self-addressed stamped envelope if you wish a response.

TODAY'S HOTTEST READS
ARE TOMORROW'S SUPERSTARS

VICTORY'S WOMAN (4484, $4.5̶)
by Gretchen Genet

Andrew—the carefree soldier who sought glory on the battlefie̶l̶ and returned a shattered man . . . Niall—the legandary frontie̶r man and a former Shawnee captive, tormented by his past . Roger—the troubled youth, who would rise up to claim a shoc̶ ing legacy . . . and Clarice—the passionate beauty bound by o̶ man, and hopelessly in love with another. Set against the bac̶ drop of the American revolution, three men fight for the̶ heritage—and one woman is destined to change all their lives fo̶ ever!

FORBIDDEN (4488, $4.9̶)
by Jo Beverley

While fleeing from her brothers, who are attempting to sell h̶ into a loveless marriage, Serena Riverton accepts a carriage ri̶ from a stranger—who is the handsomest man she has ever see̶ Lord Middlethorpe, himself, is actually contemplating marria̶ to a dull daughter of the aristocracy, when he encounters t̶ breathtaking Serena. She arouses him as no woman ever has. A̶ after a night of thrilling intimacy—a forbidden liaison—Sere̶ must choose between a lady's place and a woman's passion!

WINDS OF DESTINY (4489, $4.9̶)
by Victoria Thompson

Becky Tate is a half-breed outcast—branded by her Comanc̶ heritage. Then she meets a rugged stranger who awakens h̶ heart to the magic and mystery of passion. Hiding a despera̶ past, Texas Ranger Clint Masterson has ridden into cattle count̶ to bring peace to a divided land. But a greater battle rages insi̶ him when he dares to desire the beautiful Becky!

WILDEST HEART (4456, $4.9̶)
by Virginia Brown

Maggie Malone had come to cattle country to forge her future a̶ a healer. Now she was faced by Devon Conrad, an outla̶ wounded body and soul by his shadowy past . . . whose ey̶ blazed with fury even as his burning caress sent her spiraling wit̶ desire. They came together in a Texas town about to explode in si̶ and scandal. Danger was their destiny—and there was nothin̶ they wouldn't dare for love!